YEAR·OF·T
B

LAND OF THE DEAD

BY ANDREW BATES

AUTHOR ANDREW BATES
COVER ARTIST TOM FLEMING
SERIES EDITOR CARL BOWEN
COPY EDITOR MELISSA THORPE
GRAPHIC ARTIST PAULINE BENNEY
ART DIRECTOR RICHARD THOMAS

ISBN: 1-58846-804-6
Printed in Canada

White Wolf Publishing
735 Park North Boulevard, Suite 128
Clarkston, GA 30021
www.white-wolf.com

YEAR·OF·THE·SCARAB·TRILOGY
BOOK THREE

LAND OF THE DEAD

TABLE OF CONTENTS

PART I: LOSS AND REDEMPTION   7

PART II: SECRETS AND REVELATIONS   87

PART III: DEATH AND ETERNITY   187

EPILOGUE   277

ANDREW BATES

The god looked upon his progeny from his ethereal prison. Like he, they had all but faded from living memory in the passage of millennia, becoming nothing more than myth. For too long they had suffered the indignity of defeat by the enemy, pushed from their ancestral home, able to do nothing more than watch as the world strangled in the rapacious grasp of corruption.

Then the ghost storm had come, laying waste to the world of spirit and threatening with destruction the souls of the god's children. In this darkest hour, when annihilation was at hand, the god stirred from his long slumber and shone the light of salvation. He felt the changes rumbling through the underworld long before his attendants took up the cry. Their fear was strong, but so was their hope that he would protect them. Though the god lost many of his children to the storm, those who remained were infused with a new vigor to take up the fight against their ancient foe.

They were courageous, his progeny, but the god knew they alone could not defeat the enemy. Its corruption was too widespread, its darkness blanketed the world many times over. The only chance for redemption would come when the god walked the earth as he had in bygone times.

Yet his body was lost, scattered using dark magics that rivaled the god's own might. To be made whole, his children must recover his form, the pieces of which were hidden—and worse, in the clutches of those who would use his flesh for their own gain.

Mighty though the god was, he was powerless to influence his progeny or these pretenders to his power. He must trust in his children, and await the day when he would be restored.

Then the enemy—indeed, the world—would know what resurrection truly meant.

ANDREW BATES

PART I:
LOSS
AND REDEMPTION

ANDREW BATES

ONE

Nicholas Sforza-Ankhotep emerged from Cairo International Airport, squinting against the brilliant afternoon sunlight. His sunglasses struggled to cut the glare from the fierce Egyptian sun as he scanned the crowd flowing around him.

Ibrahim's shout barely cut through the din of jostling travelers and bustling traffic. Nicholas spotted his loyal attendant by a blue Mercedes sedan and waded through the crowd, by turns dodging, ignoring and politely refusing the hordes of guides, hawkers and drivers offering their services. He handed his pair of duffels to the wiry Limo Misr driver, who tossed them in the trunk with little concern for the contents. The small man grinned, exposing crooked brown teeth, and chattered rapidly in Arabic while he slammed the trunk closed.

One last look around before slipping into the back seat revealed nothing beyond the airport's typical chaos. The more persistent entrepreneurs took the opportunity to make a last loud pitch. With a smile and a shake of his head, Nicholas ducked in and closed the door. Ibrahim claimed the front passenger seat and kept a watchful eye as they headed toward Cairo.

On average, a Limo Misr driver was more familiar with the city than was the typical taxi driver. Still, there was never a guarantee that any driver had a clue where his fare's destination was. Ibrahim, born and raised in Cairo, was used to this arrangement and chatted with the driver while directing him along the Shari Salah Salim to their destination.

Nicholas was happy to pass on the navigation duties. He was used to the hectic, aggressive driving of Chicago, but that was nothing compared to Cairo. Driving the streets of Cairo was like being in a *Mad Max* movie. Fifteen million people driving boxy European cars at ridiculous speeds and with a disregard for even the concept of traffic laws. Automobiles careened from lane to lane with abandon, drivers with one hand on the wheel and the other on the horn. Accidents were commonplace—a car without dents or scratched paint was a cause for remark, and likely wouldn't last the week in such pristine condition. Still, those involved in fender-benders shrugged and laughed as long as no one was hurt. Nicholas did his best to lean back in the worn leather seat and stare past the traffic at the city they were headed toward.

Despite a fourteen-hour flight from Chicago by way of Munich, Nicholas wasn't the least bit exhausted. (Ibrahim, in contrast, remained conscious thanks only to a pair of Turkish coffees he'd drunk shortly before landing.) Nicholas was brimming with energy. Being within the Lands of Faith again erased any hint of exhaustion he had. It was all he could do to force himself to relax against the Mercedes' backseat. He wanted to be out there, drinking in the sights and sounds of Cairo, basking in the glory in which the city was steeped, reveling in the return to the land of his rebirth.

His heritage may have been almost pureblooded Italian, but his soul belonged to Egypt. And not in any mere poetic sense. It was only thanks to the power that flowed through the region, the mystic strength of the Lands of Faith, that he was alive today. Nicholas literally owed his immortal soul to this ancient land.

Never in his most fevered imaginings did Nicholas think his life might take the turn it had. He'd long accepted the way things were supposed to go. A third generation Italian-American, his family part of organized crime since his great-grandparents stepped off the boat after World War I, he was almost a stereotype goombah.

He'd made a half-hearted effort to strike out on his own a few years back, starting up S Securities, his own security firm. But prospective clients he approached—selected in large part because they weren't connected to the life— thought he was mobbed up. No self-respecting individual or corporation wanted to hire a company with ties to the Syndicate to handle their security. And his family thought it was the perfect front for their various shady dealings. He resisted, but a year later he had a full client list and a staff of ten… mob-approved, each and every one.

Nicholas had rationalized that he had no alternative. He settled into routine, delegating the most unsavory aspects to his employees. As if that somehow made his career legitimate. The empty days grew into empty weeks, which bled into months. Years slipped by like refuse washed down a sewer. He felt empty inside, unfulfilled; a zombie stumbling through the graveyard that was his life.

There was the joke: it took an honest-to-God zombie to make Nicholas immortal. Maxwell Carpenter, a freak out of a B-grade horror movie, returned from the grave to kill off Nicholas' entire family. Lurking for sixty years, a malevolent spirit with a grudge against Nicholas' grandparents, Carpenter arose as one of the walking dead, a bloodless devil out for revenge.

Nicholas suffered the same fate as the rest of his family. Carpenter somehow forced Nicholas to put a gun to his own head and pull the trigger.

Yet even after squandering the life he was given, Nicholas got a second chance. Mighty Osiris, the Lord of Life, sent him a messenger, Ankhotep, to show Nicholas the path of redemption, the way of Ma'at. Nicholas was dead, but he could choose to live again, live *forever*, his soul joining with Ankhotep's as one of the Undying… as a mummy.

It was an easy choice to make, but only now was he beginning to understand the full scope of it. Only now did he start to understand what immortality truly meant.

• • •

The imposing edifice of the Citadel filled the Mercedes' front window as the car headed southwest from the airport. The Citadel, called Al-Qala'a by the locals, was a grand structure dominating Cairo's eastern skyline. Salah ad-Din built the fortress in the 12th century on a steep limestone spur of the Muqattam hills overlooking the city. Originally designed to defend against hostile forces, it now served as nothing more than a military barracks and tourist attraction. Extending west from the foot of the Muqattam hills to the mighty Nile in a baffling jumble of overcrowded neighborhoods was The Mother of the World, Misr… Cairo.

Mysterious and alluring to Western tourists, to Nicholas' biased eye the Egyptian capitol was a chaos of narrow streets winding around clusters of buildings that had never heard the extreme concept of a street grid. Ancient mud brick wakalahs and elaborate mosques heavy with the weight of centuries stood cheek-to-jowl with utilitarian poured-concrete apartments and blocky office buildings. All in all, modern Cairo bore no resemblance to the ancient city of Heliopolis that had once existed at this place along the Nile. As the taxi came around the Citadel and descended toward the plain, Nicholas at last saw the only remaining evidence of that once-great metropolis.

The Pyramids of Gizah were easily visible even ten miles distant. Their massive shapes reared up in sharp relief against the lowering sun, unforgettable reminders of a proud and ancient people. Nicholas was overcome with emotion at the sight. Seeing the pyramids standing over the modern metropolis struck home that Nicholas was a child of two eras, a man of ancient past and turbulent present.

The Mercedes swung around, shaking Nicholas from his recollections as it exited Shari Salah Salim and turned south onto Shari as-Sayyida Nafisa. The area was clearly different from the cramped neighborhoods that spread out across the city to the northwest. Instead of nondescript slabs of concrete and mud brick jammed together with no room to breathe, they drove past a series of mausoleums and low stone buildings. Like any other neighborhood in Cairo, people strolled along toward various matters of business and pleasure, sat outside simple mud brick homes watching the world go by, and hawked wares by the side of the road. Except that, unlike any other neighborhood in Cairo, the people here lived and loved, ate and slept, among the dead.

They were entering the Cities of the Dead.

Entering the Cities of the Dead struck a chord in the ancient portion of Nicholas' soul. The living paid homage to the spirits of the dead, here, nurturing their memories even as they cared for the mausoleums in which their bodies were laid to rest. The piece of Nicholas that was the ancient Egyptian physician Ankhotep wept at the devotion the cemeteries' living residents showed.

Although his wiser self came from that time, Nicholas' modern sensibilities found the Cities of the Dead an odd setup. Two great cemeteries fringed Cairo's edge to the east and south—named, in prosaic fashion, the northern and southern cemeteries. Western media had coined the sensational phrase "Cities of the Dead." The southern cemetery was much older than the northern one, but both had a similar function. Not only did they have their traditional purpose—storing the remains of the deceased—but the living had long made their homes here. Entire neighborhoods of families dwelled there for centuries, beside and even in the many tombs. Squatters abounded, but the majority of residents were there legally, acting as custodians and guardians for ancestral crypts.

Although Islam was by far the predominant religion, residents of each City of the Dead still adhered to many ancient Egyptian traditions. The mausoleums themselves were a prime example. Muslim strictures called for the deceased to be buried simply, in an unmarked grave. In contrast, the Cities of the Dead were just that: cities.

Many crypts had two or even three rooms with walled courts. The bodies were laid to rest beneath the courtyard or under the floor of one of the rooms, a cenotaph marking the spot. That left a fair amount of room for the living to take up residence and act as caretakers for the mausoleum in which they dwelled. Offerings to the dead were likewise not uncommon, and relatives who didn't live with the dead often dropped by to picnic among the graves. In addition, the living residents enjoyed municipal services from utilities to post offices and police stations. It was a lively place, and one of the few areas not overrun with the enemy's putrescence.

It was not always this way. Until recently, Apophis' children infested the place, vampires and zombies feeding off the blood and fears of its residents. The environment was perfect for their habits—resting during the day, well protected by loyal attendants and rising at night to prowl the cemetery for sustenance. Upon their emergence in the modern world, the Amenti moved into the Cities of the Dead. They swept through, systematically destroying each one of their enemies, cleansing the cemeteries of corruption.

Yet, while the Cities of the Dead were liberated in the names of Osiris and Ma'at, the rest of Cairo—and, indeed, much of the Near and Middle East—remained infested with undead. From what the Amenti had been able to determine, there was a greater concentration of Apophis' servants here than in most other places around the world. This was deemed only fair, as it was here, along the life-giving Nile, that the struggle between Osiris and the Corrupter began.

The Undying wanted nothing more than to sweep through the region and eliminate every last one of their foes. They remained too few in numbers, and faced an enemy about whose true scope and influence they were ignorant at present. The Amenti were content to bide their time, gathering intelligence they used to make surgical strikes against pockets of Apepnu, slowly whittling down their numbers and sowing confusion as to who was behind it all. In Cairo, select mummies, those reborn from natives of the Middle East better able to blend in with the locals, investigated the city to discern all they could about the enemy's numbers and movements. It was a dangerous task; the Undying might be powerful, but they weren't invulnerable. A single bullet could kill an unprotected Amenti, and the enemy had far more powerful tools than guns at their disposal. Until they had a better read on the cities and its pockets of decay, these mummies tread with care, and other immortals seldom ventured outside the Cities of the Dead when they came to Cairo.

The Mercedes jerked to a stop a few minutes later. The sandy street wasn't designed with cars in mind, which made getting out rather a challenge. Pedestrians and cyclists called out heartfelt but quickly forgotten complaints as they squeezed past. Nicholas took a look around as Ibrahim paid the driver. As was customary, he had settled on a rate before they left the airport; after adding a few extra gineh as tip, Ibrahim sent the taxi on its way.

Nicholas stood near a squat, whitewashed tomb and scanned the crowd. He didn't see anything out of the ordinary. No minions of Apophis for the moment. Still, it was only a matter of time before the enemy learned he was back in town. The undead infested Cairo like rats in a landfill. Worse, the creatures had any number of mortals in their employ, watching for Nicholas and others of his kind. The Cities of the Dead were relatively safe, but there was never a guarantee where the Corrupter's minions were concerned. Despite the precautions he and Ibrahim had taken even before leaving Chicago, it was possible they were already on his trail. The followers of Apophis were sneaky and tenacious. They could infiltrate the most secure places, and once they had a scent about the only way to lose them was to kill them. Killing didn't bother him— it was why he'd been reborn, after all—but he preferred to do it on his terms. The enemy had an annoying tendency to pop up when he was in the middle of something else, and Nicholas was not a fan of complications.

He nodded to Ibrahim and hefted his duffels. They headed generally south, weaving through the flow of foot traffic and struggling against the oppressive heat that pressed down upon them. It may only be mid-March, but already the Cairene days ranged into the eighties or hotter. And humid, too. The desert encroached all around, but the mighty Nile carried shed a great deal of moisture through much of the city. Coming from the frigid clutch of winter, Nicholas found the warmth welcome at first. His Midwestern physiology just wasn't used to it, though, and soon he was sweating buckets. A ghost of a breeze offered little respite. Nicholas could only imagine how stifling it must be in the rest of the city, where the buildings crouching over narrow streets denied any chance of cooling wind. The locals bore up under the sun's rays with a kind of laconic grace. It was Allah's will to make the day hot; who were they to protest? Though he might apply a different name to the deity, Nicholas couldn't dispute the sentiment.

Approaching the tunnel entrance—a small mud brick dwelling built on a plot next to a large Muslim crypt, complete with courtyard—Nicholas sensed something out of place. He paused by a vendor hawking Harraniyyah style tapestries, Ibrahim stopping a few paces on. Nicholas allowed himself to relax, trying to slip his senses in tune with his surroundings. Mummies possessed a kind of insight, an ability to discern strong emotions in others: joy, fear, anger… and, in this case, nervous excitement. The feel of a voyeur, of someone observing something that stirred them greatly. Nicholas had sensed a similar feeling in the past. A lackey of the Corrupter was watching them.

Eyes hidden behind his Oakleys, Nicholas cast his gaze around while seeming to look over the hangings on display. The vendor pointed out choices and prices. When Nicholas indicated his preference, Ibrahim stepped in to take up the haggling as befitted his role as guide. Nicholas couldn't see anyone but was sure they were being watched. Frustrating; he'd hoped to get to the safe house unnoticed. Now, instead of relaxing before his meeting as he'd hoped, he'd have to deal with a spy. Their tail was skilled enough that Nicholas couldn't pick him out without giving away that he'd been spotted. He decided to draw the shadow along until they could set up a way to turn the tables of stalker and stalkee. The guy was bound to be a small fish; Nicholas was more interested in who he was working for.

Ibrahim and the vendor reached a mutually agreeable price, and Nicholas forked over the three Egyptian pounds while the old gentleman rolled up the small wool tapestry. Ibrahim shot Nicholas an inquiring glance as he stuffed the hanging between the handles of his duffel. At his nod, they set off again as if nothing was out of the ordinary.

Nicholas followed Ibrahim into the nondescript hovel. It was completely unremarkable, two small rooms split by a thin plaster wall and a woven hanging. A scattering of pillows was the only furniture, and a collection of pans and metal storage containers comprised the kitchen. The other room took up two thirds of the building and would be the combination living room/bedroom. Although a common enough setup for the city, it was only a front. Just as they passed inside, Nicholas felt a faint but unmistakable surge of excitement. Their voyeur was filled with eagerness, having confirmed his quarry's destination. The question was, would he stick around for a while or head back to report immediately?

The curtain parted in response to the noise of their entry, revealing sharp black eyes in a dark, lined face. A wide grin bloomed on the old man's face and his eyes lit with delight.

"Amenti Nicholas! Ibrahim! I did not expect you so soon!" The Eset-a elder spoke in English out of deference to Ibrahim. Faruq was equally conversant in ancient Egyptian, his native Arabic and English. Although Egyptian was as vivid in Nicholas' mind as English, he had only a passing familiarity with Arabic—enough to

pick it out of a lineup, say, but nothing sufficient for extended conversation. In turn, Ibrahim, like most of the cultists, knew only scattered phrases in the tongue of the Amenti. Conversations among mummies and their followers were often a patchwork of languages.

Faruq tried to give a hug and help with the bags at the same time. Nicholas waited with a bemused smile until the two Egyptians sorted themselves out, then laughed as the old guy began genuflecting while tugging at one of the duffel bag's handles.

"Hello, Faruq," he said, chuckling at the old man's antics. Faruq had the utmost respect for him, Nicholas knew, but the old guy was a born ham. Nicholas would have played along, but he had to take care of their tail first. "I'm sorry to be an ungracious guest, but we have some business to attend to."

"I am your servant, Amenti." Faruq's smile remained, but his eyes snapped to Nicholas' own with the intensity of a hunting hawk. "Tell me what you need, and I will supply it."

"Actually, you should probably stay put. Ibrahim, I want you to run an errand."

The Eset-a cultist looked confused for a moment, then nodded. "A distraction, Amenti?"

"Of sorts. Only for, say, five minutes. Run to a nearby market and pick up some fruit or something. Just make sure to look furtive when you leave."

"Furtive?" Ibrahim spoke excellent English, but his knowledge of the language was not encyclopedic.

"Uh, suspicious. Don't overdo it, though."

Ibrahim gave a sharp nod and slipped back outside. He gave a quick look around and back into the dwelling before heading off.

"Right. Faruq, let's get over to the safe house. I'll want to inform Basel and anybody else who's there."

"I am sorry, but Basel Nyambek-Senemut may not aid you at this time. And no other Amenti are at the mausoleum."

"What?"

"The struggle, it grows intense now." Faruq shrugged an apology while he led Nicholas through to the next room. "Amenti Basel fell in combat with one of the Apepnu; his body awaits his return from the death cycle. And strange things are afoot in Misr as well as the new adversity to the east. The others investigate. But the Amenti Indihar and Lu Wen are returning this evening."

A handful of the Undying and their mortal assistants could normally be found in the safe house, sharing information, planning, recuperating, and/or just hanging out. Nicholas had been so focused on his debacle with the Heart and that thieving bastard Maxwell Carpenter that he'd forgotten about the trouble in Cairo. Plus, it was hard not to know about the Israeli-Palestinian conflict, which was threatening to explode into full-blown war. Mummies and their helpers were all out pursuing one mission or another—or, in the case of Basel, awaiting the return to life.

Basel Nyambek-Senemut's death was only temporary, but the mortals who helped them in the struggle were not so lucky. Nicholas' thoughts returned to the Eset-a cultists who'd joined him on his mission in Chicago. The Eset-a were not a large group, the smallest faction of those loyal to Osiris, in fact. He left with fifteen and came back with one: Ibrahim. Grimacing, Nicholas contemplated the scope of his failure—to the men under his command, to the struggling Eset-a cult, to his fellow Amenti, and most of all to the gods to whom he owed his existence. He felt Osiris' disappointed gaze upon him every waking moment. In his dreams he cringed before the displeasure of Ma'at. He would answer to each revered power in time, that was certain.

But a more immediate matter was at hand that did not allow him the luxury of wallowing in the tragedy of the past. "Right. We'll just have to take care of this ourselves, then."

Faruq went to a battered toilet that sat exposed in the far corner. Like the rest of the hovel's rustic design,

this was common for the area. Much of the Cities of the Dead had access to electricity and plumbing, but many residents had to cobble together their own hookups. Old buildings like this, slapped together before indoor plumbing, had jury-rigged sinks and toilets, the larger ones shower stalls or even baths. The toilet was an old design with the water tank set into the wall above the bowl. The pipes went under the floor and led outside, where they were buried under perhaps a foot of earth in a channel residents dug over to the main junction. The setup would make any halfway-competent civil engineer cringe, but it got the job done.

Faruq pulled the chain hanging from the tank and, keeping the chain tugged down, grabbed the toilet bowl rim and yanked it toward him. The toilet flushed, covering the squeal as a square of the cracked concrete to which the toilet was attached tilted up. The water in the bottom of the bowl poured out in a coughing gurgle as the toilet was disconnected from its plumbing. Faruq let go of the pull chain and tilted the toilet the rest of the way over. Grabbing for support the pipe that ran down from the water tank, he dropped through the hole to the tunnel below. Nicholas handed down the luggage, which the old Eset-a cultist set out of the way of the water that had splashed down. After slipping off his sunglasses and jumping down himself, Nicholas grabbed the pipe that L'd out from the bottom of the bowl and levered the whole thing back into place. It took a little jiggling to reconnect the pipe to the regular plumbing, and when he did Nicholas heard a faint click as the panel locked back into position. Then came a gurgling as the water from the tank was unblocked and ran to fill the toilet bowl. While Nicholas took care of the toilet, Faruq felt for a switch on the wall. A dim red bulb lit up a few yards down, giving them just enough light to make their way down the tunnel.

Nicholas always felt a little ridiculous entering the safe house in this fashion, like he was playing at some cut-rate

James Bond scenario. It wasn't a game, he knew; hidden passages like this one were of vital importance to keep their hideout as secret as possible. The enemy had eyes everywhere, as their tail proved. He was in town under an hour and already someone on the enemy's payroll had picked up their scent. It was mostly luck, he knew; the Corrupter's people must have had someone watching the area already. It was for just that reason that they used the tunnel. Skulking through a smelly passageway was preferable to leading the enemy through the front door. The Amenti and their mortal helpers used a maze of tunnels to move unseen throughout the Cities of the Dead and even to certain points in Cairo and beyond.

The passage ended after fifty yards at a heavy steel door inscribed with a series of hieroglyphs. Beyond was a series of steps that let to a matching door. The protective glyphs were the work of the Kher-minu, mummies like Nicholas who specialized in the magic of amulets and wards. Bonded to the steel plate in this fashion, the symbols enabled the door to withstand anything up to an anti-tank round. There was no reason to assume an anti-tank round would ever be fired at them, but better safe than sorry.

Inside was a series of chambers carved in traditional Egyptian style. The hieroglyphs on the walls related tales of the gods and the Amenti, mixed with further protective wards like those on the doors. The central chamber was created centuries ago as the burial chamber of Beyd al-Qalarayn, a Mamluk general. This was unusual, as mausoleums typically interred the deceased aboveground—the tomb's main surface chamber even had an ornate casket. Seemed al-Qalarayn was rather paranoid, and secretly directed that his body be laid to rest where his enemies would not find it. An African scholar named Basel Nyambek knew of the now-obscure al-Qalarayn's odd interment quirk, and used it as the basis for his own retreat after rebirth as Basel Nyambek-Senemut. The leader of the Eseta in the area, he expanded the single underground cham-

ber into a number of rooms that spread out below the City of the Dead. Though run by the Eset-a, the safe house was available to all mummies and their mortal helpers. Cunningly wrought ventilation systems and electrical wiring piggybacked to the city grid, made the entire place not only livable but comfortable. The Mausoleum of al-Qalarayn remained in good repair, a large sandstone and marble tomb with a sweeping, arched courtyard long since closed off to the public. Since the only entrance to the tomb was through one of the half-dozen secret tunnels, privacy was assured.

Nicholas had stayed here after the rebirth into his third life. It felt as much like home as did the Sforza family estate on lake Michigan or Ankhotep's rooms long ago in the palace of Amenhotep III. He would have to wait to enjoy his return; for now, he had to try and turn the tables on his shadow.

As long as the man was still monitoring them, of course. If he was competent—and since Nicholas hadn't spotted him, he must be—the tail would wait around to see if the hovel was merely a stopover or if anyone else might show up. Only once he was sure they were in for good would he would report in.

Faruq had listened to Nicholas' brief explanation as they hustled down the tunnel. Once inside the main chamber, he headed for another room. "I will get something to help you blend in, Amenti."

Nicholas nodded, busy withdrawing a slim leather case from one of his duffels. Much of the stuff in his luggage would have caused alarm if customs hadn't been easily distracted with the "gift" of a stainless-steel cigarette case and Bulova watch he'd packed conspicuously at the top of his first duffel. Bribing customs was illegal and insulting, but a friendly gift was most welcome and made the whole process of arriving in Egypt run smoother for everyone.

Inside the case was a selection of gold and brass jewelry that shone warmly in the light. A few of the pieces were rendered in a traditional Egyptian style, but most looked filtered through the lens of an Art Deco sensibility. All included various hieroglyphs tooled into the surface, often with silver highlights, as part of the design. He'd fashioned these amulets himself, infused them with his own sekhem, his life force. The mystic energy could have been bound into a charm made of virtually any durable material—steel, wood, plastic, even glass—but Nicholas preferred the warm luster of gold and brass. Likewise, the style need not reflect ancient Egypt. His sensibilities remained modern in many ways after his resurrection, but he felt his art should honor the past. Nicholas had removed most before going through customs, not wanting to call attention to himself. The only amulet he wore between the airport and here was the Ankh-Meket, the scarab of life, that hung around his neck. He should have put the rest back on during the taxi ride, but he was distracted by the pleasure of being back in Egypt. He had no business calling himself an Amenti if he forgot such essential precautions.

Nicholas plucked out three rings, one designed as an abstraction of a scorpion, another with a series of hieroglyphs along its circumference and a third fashioned in the shape of the uraeus, the hooded cobra. Next he grabbed two bracelets embossed with a series of hieroglyphs, each featuring the symbol of a god—Sekhmet and Selket, respectively. Finally he took three matching necklaces with the glyph of Mentu inscribed on the back of a black scarab. That should be plenty to go after some middle management Apepnu. Then again… he *had* found himself on the receiving end of a beating in the last few fights. Nicholas dug in his bag for a velvet clamshell case and removed a pair of carved figurines.

Donning the various amulets, Nicholas felt wrapped in a cocoon of power that supplemented the protective aura of his spirit. Immortality filled him with unbridled energy as it was. Adding his protective charms, Nicholas felt ready to conquer the world before dinner.

Nicholas was draping the three flash scarabs around his neck when Faruq returned with a light robe and cloth skullcap, what locals called a djellaba and tarboosh. "These should be adequate."

"Perfect; thanks." Using the djellaba and cap, he shouldn't stand out in a crowd. Shirts and slacks were about as common among Cairene men as were the robe and tarboosh, but Nicholas' clothing had a distinctive Western cut. His skin was pale after winter in the Midwest, but Italian genes lent him a dark enough complexion and Mediterranean cast to his features that he should pass at a glance. Feeling an unexpected warmth from his scalp, Nicholas realized the tarboosh might come in handy for another reason—he no longer had hair to protect him from the sun's intensity. Maxwell Carpenter had kidnapped Nicholas and wrapped him in duct tape from head to toe. After he got free, he'd shaved his head down to stubble to get rid of the ruined tangle the strong adhesive had made of his hair. From the way his scalp felt, he might have the beginnings of sunburn. He made a mental note to buy some sunscreen and a hat after he took care of more immediate concerns. With a nod of thanks, he donned the djellaba and tarboosh and headed for a second door that led to a different tunnel.

"Amenti," Faruq asked, "do you need me with you?"

Nicholas considered. He knew enough Arabic to get by, but he wasn't familiar with the city. In contrast, Faruq was a Cairo native. Faruq was also mortal, while Nicholas was blessed by Osiris with immortality and skilled in the mystic hekau of ancient Egypt. "No, you stay put. I should blend well enough for a short while. And just in case something does happen to me, I need you to tell the other Amenti where I went. Make sure Ibrahim sticks around when he gets back, too. He's the only other one who knows about Chicago."

"I will, Amenti."

Nicholas sped down the tunnel, this one little more than a glorified conduit for electrical cables. He popped up amid a cluster of stunted date palms trees a few yards from the hovel he'd entered five minutes before. In seconds he was circling the area around the hovel. He tasted the faintest flavor of anticipation; from the shadow, it seemed, still watching. But where? That was the trick. The neighborhood wasn't very crowded, and the guy must have a good observation post. Nicholas took his time, moving as fluidly as thought. Even so, he found nobody peeking around corners or skulking behind obstructions. That left one of the two dozen people within sight—a couple street vendors selling wares, residents attending to domestic tasks, customers hanging out at an open-air coffeehouse up the road. None looked out of place, furtive, intent, or otherwise noteworthy. Taking a moment to think about it, the best possibility soon became clear. Whoever picked up their trail must have been watching the hovel even before Nicholas and Ibrahim arrived. Only at the coffeehouse— or qahwa, as the locals called it—could someone could sit for a long period of time without attracting attention.

He circled around and approached the qahwa from further up the lane. It was a no frills affair, a mud brick structure almost indistinguishable from the hovel that hid the tunnel. One wall was nothing more than a pair of large wooden doors, these currently folded back to reveal a serving counter. A trio of wobbly tables stood in a ragged line in a clear spot by the street. Two men sat at one, playing backgammon. Slipping in a bit more, Nicholas determined that the one facing him was the shop's owner and operator. Typical to relax in a game with a customer during a slow spell—which, for many of these hole-in-the-wall concerns, constituted their normal pace of business. But the old guy he played was sitting just so, allowing him to keep an eye on the hovel and almost any approach to it. Clever old fart, looking like your average Cairene with no place he needed to be and all the time in the world to get there.

There came Ibrahim, carrying a small bundle in a paper sack. He looked around then slipped in the hovel.

A few seconds later the old man waved his hands over the backgammon board. Seemed like the guy was just waiting to confirm Ibrahim before heading out. Nicholas ducked to one side in case the old man came his way. Then he heard the faint sound of a cannon. A second later, words in Arabic crackled through the air, amplified to the point of irritation by the loudspeakers scattered through the cemetery. Even with the cannon shot to prepare him, Nicholas was still startled by the Muslim call to prayer. He took advantage of the distraction to slip back to the safe house.

Nicholas found Faruq and Ibrahim talking in the central chamber. Everyone aboveground might be praying, but neither Egyptian felt the need. Faruq came from a long line of adherents to the ancient Egyptian pantheon and Ibrahim had converted from Islam years ago.

"Amenti! What did you learn?" Ibrahim asked, zeal burning in his eyes.

"Sorry, Ibrahim; nothing that requires you to take up arms just yet. I found the guy who shadowed us; wanted to pass on the word before I head after him."

"He is leaving now, Amenti Nicholas?"

"No, right now he's praying along with everyone else. He'll report in after he's done, though, so I gotta move."

Faruq was puzzled. "He is Muslim?"

"I don't know." Nicholas shook his head. "Could be. The enemy doesn't care about little things like religious preference, just that these fools can be manipulated eight ways to Sunday."

"Indihar and Lu Wen will arrive soon," Faruq observed. "What should I tell them if you have not yet returned?"

"Tell them I'm delivering a case of whup-ass, C.O.D."

"Amenti?" Faruq and Ibrahim gave him their best blank looks.

"Uh, tell them I'm off striking a blow for Ma'at."

An ideal given sentience, Ma'at was justice personified, the embodiment of cosmic order. Apophis the

Corrupter had spent millennia spreading its foul influence across the world. Ma'at cried out for cosmic balance, an equal measure of evil and good. The Lord of Life heard her call and commanded the mummies to arise. Nicholas Sforza-Ankhotep was among those blessed with the gift of a second chance and a duty greater than anything he had dreamed in either of his previous lives. Like his fellow Amenti, Nicholas was a child of Osiris, a warrior of Ma'at. He had been agonizing over his recent failure in the cause; now he was filled with the passion of retribution. He had the chance to strike a blow against their eternal enemy.

In the vernacular: To unleash a serious ass kicking on some righteously sorry sons of bitches.

TWO

The call to prayer was over by the time Nicholas got back to the qahwa. The area was returning to its normal languid activity, and the old guy was nowhere to be found.

Nicholas came in from the south and didn't see the guy, so he had to be further up the street. Nicholas hustled as much as he could without drawing attention to himself, and caught sight of the man just before he would have vanished through a sloppy intersection—the result of forming streets around haphazardly arranged mausoleums. The serpentine roads might provide local color, but they made navigating a bitch.

Nicholas was pretty good at following people thanks to the last years of his second life spent running S Securities. He had the natural charisma of the Undying, though, his vibrant life force drawing attention even when he tried to stay inconspicuous. It was like being the most attractive person in the room—not a problem as long as you're alone, but inconvenient if you're trying to fade into the background. Passersby took note and many registered the Western look of his clothing under the robe and cap. Cairenes saw stranger things than Nicholas, but even the slightest attention made shadowing someone that much more complicated. Not to mention that the old guy was skilled as well, the type who blended in with his surroundings and had the darting gaze of a hawk.

At least Nicholas had magic on his side. One of the rings he wore heightened his perception. Gifted with the eyes of a hawk and ears of a fox, he could let his quarry

range some distance ahead. Nicholas followed the tail north, the vast complex of the Citadel rising to the east. They exited the cemetery soon enough; Nicholas tried to remember the layout of this part of town. Noting the grand Ibn Tulun Mosque up ahead, he thought they might be on… ah, what was the name of it? Problem with Cairo is that most of these winding streets changed their names a half-dozen times in the space of a mile. This could be Shari as-Sayyida or maybe Shari al Hilmiya, or perhaps it was Shari al-Mu'izz. Who knew? After ten minutes, he had a much better understanding of why taxi drivers often had no idea where a destination was.

Even staying on the same roads, all the twists and turns were confusing. After twenty minutes, Nicholas had no idea how to get directly back to the safe house. He'd just have to head due south until he hit the City of the Dead and try zeroing in from there. The pounding heat didn't make trailing the guy any easier. The off-white djellaba reflected some of the lowering sun's rays, but he still felt like he was baking alive. His ancient self might welcome the heat, but most of Nicholas remained a child of the modern American Midwest. Perhaps he should fashion an amulet to protect him from temperature extremes; would keep him from getting sunburn on his tender head, too. He made a mental note to look into it.

Nicholas wiped the sweat from his face and forced himself to focus. It would help if he had an idea where they were headed; he could fashion a rough plan of approach and be alert for ambush. This just wasn't his city, though. All he knew was that they were moving north and slightly west—deeper into the city. Where the cramped streets and squat multi-story buildings suddenly replaced the area filled with pockets of grass and small mud brick and stone structures known as the Cities of the Dead.

The safe move would be to return to the Cities of the Dead. Meet with his fellow mummies, Indihar and Lu Wen—already coming by to learn how his mission went in Chicago—and pass along a description of the old man. After all, the tail might have pegged the hovel, but he didn't know about the secret passage. The Eset-a could use it to their advantage to set up an ambush. Or simply fill in the tunnel. The mummies knew arts that could clog the passage with hard-packed earth as if there had never been a hole.

But Nicholas kept going. He had spent his entire second life playing it safe. He'd been defined by taking the path of least resistance, doing what was expected. He no longer suffered that weakness; his ancient self had replaced it with the strength of resolute action. He would prove that he was still worthy of the gift he was given.

The promise of vengeance in his eyes, Nicholas Sforza-Ankhotep headed deeper into the city.

●●●

Like most of Cairo, the neighborhoods of Darb al-Ahmar didn't conform to a rigid, easily recognizable grid. The quarter occupied the eastern portion of the city below the Muqattam hills, The Citadel a constant presence rising high above. Nicholas was somewhat familiar with the area, having played tourist to check out the many mosques that peppered the neighborhood.

The street he was on was, if anything, even more cramped than those in the Cities of the Dead. Pedestrians hustled along in the waning afternoon light, running errands before heading home. A donkey cart forged its way through the foot traffic some distance up the street. Its driver was a rubabikya man, one of hundreds of rag pickers who traveled the city, recycling rubbish and reselling it. With a mixture of pride and sorrow, Ibrahim once told Nicholas that his father had been one. Ibrahim had explained the government-run trash collecting service was a joke, thanks to staggering maintenance costs and rampant corruption. A rubabikya man processed many of the things others threw away, making a decent enough living and keeping the city from being overwhelmed by the rubbish it produced.

Nicholas noted the old man stopped beside the donkey cart and exchanged a few words. Interesting. The rubabikya men would make excellent spies, covering neighborhoods regularly and probably learning a lot about the residents from the refuse collected. Nicholas wouldn't be surprised if a number of them worked for the enemy, even if unknowingly. He'd have to bring the subject up to the others, see if there was some way the mummies could use the rag pickers themselves, if they weren't already.

Sensing they were getting close to their destination, Nicholas decided to take advantage of the winding twists and turns and the shadows deepening in the gloom to sneak closer to the old man. He held back to between five and ten yards, keeping his quarry just in sight and using his hearing as much as he could. They went down a winding street past a few more houses, then around a corner to an alleyway slotted between a two-story mud-brick building and a sprawling wakalah, a kind of residential warehouse more recently converted to small shops and dwellings. Nicholas eased back as the old man flashed a look around before entering. Shuffling along with the flow, Nicholas passed the alley and rounded the next corner. A glance had shown him the alley ended at an archway into what appeared to be an interior courtyard.

Nicholas circled the block, which was comprised of the wakalah and three other buildings, all two-story mud brick residential structures. The three apartment buildings formed a U with the open end facing east. The wakalah closed up the top of the U, except for the alley entrance, to form a square. Looked like this was, indeed, the old man's destination. Here was the question: was he going to a particular apartment in one of those three buildings, or was the whole place under the enemy's influence? Best to assume the latter and re-evaluate as the situation warranted.

Now that he had the locale, Nicholas knew he should head back to the mausoleum. The sun would set in less than an hour, and it would take about thirty minutes to reach the southern City of the Dead—longer, if he got lost. But he couldn't just leave it. What if this place was a blind, like the hovel was for the Eset-a safe house? His wiser self wondered if he might be trying to compensate for his failure in Chicago, but Nicholas was too busy deciding on the best point of entry to give it any thought.

Darb al-Ahmar grew up in the days of Salah ad-Din. From what he'd seen so far, it had escaped the periodic rashes of urban renewal that hopscotched through the city. The buildings Nicholas observed appeared much like others in the neighborhood. They'd been constructed of mud brick centuries ago, rather than thrown together with concrete as an increasing number of buildings were in modern times. Dried mud was the perfect insulation, keeping the interior at a relatively even temperature—cool even in the blistering summer months and warm during the chilly desert nights. Each had a single main door set to one side and three narrow windows overlooking the street on each floor. The roofs were flat, with clusters of television aerials on each—as well as two small satellite dishes poking from one corner. Overall, seemed pleasant enough, even upscale for the area. It looked like there was once a fourth matching building where the wakalah stood. The residential warehouse covered more ground but wasn't quite as tall as the old apartments. A jumble of dilapidated buildings leaned over the street across from the wakalah, a few of them three stories tall. The setting sun threw their shadows over most of the warehouse. Considering the sun's angle and the convenient darkness, Nicholas thought that offered the best approach.

The tricky part would be getting on the wakalah's roof. Remembering an add-on to one side, a one-story storage shed or something, Nicholas slipped around and lounged in the angle where it joined the wakalah wall. Foot traffic was thinning fast as the day waned, but it would still be tough to time it right. Soon enough there was a few seconds' gap when no one was facing his way.

Drawing upon his bracelet of Selket, he leaped onto the shed's roof. Sure-footed as the scorpion that fell under the goddess's auspice, Nicholas leaped again to the top of the wakalah and made his way across its tiled roof. Nicholas moved deliberately over the ceramic tiles, careful not to dislodge them as he went. As far as he could tell, no one was watching from the apartment building roofs. He wasn't concerned with being spotted from below. People seldom looked up, especially in areas where things weren't built up that much. The cramped streets helped further; anyone on the street who wanted a decent look at the rooftops would have to crane his neck sharply. Nicholas could look at passersby from right overhead with little fear they might spot him. His perspective gave him a good view of the neighborhood, in fact. A series of mosques bordered the southeasterly portion of Darb al-Ahmar. He recognized them from his previous excursion—the minarets of the Ibn Tulun almost due south, with the Ar-Rifa'i and Sultan Hasan Mosques much closer to the east. In the distance beyond arose the imposing shape of the Citadel, its walls shining like gold in the lowering sun.

Although he still hadn't seen any lookouts on the adjoining roofs, he expected an attack at any second. He moved fast, slipping lightly along the rooftop, and was soon at the edge peering into the central courtyard. The space was tiled, with small plots of earth in each corner in which were planted clusters of ferns. A single door opened from each building into the courtyard, but there was no doorway into the wakalah. The three apartment buildings also had wrought-iron balconies on the second floor. The old man had plenty of time to get inside and Nicholas saw no other movement outside. It was impossible to tell which structure the guy had entered. Nicholas decided to give it a few minutes. See if the old man had merely dropped by to report. Nicholas hunkered down to one side where the wakalah roof met the right-hand apartment building.

A little while later, he heard the crunch of shoes—not from the courtyard, but from above. The measured pace of a bored guard. He pressed against the mud brick that rose eight feet to the apartment roof. Nicholas couldn't hide from anyone looking straight down, but otherwise a casual glance should miss him. The footsteps strolled by, growing quiet as the guard worked his way back around the roof.

Perhaps it would be best to head out. Nicholas took one last look down to the courtyard. He caught movement on the left side apartment roof and jerked back out of sight, cursing himself even as he did so. Sudden movements were the best way to get spotted. Sure enough, he heard a yell from the left-side roof. Not an alarm, at least. His Arabic was good enough to understand Lefty was calling out to the guard who'd just walked by above Nicholas.

Great, yeah, come check out if somebody's hiding down here. Nicholas scowled. If he ran now, they'd surely spot him. But what would they report? Somebody in a robe running across a rooftop. Fuck it; he was sick of running.

A stocky Egyptian torso poked over the roof lip right above him. Nicholas was ready, the surge of concern helping him pinpoint where the guard would be. He straightened, one hand grabbing the guard by the front of his shirt and yanking him down to land clumsily on his face near the roof's edge. Any doubt Nicholas had about the place or this man was wiped away at the sight of a snake tattoo that peeked out of the man's sleeve when he slapped a hand against the wall to get some leverage and regain his feet.

Nicholas faced the retainer of a Follower of Set; mortals like this often showed their loyalty with the serpent tattoo. Allegiance to one of the mummies' greatest foes left the man bereft of any mercy Nicholas might otherwise have shown. He moved with the speed of a striking scorpion and grabbed the front of the man's shirt again, yanking forward then driving back to strike him hard in the throat. Even as the first blow landed, Nicholas struck with the heel of his other hand against the man's temple.

The guard choked on whatever he was about to say, the blow to the head knocking him senseless an instant later. Nicholas kept hold of the cheap fabric and swung the twitching body over the roof's edge, then released. A cloud of dirt puffed around the guard as he hit the street.

Nicholas' sharp ears caught the other guard's scrambling as soon as the stocky one disappeared over the side. He hopped up and grabbed the roof edge above him, rolling up and over and laying flat behind the lip. An instant later he heard Lefty drop to the warehouse roof and scramble over the tile, calling, "Malik? Malik?" Concern became panic when Lefty saw his buddy Malik sprawled in the street below. Nicholas listened as the guard rushed to the edge of the roof overlooking the courtyard and yelled for help.

Nicholas peered over the roof's edge. *Bingo.* The old man and another, younger fellow, emerged into the thin strip of light that banded the west end of the courtyard. They shielded their eyes, staring up into the light of the setting sun toward the guard.

"Malik has fallen!" Lefty called down in Arabic. "I think that someone—"

"Hey!" exclaimed the younger man in the courtyard, pointing up to where Nicholas was moving, fully upright and in plain view, along the rooftop edge.

Soon as he was seen, Nicholas headed for the simple trap door that provided entrance to the rooftop. He vanished from view right away, but from the subsequent commotion it sounded like they were all converging on this building. Lefty clattered over the tiles and grabbed for the roof, shoes scraping against the side as struggled for the leverage to pull himself up. The door to the building squealed open and Nicholas soon heard one set of feet heading fast up the stairs. Too fast for the old man, so where was he? Straining a bit, Nicholas heard a shuffling step he'd tracked before. Sounded like the old guy was headed for the street to check on Malik. So far, it was going the way he'd hoped.

It would be easy enough to pick off each of these guards, but he didn't give a shit about them. The vampire they surely guarded was what interested him. The sun was setting even now; Nicholas would have to move fast if he wanted to deal with the creature before it could rise. It would be unwise to ignore the mortals entirely, though, so Nicholas decided to leave them a surprise. He dug into his pocket and tossed the pair of dog carvings to the rooftop and whispered a command in Egyptian. As he focused his will, the figurines began swelling. In a matter of seconds, they took on the form of two huge black mastiffs—Sherlock and Watson. Ebon eyes looked at him with an unnatural intelligence, awaiting his commands.

Nicholas' specialty was amulets, not effigies. He knew enough to get by, but nothing near the level of talent required to make magnificent beasts such as these. They were a gift from Lu Wen Khutenptah; the finely crafted pieces of ebony became creatures as swift and powerful as the most purebred mastiff, but possessing wits and cunning far beyond that of a natural animal. As he had to infuse them with a portion of his own life force, Nicholas used them only sparingly. He'd never had the chance to activate them in Chicago, a mistake he wouldn't repeat here.

Still speaking Egyptian, he directed Sherlock the guy coming up the stairs and Watson to deal with Lefty. All mortals in these buildings were fair game, but if the mastiffs caught a whiff of the undead, they'd get him right away. Powerful allies they may be, but the dogs were no hardier than their natural counterparts. They might give a vampire some trouble but there was little chance they could destroy one. Best to leave that to Nicholas.

Orders given, Nicholas leaped from the rooftop, the tiles shattering beneath his feet as he landed. The sound echoed through the shadows of the courtyard, triggering confused shouts from the rooftop. Then the shouts turned to screams, punctuated by low snarls. Nicholas smiled and dashed into the western apartment building.

The interior was part of a single large suite of rooms, rather than a series of separate apartments that he'd assumed. Stairs before him led up, and to his right the space opened on a large sitting room containing a pair of low couches strewn with pillows and a series of small tables. An antique writing table sat in one corner. Carpets scattered the floor and hangings adorned the walls, everything a lush Arabic decor. All very nice, but Nicholas was more interested in finding the vampire's resting place. Seemed most likely it was downstairs—having your coffin aboveground was asking for trouble. His ears, sharp as a fox's, heard stone grating on stone coming through a beaded hanging that was strung across the doorway on the opposite wall. He plunged through the hanging, into another well-appointed chamber. His gaze went to the center of a stone floor strewn with colorful rugs. One of the rugs was flipped aside by a marble square just lifting from the floor.

The creature pushing up from below saw Nicholas the instant he entered the room. Nicholas caught a flash of yellow reptile eyes, then the heavy stone slab was flying right at him.

The ancient portion of Nicholas' soul, his ka, acted as his very own guardian angel. There should have been no chance to avoid the hurtling stone, yet Nicholas somehow flung himself backward, arching his back as the marble flashed less than an inch from his face. The slab shattered against the wall as Nicholas continued his move into a backward roll. He came up in a crouch just as the vampire launched itself from its lair. The Followers of Set were dangerous predators, strong and fast and possessed of tremendous powers given them by their connection to their undead lord. Nicholas had hoped to catch this one before it emerged from its slumber; apparently it was an early riser.

The thing's skin became mottled and darkened to black scales as it came at him. It moved with hypnotic fluidity, one clawed hand flashing with deceptive speed.

Nicholas flung himself back a second time, the dark fingernails barely missing his throat. Not good, being on the defensive. Especially with his back to the door where this thing's lackeys were bound to come rushing through at any second.

Nicholas spun away and grabbed at one of the amulets around his neck. Trigger the scarab of Mentu and the vampire would be a pile of ash within seconds. The Follower matched Nicholas' speed, knocking the amulet aside just as he grabbed it. His hand went numb for a second from the force of the impact and the black scarab snapped its chain and bounced off a wall. Nicholas had no time to worry about losing the amulet, busy as he was avoiding the vampire's hand swinging in for a killing blow.

It turned out to be a feint, the Follower's left hand suddenly darting out for his throat. But Nicholas' spirit was in tune to the flow of fate. An infinitesimal shift of his balance and the vampire grabbed a handful of Nicholas' djellaba instead of his throat. The creature pulled, its mouth opening impossibly wide and needle-thin fangs extending from its upper jaw.

Having his throat torn out by vampire teeth was no more appealing than being eviscerated by undead talons, so Nicholas spun around and shrugged out of the robe. He continued the momentum, grabbing the far sleeve and flinging the djellaba over the Follower's head. The vampire snarled and tore at the cloth, but not fast enough to avoid the punishing blows Nicholas delivered with his curled fists. Got to love the avenging strength of righteousness bestowed by the amulet of Sekhmet. The creature's head snapped back, one side of its face a pulp of reptilian skin, startling white bone and dark red blood.

Then, just as Nicholas grabbed for the second scarab of Mentu, the ghul vanished. *Shit, the thing turned invisible!* He triggered the amulet with a shouted command. Blinding light and scorching heat blasted from the flash scarab and incinerated one of the couches. Nicholas cursed; his second of hesitation was all the vampire

needed to duck out of the way. The fire must have panicked it, though, for instead of feeling fangs at his throat Nicholas heard a short cry and saw the beaded curtain clatter open as a large nothingness plowed through it.

Nicholas snatched his lost amulet from the floor, then took off after his foe. Yells of pain and surprise came from the next room. Nicholas emerged to see the old man groaning where he lay by the door. *Yeah, well, tough*, Nicholas thought. *That's what you got for getting in the way of a panicky vampire.*

Heading for the door, Nicholas heard a cacophony of yelling from upstairs along with barks loud as shotgun blasts. Sounded like Sherlock and Watson had found more guards. He dashed into the courtyard and almost plowed into a guard armed with a large curved dagger. Nicholas didn't have time for this distraction; he needed to catch the vampire before it fled into the darkness. He grabbed the guard's wrist and twisted, using his momentum to drive the dagger into the man's chest as he pushed past.

Nicholas cast about with his heightened senses. He ignored the guard's gurgling gasps and the barking and screams from inside, ears straining to catch the telltale scuff of footfalls. Nothing. The Follower couldn't have gotten beyond earshot so fast, not from Nicholas' hearing, anyway. So it was likely the creature was still—

The rage was a palpable force, alerting Nicholas in time to spin. Pain flared along his shoulder, just missing his neck as he ducked. The wound went numb immediately, a strange lassitude threatening to overtake him. Nicholas leaped across the courtyard, turning to face the general area the Follower of Set was hiding. He fired off the flash scarab, the blast doing nothing more than scorch the wall. In the next second, he grabbed the last scarab of Mentu that hung at his neck and triggered it toward the opposite end of the arc from where he'd just fired.

That did the trick. The vampire's instinct to avoid the flame sent it away from the first blast and caught it in the second. The creature flickered to visibility shrieking in agony, its side aflame from catching the edge of the blast. Still, it had plenty of fight left. Even as it slapped at the flames, the vampire ran at Nicholas, its tongue flashing at him again in a deadly fork. The poison from the first strike was making Nicholas sluggish, but with an inspired twisting roll, Nicholas flung himself out of the way. He came up a crouch as the tongue darted at him again. Although focused on avoiding the attack, Nicholas noticed the old man had stumbled from inside—with a fire extinguisher, of all things—and ran toward them to spray liberally at the flames eating into the vampire.

Anger gave Nicholas renewed energy. His hand darted out as the tongue struck, grabbing it behind the fork. The undead screamed in rage and pain as it tried to draw its tongue back, but Nicholas held fast. The vampire might match his speed, but Nicholas had the edge on strength. Now would be the perfect time to fire off another scarab, but since he didn't have one, Nicholas improvised. Taking advantage of the momentary stalemate, he wiped his free hand across his brow, then inscribed a quick combination of hieroglyphs into the air. The sweat on his fingers hung sizzling in the air as he fashioned the warding. The vampire realized what he was doing and tried to close the remaining distance between them, but it was too late. Nicholas sketched the last symbol—the sign of the god Mentu, the personification of the sun's destructive heat—and a brilliant flash went off. It lasted only a second, but it was enough to engulf the end of the Follower's tongue in flame.

The fire flashed up the tongue's length like it was primer cord. Golden serpent's eyes grew wide in the vampire's face as the flames rushed at its face. Hissing and screeching, the creature flailed in confusion for a precious second, then bit down. Its burning tongue fell away, spewing a gout of blood. But the flames were too hungry to be denied. They surged across the gap to engulf the vampire's face.

A piercing shriek blasted Nicholas' eardrums as the Follower of Set flung itself around in an agonized frenzy. The old man tried to direct the fire extinguisher on his master, but the creature wouldn't oblige him by standing still. Then a dark shape sped from the apartment building and launched itself at the old man. He saw the mastiff in time to make a clumsy swing with the extinguisher. Sherlock ducked below the blow, then lunged forward to clamp his huge jaws on the old man's groin. Two vicious shakes and most of the old man tore away, describing a short arc that ended against the courtyard wall. There was a wet crunch and he crumpled to the cracked tiles, the extinguisher giving a hollow *thunk* as it landed beside him.

Nicholas moved to grab the fire extinguisher in case the burning vampire was aware enough to go after it. He was halfway to the container when the creature's head blew into a hundred chunks of flaming gore. The thing's body staggered, fire coursing over its torso, then collapsed. A minute later all that remained of the Follower of Set were blackened chunks of flesh.

THREE

Defeating one of Set's children didn't absolve Nicholas of failure in Chicago, but the memory of his victory against the vampire was a balm to his soul. He'd single-handedly destroyed a nest of the enemy. Hell, he would have torched the place if he hadn't been worried the fire would spread through the entire neighborhood. The disaster in Chicago had made him doubt his abilities, had made him doubt his worthiness as a warrior of Ma'at. Destroying the Follower of Set and its subjects had restored his confidence. It didn't erase the pain he still felt at losing fourteen men, but there was little he could do for the loyal Eset-a who fell in his service but carry on the fight.

He stepped out of the shower and toweled off, then trotted into the Spartan chamber that served as his bedroom. Sherlock thumped his tail in greeting, looking a little lost without his partner. Watson had reverted to statuette form in the fight, having suffered too much damage after stumbling into the guards' off-duty room. The figurine was a mess of gouges and cuts, but the damage could be repaired. The six guards Watson fought weren't so lucky. Nicholas had decided to maintain the enchantment on Sherlock for the time being; things were bound to be dicey for a while longer, and a loyal hound would be of great comfort.

After a minute of sifting through his duffel, he chose a pair of tan cotton slacks and a blue long-sleeved cotton crewneck shirt. Before dressing, he removed another small case and took out a roll of fine linen which he began wrapping up his arm. Starting at his injured

shoulder, he wound it down to his sprained wrist, then pinned it with a couple of stays. Thanks to the bandage's enchantment, his wrist should heal in a few hours and the ugly cut on his back wouldn't even leave a scar after a few days. Nicholas then slipped on his slacks, shirt and a pair of deck shoes. He was selecting his scarab necklace and the bracelet of Sekhmet from his somewhat reduced stash of amulets when he heard voices from down the corridor. A last look at his shaved head in a mirror over the simple dresser, and he declared himself ready for what as to come.

He strolled down the narrow corridor, Sherlock clicking along behind, and entered the main chamber. Faruq stood speaking with two women while noises from a set of narrow stairs suggested Ibrahim was up in the tomb. The woman to the right was a slight Asian with short-cropped hair and wearing a light long-sleeved top with a shallow scooped neck, capri pants and sandals. She carried a battered satchel over one shoulder. The other was a tall Egyptian in long-sleeved blouse, shawl, floral-print long skirt and flats. "It is good to see you also," the Egyptian said in Arabic, greeting Faruq. Seeing Nicholas enter, she inclined her head, her heart-shaped face expressionless. "Nicholas Sforza-Ankhotep."

"Indihar Nabih-Hentempet." Nicholas gave a shallow bow, repeating it a second time for the Asian woman. "Lu Wen Khutenptah."

"We did not expect you here already," Indihar said, switching to English. Nicholas' command of Arabic was weak; while the three mummies could talk comfortably in Egyptian, their mortal helpers might have some trouble. English served as a convenient default so that everyone could take part in the conversation.

"We took an earlier flight than what we'd told Faruq, just in case someone was listening in."

Lu Wen patted Sherlock's side in greeting. "How do you like Sherlock and Watson?"

"They're great; thanks. Unfortunately, I haven't gotten as much use out of them as I would've liked." He decided he'd tell her some other time about Watson's condition. "How is Xian?"

Lu Wen's face flushed with pleasure. "He is very well; thank you for asking. I sent him on a scouting mission recently, so I am having him rest now." Like others of the mummy caste known as Sakhmu, Lu Wen was a master of the art of effigy. She had fashioned a number of enchanted figurines and statues, including Nicholas' mastiffs. Perhaps her greatest creation was the small dragon, Xian. In its inert form, the creature was a breathtaking work of art, carved in exquisite detail from a ten-inch long block of ebony. Lu Wen had but to command the change, infusing her creation with a portion of her own spiritual energy, and Xian transformed into a miniature version of a dragon from Chinese folklore. It was a lithe, two-foot length of solid muscle, with a dramatic pair of feathered wings that extended from its snake-like body. The scales of its body and feathers of its wings were black, with a lush rainbow sheen like oil on water. The creature was as intelligent and perceptive as Lu Wen and handled a variety of tasks for her, from reconnaissance to guard duty to delivering messages.

Although from different castes, Nicholas and Lu Wen shared a creative temperament, and could pass the hours discussing the finer points of their respective arts. Indihar was of a more scientific bent, and endured only a few minutes of their chatting before she broke in. Directing a puzzled look at Nicholas' lack of hair, she asked, "Is this the style in America now?" Indihar wasn't known for her tact.

"Long story; I'll tell you later." Pointing toward the narrow stairs that led to the mausoleum courtyard, Nicholas continued, "Speaking of which, should we…?"

The two women were here as representatives of other factions within the Amenti, and were understandably

eager to learn how things went in Chicago. Nicholas wasn't looking forward to explaining how it had all gone wrong, but neither could he put it off any longer.

The stairway ascended behind a mural wall in the Mausoleum of al-Qalarayn, accessed by a false panel at one end. The old Mamluk interior murals had been redone in Egyptian decor, including four statues of Egyptian warriors placed in the corners and an ornate sarcophagus in the room's center. The face on the lid was a stylization of the tomb's new owner, Basel Nyambek-Senemut. Faruq had mentioned the Eset-a leader's body rested inside, awaiting a return to life. There was no timetable as to how long a resurrection took—for some, it was a matter of days, while others took months. There was no tried-and-true method for determining the time of resurrection… other than dying. And even the most masochistic mummy didn't look forward to finding out. Until Basel's soul gathered sufficient strength to return to its flesh, his body would rest within the sarcophagus. The mummies paused on the way through the chamber, each placing a hand on the sarcophagus in honor of their fallen comrade.

The next room was an antechamber, meant for offerings to the dead. Like the mausoleum's exterior, this had been left in the style popular among the Bahri Mamluks. It opened onto the mausoleum's courtyard, a tiled square that looked upon the vast expanse of stars above. Aside from the occasional sound of passersby on the surrounding streets and the distant murmur of vehicle traffic a half mile away, they felt the calm of isolation.

A stone wall ten feet high surrounded the courtyard, with a dry fountain in the center, its trio of Mamluk soldiers carved to life size. A scattering of lights was strung around the wall, shedding a soft illumination in the cool Egyptian night. The three mummies took seats on padded chairs Ibrahim had arranged around a low table on which sat a tea service and tray of hors d'oeuvres. Sherlock roamed around the perimeter; finding everything satisfactory, the enchanted mastiff thumped on his side by Nicholas' chair.

"The fountain is new," Nicholas remarked as Ibrahim poured each of them tea. He breathed in the aroma from his cup. With nightfall came a drop in temperature, making the tea a welcome shot of warmth. Even with the gravity of the impending conversation, he felt a great sense of calm. He hadn't felt this relaxed since… well, since he'd last left Egypt.

Lu Wen nodded. "Yes. I installed it a few weeks ago."

"Your design, or…?"

"Yes, it is my own. It looks authentic, does it not?"

"It does indeed." Nicholas often marveled at Lu Wen's skill, not in the least because she didn't restrict herself to one style. Many of the Undying—including Nicholas—created amulets and effigies in the Egyptian tradition. But Lu Wen drew as much upon her modern Asian sensibilities. And, as the Mamluk fountain indicated, she was expanding even beyond this. "Does it work?"

Lu Wen favored him with a Mona Lisa smile. "When it needs to."

"You may share tradecraft later," Indihar said, waving a hand as if to clear the conversation from the air. Both women had reputations for being blunt and plainspoken, but Indihar wasn't known as the polite one. "We are most curious why you have returned to Egypt so suddenly. Two months ago, you reported success. Yet you return empty-handed. What happened? Where is the Heart of Osiris?"

The Heart of Osiris—ab-Asar, as it was known in Egyptian. The mummies no longer spoke its ancient Egyptian name. Calling it simply "the Heart" was by no means a brilliant subterfuge, but its true name held too much power to be uttered. The same held for the other pieces of Osiris that were long ago scattered across the land. For the Heart was, in fact, a piece of their god. Osiris was eternal, but his jealous brother Set had sundered his body, thereby barring his return to the living

world. Only a power equal to Osiris' own could have kept his body from re-forming, and this Set had done with damnable effectiveness.

With mighty Osiris barred from restoring his flesh, it fell to the mummies, his progeny, to recover his long lost pieces. Once reassembled, the God of Life would walk the earth as he had millennia before. Osiris would rise and beat back the corruption of Apophis with the light of justice. Yet it was not a task the mummies could easily accomplish. Their enemies were legion and had an active hand in making sure Osiris' body remained lost. Even the venerable Imkhu, the Revered Ones who were the first to be resurrected in the days of ancient Egypt, had yet to collect more than a handful of the artifacts. Most often, rumors of one of the pieces turned out to be nothing more than a mistake, a hoax or a trap.

Nicholas' fellow mummies had assumed the same in this case. Indihar and Lu Wen represented other groups within the Amenti, just as Nicholas allied himself with the Eset-a. Indihar was the primary agent in Cairo of the Shemsu-heru, or Followers of Horus. Lu Wen was loyal to the Cult of Isis, those mummies most skilled in the ancient mystic arts, or hekau. They were all disciples of Osiris, but each group had its own view of how best to fulfill the god's wishes. Though united in the battle against Apophis and its minions, each faction operated on its own as much as it worked with the others. But the groups did at least keep one another abreast of their efforts… most of the time, anyway. Even the Undying weren't immune to the machinations of internal politics.

Nicholas' mission was not secret within mummy circles, and he was expected to forward reports of his progress if he encountered anything of note. None anticipated he would confirm that he'd actually found the Heart. Nicholas made quite a coup with his announcement. The other groups were understandably interested in such a significant find. Then he returned to Egypt, weeks earlier than planned. His contemporaries expected him to head straight for Saqqara, Abydos, Edfu, or some other mummy stronghold, the Heart clutched protectively against his breast. In coming to the Cities of the Dead, and without the Heart in his possession, it was evident something had gone grievously wrong.

"Your call announcing your return revealed little," Lu Wen added when Nicholas didn't speak immediately. "You understand that we are curious."

Nicholas leaned back in the chair and sighed. "First, let me apologize for being so brief over the phone. Seemed best to wait until I could speak with someone face-to-face."

Indihar waved one hand, rings flashing in the light. "We understand the need for caution. We are here now, so you may speak without reservation."

"Remember when I first left for the States? Following the rumors that one of the Osiris fragments was in Chicago. Having spent my second life there, I figured I had an edge on tracking down any leads." He paused, recalling what a long shot it was, that one of the greatest artifacts of the ancient Egyptians would be secreted in northern Illinois. Nicholas had gone to the States with little fanfare. "Six of us at first, myself and five of the Eset-a. No other immortals to spare chasing after hearsay, right? I understood the skepticism. I wasn't positive the Heart was in the area myself. But we had everything to gain by investigating. And I learned the rumors were true—it was stashed in the Temple of Akhenaton, all right."

Even now, millennia after the followers of Akhenaton had ceased being a threat to the mummies, anger stirred within Nicholas. His wiser self, Ankhotep, had lived in that dark time of the 18th Dynasty, when the Cult of the Sun-Disk arose to become a bitter enemy of the Undying. He was a mortal, a physician dedicated to serving the divine pharaoh in the court of Amenhotep III. His service continued when the son took the throne, but he soon saw Amenhotep IV was nothing like his father. The new pharaoh changed his name to Akhenaton, spurning Osiris and the other gods in favor

of the hopeful usurper Aton (or Aten, depending on how you chose to translate from the ancient Egyptian). A deity without gender, embodied in the rays of the sun, Aton was declared the only true god, the creator of all life and ruler of all… with Akhenaton as his divine counterpart.

It was a revolutionary idea on many levels. Aside from sending shock waves through Egyptian society that shattered generations of religious and cultural traditions, Akhenaton's new faith dared defy the eternal power of Osiris. Immortal defenders of Egypt, the mummies were appalled to hear that anyone, especially Pharaoh himself, would attempt such a thing. Egyptian priests may have labeled Amun-Ra as the king of gods, but that was little more than political maneuvering among the temples. Even they dared not dispute the unrivaled might of Osiris, Lord of Life.

The physician Ankhotep was one of many shocked by the strife that arose in the wake of the pharaoh's bizarre behavior. Generations of peace and enlightenment seemed in danger of being buried under the brewing disharmony. The conflict was most fierce between Pharaoh Akhenaton and the mummies. The Undying tried to reach a reconciliation. Akhenaton and his followers worshiped light and life just as they did. Was devotion to Aton so different that it could not reconcile with the greater pantheon? Akhenaton's rebuffs seemed to indicate so. The mummies were baffled, some suspecting Akhenaton might be an agent of Apophis—despite the Corrupter being a creature of darkness, not the light that Akhenaton revered. Their peaceful efforts went for naught, and scuffles broke out with increasing frequency. Ankhotep bandaged the wounds of the pharaoh's guard, becoming ever more ill at ease with the events unfolding around him.

Then came the day that the pharaoh challenged the Undying outright. They served false gods, Akhenaton claimed, and so were heretics to Aton and its followers. These claims were matched with powerful magic

Akhenaton and his priests directed at the mummies—
some altered form of the very hekau the Undying used.

Egypt was on the verge of religious civil war, with
Akhenaton and his bride Nefertiti on one side and the
Undying on the other. It should have been no contest,
but the Cult of the Sun-Disk tapped into powers greater
than the mummies would have though possible. Although the mummies were confident of ultimate victory,
the struggle would likely destroy the empire. Rather than
trigger outright warfare, the Undying faded into the background, leaving the pharaoh the seeming victor. They
did not want to see the great empire ravaged by internal
strife, but neither could they allow Akhenaton to defy
the will of Osiris. The argument over what action to take
went on for some time. Finally, they decided they had
no choice but to engineer Akhenaton's death and destroy the cult.

It was not a course undertaken lightly, and the sen-
tence was carried out only against Akhenaton himself
and his most loyal followers. His wife, Nefertiti, recanted
her claims of loyalty to the Sun-Disk, Aton, and so was
spared her husband's fate. The Undying hastened to place
her on the throne to take up rule of Egypt… only to
learn a few short years later that Nefertiti secretly continued her heretical worship. She vanished soon after,
along with the remaining followers of Aton. The child-
king Tutankhamen received the crown next. Ankhotep
was one of a handful of retainers who nurtured the young
pharaoh as best they could in the years following. Strife
on the throne of Egypt continued with Tut, though, as
he fell to Set's agents a short time later.

Like most citizens of the day, Ankhotep was con-
flicted about the rise of the Aton-u, the sun-disk cult.
He was disturbed by the thought that any force could
supplant Osiris and his deified brethren; yet how could
Aton's supremacy be contested if even the powerful mummies bowed to his might? Only later, after Ankhotep died
trying unsuccessfully to protect the young pharaoh

Tutankhamen from assassination, did he learn all that the mummies had done. Ankhotep's spirit lived on in Duat, the underworld kingdom of Osiris. There he heard the full tale from Sahura, one of the first mummies, during one of that venerable one's death cycles.

After Pharaoh Akhenaton's death, the mummies did what they could to eradicate all memory of his cult, but Nefertiti and the other disciples continued worship of the Sun-Disk. Soon enough the Undying had more important matters to attend to, as Apophis and Set continued growing in power. It was only centuries later that mystics in the Cult of Isis, one of few Egyptian sects who survived the passing of the ages, found compelling evidence that Nefertiti had taken a treasured artifact of Egypt and the Undying: the Heart of Osiris.

Learning that the heretical Aton-u possessed this most holy of items incensed the immortals. But the Undying were few in number. In addition, by this time they could no longer call upon the Egyptian empire for aid. The great civilization had been conquered by multiple peoples and had lost touch with its past. With only scattered loyalists for assistance, the immortals did their best to track down the Heart as well as the other lost artifacts. It would not be a task accomplished quickly, yet immortality offered a wealth of time.

When Osiris awoke, Ankhotep was among those commanded to join with a modern soul to form a new age of immortals. As he was born into his third life, Nicholas Sforza-Ankhotep vowed that he would let nothing stand in the way of restoring Osiris to his place of supremacy.

"And did the Cult of the Sun-Disk give you trouble?" Indihar asked, trying to guess as to what went wrong.

"They didn't even know what they had. The mighty have fallen quite a ways," Nicholas observed, the past—recent events and ancient history alike—weighing heavily on his mind. "Pockets of them still cause us grief, but the Chicago cell was full of sycophants playing dress-up.

Granted, the temple was impressive; designed by some-one with mystic talent. The Heart was kept in a sealed sarcophagus inside, the entire place designed with mystic wards that shielded it from detection. No wonder we'd never found it before. Just lucky that word of mouth brought it to our attention. But the people who were us-ing it when I investigated?" He shook his head. "They didn't have a clue."

Nicholas sipped tepid tea. "After I realized the Temple of Akhenaton really did hold the Heart, I re-vised the plan. The thing radiates unmistakable power. Once we removed it from its protective sarcophagus, every supernatural in the area with the slightest bit of sensitivity would've picked up on it. No way I could have gotten it back here safely with only five mortals as backup. But since everyone here was gearing up for the assault on the Dead Sea… well." From what little he'd heard, the Dead Sea affair—an assault against a major gather-ing of the enemy—had been a tremendous undertaking. He was curious as to how it had turned out, but now was not the time to ask. And his interest paled in compari-son to the frustration and anger he felt at being left in the cold in his own venture. If he'd had even one mummy to help him, it might have made all the difference.

"I was not aware that you had need of such aid at that time," Lu Wen said.

"I told Basel, but he said there was no one available. He sent me ten more Eset-a instead—half the number operating in Egypt, as I recall. Still, fifteen cultists don't compare to one mummy—no offense to Ibrahim and Faruq." He nodded to the two cultists, who nodded their understanding. He sighed, trying to let the anger go. "And I admit, I didn't think it was a big deal; the Heart was secure where it was. I decided to leave it safe for the moment and move forward with another plan we in the Eset-a had talked about: setting up a secure base in the States for us to work from. And what better place than something already well-equipped with mystic defenses?

"Gamal and I had already infiltrated the temple. We knew the current staff had nothing to do with making the place secure. It'd degenerated into little more than a community center. It wasn't difficult persuading the 'high priest' to sell, and we cleaned house once the papers were all signed and legal. With a little of Ibrahim's computer wizardry to help, I routed things through my old security company to avoid some hassles with permits and the like…" He realized he was getting off-track. They didn't care what he'd done to gain possession of the temple; they just wanted to know what happened to the Heart. "Anyway, the Heart was safe in the Temple of Akhenaton ever since the building's foundation was laid in the 1920s. With it under our control and with more advanced security measures in place, we were fine to wait until a few Amenti could reach us and help bring the Heart back. Despite that, I started feeling a… I guess I'd say an *urgency* that I should get it to Egypt as soon as possible. Gamal and Ibrahim were making the plans when we got a visit from three people claiming to work for one of the Chicago newspapers."

"The media?" Indihar was prepared to be upset. "Were you not to… what is the expression? Keep a low profile?"

"I *was*," Nicholas grumbled. "Okay, let me back up a few steps. As far as anyone knew back home, I was missing, possibly dead, although there was no conclusive proof of my death. Long term, I planned to re-establish contact with my old life; I have some useful contacts through my remaining family and my security firm. But for this mission, it was best if I operated below the radar. So I didn't go to my house or my old neighborhood haunts, nothing like that. I dealt with my firm through phone and modem lines Ibrahim jazzed up to display as overseas exchanges. And once we had the temple, I stayed on site to oversee the security upgrades and protect the Heart."

The women nodded their approval, assuaging Nicholas' irritation somewhat. They understood the limitations he'd been working under and the choices he'd made. He'd have to see if that understanding would continue when he explained how it had all fallen apart.

"My firm probably could've tracked me down, but they thought I was on a long-term surveillance gig and would be incommunicado until further notice. Besides, they got their paychecks every two weeks, so what did they care what I was doing? Otherwise, far as anyone knew, I hadn't been in town for months. But somebody found out I was back. We picked up someone casing the temple; even got some decent images of him. I routed the guy's face through my firm and had them dig up whatever they could find. Not a lot to work with, just having a face, but we finessed some search time with government databases—FBI and Interpol, that kind of thing—hoping to get a match from a mug shot or a government employee ID or something. But we got nothing. So he didn't have a criminal record and didn't work for a government agency. Then I figured it out." He laughed without humor. "You'll love this.. You know how I died my second death; couldn't even recall what possessed me to shoot myself, right? Turns out it was the man who raided the temple.

"Though calling him a 'man' is a misnomer. For lack of a better word, he's a zombie."

Indihar look at him, then cast her eyes over at Ibrahim.

"It is true, Amenti," Ibrahim asserted. "A bloodless devil killed many and fled with Nicholas as his hostage."

"He calls himself Maxwell Carpenter," Nicholas explained. "He had a history with my grandmother—far too long a story to get into now. Suffice it to say he returned from the grave with the idea he'd kill off my whole family. And he pretty much has, too." He rubbed his face, uncomfortable with the recollection. "Anyway, I wasn't too worried. We were secure in the temple and I created a prison to store him in if he was dumb enough to come after me.

"Then these so-called reporters showed up claiming they knew I was there. This, I was not expecting, but I couldn't ignore it."

"You say 'so-called.' They were not real reporters?"

"Nope, though I still don't know who they really were. Gave us bogus names at first, but one of them caved right off when I called them on it. A woman who they called Thea—exotic-looking; Arabic, but with some other flavor mixed in. Then two men; an Asian named Romeo, and a young black guy named Jake. Never got the chance to find out their last names. Odd, multi-cultural group, they were. I wasn't sure they were connected to the other guy, the one who'd been casing us. Regardless, we had to find out what these people were up to. So I had Gamal bring them inside—"

"What?!" Indihar's cry was a rather unattractive squawk.

"We had them covered, and the detectors didn't indicate any weapons. They were curious but I didn't sense they were a threat. But before I could find out what they wanted, someone launched an attack on the temple. We were on guard, but we were focused on the people inside. A full-on assault through the front… well, it surprised us. My fault; I was overconfident. Didn't think anyone would be so bold. The men recovered quickly and converged to protect the Heart, though, and it all would have been fine. Except, this Carpenter I mentioned? He chose that moment to make his own move. So while the 'reporters' were gunning for the Heart, the other guy was after me."

Indihar's frown made a drawn bow of her full lips. "So you fought this zombie. And meanwhile, the Heart…?"

"The 'reporters' swiped it. The Eset-a left alive after the Temple attack tracked them down and tried to recover it. They had it, too, but— the thing gives off a unique energy signature. Some undead in the area sensed it and swooped in to grab the Heart for themselves."

"Wait." Lu Wen was baffled. "Why were you not there to recover it yourself?"

"Because Carpenter…" Nicholas' face flushed. "He kidnapped me. A series of bad luck, overconfidence, and underestimating the enemy. Believe me, I won't make the same mistake again."

The women exchanged a look. "And how did you get free?"

"He ended up accidentally killing me. After I was resurrected, I got away. While he had me, though… he interrogated me. He used a strange power that forced me to reveal some of our secrets. I could not… I was unable to resist it."

A shocked silence lay over the courtyard. Nicholas could sense powerful, conflicting emotions emanating from the others like a fatal dose of radiation.

"He learned very little, but it was enough that he became interested in the Heart of Osiris. He came after it, with other creatures like him for support. I had only Ibrahim, Saled and Duri, but even then we might have defeated him. But we were… I was caught off-guard. Focused on getting the Heart back from the vampires, and Carpenter surprised us. We fought, and he ran, but…" Nicholas took a deep breath, the pain of it too much to get the words out the first time around. "He captured the Heart when he fled."

This time the silence was so profound Nicholas could almost hear cells divide.

Indihar was in a veritable frenzy. "Do you know where this creature has gone? Do you know where the Heart is now?"

Nicholas shook his head. "The compass scarab was destroyed in the fight. But I have a good idea of where to find it."

"Well?" Indihar demanded. "Where?"

"Here. He's coming to Egypt."

•••

Silence fell as the women looked at Nicholas and one another. This was a lot to take in, and he sensed from their turbulent emotions that it would take a while

to process fully. Indihar made no effort to conceal her reaction, her face a window on the feelings roiling inside her. Although as shaken up as the Shemsu-heru agent, Lu Wen was the picture of composure, but for a tightness around her eyes. Nicholas sensed strong concern from Faruq, but nothing on the level of the two mummies. Ibrahim must have given the old Eset-a a quick run-down of things while Nicholas was out earlier.

"How?" Indihar finally choked out. Her voice rose in volume and pitch as the words tumbled from her lips. "How could you allow this bloodless devil, this zombie, to murder fourteen of Osiris' faithful, learn the secrets of the Amenti from one of our kind, and steal one of our most sacred artifacts?!"

"Hey!" Nicholas snapped. "Don't make me the scapegoat. This whole thing could have been avoided if I'd gotten the support I asked for!"

"You were sent many Eset-a—"

"Who, capable as they are, don't even compare to one of us! We're talking about a major find, but you Shemsu-heru were too busy getting all pumped up about some Apepnu picnic to lend us a hand. The Eset-a getting screwed, like always!"

"That is excessive," Lu Wen interjected in a strong but calm voice.

"Is it? Everyone else thinks we're a bunch of radicals. We seldom get help from the rest of you, even on the simplest deals. I would've thought something this important would rate some assistance, but no!"

"You *are* radicals," Indihar retorted. "You Eset-a blunder around after the Osiris fragments with no thought of the consequences of your actions. We must operate with caution, choosing our battles carefully, until our numbers are sufficient to face the enemy on equal terms."

"Except that dragging our feet like that, we'll never catch up. Our top goal has to be restoring Osiris. I can't think of anyone who denies how vital that is to the cause.

Yet it seems like we're the only ones who bother trying to make it happen!"

"Watch yourself, Ankhotep," Indihar growled.

Lu Wen broke the staredown, leaning forward to grasp Nicholas' uninjured hand. "We will not solve these differences tonight. We do not think the Eset-a is unimportant, but your methods can be more extreme than warranted."

Indihar frowned, but gave a grudging nod. "Agreed. Your people can be helpful as long as they take direction. The Dead Sea assault, yes? Every caste was involved; even the Eset-a took part as its limited numbers allowed."

"It is unfortunate that the timing," Lu Wen said, "mobilizing when your request for support came… How could we have known what would happen?"

"Exactly!" Nicholas said. He was ready to unload further accusations, but instead slumped in his seat. He wasn't interested in pointing fingers. *Just get pissed when they're all pointing at me, is all.* In a more reasonable tone, he repeated, "Exactly. Look, no one saw this coming. The only ones who might have are the Mesektet, but I bet the sky priests were busy with the Dead Sea."

The Mesektet, or Midnight Suns, was a faction of the Undying skilled in the Egyptian art of divination. The sky priests could read portents in the sky, and were often consulted prior to major undertakings.

"Yes," Lu Wen said. "Everyone here was focused on the Dead Sea. Important as your discovery was, it… well, as you say. The other sects agreed it would be safe there for the time being."

After a beat, Indihar said, "This is true."

Nicholas looked at the others, holding his gaze a bit longer on Indihar. "Okay, fine. I know this isn't the time to place blame. Hell, I made some mistakes—and I'll never forget the men who died because of it. But I didn't come here to be judged or to look for absolution. I need your help to pass the word along, keep a lookout for Carpenter's arrival and recover the Heart as quickly as we can."

Lu Wen patted Nicholas' shoulder, directing a measured gaze at Indihar. "That is best, yes. People watch for new arrivals on the hajj. We can try to contact them, and warn those at the resurrection sites."

Nicholas knew from his own resurrection that the Amenti kept an eye on various points of entry into Egypt. Small teams of mortal helpers assisted a mummy in watching for the arrival of prospective immortals on the hajj. The term was culled from the Islamic tradition wherein Muslims journeyed to Mecca. For mummies, though, it referred to the recently dead who had joined with one of the tem-akh, the ancient Egyptian spirit fragments. Not yet immortal but no longer alive, they stumbled like zombies—and, indeed, were nothing more than animated corpses—toward Egypt, drawn by the power that suffused the Land of Khem. The Amenti waited to take them into their care and ferry them to one of the secret sites where the Spell of Life could be performed. The resurrection ceremony joined the modern and ancient souls and bonded them to the flesh, creating one of the Undying, the deathless Amenti.

Notifying these groups was easier said than done, since it wasn't as if they could just get on the phone and call everyone. Egypt's phone systems were a mess to begin with; plus, mummies typically holed up in places that lacked direct phone connections. The news would pass by word of mouth, as mummies and mortal helpers traveled from group to group on their normal course of business.

Indihar was silent for a few seconds, her emotions cooling and difficult to discern. At last, she stood and looked up at the cool night sky. "Indeed. What is past is past. We must plan for the future, as always. You are right that we must pass word along immediately, Ankhotep. In fact, I think it best if you would explain it all to the Imkhu yourself. They should know the full details of what has transpired."

The Amenti lived by the law of Ma'at and the grace of Osiris, but they didn't have a single command structure on earth. Hence the bickering between groups like the Eset-a, Shemsu-heru, Cult of Isis and others. The closest thing to a ruling hierarchy was the Imkhu. The Revered Ones were those mummies who enjoyed the gift of immortality since the ancient days. First among their ranks was the son of Osiris himself, Horus, a living god on earth. They were the inner circle of those loyal to Horus, the Shemsu-heru, the Followers of Horus. Horus and the rest of the Imkhu had spent recent centuries in seclusion, waiting for the time to emerge again as agents of justice. That time was upon them, and the Revered Ones were dedicated to leading their brethren to victory against the forces of corruption sweeping across the planet.

Those brethren willing to serve under the Imkhu's orders, that is. Nicholas was among those who respected the elder immortals, but who felt that they had fallen out of touch with the modern world. The wisdom and might of the Imkhu was vital to the struggle to restore the cosmic order, but Nicholas felt he knew better how to act against the enemy in the new millennium. Plus, it seemed that Horus was perhaps a little too enthralled with his unique role as living god, while his father, the great Osiris, remained caught between the worlds of spirit and flesh. Nicholas didn't doubt Horus' dedication to the struggle against Apophis, but he had to wonder why the Avenging Son wasn't more interested in bringing back Osiris. For his part, Nicholas felt returning the God of Life to the physical world was the mummies' absolute top priority if they were to defeat the enemy. It was this attitude that placed him in the less influential group of the Eset-a, rather than the Shemsu-heru.

A nervous chill coursed through Nicholas. To meet with the Imkhu was to hand off any control of his mission. But he knew Indihar was right. They needed that influence now. He still felt the need to redeem himself to the souls of his fallen men and in the eyes of Ma'at, but the most important thing was to recover the Heart of Osiris. His personal redemption could wait.

FOUR

Despite the long travel and time change, Nicholas awoke at dawn the next morning, refreshed. He joined Indihar, Lu Wen and Ibrahim for breakfast in the courtyard. Everyone was up early, as Faruq was making traveling arrangements to Edfu, home of the Imkhu, and it was likely Nicholas and Ibrahim would have to leave soon. Indihar was going to contact her fellow Shemsuheru in the Nile Delta to warn them of the Heart's possible approach, so she would not present Nicholas to her superiors. Lu Wen was part of the Cult of Isis, and had no interest in traveling to the Followers of Horus' stronghold. Instead, she would meet with her counterparts in the area and pass the news along as Indihar was. Face-to-face communication took time, but there was little alternative, thanks to sporadic telephone and cell phone coverage in the region.

The women had quite a bit of ground to cover, but Nicholas and Ibrahim would travel the farthest distance. Edfu was almost four hundred miles south of Cairo as the crow flies. The closest major airport was in Luxor, about seventy-five miles down river from Edfu. After reaching Luxor, they would rent a car to cover the rest of the way to Edfu. Tourists took the trip often, usually in the safety of recognized tour buses and such. Solitary travelers were safe for the most part, but violence had a tendency to erupt every so often in Upper Egypt. Nicholas wasn't much worried, even if he wouldn't have the other Amenti along for the ride. Not having Indihar along didn't bother him much, as she wasn't the most enjoyable traveling companion. He

had been looking forward to spending time with Lu Wen, but resigned himself to waiting until after the matter of the Heart was dealt with. He had to remind himself that there wasn't a shortage of time for beings such as they.

Early as it was, breakfast was a more relaxed affair than the previous evening. A night's sleep helped to calm them all and gave them time to process everything Nicholas had related.

Noticing Nicholas' hand reaching for the coffee pot, Indihar asked, "Why do you wear wrappings, Ankhotep?" Most mummies weren't sticklers about whether they preferred to be called by the name from their first or second lives. It fell to whatever most suited the speaker's temperament. Nicholas was among those with a more modern sensibility, Indihar at the other end of the spectrum. Lu Wen fell somewhere in the middle.

"I took a stroll into the city yesterday afternoon."

"Faruq had mentioned something of this when we arrived," Indihar said as she and Lu Wen looked at him with faint concern. "You know it is not safe there, even for us. Cairo is polluted by the presence of the enemy."

"I know. Although as of last evening, there's one less enemy to worry about."

"Ahh. Faruq had said something about 'whooping ass'?" Lu Wen observed.

"Oh, right!" Nicholas laughed. "I told him I was opening up a case of whup-ass. Smackdown, ass-kicking, that kind of thing. You know?" The women smiled politely, reminding Nicholas he wasn't just dealing with a debriefing. His modern self came from a distinctly different cultural background than either woman did. Indihar was a native of Cairo, and Lu Wen spent her second life before her rebirth in China.

"And how did it go?"

Nicholas explained how he'd noticed the old man tailing him and Ibrahim and decided to turn the tables. "I discovered a vampire; Follower of Set. And some attendants. I hadn't committed to attacking until a guard forced my hand. But they won't trouble us again."

Indihar frowned, nodding her approval. "Those creatures grow ever more bold."

Nicholas cocked an eyebrow. "How do you mean?"

"The Dead Sea," Lu Wen said.

"Right. All Ibrahim and I heard was that there was some major undertaking against the enemy near the Dead Sea. Considering, well, y'know…" he shrugged away the tension of the previous night's meeting. "It must have been a serious deal."

"It was. As they ever have, the servants of Apophis draw out the worst that lies within mortal society." Indihar's grim look lent her a cold beauty. "The conflict that flares again between the Israelis and Palestinians is but their latest effort."

"What, the renewed fighting in Israel? You're not saying the undead are behind that."

"Even the Corrupter's agents cannot claim credit for having begun that struggle," Lu Wen clarified. "But our enemy is not above using it as an opportunity. The Apepnu and the undead alike have been encouraging the old hatreds between the Israelis and the Palestinians by playing the sides against one another."

"Sounds familiar," Nicholas grumbled.

Indihar nodded. "They surface on either side to perform their atrocities. The victims think the other side made the attack, and so the violence escalates."

"I suppose we are fortunate it is no worse," Ibrahim observed. He'd been intimidated last night, not wanting to jump into an argument with three mummies. This topic was more up his alley. Having grown up in the area, he was familiar with Middle East tensions. "The enemy would like nothing more than to push outright war throughout the region."

Indihar's eyes flashed with pride. "Indeed. We believe that is what they planned. Our ambush was the

greatest blow against the enemy since Osiris has awakened. It is unfortunate you were not here to join the battle, Ankhotep!"

Nicholas knew full well why he hadn't been on hand. He was busy in Chicago recovering the treasured ab-Asar. And then losing it. No sense poking the wound now. He poured some cream in his coffee. "So what did happen?"

"One of the Mesektet saw portents that the enemy was gathering near the Dead Sea, a force in size unknown since the days of the New Kingdom."

"On both sides of the sea," Lu Wen explained. "It was not easy to detect, as I understand—the Apepnu amassed powerful magic to disguise their presence from view, both mundane and mystic—but with aid from the Cult of Isis, we gleaned the locations."

Indihar inclined her head in thanks. "They intended assaults on multiple locations throughout the territory. Not only the contested lands of Israel-Palestine, but eastward into Jordan and north into Syria. The western forces were combined of perhaps five hundred mortals and thirty Asekhsen under the command of Hau-hra and Hemhemti."

"Holy… Basel and I ran into Hau-hra a while back." Nicholas shivered at the memory. He was one of a growing tribe of immortals in service to eternal Osiris and wise Ma'at, servants of balance in nature. The Apepnu, the Bane mummies, were their antithesis. Seven powerful mockeries who used a dark version of Osiris' gift to attain immortality, these creatures' sole purpose was to spread corruption through the world. The Bane mummies were the first and most potent of the Apepnu— the servants of Apophis—and their very existence was an outrage. Each of the Bane mummies' bodies was twisted in some gruesome fashion, outward evidence of the depravity that possessed their souls. Nicholas' encounter with one of their number was the most terrifying experience of his existence. It was but a few weeks after his rebirth as one of the Undying, on a day trip with Basel Nyambek-Senemut up the Nile. They'd stumbled across an attack on the river—Nicholas still didn't know just what was happening; the thing went to chaos too fast for recollection.

One thing remained burned in his memory: The horrid creature known as Hau-hra of the Backward Face. A ridiculous name, but scarily accurate. At a glance, the Apepnu's bald head appeared reversed upon his body, the face looking out over his muscular back instead of forward. Yet while the creature's skull did face the proper direction, his features were somehow… *moved* to the opposite side. The front was a mottled expanse of discolored flesh, with only the vaguest of hints of what might once have been a brow ridge, nose and jawline. It was as if the face on that side had dried up and blown away, leaving only the ears in their normal place. The back of Hau-hra's skull showed eyes bulging from shallow ocular cavities and a flattened lump of flesh with two gaping holes that formed his nose. A horizontal crease split the skull below the nose, an obscene slit that served as a mouth. A vestigial jaw, seemingly slapped on at the base of the skull, enjoyed only limited movement. It looked like something a sculptor with little talent and working without any reference material might put together. The rest of the creature's body retained a more conventional shape—two arms and two legs in their proper places and of normal shape and length. In fact, aside from his head, Hau-hra had a good physique, the lean and well-muscled body of a marathon runner. Having his features slapped on the back of his head appeared to hinder him not at all. His body was double-jointed and quite flexible, showing equal mobility walking forward and backward.

"Hau-hra was… well, just remembering the glimpse I had gives me the shakes. He had us outgunned so we ran back here like a couple of punks." Nicholas had never met the Apepnu called Hemhemti, but the Bane mummy was purported to be as frightful in his own way as Hau-hra was. Just one of them was threat enough, but for two to come together and lead such a force? Nicholas gave

thanks to Ma'at that his fellow mummies uncovered the plot in time to stop it. "Sounds like they did a serious recruiting drive since then. I can just imagine how nasty such a force would be with a second Apepnu and a so many reapers along for the ride."

The numbers weren't worthy of being called an army. Still, they were significant in terms of saboteurs, assassins and provocateurs. The Corrupter's children preferred to work their evil by manipulating others from the shadows. With a force of that size, they could wreak all manner of havoc throughout the already turbulent Israeli/Palestinian region. The groups must have been brought together for some conference otherwise impossible to hold remotely... or, knowing the tactics preferred by Apophis' lackeys, so that some dark enchantment could be performed on them. Not that the thousand mortals would have any idea of their true role in the matter. They were more likely mercenaries and zealots, ultimately ignorant of what they served. Nicholas assumed the living were Palestinians and/or Israelis—probably both, split into the two groups—seduced by promises and lies. The Apepnu were loyal to a faith far older than Islam and Judaism, but were not above masking their true beliefs to further their goals. Each force must have thought it was coming together to strike a blow for its people, when in truth it was nothing more than a tool spreading Apophis' darkness.

The hundreds of mortals were nowhere near as disquieting as having that many Asekh-sen in one place. The creatures, also called reapers, were the result of a Bane mummy's efforts to create more evil immortals after their original ceremony was lost. The monster Kharebutu bound ifrit, or evil spirits, to human corpses in a poor attempt at immortality. Asekh-sen made powerful shock troops, strong and relentless... and able to return to life after being slain, just as an Amenti could. That the Asekh-sen were capable of only four resurrections, each more twisted and horrific than the last, did little to lessen the threat they posed. Nicholas understood why all the Amenti in the region had mobilized to battle this threat. "You said 'western force.' More of the enemy than that, even?"

"Yes. A force on the Dead Sea's eastern shore comprised an equal number of mortals, led by a dozen ghuls under the direction of a Follower of Set named Zainab Jinnah."

Nicholas paused, a forkful of mixed fruit halfway to his mouth. A second force made up of ghuls—vampires? These creatures were almost equal to the Bane mummies in enmity to the Undying. Most hated were the Followers of Set, bloodsuckers who worshipped the brother and murderer of Osiris himself. Nicholas' immortal cousins would be quite eager to destroy a baker's dozen Followers. "I can see what you mean by them getting bold. Can't say as I'm familiar with this Zainab guy."

"It is—was—a woman. She is an old ghul, the face of an angel but with a heart as black as Set himself," Indihar spat.

Lu Wen chuckled. "Well, not any longer. I was with those who struck the eastern force. We did not destroy her in the attack, but neither did she escape unscathed. She was struck with flame across her precious face before she fled."

"In time, we will find her," Indihar promised.

Time indeed. For the immortal Amenti, it was ever a matter of *when*, not *if*. "Interesting that the Bane mummies and Set's followers would be working in concert like that," Nicholas said.

"Yes; for all that each is a tool of Apophis, they do normally squabble amongst themselves. We believe they worked out an arrangement. The Corrupter would grow bloated on death if the Arab nations and Israel erupted in violence."

"Even drawing in Europe and the US, depending."

"As the saying goes, 'the more, the merrier.'" Indihar's brow darkened. "Mortals inflict horrors enough on one

another that they may accomplish the same goal on their own in coming months. But the Apepnu are not above rushing things."

Nicholas nodded. "But what would the Followers of Set get out of it? I wouldn't think they're interested in stirring things up that obviously. Hurts their food supply, you know?"

"Of that, we are not as sure," Lu Wen admitted. "But we think they agreed to push into the Arab lands as part of an effort to oust the creature Talaq and expand their base of power."

"Who?"

"It is unclear what he is," Faruq said, emerging from the underground complex. Although mortal, Faruq was one of a handful of cultists who dedicated his life to the mummies' cause. He had long studied ancient tomes and modern rumors alike, keeping tabs on the forces of Apophis for the day when the scion of Osiris would return. His knowledge was coveted even among the wise Amenti. Nicholas knew it irked the other groups within mummy society—especially the Shemsu-heru and Children of Osiris—that Faruq had pledged his aid to the fringe Eset-a. "If half the words I have heard on the subject can be trusted, this Talaq has ruled Jordan in secret since the nation was established. He is not one of your kind, but perhaps neither is he a ghul. He is associated with the Hashashin in some way, however, so it may be his is one of the undead." Faruq shrugged. "All that is clear of late is that much activity in that region is directed at him."

Nicholas filed the information. He had heard of the sect of vampires who'd come to be called Hashashin, the term from which the modern "assassin" was derived. Not hated as greatly as the Followers of Set but no less dangerous to mummies, these undead killers-for-hire had carved out a power base throughout the Middle East. If anything, they were even more secretive and insidious than the Followers were, and proving just as hard to locate and eradicate. He doubted he would run across them or this strange

Talaq person, seeing as how Nicholas' focus was the New World, but it didn't hurt to learn all he could. Who knew where he might be a century or two down the road?

"All right, so the Apepnu were gunning for Israel while this Zainab and her people had their sights set on the Arab nations," Nicholas prompted. "Until you charged in and pounded them into the ground."

"Indeed." Indihar's tone was matter-of-fact but her eyes flashed with the recollection. "They grew complacent over the centuries, and overconfident in their mystic prowess. We swept down from the clouds, using the enemy's precious darkness as cover for our approach. They were greater in number, but we are Amenti. They could not hope to stand against the strength of our hekau."

Nicholas had mixed feelings as he listened. He hadn't taken part in the Dead Sea assault because he'd been pursuing his own mission in America—a mission he was forced to try completing with insufficient backup thanks to the raid on the Dead Sea. With what Indihar and Lu Wen were saying, it sounded like they had enough firepower; they couldn't have spared a single mummy? If they had, Nicholas would be returning in victory, not disgrace. All part of the politics. The Eset-a were often the odd group out, considered too zealous in their pursuits of the lost artifacts. The other mummy groups worked with Eset-a members, but there was a base level of mistrust. And what resources the Amenti and their allies had were seldom allocated equally to the Eset-a, despite what the others might say.

Wallowing in self-pity as he was, Nicholas almost missed Indihar's comment. "One of the Apepnu was slain?" This was big news.

"I saw it myself," Indihar said. "Hau-hra of the Backward Face, struck down while battling Senemut."

"So that's how Basel died? Taking Hau-hra down?"

Indihar nodded, casting a look back into the mausoleum. "He fought valiantly. As we were recovering his body, a pair of the accursed reapers fled with Hau-hra's corpse."

Lu Wen frowned. "Hemhemti escaped as well, fleeing under cover of a cloud of his own stench."

Nice to hear I'm not the only one making mistakes, Nicholas thought. A surprise attack and they didn't capture even one of the Bane mummies? Being mummies meant they were immortal, obviously, so the damn things were as hard to kill permanently as the Amenti were. So the Amenti now tried to capture them. Held captive, the Apepnu would at least be kept from wreaking havoc until they could be destroyed. "Does anyone know how long it might be before Hau-hra returns to life?"

"Unfortunately, the Bane mummies need not stand in judgment before Ma'at, so sooner than is common for us."

Ma'at was the Egyptian deity of justice, the faceless entity that enforced the balance upon nature. The god of justice commanded a council of forty-two judges who dwelled within the spirit world the mummies called the Duat. They determined which immortal souls were worthy of returning to life. Basel's soul had descended to this place and was even now standing before the Judges of Ma'at. Nicholas had done the same recently, after his death at the hands of Maxwell Carpenter. Unlike Basel, he had been resurrected after only a short time in the Duat—perhaps less than twelve hours. An amazingly short duration, he knew, considering most mummies had to wait for weeks—or, more commonly, months—before their soul gathered the strength to push across the barrier separating the spirit world from the living and re-inhabit their body. He didn't know if his rapid recovery was a gift of Ma'at. Considering Carpenter recovered from his own injuries not too long after, Nicholas suspected it might be. Whatever his particular circumstances, the basics held true for the Bane mummies also. While they didn't face Ma'at's judgment, the Apepnu spirits had to gather sufficient spiritual energy before they could return to their bodies. Hau-hra would be back, and soon.

"Well, that sucks just a bit."

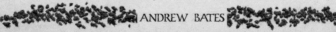

Lu Wen shrugged with one shoulder and shifted the satchel on her lap. "The leaders escaped, but seriously injured. It will be some time before they return to their full strength."

"And the remainder of the forces?" The way this was sounding, Nicholas couldn't account for why they would be so pleased with the raid.

"We decimated them. Utterly," Indihar confirmed in response to Nicholas' implicit challenge. "We even recovered most of the reaper corpses so that they may be destroyed again as soon as they rise."

"Perhaps one or two wounded undead slipped away in the struggle," Lu Wen added, "but no more. The rest were staked and destroyed in the hills where we fought."

"We are also confident that we have set back their plans. Until that assault, we are sure the Apepnu had no idea of our strength. They assumed we were still the handful of immortals we have been for centuries. Too few in number to challenge any of their efforts directly. Now they know otherwise."

"I'd wondered about that. The Imkhu didn't think it might be wiser to, say, wait until the forces dispersed and pick off the smaller groups one by one? Disguise our full strength?"

Both women shook their heads. "There was some discussion," Lu Wen admitted, "but we could not take the risk of letting them disperse. And even now the enemy does not grasp our true numbers. By striking so forcefully, we are confident they think we are far stronger than is the case."

"A show of force would make the enemy tread in fear in the future," Indihar said. "Thinking we are everywhere and know of their every move, they would be tentative, unsure of their best course of action. They would lose the confidence that has been among their greatest tools. Fill their hearts with fear and we are assured of victory."

Nicholas gave a grudging nod. Before his rebirth, his natural inclination was to take baby steps; now he saw the

merit of taking bold, decisive action. Unfortunately, doing so meant you didn't always see complications until they ran you over. The Dead Sea assault was a good example. If the Amenti had taken a subtler course, who was to say they would not have caught the Bane mummies, or this vampire Zainab? Hindsight was 20/20, as they say.

"I do not wish to cut your breakfast short, Amenti Nicholas" Faruq interrupted, "but I have scheduled you and Ibrahim on a flight south. You should leave soon if you are to reach the airport in time."

"I was able to contact them last night, so they are expecting your arrival," Indihar promised as Nicholas made his good-byes. When he began with a lackluster thank you, she waved him to silence. "I know there is little love lost between us. No, do not protest; you are not the only one to sense strong emotion, yes? But I bear you no malice, and do not begrudge you your failures."

"Gee, there's a pep talk."

"You know what I mean, Ankhotep. Despite failure, Osiris does not give up. One may win battles but still lose the war, correct? Apophis is not invulnerable, and neither is this Maxwell Carpenter. Remain true to Ma'at, and you will prevail."

Nicholas was speechless. Indihar wasn't the warm and cuddly type; he didn't know how to respond to her words of support. He cleared his throat and muttered a subdued "Thank you."

Lu Wen arose from her seat then and offered words of farewell. Nicholas remembered something then, and dug the carving of Watson from his pocket. "I broke him," he apologized. "You think it's fixable?"

She cast a critical eye over the scarred and pitted figurine. "This is not so bad. It would take some time, but I could repair it. Of course, if you became just a little more skilled in crafting these things, you could fix it yourself."

"I know. But I don't expect I'll have the opportunity any time soon."

With a smile, Lu Wen handed the carved dog back. "You will find the time someday. Perhaps as you travel, you can practice on fixing the minor damage."

"Good idea. Thanks."

"You are welcome, Nicholas. And Indihar is right. We are not judged by a single event, but by the actions of a lifetime."

He had to smile. For a mummy, that lifetime never ended, and only Ma'at could make the final judgment.

• • •

Settled in their seats of Egyptair Flight 133, Nicholas nudged Ibrahim. "You've been awfully quiet. What's on your mind?"

"It is nothing, Ame— er, Nicholas."

"Uh huh. So, what? You think the brooding look will help you get women?"

Ibrahim frowned in puzzlement. "You can be very strange at times, Nicholas."

"Don't change the subject. We're talking about you right now."

"It is nothing, really. Just that…"

Nicholas made drawing out motions with his hand. "Come on, you can do it."

Ibrahim looked around the cabin. It was a morning flight in the tail end of tourist season; a scattering of business travelers sat among tourists planning a full day of sightseeing. Leaning close to Nicholas, he murmured, "I do not understand why I was spared."

"Spared? You mean in Chicago?"

Ibrahim nodded. "I have done my best to learn the combat skills, but my talents lie in computers. Gamal or Omar, or Duri most especially; they would be much more helpful to you now than I. Experienced warriors, they are."

Nicholas had been so caught up in his own situation he hadn't even considered how it might have affected Ibrahim. Immortality didn't automatically provide

total enlightenment. "Not a good idea to start thinking along those lines, Ibrahim. It doesn't accomplish anything but get you depressed."

From Ibrahim's expression, Nicholas' words weren't that helpful.

"Look, you have what's called survivor's guilt. You're glad you didn't die, but you think you're a bastard for feeling that way because other people got killed. There's no easy answer for it. Just need to come to terms and move on. I feel the same way, having become what I am. I've lost a lot of good men. Not only that, I'm the last one of my family, all because some freak had such a hard-on for revenge he couldn't stay dead." He laughed and rolled his eyes. "Maybe not a good example—me, I mean."

Ibrahim cleared his throat. "You remember when I said you can be strange, Nicholas?"

"Okay, okay; I'll shut up."

● ● ●

Luxor was a short hop by plane, and they were in an old Volvo and heading south before ten that morning. Ibrahim drove, leaving Nicholas free to watch the Nile go by and ponder his upcoming meeting with the eldest and most venerable among his kind. He had yet to come face-to-face with one of the Imkhu. There weren't many of the Undying, but neither were they a close-knit bunch. They were reborn with a mission, and even with eternity in their grasp, that didn't allow for a lot of hanging out and chatting. For his part, Nicholas was occupied after his resurrection with coming to grips with his immortal nature, mastering Egyptian hekau and understanding the full scope of the conflict into which he'd been drawn. This, his first meeting, would be held under less than favorable circumstances. He felt like a child going to the principal's office. With an effort, he suppressed his agitation.

They crossed the Nile and made Edfu before noon. The ancient site had spawned a small modern city of over sixty thousand people. Modern-day Edfu was situated in the lush greenery next to the Nile, and served as a trading center for grain, dates and cotton. Still, tourism was the main source of income—or it had been, before Horus the Avenger and his Shemsu-heru returned to Egypt. They took control of the Temple of Horus and the surrounding excavations, including the ancient city and its surrounding necropolis, and promptly closed the entire area off from any public access. Presumably due to a combination of bribes and subtle application of magic, the Egyptian government announced the site closed for further excavations. Some noise was made about efforts to buttress structural instabilities to the temple's high stone walls. Rumor suggested that a major new site had been found and was being uncovered in secrecy. This was all true enough, in its way.

The Temple of Horus was, in fact, in excellent condition for its age. Situated in the desert just beyond the Nile's influence, its sandstone walls had suffered very little erosion through the centuries. Towering figures of Horus inscribed in the walls were almost as sharp as when they were first carved in the Ptolemaic dynasty, a few centuries before the birth of Christ. Still, wear was unavoidable, and Horus had directed a small staff of mummies and mortal helpers to repair all damage. It was an impressive effort in itself, yet the focus of the Avenger's attention was on the complex buried *beneath* the present site. From a time over one thousand years before the existing Temple of Horus was erected, the barest fraction of it had been uncovered by modern archaeologists. Horus was determined to restore his original temple city to its former glory—to a city fit for the son of a god.

With arcane hekau at their command, the mummies were making significant progress. And, to distant observation, they looked like nothing more than a large, very well organized archaeology crew.

A man waved the Volvo to a stop along the road that led to the temple. The Shemsu-heru cultist was dressed in Egyptian military garb—and, for all Nicholas

knew, was actually in the army. Once he confirmed their identities they were waved through. The solitary guard in his little mud shack was typical of lackluster checkpoints throughout the region. There were no fences or other visible barriers keeping the curious out; the desert did an excellent job of that. Nicholas knew subtle defensive measures ringed the area, amulets that would alert the Shemsu-heru of intrusion. Patrols circled the site as well, dressed as Egyptian military and armed with weaponry mundane and mystic.

As they bounced along the road the last half-mile, Nicholas was again frustrated by the choices groups like the Shemsu-heru made. Edfu was an impressive stronghold, but did their cause truly require restoring an old temple complex to this degree? It was stirring, seeing relics of his first life returned to their former glory, but would not the struggle be better served directing all these resources to fighting the enemy? He'd made a similar effort to establish the Temple of Akhenaton as a stronghold in America—only to be overrun, kidnapped and robbed. The Temple of Horus was far more secure, but Nicholas felt the lesson was valuable nonetheless. If he could find the nerve, he would make this case to the Imkhu.

A collection of tents and old mud brick buildings housed most of the residents. Enough of the original Horus complex was restored that the Avenger himself, as well as most of the Imkhu and a number of younger mummies, had moved there. Parking next to a collection of Jeeps, Land Rovers and a few Humvees, Nicholas and Ibrahim made their way through the temple toward the restored chambers. Temple walls rose to either side of the main entrance like two great wings. The lines were crisp without any crumbled sandstone gaps. The bricks were again as sharply squared-off as they'd been when first stacked three thousand years before. Images of Horus stood in sharp relief along the wall. The sun blazed along the temple surface, turning the yellow bricks to gold. The temple's interior was no less impressive, all the pylons, columns and the inner temple restored almost exactly as they'd been when first constructed. It was a sight to take the breath away.

Above it all a dozen falcons floated on thermals. Nicholas suspected a number of them were creations like Sherlock and Watson, unflagging sentries watching the terrain for miles around, alert for any incursion. Nicholas patted the pocket of his slacks where he'd stowed the mastiff carvings. Sherlock was again a figurine to make traveling easier. It would be a simple enough matter to animate him again. Watson would have to wait until Nicholas found the skill to repair his damage. An effigy that could fly would come in handy. He was talented enough in hekau that he could fashion a small beast, like a bird, but it would lack the cunning of his mastiffs. He could ask Lu Wen to create one, but it would be best to do it himself. Just have to wait until he developed greater mastery over his art.

A Shemsu-heru cultist met them just inside the underground corridors leading to the chambers devoted to the Imkhu. She was a plain woman, her face weathered by the years. Nicholas had trouble pegging her age; anywhere from late thirties to mid-fifties. "Nicholas Sforza-Ankhotep?" she inquired, inclining her head.

"I am, yes. This is Ibrahim Rassul."

She nodded again. "I am Zabeya. Come this way; the lord Mestha wishes to see you immediately."

Nicholas gestured for her to lead the way, then removed his Oakleys to wipe the sweat from his brow. The heat faded as they went along, but Nicholas didn't stop perspiring. Each one of the Imkhu was impressive in his own right, but Mestha was unique. The old farmer lived in the days of Osiris' earliest rule. He had walked the Land of Khem even before Horus was born, and had long been a loyal servant of Osiris. Such was his dedication to the Lord of Life that he offered to be the first to undergo the original Spell of Life to ensure its effectiveness. A humble farmer in his first life, Mestha was now the highest of the

Mesektet, the great sky-priests. These mummies were distinguished by their ability to read portents in the stars and command the tempestuous power of the weather. Other Amenti said Mestha's wisdom was matched only by the greatest of Ma'at's judges, and that he consulted regularly with the spirit of Osiris. Nicholas was humbled even before Zabeya presented him to the wizened Imkhu.

Mestha was already well into old age by the time he received the gift of resurrection. He appeared as a wiry old man with skin darkened and wrinkled from many seasons of hard work under the harsh Egyptian sun. Despite this, he moved with the vigor of youth. The venerable mummy was clad in a simple peasant tunic, cotton slacks and sandals. He stood barely over five feet in height, but his presence was that of a giant. He strode across the sitting room in which they had been shown and grasped Nicholas' forearms in his own. "Greetings, Nicholas Sforza-Ankhotep," Mestha said in Egyptian. "It pleases me to meet you."

"Mestha," Nicholas replied. "It is an honor to be in your presence."

Mestha chuckled, giving a brief squeeze before releasing Nicholas and waving a hand. "We are equal in the eyes of Osiris."

Nicholas doubted that, but appreciated the sentiment nonetheless. "May I present Ibrahim Rassul of the Eset-a?"

Mestha nodded a greeting, and Ibrahim did his best not to collapse from awe. "Zabeya, please bring us refreshments." As the woman slipped from the chamber, Mestha indicated Nicholas should take a seat. They moved to a pair of low cushioned couches that faced one another across a polished marble table. Ibrahim followed with some hesitation and stood a few feet away, off Nicholas' left shoulder.

"I'm very impressed with what you've done with this complex," Nicholas said. The chamber they sat in had been refurbished, the murals along the walls positively glowing with color and the furniture, while new, modeled in ancient designs. Technology was used in subtle fashion to provide further comfort without spoiling the illusion they were back in ancient times. Electric lights hung in simple lanterns where torches had once sat, providing warm yellow illumination. Nicholas even spied a vent behind a papyrus accordion screen, part of an air circulation and climate control system that kept the entire underground complex quite comfortable.

"Thank you… well, first I must ask: by which name do you prefer to be called?" Mestha might be among the most powerful immortals, but he had a low-key, grandfatherly demeanor that was fast putting Nicholas at ease.

"Uh, I usually go by Nicholas."

Mestha slapped his hands on his knees. "Then that is what I shall call you. Thank you, Nicholas. We have worked hard to restore the Avenger's temple. Similar efforts are underway elsewhere at sites important to us. Though none are as advanced as this, soon we shall have a number of strongholds that pay homage to our origins while availing themselves of modern comforts." He chuckled. "Electrical power is still a marvel to me. Imagine! So much more useful than smelly oil and fire, don't you agree?"

"Well, fire still has its uses."

"Ah, quite true; quite true." Mestha pointed to the table as Zabeya entered carrying a tray with a pitcher, glasses bread, and bowls of pasta with lentils and a spicy sauce. She set the food before the two mummies with a third before another of the couches, poured water for each, then left with a slight bow. Mestha thanked the departing cultist and gestured to Ibrahim, indicating the third seat. "Come," he said in flawless Arabic, "you must be hungry after your trip."

Nicholas wasn't sure which of them was more surprised. The cultists played a vital role—only mortals could perform the Spell of Life; it functioned not at all when performed by any supernatural, including one of the Undying. Without mortal allies, the mummies would never be able to increase their ranks. As such, cultists were accorded respect. But they were, in the end, mortal, and defaulted to a second-class status among the Amenti. Nicholas had met a few mummies who treated the cultists as glorified slaves or ignored them altogether. Mestha's invitation humbled Nicholas as he recalled how he'd taken for granted his Eset-a group on more than one occasion.

"I would prefer to speak with you of topics ranging far and wide," Mestha said to Nicholas, returning to Egyptian. He picked up the bowl and readied a spoonful of pasta. "I fear that must wait for another time. From what Indihar Hentempet said, you have news of the greatest import."

Nicholas nodded. "I'll dive right in, then." After some healthy gulps of water, he related his mission to Chicago in pursuit of rumors of the ab-Asar, establishing the Temple of Akhenaton as a mummy stronghold, the raid by Maxwell Carpenter and the mysterious reporters, Nicholas' capture and subsequent torture. He paused then, the memories still raw. Gathering his will, he pushed on, describing his rapid resurrection and escape, returning to find only three of his men remained alive and the Heart of Osiris in the hands of vampires, who had themselves stolen it from the "reporters." Then came Carpenter's return and their fight in the street before the Sears Tower, the Heart suddenly falling toward them from high above. Almost within his grasp—then Carpenter had knocked him away and run off with it. Nicholas and Ibrahim had fled before the police arrived, leaving a bizarre aftermath of burning vehicles and bodies fallen from skyscrapers. "We searched the city as best we could afterward, but it was impossible to pinpoint the Heart's location without the amulet I'd created. Its aura is… it's like a dust storm. You can't help but sense it from a distance, but as you get close the power is so pervasive you can't find the center. Anyway, I felt it moving away, heading east. When I realized where Carpenter was headed, Ibrahim and I hopped on a plane and came here."

Mestha had said nothing while Nicholas spoke, taking small bites and sipping water, his dark eyes locked on the younger mummy. Nicholas downed another glass of water in the ensuing silence. Talking was thirsty work, and the arid climate didn't help any. He found he wasn't hungry but forced himself to begin eating so as not to be impolite. Glances at Ibrahim while he related recent events showed the Eset-a cultist was having similar trouble with his composure and appetite.

"And you are certain it was the Heart of Osiris that you had found?" Mestha asked.

Nicholas was puzzled at the question, but forced himself to review what he knew before replying. "As certain as I can be. I did not remove it from the Coptic jar in which it was stored, but from the emanations I had little doubt."

Mestha nodded, contemplating. "It was not originally in such a container," he murmured, as if to himself, "nor would it have been small enough to fit. But many centuries have passed since that time of Set's treachery. There is no law stating how the Heart must be stored."

What did that mean, "Nor would it have been small enough to fit"? The container was large enough to hold a baboon heart. Nicholas opened his mouth to ask, but Mestha spoke first.

"I thought your kind believed the Heart to be that stone in Israel."

Nicholas was caught off balance, then understanding clicked. "The Ka'bah? Some of the Eset-a think that. Perhaps because I'm recently a 'child of the West,' that just didn't wash with me. I don't know. It's possible that the Ka'bah is some other part of Osiris, but I can tell you, based on first-hand knowledge, that it's not the Heart."

Mestha pursed his lips and looked into the distance as if weighing options. "The events you describe are tragic indeed, but not as dire as your expression indicates. This amulet you made, to track the Heart. You could fashion another one?"

"Unfortunately not. I made the first by capturing some of the energy bleeding off the jar in which the Heart was kept. Without that to build upon, it'd be nothing more than a paperweight." Making such a device wasn't difficult in and of itself, but one that could sense the body of Osiris was far from a typical working of hekau—otherwise the mummies would have tracked down the various pieces of their god long ago.

"That is, indeed, unfortunate." Mestha rose and paced the length of the chamber, still looking thoughtful. After a minute or so, he stopped and faced Nicholas. He looked at the younger mummy with such intensity that Nicholas flinched. "Very well. I must admit your news does not please me, but it is clear you could not control everything that happened. I will make sure word of this is passed along to the others so that we may all prepare for this Maxwell Carpenter's arrival. Further, I will speak with my fellow Mesektet. We will scry the heavens to find evidence of the creature's passage. The Osiris fragments are notoriously difficult to perceive by means of even the most powerful hekau, but we may at least narrow where we search."

He sighed, the spotlight of his attention sliding away from Nicholas. "It is unfortunate Lord Horus is gone with a contingent to China; their power would be useful in this venture."

"China? What are they doing there?"

A flash of steel showed beneath the amiable farmer's demeanor. "That is none of your concern."

"My apologies, Mestha." Unsure of how to recover from his faux pas, he said, "Is there… what else should I do to help?"

"I believe it best if you return north. We will notify you if we have need."

Nicholas knew a brush-off when he heard one. Old Mestha might be surprisingly understanding, but he was still influential Imkhu and Nicholas was still radical

Eset-a. He and Ibrahim bowed their thanks and headed for the door.

Mestha's voice stopped them on the threshold. "I must admit that I find it puzzling this creature would come here so boldly, to the land where we are strongest. What would this Maxwell Carpenter hope to accomplish but his own defeat?"

"He'll be tougher to catch than you might think, wise Mestha," Nicholas said. "He has one hell of an incentive. Being a walking corpse isn't enough for him. He wants to become immortal."

● ● ●

Mestha had as much as told Nicholas he was off the pursuit after the Heart. The overzealous Eset-a had again proven themselves too reckless to be relied upon. Nicholas had no intention of sitting back and doing nothing, but it would be tough to accomplish anything without the assistance of the other Amenti castes—a difficult proposition under normal conditions. One step at a time seemed the best approach. First head back to Cairo; he wouldn't be much good hanging around so far up the Nile in Edfu. Hopefully, he'd think of the next step by the time he got back to the city.

Since he no longer felt the pressure of time, Nicholas decided he and Ibrahim could save the few hundred dollars on a return flight. He checked around the Edfu complex and found a mummy who'd recently driven down from Cairo who was willing to trade rentals. That afternoon, Nicholas and Ibrahim piled into a Land Rover to begin the four hundred mile trek north, following the Nile's course by road. They should be able to get at least a third of the way back by nightfall, and finish up the next day. Plenty of time for Nicholas to consider options.

Since Ibrahim had a weak grasp of Egyptian, Nicholas filled him in on his conversation with Mestha as the drove along the dusty, sun-scorched road. Considering Ibrahim's pensive look, Nicholas figured the cultist had

something to say. He waited patiently for Ibrahim to speak, but a good thirty minutes passed in silence. Finally, Nicholas said, "Something on your mind?"

Ibrahim shot Nicholas a look, then returned his attention to the road. "You said that you told Lord Mestha the compass scarab was ruined."

"Yeah. Carpenter smashed it."

They bounced over a series of potholes. "And you cannot make a new one?"

"I'd need to capture more of the Heart's energy first," Nicholas grumbled.

"Could you not get what you need from the first one?"

Nicholas exhaled in frustration. He had considered gleaning something from it when they were back in Chicago, but it looked like a lost cause and they'd been hustling to get to Egypt. "Hard to say. The thing was pretty well demolished. A moot point anyway. I tossed the thing in a drawer at the safe house before we left Chicago."

"Actually," Ibrahim said, "I packed it in my bags. I thought it best not to leave something so valuable behind, even if it was ruined."

"Point taken," Nicholas admitted. This was Ibrahim's way of noting that Nicholas hadn't been thinking very clearly then, worked up as he was after losing the Heart. Part and parcel of the mistakes he'd made in pursuit of the Heart. But if the compass scarab was *here*... There was an outside chance he could glean enough residue of the Heart's aura to fashion a new one. No guarantees, but it was better than sitting around waiting to hear if some other group stumbled across Carpenter.

Nicholas let out a whoop and did a drum roll on the Land Rover's dashboard. "Hot damn! You might've just saved the day, Ibrahim."

PART II:
SECRETS
AND REVELATIONS

PART THREE
OF
MANIFESTATIONS

FIVE

Beckett looked at the ruined thing seated across from him and thought about mortality. He'd regarded the subject often enough, ranging from philosophical conjecture to practical contemplation. This time was a mixture of the metaphysical and the physiological.

By rights, the creature he faced should no longer retain the spark of life. Not the limited conception of "life" as defined by mortals, but the broader spectrum including the supernatural, things like ghosts and zombies and vampires. Considering such beings were collectively called undead, perhaps "unlife" was a better term to use in this circumstance.

Beckett was interested in what it took to separate that unlife from a vampire's body. Fire and sunlight were sure bets. A stake through the heart at least paralyzed if it didn't kill outright. Lopping off the head left little room for doubt. If none of those options were available, massive trauma—a few dozen gunshot wounds, being run over multiple times, falling from a great height—did the trick.

All accurate enough as far as general vampiric lore was concerned. However, Beckett had firsthand knowledge of anomalies to each of them. The thing sitting before him was just the latest evidence that every rule had an exception.

It came down to blood and age. A vampire's blood aged like the finest wine, growing more potent by orders of magnitude with each passing century. The blood dictated everything from the extent of a vampire's powers to how difficult he was to destroy. Beckett, himself considered mature in undead terms, enjoyed significant supernatural might. Yet even with his great fortitude, he could not hope to survive a fall of seventy-three stories. In contrast, Critias, primogen of the vampire clan Brujah, had done just that.

The undead was old by any reckoning—Embraced four hundred years before Christ was born. That Critias wasn't lumpy red paste after plummeting such a distance was a testament to the power of the blood. That Critias was even *conscious* after only five nights was all the more impressive. A vampire's natural response after suffering extreme injury was to slip into torpor. This trance state was deeper even than the deathlike repose that passed for sleep among the undead. Virtually nothing could wake the undead until his body finished restoring itself.

Beckett sensed that Critias was doing all he could to resist the lure of that restorative slumber. The aged vampire had important matters to deal with before he could succumb to unconsciousness. Which was why Beckett found himself sitting across from the bruised and broken figure in the armchair.

Critias had requested Beckett come for a private audience, ostensibly to thank him for saving the primogen's unlife after the fall from the Sears Tower almost a week before. Beckett suspected that was just pretense. In the five nights since the event, Chicago's vampiric population had been stirred to a veritable frenzy. Of particular note were Critias' underlings in Clan Brujah and those of his closest friend and greatest rival, Khalid al-Rashid, primogen of Clan Nosferatu. Both groups were combing the city, searching for a trio of mortals and an artifact of incalculable power. Aside from grievously wounding Critias, these mortals had destroyed one vampire and injured another in the fight at the Sears Tower. It was the crowning effort of a year in which the self-styled "monster hunters" had tracked down and destroyed almost a dozen other undead in the area.

The artifact that was getting everyone so excited had been a mystery to Beckett, but he'd been busy the past few nights digging up all he could to cure his ignorance. He wasn't sure he was as knowledgeable on the subject as Critias or Khalid. That was fine; Beckett suspected he knew more than they about two additional players in this drama. He'd stumbled into an interesting situation, that was certain.

There was a liquid rasp as Critias cleared his throat. "Greetings, Beckett. Thank you for coming to see me."

It was the first thing Critias had said since Beckett was shown into the study ten minutes before. Beckett wasn't sure if the primogen had been wandering in a haze of pain, thinking about other matters or was just testing him. It mattered little enough; Beckett had waited far longer for far less important matters.

"First, I must apologize for recent accusations. I erred in suggesting that the Gangrel were conspiring with mortal agents to attack our kind."

Beckett hid his combined amusement and irritation behind a polite nod. Thanks to Critias' "error," the entire undead contingent in Chicago had been given the impression that Beckett and his fellow Gangrel were in league with vampire hunters. Beckett knew the idea was ludicrous, just as he knew it was pointless to straighten out the matter. He had more important things to do than trying to educate a score of misguided undead. Curious that Critias would step up and admit a mistake, especially since he'd believed so staunchly in the conspiracy not one week ago.

"Viewed through fresh eyes—" Critias' joke turned his chuckle into a fit of coughing; Beckett allowed himself a sympathetic smile. Critias' eyes had been blown from his skull with the force of impact. His regenerated eyes were a brilliant blue glaring from the ruin of his face. After wiping bloody spittle from his mouth with his left hand—seemingly his only limb capable of movement that didn't cause excruciating pain—the primogen continued. "Viewed through fresh eyes, I see now that those who hunt us could not be in league with Cainites. They are possessed of strange and terrifying abilities that prove they have no need of outside aid."

Beckett was quite enthralled by Critias' monologue thus far. In the space of a few minutes, the elder vampire had admitted to mistakes and fear, and was even trying his hand at humor. Perhaps the fall knocked some humility into him. "Thank you, primogen. Know that I don't bear you any ill will on the matter. Life is too short to hold grudges over such misunderstandings."

Critias offered a very crooked smile at Beckett's own wit. "But that is not why I asked you here tonight."

"Oh?" Beckett was all guileless curiosity.

"I spoke with Khalid al-Rashid this past night. He explained that you had learned of the Methuselah who sleeps beneath this city, a creature of such power that his mere awakening would result in Chicago's complete destruction. It may interest you to know that, until a few nights ago, I was ignorant that this being still existed. For this Methuselah is one who I had thought perished in the sack of Carthage two millennia ago." Critias leaned forward to emphasize the import of his next words. "He is the one who gave unto me the gift of unlife. He is Menele, my sire and creator."

Beckett felt the Beast within him surge in a combination of surprise, fear and confusion. He had learned a few weeks before that an impossibly old vampire slept under the streets of Chicago—had done so since even before the city was established, in fact. He knew that this same creature, Menele, used its vast powers to influence the living and undead in the area. Beckett would have been caught in its thrall as well if not for his finely-honed survival instincts. He had fled Chicago the instant he recognized the insidious touch of a powerful mind upon him. Only after he armed himself with a bracelet that shielded him from the Methuselah's rarefied senses did Beckett return to Chicago.

Critias was among Menele's most powerful agents, although Critias had long operated with no knowledge of the Methuselah's influence upon him. Or so Beckett had thought. Beckett could think of one reason why

Critias would reveal the connection to his sire: The Brujah primogen had discovered Beckett learned the secret of Menele. Not only that the ancient creature existed but where it slept, protected by a cadre of Native American warriors who had cared for the ancient since it first fell into torpor two centuries ago.

Any second now, vampires would rush into the study and tear Beckett asunder, ensuring that Beckett could never pass on the secret to anyone else. His hands, long ago disfigured into hairy, vicious talons as evidence of his feral nature, clenched the arms of the chair so tightly his claws pierced the rich leather. His nostrils flared and his crimson eyes darted behind his dark glasses, searching for attackers. A sense deeper and more primal even than the fight-or-flight instinct was all that kept Beckett from lunging across the low table at Critias. Then the telling moment passed. No assassins launched themselves from behind secret panels. Critias remained where he sat, silent and still. Beckett allowed that he might be indulging in paranoia. Still, Menele was possibly the most powerful creature he had ever encountered, and being within its sphere of influence kept him wound tight with caution. Part of him thought leaving might be a good idea, but the much larger rest of him couldn't leave without satisfying his curiosity. "I'm sorry, Critias, but I don't understand why you're telling me this."

"It is not to paralyze you with fear prior to having you destroyed," Critias chuckled again, this time swallowing down the coughing fit. "Please, you may relax. I bear you no malice."

Having his shock pointed out to him turned his unease into irritation. Removing his claws from the leather, Beckett steepled his fingers and looked at Critias from over the apex. "Thank you for clarifying. But you haven't answered my question."

"It is simple enough. As you have no doubt suspected, I, like many other Cainites in this city, have been Menele's unwitting agent for some time now."

Newly reconstructed nerves on the side of Critias' face twitched a painful frown of recollection. "I was almost destroyed by the fall from the Sears Tower—indeed, without your immediate aid I believe I would have faced the final death. But it took the massive injuries I sustained from that... accident... to break free of my sire's influence."

Curious. Another lesson in age and the power of blood. "And doing so, you became aware of Menele's influence upon you all that time?"

"Exactly. It has been thus for so long that I doubt I would have realized it otherwise. Especially believing he was destroyed when Carthage fell." His twisted face assumed an expression that may have been longing. "Centuries ago, and I learn only now that he did not perish."

Silence grew. Beckett gave a helpful cough when it appeared the primogen had drifted off somewhere other than here. Critias' head jerked and he continued as if there was no pause. "This influence explains why I made many choices—why I came to Chicago to begin with, for example."

"Or why you would fling yourself out a skyscraper after a bauble with no thought of the consequences?"

Critias nodded. "Perceptive as always, Beckett." He used his good arm to straighten himself in the chair. "Do you know the significance of that 'bauble'?"

Something in Critias' tone put Beckett back on his guard. "Khalid said it was an Egyptian artifact."

"It is that and more. I understand now that Menele wanted me to recover the Coptic jar for him. It contains incalculable power. As you know, rousing oneself from torpor leaves a Cainite weak for some time, the transition to full wakefulness draining his power temporarily. For Menele, control over those he influenced would lessen and he would be vulnerable to attack from his rival, Helene, until he regained full strength." Critias' sharp eyes bored into Beckett's own. "Channeling the energy from the Coptic jar would enable Menele to awaken at full strength. More than that, its power would make him unstoppable, a god in the modern world."

Beckett waited a beat, then asked, "And what do you think of that?"

A smile tugged at the primogen's lips. "Before my fall, I would have done anything in my power to make it happen. Now I understand the danger Menele's awakening represents. For all that he was my sire and mentor, I cannot allow him to rise. He must not get the jar."

"I don't think that will be a problem. From what I understand, the creature who has the jar is not under Menele's thrall." Beckett also knew the creature was no longer in Chicago, but he saw no reason to pass that detail along without first collecting an equal amount of information in exchange. Or at all, depending on how the remaining players in this drama established their positions.

"That is why we speak now; you understand what is at stake. I cannot rely on even my most trusted lieutenants, for they are under Menele's sway. Only you know—"

"Wait. How can you be sure I am not also?"

"The pain of my injuries keeps my mind sharp. I perceive things with a clarity I have not known for some time. I can sense that Menele knows I have suffered injury, but is not aware that I am free of his control. I can feel the weight of Menele's influence pressing around me. I can sense that, like me, his aura flows around you, but not within you. Only you can be trusted to recover the artifact and keep it from Menele's grasp." Critias gestured at his twisted form. "I would do it myself, but…"

"What of Khalid? It was he who explained all this to me. He and a few of his underlings are free of Menele's control and he already hunts for the Egyptian jar. Why not leave it to him to take care of it?"

Critias' eyes narrowed. "Because despite his claims, Khalid is as much a creature of Menele's now as I once was."

• • •

Beckett rode the El to Chicago's Graceland Cemetery in a state of distraction. A month ago he'd been pursuing his ongoing research into the origin of vampires. Now he was embroiled in an affair involving multiple vampire clans, ancient undead, powerful artifacts, mortal monster hunters, the walking dead, and mummies. His Cainite research seemed quite prosaic by comparison.

He was surprised with the direction the meeting with Critias had gone. It served as an interesting counterpoint to the talk he'd had with Khalid al-Rashid following the battle at the Sears Tower five nights before. The Nosferatu primogen had chased the Egyptian artifact after it was thrown from the skyscraper's 73rd floor, while Beckett recovered the injured Critias—who'd flung himself out the window after the Coptic jar. Khalid admitted defeat when he and Beckett met a few nights later. The artifact had vanished. For a master of intelligence gathering, the failure must have been galling indeed.

Beckett commiserated with Khalid, deciding not to share what he knew about the artifact. It was never smart to divulge more than necessary, and things had gotten complicated enough that Beckett wanted to find out as much as he could about the artifact—and everyone involved—before he took another step.

The night of the battle, Beckett had arrived at the point of impact below the Sears Tower before Khalid had. He'd seen immediately that the artifact was already gone. Someone had grabbed it from where it had fallen, just a few feet from the bloody mess of Critias' plummet, and run off. Frustrating, but the question arose as to who had made off with the thing. Beckett knew only one person had reached the parking structure where the jar landed before he did—excepting Critias, who was in no shape to do anything after his fall but bleed. That person hadn't been a vampire; they were all in the Sears Tower. It wasn't one of the hunters, either. All but two of those mortals were dead, and one of the pair had thrown the artifact from the Sears Tower to begin with.

Khalid had assumed it was the mysterious mummy, the artifact's apparent guardian to begin with. Beckett knew otherwise, having run into the mummy just after landing in his bat form on the parking structure. The mummy had looked like a typical human, but his scent was of something... other. Likewise, the mummy couldn't help but see Beckett for what he was, as he was in the midst of returning to his human shape when they met. But the mummy was more concerned with recovering his artifact than dealing with a vampire. The immortal had circled Beckett with hands raised, his attendant trailing, and taken off for the opposite end of the parking garage. From the shouted words the mummy had exchanged with his lackey as they left, it seemed someone named Carpenter had run off with the Coptic jar's contents mere seconds before.

The following nights Beckett spent making numerous calls and going to certain little-known locales on the Internet, checking with sources mundane and mystic to uncover what he could about Egyptian artifacts and the self-styled followers of the heretical pharaoh Akhenaton. He pored over rumors, conjecture and myth, at last arriving at fragments of legend about a theft soon after Pharaoh Akhenaton's death. The tales he uncovered disputed whether the pharaoh was murdered, committed suicide, or suffered from some manner of ailment—but all agreed that priests later discovered a treasured artifact was stolen from his palace. The ab-Asar, the Heart of Osiris. Beckett pursued other threads of investigation to see if his hunch bore out, and after some time felt he had enough to connect the stolen object with the thing taken from the broken Coptic jar. Adding Khalid al-Rashid's allusions to a "heart" and the involvement of mummies, this allowed for at least a working hypothesis. His sources disagreed as to whether it was truly a piece of a dead Egyptian god—for his part, Beckett had yet to find conclusive evidence that any gods existed, just many pretenders to the throne. Regardless, there was little dispute that the Heart was quite powerful. Just what it was doing in Chicago was anyone's guess.

He'd also learned a bit about the mummy. Khalid had explained before that mortals attacked the Temple of Akhenaton in downtown Chicago—where the mummy was apparently guarding the artifact—and stole the Heart from under the immortal's nose. After more long hours of searching, Beckett confirmed that the mummy and a man by the name of Nicholas Sforza were one in the same. Quite a curiosity, was this Sforza. Ties to organized crime, vanished under mysterious circumstances a year ago—after everyone else in his family had suffered fatal accidents, lethal assaults, or suicides—and not seen since. Not until a frigid night in March on the top of a parking garage next to the Sears Tower.

That left Carpenter, the thief, about whom Beckett knew nothing. Not surprising, considering the only thing he had to go on was an overheard snatch of conversation between the mummy Sforza and his attendant. Rather than waste time with futile searches, the night prior to meeting with Khalid, Beckett returned to the parking structure. He wouldn't have to become a wolf to track the artifact; his human nose was preternaturally sensitive enough to catch its peculiar aroma. He doubted he would ever forget the unique and disturbing odor. There was no mistaking, it was something from the time of the pharaohs. Beckett trailed the scent southwest for a few miles to the fringes of the meatpacking district. His hackles raised as he approached a darkened warehouse; he knew nothing about this Carpenter, but the mummy Sforza had appeared exceedingly distraught regarding the fellow. No telling who—or what—Carpenter was. Beckett wondered if he was one of the hunters, not captured with the others. That would jibe with the mortals' attack on the Temple of Akhenaton and original theft of the artifact. If so, that might mean he wouldn't be dealing with just one man if he caught up to the Heart. Not to mention that these hunters had abilities that proved especially effective against the undead.

Beckett had no interest in waltzing up and getting staked. But his curiosity demanded that he not scamper away in fear. After all, he had single-handedly tracked the great Menele to his secret lair and escaped unscathed. Compared to counting coup on a Methuselah, what were a handful of "monster hunters"?

Menele remained on Beckett's mind as he drew closer to the warehouse. He was shielded from that ancient thing's awareness by the enchanted bracelet he wore. Surely he was no longer unknown to the Methuselah—Menele's mortal agents might even be tracking him down through more conventional means. Protected from mystic scrying Beckett might be, but two of Menele's Indian guardians had seen him firsthand: the guard he'd injured while investigating Menele's lair and William Decorah. The latter had been a mole in service to Beckett's fellow Gangrel, Augustus Klein, and subsequently held captive by Critias. Beckett had favored Decorah with enough undead blood to heal his injuries and escape back to his fellow Indians, but Beckett had no illusions that the act gave him a special dispensation. He allowed himself a smile. Yet another reason to wrap things up here as quickly as he could and move on.

Beckett shook off his contemplation when he scented the Heart's trail leading away from the warehouse. Given that, it was doubtful there would be trouble still inside. Before following the scent, Beckett decided a look in the warehouse was in order. The more he could learn about his quarry, the better. As he went to pick the lock he noticed the hair-thin glimmer of security wire in the window glass. He debated with himself for a few seconds, then decided to go ahead. He should have five minutes to search the place before security arrived—plenty of time if he didn't finesse it. And, at this stage of the game, he felt like being a bull in a china shop. He put away his lock picks and knocked in a pane with his elbow, then unlocked the door and slipped inside. The place was empty, a large two-story open space with a pair of garage doors on the front and an office built into an upper left corner. The Heart's pungent scent hung heavy in the place. But, like the trail he'd followed here, it was a few nights old. A quick look upstairs confirmed that the warehouse was deserted. Checking out the Spartan office, Beckett caught traces of a second, fainter scent. It was difficult to isolate thanks to the overpowering smell the artifact left behind, but he finally trailed it to a bloody, torn suit shoved into one of the desk's bottom drawers. After one good whiff, an epiphany flashed through his brain.

He held the clothes belonging to the figure he had encountered in an alley a few weeks before. Beckett was tracking the hunters at the time and stumbled across a man clad in black, a figure who reeked of old death and the cold of the grave. Not the subtle tang of a vampire, but the bitter stench of the restless dead. This Carpenter was a walking corpse, a zombie. A zombie that had used some mental compulsion to force Beckett to run away. A zombie that had dared force its will upon Beckett. A zombie that was on the run with the Heart of Osiris.

Beckett had wondered what the zombie was doing near the hunters that night. It seemed the mummy artifact was the connection. Perhaps this Carpenter had known the mortals were going to raid the Temple of Akhenaton and lurked around the periphery till its chance came to steal the Heart. Beckett suspected there was more to the story, but he'd yet to determine what it was. Frustrating that the walking corpse hadn't stayed in town to answer his questions.

Once he realized just who—or, more properly, *what*— he was tracking, Beckett scrambled back on the trail. Straight as an arrow, it led southeast. The industrial sprawl of the docks soon gave clear indication of where Carpenter had gone, but Beckett nonetheless followed the scent all the way to the pier, where a massive container ship reared overhead.

A security guard approached who wasn't sure what to make of Beckett. Lean, muscular physique and well-worn clothing indicated a laborer, possibly a dock worker or deck hand looking for employment. But Beckett's lustrous dark hair and round smoked glasses hinted at a pretty boy slumming. A short conversation followed, wherein each tried drawing the other out. Beckett was the slicker of the two, having had a few centuries to practice. He learned what he needed while giving the guard no indication of who he was or what he was doing there.

The guard—whose name tag read WALPERT—confirmed that freighters docked there all the time, offloading bulk cargoes and shipping out durable goods. "Ayuh, a freighter by the name of the *Meroe Atlantic* left from that berth a few days ago. Comes through on a regular route, don't ya know. Should be most of the way through the St. Lawrence Seaway by now."

"Do you know where it is headed?" Beckett asked, though by now he an inkling.

The big man shrugged, making a lazy loop with his finger. "Different companies got different routes; swing out to some 'nother country, swap cargo, come on back. I think Meroe Global ships around to one or a couple a them Arab countries."

"Including Egypt, perhaps."

Another shrug. "Ayuh, that sounds right."

"The vessel travels from here to there without stopping?"

"Nah, all a them ships make stops at different ports along the way. Take some cargo from here to New York or Norfolk or Charleston, then over to Spain or Italy or wherever and around to Turkey or what you said, Egypt. Come 'round back in reverse."

Other ports meant stopovers; add in time to transfer cargo and it should take a ship some time to get from Chicago to the mouth of the Nile. "On a regular basis, you said? How long does it take for the *Meroe Atlantic* to make the circuit?"

Walpert scrunched up his face as he considered. "Man, I don't know 'bout that ship in particular, but there's a

general kinda range with them container ships. There and back, altogether? Maybe two months, give or take."

Beckett nodded. Which meant a month, possibly less, one-way. Plenty of time to see what else he could learn in the area. He thanked the guard and started away from the pier, courses of action running through his mind.

"Listen," the guard yelled after him. "You lookin' for work you swing by in the mornin'. They got offices right over there."

"Maybe I'll do that."

"Hey, mister. You mind me askin' why you're wearin' sunglasses in middle a the night?"

"Not at all," Beckett called back with a farewell wave.

•••

Beckett was jerked back to the here and now when the elevated train shuddered to a halt, the driver applying the brakes a little too hard. A look out to the platform showed he had two stops to go before he reached the cemetery.

Beckett surprised himself with how deeply he'd fallen into his remembrance of the past week. Much as he hated to admit it, the zombie named Carpenter had gotten under his skin. Beckett had faced down princes and elders; he'd seen horrors that would terrify the most depraved of vampires. That a pathetic walking corpse would subject him to a parlor trick compulsion? Among the more unpleasant shocks he'd ever had.

And the surprises kept coming. Take Critias and their recent heart-to-heart. Ostensibly a puppet of Menele, the Brujah primogen claimed to have shaken off his sire's control by almost suffering the final death. In the next breath, Critias suggested that his fellow primogen and rival, Khalid al-Rashid, was not free of the Methuselah's influence as he had previously declared. It didn't take a genius to realize each was manipulating Beckett in hopes he would recover the Heart of Osiris for him at the exclusion of the other. Of course, they'd each assured

Beckett they were only interested in keeping the artifact out of Menele's hands. On that, at least, they could all agree. But Beckett did not plan on delivering the thing to Critias or Khalid. It seemed likely that Critias was his own man—well, creature—again, but that didn't make him a suitable guardian for the power the Heart evidently possessed. And there was no telling if Khalid was free of domination or if he was toady to a sleeping demigod. All things considered, Beckett thought it best to avoid the issue of control altogether. It would be best if the artifact was put someplace secure where no one would get at it.

Beckett would track down the artifact, but not for the reasons his contemporaries wanted it. He wasn't interested in amassing power and prestige; he left such pursuits to others of his kind. His passion was knowledge. While the Heart of Osiris interested Beckett greatly, it was on an intellectual level, not as a tool with which to attain omnipotence.

The problem was, although he knew the zombie was on its way to Egypt with the thing, he didn't know exactly where or why. Beckett would have asked Nicholas Sforza, but it turned out the mummy had recently left for Egypt as well—though by plane, not freighter. He considered asking the hunters—he had the woman's scent, and it wouldn't be difficult to track her down—but his instincts told him they had no idea what was going on. Plus, they'd proven on more than one occasion that they were a match for vampires. Beckett didn't feel like taking the chance that they wanted to talk rather than fight.

His best prospect at gleaning a solid lead lay in the only fellow Gangrel he knew of in the region—and the one who dragged him into this mess to begin with: the ancient vampire Inyanga.

●●●

Beckett exited on Sheridan and made his way to the Graceland Cemetery. He hoped Inyanga was still in the area. She was known to roam around the Midwest and

Great Plains for weeks at a time. Normally, he had no problem waiting a week or two in his pursuits; time was not a precious commodity for one such as he. Events surrounding the Heart of Osiris were accelerating, and Beckett sensed he had to move fast if he wanted to keep up.

It seemed Inyanga felt the same momentum. Beckett found her waiting by the tomb to Mies van der Rohe, the same spot he'd encountered her when he came to Chicago a few weeks before.

"Mother Inyanga," Beckett said, nodding in greeting.

The crone stepped forward with an economy of movement common to elder undead. "You have been busy these past weeks. What have you learned?"

Beckett wasn't put off by her abrupt attitude, Inyanga having a reputation for being plain-spoken. Still, was there something more to her tone…? Perhaps the recent talk of Menele was making him paranoid. Beckett fell in beside the wizened Gangrel, collecting his thoughts as they strolled through the cemetery. Beckett had come to Chicago to interview Inyanga about her past to add to his collective understanding of the undead. Before sharing that information, she had asked him to research the matter of kine hunting Cainites. Such trades in service were common among vampires, and he'd been interested in the rise of mortals who hunted his kind, so Beckett had considered it a win-win scenario.

Investigating the hunters had led to the matter of the Heart of Osiris and the attendant mysteries of the zombie Carpenter, mummy Nicholas Sforza and the Methuselah Menele. The kine fast became a footnote in the larger scheme, as Beckett found himself occupied with trying to make sense of the bizarre melodrama unfolding in the city. As a result, he had not progressed far along the assignment Inyanga handed him. He hadn't discovered how the mortals could perform the unusual powers that proved so devastating against Cainites. Neither had he learned how they knew so much about the habits, strengths and weaknesses of the undead. He suspected that the answers were not to be uncovered easily, and would require far more time and diligence than he'd devoted thus far.

He wasn't there to deliver a final report, though, but to enlist Inyanga's aid in tracking down the Heart of Osiris. She was rumored to be able to speak to spirits; Beckett thought it might be informative to call up the shade of one of Sforza's attendants. From what he understood, the mummy had had quite a crew in town, a number of whom died in an attack on the Temple of Akhenaton, others of whom fell assaulting the hunters shortly thereafter.

As he began relating the events of the past few weeks, Beckett again sensed something more to Inyanga's attitude than the restrained curiosity she'd shown in their previous meeting. It was difficult to read a vampire of her age; like her fellow primogen, Critias and Khalid, Inyanga had existed for long enough to keep a tight rein on her emotions. And it was this, Beckett realized, that was disturbing him. He shouldn't even be able to pick up the… eagerness? Hunger, even, that he sensed from her.

A nasty suspicion clenched his atrophied guts. He stopped speaking as thoughts thundered through his mind. Was Menele influencing her as well? Beckett had considered the possibility a few nights before, but thought that her ability to wander far from Chicago for great lengths of time and her sense that there were strange events afoot in the city indicated she operated of her own free will. But she kept returning to the Windy City and had urged Beckett into an investigation that ultimately led him to the Heart of Osiris. Could that be evidence of Menele's sway?

The power required to manipulate three ancient Cainites, not to mention a score of lesser creatures, would be staggering. Beckett felt the chill of fear spread through

his long-dead bones as he wondered just how useful his bracelet was at protecting him from the Methuselah's control.

Inyanga's piercing gaze upon him, Beckett decided he couldn't take the chance that she—or any of Chicago's primogen—were subject to Menele's influence.

So far he'd told her about Critias' accusation that the Gangrel might be in league with the kine, and his subsequent investigation of the site of the vampire Augustus Klein's final death. He picked up the thread of his tale, explaining that he had trailed the hunters from there to an apartment building engulfed in flame. Each site he tracked them to, he arrived to find the place had been attacked and more of the hunters killed. "Finally, a few nights ago, I learned that Critias had captured the remaining two kine. He had them in his offices in the Sears Tower, where they apparently tried to escape. It may surprise you to learn that they seriously injured Critias and destroyed one of his people, Graham, before escaping."

Beckett said nothing about having discovered Menele's lair, nor about the Heart of Osiris. Technically, neither detail fell under the assignment Inyanga gave him.

"Do you know why Critias captured them instead of slaying them outright?"

"I believe that, like you, he was interested in learning their secrets." A moment's hesitation as he decided whether he could avoid mentioning the Heart. He had no problems lying if it benefited him. But it would not be difficult for Inyanga to learn of the artifact's existence from other avenues—assuming she didn't already know of it. Either way, she would not be favorably disposed toward Beckett if he held back the information. Watching her through his remarkable peripheral vision, Beckett added, "It appears he found an artifact in their possession as well, something called the Heart of Osiris."

Inyanga's eyes narrowed, which for her was being highly expressive. "I heard of such a thing long ago... what has come of it? Does Critias still have it?"

"No. It was lost when the kine made their escape. It's possible they have it again." *If they somehow boarded the freighter Carpenter was on and wrested it from him*, Beckett thought. An extremely slim chance indeed, but possible.

"What do you plan next?"

He still couldn't get an accurate read on Inyanga, so he kept it vague. "I think the mortals who remain may have fled the area. They should have an interesting story to tell if I can find them."

Inyanga's head inclined the merest fraction. "I look forward to your further discoveries."

Beckett took that as a dismissal and became the wolf, heading for the disused mill where he made his lair in Chicago. A mile out he changed his mind and turned south. Two hours later he was on a redeye to New York. He'd get in to La Guardia by 4:30 AM and would be safe underground within a half hour afterward. A margin for error in case of delays, but Beckett felt uncomfortable being in a plane so close to sunrise.

He'd felt a sudden, tremendous need to get out of Chicago immediately. It was as if he was in the center of converging forces but without a clear idea of where anything was coming from. The only things he was sure of were that Menele must remain in torpor; that the Heart of Osiris was on its way to Egypt; and that he could only trust himself to make sure the Methuselah didn't get the artifact that would make him a god on earth.

SIX

Thea Ghandour had long thought that pinching yourself to see if you're dreaming was stupid. She also thought the expression was dumb—"Pinch me, I must be dreaming…" come *on*—but it was actually doing the pinching that didn't work for her. She'd never had trouble knowing when she was dreaming; in fact, she could often make things happen in dreams the way she wanted. Likewise, she'd never mistaken her waking life for a dream.

Well, up until about a year ago. After coming face to face with the horrors of the supernatural, Thea was willing to try anything to see if she was just going through a long, bad dream. After pinching herself the first few times, she decided she'd been right in the beginning. All pinching did was hurt, and you weren't any better off than before.

Considering Margie Woleski's dazed expression, Thea figured her best friend was still in the "try anything" stage. If Thea could have spared Margie from seeing the stark truth that hid behind the veneer of the world, she would have. But now that the damage was done, Thea thought the best thing was to work through it. That's what she'd been trying for the past few days, but Margie didn't feel like playing along. She was relatively responsive, recognizing when she was being spoken to, eating when food was put in front of her, bathing when stuck in the shower with the water pounding down. But Margie didn't speak, and generally spent her waking moments staring. At the wall, out the window; made no difference to her.

Already concerned to begin with, Thea was growing frantic with worry. Margie was a couple steps up from being a vegetable. She needed help.

"I'm not arguing with you, Thea," Jake Washington said, looking up from his laptop. "But we can't take her anyplace. Not around here, anyway, not right now."

"She's just an innocent bystander, Jake," Thea replied with some emotion. "*We're* the damn monster hunters, *we're* the ones they're looking for."

"You know that's not true. The rots're bound to have an eye out for Margie as much as for you and me. They kidnapped her to try and make us talk; what makes you think they wouldn't do it again? Or, forget her even being a hostage. She had a front-row seat to seeing honest-to-God vampires in action. You think they're going to ignore that?"

Thea pinched the bridge of her nose, fighting back tears. Jake was right; she knew he was right. She'd told herself the same thing. It was ripping her apart inside, seeing Margie reduced to such a sorry state, and all because of her. "We can't just do nothing, though. And not just about Margie. It's been four days of us hiding out at this friend of Lupe's. They're sick of us being here, I'm going stir crazy, Margie's not getting any better, and you spend all day on the damn computer!"

Jake sighed. "I've been talking to other people on hunter-net. Getting help on this whole situation—help for us and for Margie."

"And?" Thea frowned. "After all that time, what have you come up with?"

"Not as much as I'd've hoped," Jake admitted, giving the Compaq a disappointed look. "Folks were interested in what happened with the vampires—them holding us hostage in the Sears Tower instead of killing us outright, using Margie as leverage to find out what they could about who we were, like that…"

"You also told them how they seemed about as scared of us as we were of them?"

"Yeah, they loved that. Although knowing we're starting to frighten monsters is small consolation for losing the rest of the Van Helsing brigade."

Thea felt like another hundred pounds was added to the weight of guilt already crushing her down. "About that, then. Anything on the Temple of Akhenaton or the Egyptian guys or Nicholas Sforza?"

"Nothing more than we already knew. Akhenaton's some obscure cult, presumably the Egyptians who attacked us are part of it, and I still haven't figured out how Sforza figures into it."

"During that attack, they'd said something—yelling about the Heart I threw out the Sears Tower. And wanting to know where the... damn, what was it?"

"'Amenti.' Like 'amen,' right?"

"Yes, you're very perceptive, Jake." She favored him with a smile, her first in days. "I've had a lot on my mind, okay? So anything on that?"

"Lots that wasn't useful, but something interesting. People say A-M-E-N at the end of prayers, right? But it's also one of a few ways to spell the name of an Egyptian god—you know, Amon-Ra? Some think that's where the custom came from, even. I think it's more common with an 'O' or a 'U', but whatever."

"Keeps coming around to the Egyptian stuff." Thea had rolled around a thought for some time now, but it sounded too out there—even for what they were involved in—to say aloud. She decided to approach it cautiously; maybe that way she could get Jake to say it first. "You know Sforza was wearing Egyptian jewelry when we met him in the temple?"

Jake gave a slow nod. "And you said he made some strange marks on his chest after Romeo shot him."

Thea felt a flash of vertigo wash over her, Romeo's loss still acute. It reminded her of the son of a bitch who'd killed him; who'd begun this whole nightmare, in fact. "Carpenter. Remember when Carpenter abducted the guy? The shattered sarcophagus in Sforza's office? Makes you think, eh?"

After a few seconds of staring at one another, Thea surprised herself by bursting out laughing. A puzzled smile wandered across Jake's face. "What?" he asked with a chuckle.

"You're thinking the same thing I am!" Thea accused. The laughter had a touch of the hysterical, but it felt great. She'd needed a release like that, anything to ease the tension that'd been mounting within her for far too long. She let out a sigh and pointed a finger at Jake. "You're thinking 'mummy,' but you didn't want to say it 'cause it sounds too goofy."

Jake's smile widened. "Well, maybe not because it sounds *goofy*. I just don't know, y'know? I mean, you look on hunter-net, and who's ever said anything about a mummy? And you think about it, a mummy's just another word for a zombie, isn't it? Dead body arisen from the grave, right?"

"Mmmhmm," Thea countered, lips pursed in thought. It wasn't physical action, but their discussion gave her a sense of activity, of *doing something*, that she'd missed. "Mummies keep coming back, though, don't they?"

"In those old movies, sure. But based on what I've learned so far, I don't think they're any different than your typical hidden."

"Not *my* hidden."

"You know what I mean. Hidden like Carpenter," Jake clarified. The mirth faded from his face. Maxwell Carpenter would be a sore spot for them both for some time to come. "Romeo never told us what he saw in Sforza, did he? Whether the guy was, well, a *guy* even. Instead of a rot or something."

Thea grimaced, shaking her head. "Never... never got the chance."

"Something to the guy that sounds different, like a wizard... now how's *that* for sounding goofy? But, I don't know. If the Egyptian connection is valid—and considering all the other evidence I'd say it is—makes more sense to me that Sforza's some kind of rot." Jake spoke slowly as he puzzled out the logic. "Think about the circumstances surrounding his disappearance; that fits, too. Vanished under suspicious circumstances—his death? Carpenter was hunting down the guy's entire family; maybe he got Nicholas Sforza, too. Except that Sforza comes back for revenge just like Carpenter did. And if anyone knows what a zombie's capable of, it's Maxwell Carpenter. So instead of charging in himself and dealing with a fellow undead and the nifty mystically-defended hideout he's thrown together, he ropes us in as cannon fodder."

"I guess that makes sense." Still, Thea couldn't reconcile it with all that had happened. "But it doesn't answer everything. I keep coming back to the Egyptian angle. Sforza's Italian. Italian-American. Whatever. If he rose from the dead like your average zombie, what's he need with temples and murdering cultists and way powerful Egyptian artifacts?"

"Yeah, I don't know why the cross-culture thing, either. And the Heart those cultists and the vampires were so excited about…" he shrugged. "You said it radiated some kind of power?"

"And did something to my sense of perception. When I was fighting the vampire, I could see, like, five moves ahead. As if my sixth sense was boosted by an order of magnitude."

"Boy. That could be almost anything."

"What, you hear about strange artifacts every day?"

"Lately, yeah. I meant that there's no telling what this so-called 'heart' actually is."

Thea smiled. "Sounds like we should do some more research on the whole mummy possibility."

"And, by 'we,' you mean 'me.'"

"Hey, you're the one with the computer. All my cool toys are at my apartment." It occurred to her that her laptop was the only toy she had left (not counting the purely entertainment-related gadgets like her DVD player and stereo system). She'd lost her cell phone, palmtop and diving

watch in the past month fighting the undead. And, for all she knew, vampires had ransacked her place and taken the rest of her stuff. She had no idea what condition her apartment was in. Aside from traveling from Jake's efficiency to their current hideout the day following their escape from the Sears Tower, they hadn't gone outside in days.

It wasn't a bad spot, here in Harold Casey's furnished basement in the suburb of Oak Lawn. Casey was a veterinarian and part of the loose network of hunters Jake's pal Guadalupe Droin worked with around the south side of Chicago. The south side hunters were not as cohesive a group as Thea's north side gang had been. Lupe and Howard were among about a dozen or so who covered the area from as far west as Aurora all the way east through Gary, Indiana. Not that the "north side" and "south side" labels indicated firm boundaries; they were more references to where the hunters lived. Madison Street split the city of Chicago horizontally, creating a convenient reference point for patrolling. The two hunter groups didn't recognize it as a formal barrier, though; if the hunt led to Oak Lawn or the University of Chicago, Thea wouldn't hand the job off to Lupe. She might contact some of the south side hunters for an assist, but there was no reason for anyone to get greedy. Plenty of monsters to go around.

That was the way it used to be, anyway, before the rest of the Van Helsing brigade got dead.

Backs against the wall, Thea and Jake naturally turned to the south side hunters for aid. Crashing at the veterinarian's house was a short-term solution, a place to regroup and decide on the next course of action. The situation, already tense, got more complicated—Thea and Lupe didn't get along, and this Casey guy kept hitting on Thea. Plus, the vet was supposed to get his kids for the weekend. They needed to find another place to crash by the next day, Friday.

A week since they'd been attacked by Egyptian cultists and held captive by vampires. Barely four weeks since they'd first encountered Maxwell Carpenter and been suckered into being his pawns. One month. Romeo, Parker, Carl, Lilly, Dean, Dean's lover Wayne— one month ago they were still alive. One month ago Thea's best friend was happily making her way through grad school. One month ago Thea's world still made some flavor of sense. With an effort, she tore her thoughts from the past. *Nothing to be gained by wallowing, right? Focus on the future.* "I wouldn't think it'd be too hard, Jake, checking into this. Sounds like you've already done some digging."

"Well… not as much as you'd think. I was more drawing on past research, stuff I've learned about rots in general. Past few days, I've been too busy checking into the Temple of Akhenaton and vampires and whatever… Speaking of which." Jake directed a sharp look at Thea. "One thing I've been wondering about."

"Just one?"

"Ha ha. No, about the temple and, well, and your mom."

Thea frowned in surprise. She'd been so preoccupied with fleeing from strange cultists, fighting vampires and caring for Margie that her mother's bizarre reaction to the Temple of Akhenaton had slipped her mind. "Okay, fire away."

"You said she freaked out when you mentioned the place, right?"

"Yeah. Covered it fast, but there was no mistaking. Something about the place rattled her." Thea looked into the middle distance, trying to recall what Newa Ghandour had said. "She seemed terrified of me going to the temple, but wouldn't say why."

"You don't think she knew what might happen?"

"What, you mean like she had a vision?" Thea smirked. "No way. Mom's not psychic. Far as I know, I'm the only one in our family with that trick."

Jake played around with the angle of his laptop screen. "I was thinking more along the lines that maybe she knew who—or what—might be there."

"You mean like what may be a mummy? Or the what-ever-it-was in that Coptic jar? The Heart everyone was so excited about?"

"Something like that, yeah."

Thea sat up straight, determination flashing in her eyes. "You know what? I think it's time we found out."

•••

Thea wanted Jake to come along. She was a pretty good independent journalist, even had the potential to be great. Given time and experience, dedication and perseverance—and not getting clipped by a nasty—she could make a name for herself. But when it came to standing up to her mother, she reverted to childhood patterns. For all their differences and Thea's acts of rebellion through the years, she retained a core of respect (and fear) toward her mother. Even pissed as she was at Newa Ghandour, Thea wasn't sure she could ask the tough questions.

Having Jake along would help her steel her nerves, stick to her guns, keep her eye on the prize, whatever cliché was appropriate. Although uncomfortable getting drawn into what might end up being nothing more than a family squabble, Jake promised his support.

"But what do we do about Margie?"

"I'm thinking we should take Margie with us," she said.

Jake looked at her over his glasses. "You sure that's a good idea?"

"We need to keep an eye on her, right? Help her get better, make sure she doesn't get into trouble." Thea sat next to her friend on the old couch that faced the fooseball table.

"That's fine, but won't your mom freak seeing Margie like this?"

"She and Mom get along pretty well," Thea said, giving Margie a one-armed hug that Margie returned with a tentative squeeze. Then she laid her head on Thea's shoulder, her stare still locked on the nothing of the middle distance. "Maybe it'll help Margie come all the way back. I get the feeling she's trying; she's just too scared right now to take the last couple steps." Unvoiced was Thea's hope that, if her mother *did* know something but was unwilling to talk about it, Margie's condition might provide the leverage for Newa Ghandour to spill. Eyes moist, Thea looked at Jake. "We have to do whatever we can to help her."

"Yeah, okay. We still have to find a new place to stay by tomorrow."

Thea nodded. "I'm thinking it might be best to hole up in a hotel room for the weekend. Nice and anonymous, no worry of something jumping us."

Jake didn't look thrilled with the idea. Hotels cost money, and Thea was broke. Jake got a decent amount of cash from the accident he'd suffered a couple years back, but he'd been living on that for a while, and nothing lasted forever. "We still have to figure out something long term. I mean, my whole thing was to wander around, helping hunter teams. Didn't do too good a job of that, here." Jake gave a noisy exhale and a humorless laugh. "Not that I'm going to leave before I've helped make all this right."

"I don't think it'll ever be right again, Jake."

"You know what I mean. Right as we can make it. But it's going to take longer than the weekend, and we can't hop around from place to place indefinitely."

"Yup. We're smart; we'll figure something out."

They left it at that for the moment. That evening, Howard Casey—who Thea had decided was enjoying his second chance at bachelorhood, evidenced by the various gaming tables and expansive home entertainment system in his basement—brought home Chinese food. Lupe Droin came by as well and they had a nice, dysfunctional hunter family dinner. The food was a bland American interpretation of Chinese dishes, but the association was enough to raise painful memories of Romeo Zheng in Thea. She did little more than poke at the kung pao on her plate. Margie seemed to enjoy the food at least, coming out of her shell enough to spear a potsticker off the plate halfway across the

table. These carefree flashes gave Thea hope that Margie was in a prolonged shock rather than a permanent fugue state. Professional help would surely hasten her friend's recovery, but Thea couldn't take the chance of drawing the attention of the undead. The rots were bound to be looking for that sort of thing. She had to hope that their current course would enable Margie to recover with no lingering problems.

During the meal, Jake explained their plan to Lupe and Howard. The vet became more animated with the news, clearly relieved to get his house back. Thea bit back some choice comments. This guy was supposed to be on the hunt like the rest of them, but he was more upset about a few squatters than that monsters had killed off a half-dozen hunters and left Thea's friend in a fragile emotional state. *Fuck him*, she thought. *If he's more interested in scamming on the single women who bring their pets in for flea baths, I don't want him watching my back.*

Lupe thought their plan was reasonable, but seemed skeptical of the good it would do. "You said yourself you weren't sure if your impressions of the Temple were memories or just run-of-the-mill déjà vu," Lupe told Thea before popping a mouthful of sweet and sour pork.

"So how do you explain my mom's reaction?" Thea tried not to let Lupe bait her—for that *had* to be what the woman was doing—but she couldn't help but respond. Lupe knew how to get under her skin.

"Maybe she's just looking out for you." Lupe shrugged. "Not everything has meaning, you know."

"I *know* that, Lupe." After counting to five (Thea lacked the patience to make it all the way to ten), Thea continued. "Look, you have to know my mom, how she's always reserved and in control of everything. She never talks about her feelings or her past. Her reaction was way out of character. There's something there."

"Hey, we know it might not come to anything." Jake took up the role of diplomat again. "But we're not going to know until we check into it, right?"

Thea couldn't help feeling that the nods around the table were more a sign of dismissal rather than agreement.

• • •

Thea felt it was safe during the day to make a run to her place. There was no reason to think that nasties had the place staked out six days after the Sears Tower battle. No reason except the bastards had proven themselves sneaky and patient. It was a foregone conclusion that the undead would have somebody watching the place—in the daytime, most likely a Renfield in the vampires' employ. Thea hoped whomever it was would be bored and growing lax after almost a week of nothing.

The others didn't think it was worth the risk just to get clothes and toiletries for her and Margie. Thea pointed out it would also be good to recover her computer and the weapons they'd stashed after the raid on the Temple of Akhenaton (if any of that was still there). Considering she'd kept relevant notes on the laptop and guns always came in handy on the hunt, the others soon acquiesced.

The next morning, the good pet doctor wished them well in a tone poorly disguising his relief at having them out of his hair. The feeling was mutual, far as Thea was concerned. Lupe pulled up in her taxi and Jake hopped in the shotgun seat while Thea slipped into the back with Margie. State highway 50, which became Cicero Ave, was a straight shot up to North Avenue. They hung a right and Thea directed Lupe to her block in Wicker Park. They cruised through the late morning traffic, tension mounting as they neared the apartment. It was frustrating for Thea that, despite all the effort she'd gone through to keep her place secret, the enemy still tracked it down. Thanks to Margie; not that Thea blamed her friend. Margie was under a vampire's influence, hypnotized to do his bidding. Thea was at least consoled by the fact that she and Jake had sent the bastard on a fatal swan dive out the Sears Tower.

Margie perked up as they cruised through Wicker Park. Seeing familiar places seemed to do her good. Thea

considered taking her inside, but there was no telling if they'd run into trouble, and there was no damn way she was putting her best friend in danger again. Instead, Lupe pulled the taxi to the curb and Thea and Jake got out like a typical fare. The cab pulled away, Margie in the back looking bewildered. The plan was, in and out in five minutes. If there was trouble, Jake would call the cab on the cheap Radio Shack walkie-talkie Lupe gave him. It was only good for a mile or so, but Lupe would be parked a couple blocks away, waiting with the walkie-talkie's twin.

It was a crisp, cool day, promising spring would arrive soon. Raised in the Midwest, Thea knew that was about as likely as a junkie promising to get off the smack cold turkey. They could expect at least one more big snowstorm, probably a few days after spring. Still, it was brilliant out now, and Thea drank in the clean sunlight and chilling air. She scanned the area, including a hard look at the plastic covered windows of the burned out old mansion across the street. Even after summoning her sixth sense to tweak for trouble, she saw nothing out of the ordinary.

They ventured inside, Thea in the lead. The stairway was empty, but they didn't expect a guy to be camped out in the hall. After a nod to Jake confirming he was ready, Thea unlocked the apartment door and slipped inside. She wasn't sure what to expect—a squad of goons, a vampire who could resist daylight, a note saying BOO. What awaited may not have been dangerous, but it was a surprise indeed.

The place was a mess. The living room furniture was covered in the feathery guts of a dozen pillows. The TV looked up at Thea from the floor, its screen a shattered accusation. The VCR and DVD player fared no better, their metal casings peeled back like the skin of a fruit, the interiors a broken jumble of circuit boards and wires. The stereo lay on the floor near the kitchen counter, pounded into a flattened mess of metal and plastic. Pictures were torn from the walls, frames rent asunder, glass shards scattered like lethal confetti. Plants had been savaged, fronds and clumps of potting soil scattered around in floral dismemberment.

The kitchen fared little better, the refrigerator pulled from the wall to lie on its side in the hallway leading to the bedrooms. The stove coils were yanked from the stovetop and flung around. The microwave, bread maker, coffee maker and other appliances were now an unrecognizable pile of junk scattered across the countertops. Holes were gouged into the wall, exposing lath and plaster and giving a good view into the closet just off the kitchen. The hallway hinted at more of the same for the rest of the place, pictures strewn across the floor and more holes smashed along the walls.

Considering the extent of the damage, ransacking the apartment must have caused one hell of a noise. She was surprised the cops hadn't been called, roped the place off, the whole bit. But then the nasties surely had the police in their pocket and had taken care of all that. It was hard to tell just when the violence occurred, but Thea suspected it happened when that fucker Graham snatched Margie. She picked her way through the wreckage toward the hall, giving Jake room to enter.

"Why don't you get Margie's things," she said, pointing to the first door past the bathroom. "Hopefully they didn't rip up all our clothes. A bunch of comfortable stuff, some sweaters, shoes and a coat."

Jake nodded. "She have a suitcase?"

"Should have; check the hall closet if there isn't one in her room." Thea headed down the hall, stepping around glass shards and plaster dust. "I'll get things together in my room."

A ripple of sensation flowed out from Thea as she was about to push the partly-open door to her bedroom. Her hand an inch from the wood, she focused on the feeling. Subtly different from what she discerned when facing a monster, it nonetheless gave the same sense of potentialities lying before her. The easy part was recognizing that

danger lurked in the next room; the trick was identifying the best choice to make. *What was it, a bomb? A guy? Yeah, that feels right. Someone behind the door.* And he had to have heard them talking, so Thea couldn't surprise him. The danger flared then—*he's coming!*—and Thea suddenly knew what to do.

She stepped to the side and yanked up a throw rug from the hallway floor. The bedroom door swung open that same instant, its motion swirling air inward that carried the glass and plaster dust billowing up from the rug. The debris wasn't harmful, but the man who stepped forward flinched reflexively, swearing and trying to protect his eyes with his off hand. Thea tossed the rug right after, and as the guy batted it away to clear his line of sight she spun to the other side of the narrow hall. She crouched to send a kick at the man's sternum, visualizing the attack ending with her foot six inches past the man's spine. The kick fired him back over the bed to crash against the floor.

Thea dashed forward as the man struggled to his knees, gasping for breath and raising a submachinegun with a large silencer attached. She was on the bed in two strides, standing smack in front of the guy—not that he had a chance to take aim. Her left fist came down with the weight of her body behind it and smashed across his face. Thea was hoping to feel the warm flare of the tattoo on her hand but got nothing more than a solid punch. That proved the guy was mortal, as her tattoos reacted with intense flashes of light and heat in contact with the supernatural. The realization brought with it a moment of hesitation—she didn't want to kill this guy if she could help it. He took advantage of that instant, swinging his gun hand around and up sharply—not to fire, but to catch Thea around the back of the knee and knock her down.

She collapsed on the bed and struggled for leverage even as the man lunged atop her. One hand grabbed the side of her head, thumb jabbing painfully along her jawline while the other hand shoved the SMG under her chin on the opposite side. Thea struggled, but his strength was tremendous. She tried to unbalance him but she was sunk deep the soft mattress, limbs stuck amid the comforter's heavy folds.

"Neat trick," the man said, squinting at her from inches away. "Think you got some glass in my eye. Now—"

"Hey!" Jake yelled from the doorway, pulling out the Sig Sauer 9mm automatic Lupe had lent him.

The man reacted in a flash, swinging the silenced submachinegun across—an H&K MP-5, Thea saw from the lettering on the side as it hung an inch before her eyes. Thea recognized Jake's move for what it was and flexed hard, pitching up her hips and shoulders to throw the man off-balance. His left hand squeezed so hard that Thea couldn't breathe. The SMG stuttered like a stuck toaster as it fired, spitting sizzling casings just over her forehead to scorch her hair. She ignored the pain as best she could, bringing a knee up to smash into the man's balls. He lurched forward and landed with his belly over her face. Buried by a 250-pound thug, Thea heard his roar of pain as a distant rumble. Fighting the soft mattress and lack of air, Thea shoved again with her legs and snapped her hips in a clumsy roll onto the guy's back. She scrambled back like a crab to position her knees over his flailing shoulders and hold his face down by sitting on the back of his head.

Thea had all she could do to stay on him as he churned forward with his legs. He was much too strong for her to control, so she aimed a series of sharp strikes into his kidneys. The first two probably did the trick, if his strangled cries were any indication, but Thea kept nailing him to be safe.

Then Jake was there, pulling her off and calming her down. She realized she was wheezing, having trouble breathing. *Feels like the bastard collapsed my throat*, she thought. Hunching over and massaging her throat, her breathing began approaching normal. It hurt to swallow but she'd live.

In the meantime, Jake had disarmed the man and had him sitting on the mattress, legs out straight in a V and leaning forward to grasp his calves. Thea chuckled at the pose, then gasped as the laugh pulled at something in her throat. Jake gave her an embarrassed shrug. "I figure he can't try anything sitting like that."

She took the MP-5 Jake offered, her other hand probing her side. The gunshot wound she'd suffered a week before was still tender, but it looked like the struggle hadn't aggravated it. *Just add it to the list of aches and pains.* "You think— ow, damn that hurts…" Her voice was the rasp of sandpaper. In a softer tone meant to spare her throat, she tried again. "You think anybody heard those shots?"

"No telling. Silencer still made noise but this looks like a sturdy old building." Jake ran a hand over the ragged line of bullet holes in the wall dividing Thea's room from Margie's. "This'll take some work to repair, but at least we don't have to worry about the slugs flying into the street and hitting somebody. So maybe we're okay, but I don't think we should take any chances."

"Great minds. Wish we had time to question the guy, but guess we'd best haul ass. Grab what we can and get out of here in the next minute." Whatever rage had fueled the destruction in the living room had abated somewhat by her bedroom, so she only had to cope with minor things like the dresser with its drawers pulled out and clothes strewn around like a cyclone had swept through the room. Not too different from normal, really.

She grabbed her internal frame backpack from the closet and shoved a selection of clothes into it. From a box on the shelf she dug out what few pictures she had of her and her mother, a packet of love letters from her first boyfriend, and the "emergency" American Express card her mom got her years ago. After stuffing the items into a side pocket, she propped the pack by the door. "Get Margie's stuff together, Jake; you have a minute. I got this guy."

Jake dashed back down the hall. Thea stepped up to the edge of the bed, submachinegun pointed squarely at the man's chest. Despite being in obvious pain from the kidney blows— which being hunched over like that did nothing to help— the guy was alert, watching her as best he could.

"What's your name?" she asked.

He smiled and shook his head, but replied, "Earl."

"Okay, Earl. Where's my laptop and the bag full of guns that was in here?"

"Where do you think?"

Thea nodded, figuring as much. "Right. Look, you'll be fine long as you don't try to come after us. Don't want to kill you, but I will; got me?"

Earl just looked at her. *Tough guy; fine.* "Okay, Earl, I want you to lean as far forward as you can and put your wrists together between your feet." The big man had to put his head down to reach a full extension, so Thea was spared any further inscrutable looks. "Jake! How's it coming?"

Jake hustled back a half-minute later, stuffing a sweater in a Samsonite carry-on. "Shoot him if he moves," Thea said. She shoved the MP-5 into the awkward holster the straps of her backpack made and unclipped a bungie cord from a side pocket. She approached Earl carefully. Though bent almost double and mired in the soft mattress with no leverage to attack, he could lean back and drag her with. She was counting on him believing Jake would shoot. Thea hooked one end through wrought iron bedpost, looped it tightly in a figure-eight around his wrists, back through the frame, then pulled down *hard* to attach the straining other end to the frame under the bed. Earl could get free with some effort, but it'd hold him long enough for them to make a clean getaway.

But before they left, Thea wanted to try and get something, anything, from this guy. She and Jake were operating too much in the dark for her comfort. "Look, Earl, you can see we got nothing against you, so work with us and you'll come out of this smelling like a rose."

"I'm not going to tell you anything, lady," Earl replied, voice muffled by having his face shoved against his knees.

"No? Yet you're here to take us back in and spill our guts. Double standard, don't you think?"

"Ha. Ha. You're a real riot." A pause, during which Jake urged her to haul ass. "All right, I'll give you something, honey. Doesn't matter what you know anymore; you're considered too dangerous to live."

A chill coursed through Thea. "Who do you mean?"

"What? All of you, you daffy broad. You, your pal there, the blond chick; all the rest of you who're left."

Thea gaped at the man. Jake and herself she could handle, but she hadn't thought they'd come after Margie. Hadn't *wanted* to think it. Really, it made perfect sense. Margie was a witness. Under other circumstances they might have written her off—who would believe what sounded like a drugged-out story about vampires in the Sears Tower? But she'd been connected to the hunters, and it was clear the nasties were in serious revenge mode now. Her best friend's life was ruined, and all because of her. Unless… it was an outside chance, but maybe she could make it work. Catching her breath, Thea let outrage overwhelm her.

"You know who's left? Just the two of us! No 'blond chick,' not anymore. Your bloodsucking pal Graham murdered my best friend, you bastard!" She launched herself at him, smashing her fists into his side and face. "She never did anything to anyone, and you had her killed!"

"Thea!" Jake cried, grabbing at her flailing limbs. "Jeez, come on! We got to get going *now*."

"Yeah, you run." Earl chuckled, licking away a trickle of blood. "Thanks for the update, sweet thing. I'll be sure to pass it along."

Thea let Jake pull her away. "You want to pass something else along, tell your masters she's the last. I'd start looking for a new gig, Earl. Your bosses are going to be out of business real soon."

Earl's laughter, hearty despite being bent double with bruised kidneys, followed them out of the apartment and down the stairs.

●●●

Jake had the walkie talkie out as they made their escape. The taxi roared toward them as they reached the building's front steps. Thea and Jake wasted no time tossing the luggage on the floor of the back seat and piling in. "How'd it go?" Lupe asked as she steered them west on North Avenue.

"The rots had a guy staked out, waiting for us in Thea's room."

"What happened?"

"His weapon went off while we were subduing him," Thea said, puzzling over the MP-5 for a few seconds till she figured out the correct way to remove the silencer. She popped the clip and jacked the slide, then shoved everything in her backpack. "We left him tied up." A sharp look in the rearview showed Lupe's opinion of that. "What, you rather we killed him? He may be working for the undead but he's still a human being."

"Relax, sister," Lupe said, turning right. "Just wishing you'd had time to get some answers out of him."

"Me, too," Jake said. Thea imagined his reasons for questioning a servant of the undead were likely different from those of the pragmatic Guadalupe Droin. "Still, we got enough to know the rots are no longer interested in *talking* to us."

Lupe nodded and concentrated on steering them around in a loop designed to lose any tails and bring them to Newa Ghandour's Gold Coast condo from the north. After looking over the large pistol he'd been given, Jake stuffed the Sig Sauer back in his jacket and stared out the window, lost in thought.

"What was that about Margie?" Jake asked after a few minutes. "Trying to put them off the scent?"

"Trying to, yeah." Patting her friend on the back, Thea explained to Lupe, "They wanted her, too. Witness. Maybe if they think she's dead they won't worry about her anymore."

She didn't have to fake the show she'd put on for Earl. The trauma Margie suffered stirred Thea to thoughts

of violence she could never have imagined herself capable of. Convincing as it might have been, there was no telling if the guy and his masters would believe it. But she'd had to try. It was the least she could do for Margie.

Another twenty minutes brought them to Thea's mom's place. The condominium was part of a row that commanded a respectable view of Lakeshore Drive and Lake Michigan. It was before noon on a Friday. Thea knew her mother would be doing whatever it was marketing directors did for another eight hours at least. Newa Ghandour was in her mid-sixties, but she still put in solid fifty- to sixty-hour work weeks at the pharmaceutical company Panflex. Jake had wondered about showing up so early, not to mention unannounced. They hadn't lined up another place to stay. Thea thought it'd be good to go straight to her mom's instead of running around, booking a room and then showing up. She wanted to take the time to prepare herself. They could get a cab to a hotel afterward easily enough.

Thea's key got her inside with no trouble, but she had a moment's panic recalling the security system code. She got Margie settled in on the couch while Jake followed with the bags, Lupe heading off to return to her route after a last wave of good luck.

The afternoon was spent with Jake hunched over his computer doing research while Thea cared for Margie. Her friend showed a perceptible improvement. She'd been to the condo often in the past, and it was clear the familiar environment was a calming influence. Thea could only imagine how comforting Margie's own parents' home would be. But to take her home in this condition would raise uncomfortable questions. Questions for which the answers would not ease the comfort level any.

Thea expected she would feel similar unease when she confronted her mother in a few hours.

• • •

Thea had to hand it to her mom. Coming home to find your daughter—long since moved out years ago—

there with her best friend sitting in some zoned-out fugue state, not to mention some black kid barely out of his teens who you've never seen before, and a parent would be understandably surprised.

But Newa Ghandour was not a woman who lost composure easily (notwithstanding her outburst regarding the Temple of Ahkenaton). Entering the condo that evening, she stopped short when she saw Thea and Margie on the couch watching television, with Jake at the dining room table working on the laptop. After absorbing the unexpected tableau, Thea's mom said simply, "What has happened?"

"Hi, Mom. Good to see you, too." Thea came around the couch and leaned against its back, matching her mom's composure. She waved Jake forward, continuing, "Mom, this is Jake Washington; Jake, this is my mother, Newa Ghandour." Jake smiled and murmured a hello, unsure of how to greet the woman whose home he'd invaded. For her part, Margie was engrossed in *To Catch a Thief* on AMC, oblivious to Newa's arrival behind her.

Although her beauty had faded with time, Newa Ghandour was still a handsome woman. She had grown broad in the beam and her face showed the lines of age and determination, but she retained the healthy caramel skin and lustrous black hair of youth. Newa favored Jake with a polite "Pleased to meet you," then focused on Thea. "Your neck is bruised. Are you all right?"

"I'm fine. But there are some things we need to talk about."

Her mother rolled that around before nodding again. "I will make us dinner."

Jake shot Thea a glance, wondering at the odd formality between her and her mother. With a shrug and a quick smile she indicated this wasn't all that different from normal.

They left Newa alone in the kitchen. Even under normal circumstances Thea's mom preferred to operate alone when preparing meals. Cooking was her big hobby, and having anyone else around disrupted her creative

flow. It was telling of their relationship that, in comparison, Thea had trouble boiling water without burning it.

Jake put away his laptop and joined the women in the living room. Thea divided her time between the television and keeping an eye on Margie. Hope fluttered around in her chest. In the few hours they'd been at the condo, Margie had relaxed dramatically. She was snuggled on the couch in her typical movie-watching pose, her feet kneading Thea's thigh like a cat and chuckling along with the funny parts of the movie. Aside from not speaking—Margie liked making observations about what she was watching, from the actors and sets to what the screenwriter was thinking with a given piece of dialogue—she could have been mistaken for her typically mellow self.

Hearing the clatter of serving dishes, Thea hopped up and set the dining room table. Jake scrambled to help, but she waved him to stay put. A few minutes later Newa Ghandour presented them with a casserole she'd cobbled together from odds and ends. She noticed how Thea led Margie to the table but said nothing, merely adding Margie's silent compliance to the mysteries before her.

A similar silence hung over much of the dinner. It was customary for Thea and her mother to keep any talk of substance till after the meal. Each had a lot on her mind, so even attempts at small talk died a quick death. Jake was a stranger in a strange land and wasn't the most extroverted person to begin with, so he didn't take the chance of kicking off any topics aside from complimenting the elder Ghandour on the meal. Margie seemed happy enough enjoying the meal and continued her trend of silence.

This dance continued until after-dinner coffee. Thea was almost ready to start when her mother took the initiative. Beginning to her left with Jake, Newa Ghandour swung her gaze around to Margie and then Thea. "All right, Thea. I would gather that you are here because of something to do with the news I saw of someone attacking the Temple of Akhenaton."

Thea realized she shouldn't be surprised. She had asked her mother about the temple, and the next day there was a massacre there. Newa Ghandour wasn't stupid. She was bound to suspect there was a connection on some level. Thea supposed she should be surprised her mom remained cool and composed while firing off such a volatile question.

"You gather right, Mom. But maybe not in the way you think." A pause as Thea considered. If her mom thought her daughter was involved in some fringe group committing violence, then it *would* be in the way she'd think. Thea's job was to get some answers from her mother as best she could without revealing the complete scope of the insanity she and Jake were involved in. After hours of discussion, they hadn't come up with anything that didn't sound at least mildly nuts. Thea led off with the most reasonable of those, hoping she could jump from there to grilling her mother about the temple before Newa had a chance to spot any major flaws in their tale. "Okay, look. Jake and I, we've been looking into something for a while now, a group—I guess you'd call them a secret society—who—"

"The Cult of the Sun-Disk," Newa interjected.

Thrown off-track just as she was getting rolling, Thea could only direct a surprised look at her mother.

Newa Ghandour looked into her coffee cup, then raised her head. Her eyes held a great weariness. "I had hoped to protect you from all this, but I understand now that is not possible. One of the Aton-u found you and told you of our past, yes?"

Actually, Thea was using "secret society" as a metaphor for the undead. Considering her mother was revealing what they'd hoped to learn, Thea didn't think it was worth correcting the misunderstanding. "Aton-u. That's not Arabic."

"No, it is Egyptian. Aton-u, the Children of Aton. The Cult of the Sun-Disk. It formed long ago, in the

time of the Egyptian dynasties. Its members worshiped a heretical god, and were persecuted for it. They went underground and survived the passing of years. Even as the recognized Egyptian gods passed into the land of myth—as is their proper place—their worship of Aton endured. In time, the cult came out of hiding, re-forming as something akin to the Freemasons. But, in secret, the cabal continued its homage to Aton."

"Oookay. So how do you know all this?"

Newa opened her mouth to reply, then frowned. "You should know that, otherwise why the violence against the temple?"

"That wasn't us," Thea asserted almost truthfully. "Like I said, we were investigating a lead. We got caught in the middle when everything went to hell. Honestly, Mom, I have no idea how you tie into all this."

Newa Ghandour scrutinized her coffee cup. Perhaps a half a minute passed, the only activity the thoughts scampering across the older woman's face and Jake fidgeting in his chair. Finally, with a heavy sigh, Newa raised her head to point a pair of anguished eyes at her daughter. "I used to belong."

SEVEN

Spring might be a week away, but winter had yet to relax its grip. Sunset descended in the late afternoon to find Beckett already working out of the earth's embrace. Salmon and violet still tinted the western horizon as he slipped from his resting place behind some maintenance sheds at La Guardia. He emerged refreshed and with renewed purpose. His lingering paranoia suggested the feeling was due to escaping Menele's pervasive aura. He doubted it was thanks to a day spent resting in ground soaked with smog, soot and oil from thousands upon thousands of jets making their way to and from the airport.

He headed for the taxi stand and, with an area map for reference, directed a cab to the New York offices of Meroe Global Shipping in Red Hook. Beckett had some experience with trans-Atlantic voyages. The undead typically booked passage as cargo on planes and ships to cover long distances. (His two recent flights as a passenger were done out of necessity rather than preference. He was uncomfortable being stuck in a seat so high up, unprotected from possible exposure to the sun. Resting in a shipping crate, it didn't matter if the jet suffered a delay or rerouting that kept it from disgorging its passengers before the sun rose.) He was less familiar with the St. Lawrence Seaway, but he had a good head for navigation. By his reckoning, it would take a large cargo vessel between three and five nights to cover the distance from Chicago to New York. *Meroe Atlantic* would come into New York Harbor within the next twenty-four hours, if it hadn't reached port already. Even if it had come in the previous day, it should stay in dock for some time to transfer cargo. Either way, the zombie Carpenter was close by, and with it the Heart of Osiris.

The docks stretched along the coasts of New York and New Jersey for miles. Sniffing out the Heart from amid that mess would be difficult to say the least, and would take time Beckett didn't have. So, armed with the name of the shipping company and of the container vessel on which his quarry had stowed away, he'd do it the easy way. It had been a simple matter to get the number for Meroe Global and cull its address from the automated after-hours message he'd called after arriving in La Guardia that morning before dawn. The tricky part came now—slipping into the offices and finding *Meroe Atlantic's* shipping route and present berthing slot. It wouldn't have a berth assigned if it hadn't reached the harbor, but that was simple enough to follow up on.

It was after five o'clock when he approached the Meroe Global offices. The place was still open, so Beckett would have to wait for a few hours if he wanted to break in and look for the information without interference. He felt the time was precious—and besides, he didn't know where they might keep such files—so he just walked inside and asked his way over to a clerk who could help.

The man had the large frame of a dock worker, but the forty extra pounds around his middle indicated he'd traded ships for his desk years ago. A cheap nameplate on the desk confided his name as WALTER ZACKOWICZ. Beckett liked the modern habit mortals had of labeling themselves so conspicuously. For some reason, having their names on display, they seldom asked for his in return. Beckett preferred anonymity.

"Help ya?" Zackowicz asked. The man cast a weary gaze his way, brows furrowed in a blend of curiosity and irritation—curious no doubt due to Beckett's sunglasses and pale complexion, irritated at having to deal with one more thing so close to quitting time. Beckett could tell the man's mind was already on the burger, onion rings and two or three boilermakers he'd be having for dinner. Given this fellow's distracted state, it shouldn't be difficult to learn what he needed.

"Looking for a ship of your line," Beckett said.

"Why?" A man of few words, it seemed, was Walter Zackowicz.

"Got a buddy working on it," Beckett improvised, adopting the fragmented speech patterns and aggressive tones he recalled were common to the East Coast. He slouched in the molded plastic chair next to the desk and pointed toward the docks. "Remembered it should hit town sometime soon. Figured we could get together, catch up for a drink."

"Don't bullshit me, pal," the man said after a beat, his face a textbook expression of suspicion. "Ain't nobody comes in here wanting to catch up with some 'old friend' works one of our tubs." Before Beckett could toss out a new line, Zackowicz continued: "So, what? This 'buddy' owes you some money, is what I'm guessing."

Beckett had to laugh. "You got me."

"Uh huh. Don't think I'm gonna tell you where to find a guy and have him end up taking a beating so he can't finish his run."

"I'm not looking for trouble," Beckett replied with a shrug. He dug a much-abused twenty from his sheepskin jacket and laid it on the desk. "Don't want to jam up your operation; just want what I'm owed."

Zackowicz looked at the bill and pursed his fleshy lips, then slapped his hands on the desk and shoved his chair over to a computer terminal behind him. The twenty disappeared in the process. "What's your 'buddy's' name?"

"I only know him by Joey," Beckett said. "Why I'm having trouble finding him, you know? I do know he's on the *Meroe Atlantic* coming in from Chicago."

There was a noncommittal grunt and the tapping of keys. "Okay, yeah. Got in maybe six hours ago." Zackowicz shoved his chair back over to the desk and scribbled down the berth. He slid the paper toward

Beckett, fingers holding it down where the twenty was a moment before. "I know you got bills to pay, but so do we. You get me?"

Beckett nodded, making no move to take the paper until the mortal felt he'd made his point and removed his hand. Slipping the address in his pocket as he stood, Beckett thanked Zackowicz.

"Hey, pal, some free advice," the man said as Beckett turned for the door. "Wearing sunglasses at night don't make you look cool. You come off looking like some kind of pansy."

"Thanks for the tip," Beckett replied with a smile, wondering what Walter Zackowicz would say if he could see what the glasses hid.

•••

Beckett ran very fast. Bustling though the docks were, even heading into night, most of the workers were busy enough with their tasks that he was gone from sight before they had time to register his passage. He would cause some remarks, moving at such a rate, but mortals were good at rationalizing almost anything. Not worth worrying about, all things considered.

He passed a series of mammoth ships with crews swarming over them like so many flies on an elephant's hide. There was a gap every so often, an open berth waiting the arrival of another big container vessel and its cargo. Activity was dying down as the day shifts knocked off, but operations never stopped completely in a harbor busy as this one.

Six hours. The Heart was here, not more than a mile away. It would be a day or so before *Meroe Atlantic* left New York Harbor. The zombie was probably hiding in some disused portion of the ship's hold, waiting for the vessel to get underway. Beckett could be in, dispatch Carpenter, and away with the artifact within thirty minutes. Plenty of time. But instinct said he had to move, that time was still of the essence.

Moving at speed, Beckett was aware of a growing hunger. He'd been busy with one thing and another and had forgotten to feed in the past few nights. Although he could comfortably go for more than a week without requiring blood, he preferred to feed every few nights. A regular diet ensured he was never caught in a weakened condition. Still, he was confident he was strong enough to face Carpenter. Zombies could be formidable opponents in the realm of brute power, but they lacked the array of powers vampires enjoyed. A Cainite like Beckett had a number of aptitudes upon which he could draw. The zombie had shown a disturbing talent for mental compulsion, but Beckett could negate that by avoiding eye contact. Even so, he would have felt more comfortable with fresh blood flowing through his veins.

Nothing to be done about it now. A few dozen yards away rose a massive hull, indistinguishable from the rest except for the name that marched across the stern. The *Meroe Atlantic.* Cargo containers rose a good twenty feet above the deck like children's building blocks. Workers moved around on the bridge, silhouetted by interior lights. That was the only activity Beckett noticed on the ship; the cargo transfer must not begin until the next day. That should give Beckett free run of the ship to hunt down the Heart.

Drawing toward the gangway, Beckett caught the artifact's unmistakable scent. It wasn't wafting from the ship—instead, a trail lead further down the docks. The scent was a couple hours old.

Beckett was on the trail in a flash, every loping stride taking him that much closer to his quarry. As he ran, he wondered what Carpenter was doing leaving the tanker. Seeing a few sights while it waited for the ship to depart? Or was Beckett even following the zombie any longer? The Heart's odor was so strong to his human nose that it overshadowed any other scent. He supposed it was possible someone else had the artifact now. Khalid had explained the Heart resonated with an aura that those with supernatural sensitivity would feel. Beckett wasn't one of those types, but he knew there were a lot of them in the Big Apple. It would complicate things if some local

force had sensed the artifact and come after it. Indeed, that was putting it mildly.

Conjecture would get him nowhere. Best to see where the trail led and act accordingly once he had a better sense of the situation.

The scent traveled parallel to the docks for about a half-mile. Beckett was moving at a slower rate than before—equivalent of a fast jog for a mortal—but even so he overshot the trail when the odor took a sudden turn. He scrambled back, scenting that the Heart had gone down a pier. Puzzled, Beckett trotted forward. The berth was empty, so where did the trail lead?

Then Beckett noticed the water. It rolled in gentling waves… a wake. He put on a burst of speed, reaching the end of the pier in an instant. Without a docked ship obstructing his view, Beckett saw it: Perhaps a hundred yards away was a huge blocky freighter—the NORTH LLORCA, its stern declared—churning toward the channel that lead to open sea. A snarl ripped from Beckett's lips. He ran at full speed back down the pier and around to the second berth along. Ratcheting his pace up a notch, pushing himself to the limit, Beckett charged up the gangway and leaped atop the nearest cargo container. A handful of deckhands saw a blurred shape streak across the tops of the containers toward the bow—and disappear over the side.

The leap was tremendous, but it carried Beckett merely half the distance toward the departing *North Llorca*. He would have plunged into the frigid waters of New York Harbor, but on the descent he willed his body to fold in upon itself. In seconds Beckett was a bat flitting toward the ship. He was playing a dangerous game, performing superhuman feats within view of the living. There were a few shouts of surprise and confusion as he leaped, but he relied on his rapid passage and the darkness blanketing the harbor to conceal his efforts.

Just getting underway, *North Llorca* was not speedy here in the channel. It chugged along fast as a man could run. Beckett's leap cut its lead, and it wasn't long before he was flapping over container ship's huge deck, stacked four- and five-deep with semi-trailer sized cargo bins. He assumed people were in the bridge that arose in mid-deck, but his natural sonar picked up no movement elsewhere on deck. Made sense; the containers were packed together tightly and fastened down, leaving hardly any room to maneuver. The crew would seldom venture out of the central area, Beckett imagined, especially on such a chill night. He angled down to the aft deck to a spot where the containers weren't stacked quite so high. He shifted back to human form, dropping to the container without a sound.

"Now that is one hell of a trick," a cold voice said.

Beckett turned to the sound of a gun cocking and saw a man step out from the shadows of an adjacent container stack. He looked like a merchant marine from a bygone time, dressed in work boots, dungarees, thick wool turtleneck, gloves, navy pea coat and watch cap. Beckett recognized the narrow face, dark hair, mocking lips and eyes burning with intimate knowledge of death. "Carpenter."

The zombie's eyebrows arched in mild surprise. "My reputation precedes me, it seems. So who're you, then?"

"You may call me Beckett," he said, ignoring the automatic pointed with casual confidence at his head. "I would have expected you to be hidden somewhere in the hold."

"Never been to New York," Carpenter replied, nodding over its shoulder without taking its eyes off Beckett. "Thought I'd take a gander at the skyline."

Manhattan's distinctive silhouette towered behind Carpenter, a million lights glittering in the night. The zombie must have stood by the corner of a container, inadvertently shielded from Beckett's sonar. It was the mistake a vampire new to unlife would make, not double-checking before changing form. Rather than berate himself, Beckett channeled his anger into a plan of retribution.

"I have a good idea why you dropped by," Carpenter said, "and it wasn't for chitchat. Let me save us both

some trouble. You're not going to get what you came for, so why don't you save yourself from getting your ass kicked and head back to whatever hole you crawled out of?"

Beckett avoided looking directly at the zombie, so he didn't know if the thing had inserted a command into its suggestion. As long as there was a dialogue going, he decided to see if reason and persuasion might prove useful. "I don't know what you plan to do with the Heart, but you must know you won't succeed. It is a beacon to the supernatural. You can't hope to hold onto it for much longer."

"What can I say? I feel lucky."

Reason and persuasion didn't seem to offer much chance of success. Beckett saw no recourse but violence. It appeared Carpenter had the same opinion, for the pistol fired the instant Beckett started moving. The bullet tore a chunk out of his shoulder as he flung himself to the side. Ignoring the burn of the wound, Beckett leaped atop a container and ducked out of the zombie's line of sight. The gun was nothing more than an irritant, but Beckett didn't much feel like getting shot up. He circled around, leaping lightly from one container to another in hopes of attacking from an oblique angle.

If the running footsteps were any indication, Carpenter wasn't willing to be a stationary target. The Heart's scent filled the area, making it impossible to tell exactly where his opponent was. Tracking by sound instead, Beckett ran forward. A beam of light speared through the darkness, startling him. It wasn't fire or the sun, but instinct demanded he avoid the light. Fluid as thought, he rolled off the side of the container just as the bridge spotlight swept where he'd been. Beckett was surprised that weak mortal ears could hear the gunshot over the sound of the ship's throbbing diesels. He suspected Carpenter was trying to avoid being seen as well—crews took a dim view of stowaways—and used the spotlight to his advantage, slipping fast around containers to come at the zombie from the opposite direction. On the way, he focused to knit the wounded flesh of his shoulder back together.

The spotlight made another pass, then clicked off just before it reached Beckett by the port side. His ears strained to hear the scrape of a boot or other telltale indicator of Carpenter's location. Nothing. They could continue this cat-and-mouse for hours, but Beckett wanted to recover the Heart before the ship made it through to open sea. An idea sprang to mind. Falling into a momentary trance, he sent out an urgent call, then settled back to wait.

A few minutes passed. He took advantage of the time, stuffing his sunglasses and gloves in his jacket and removing his boots and setting them to one side. His feet had claws as wicked as those on his hands. A few seconds later he heard a yell of surprise, faint over the drone of *North Llorca*'s engines. Beckett was off like a shot, tracking the voice that soon turned to cursing. Bounding over the final container in the row on the starboard side, Beckett couldn't have asked for a better opportunity. The zombie stood two yards away, facing the other direction, kicking and swinging at a cluster of some-things that squeaked and chittered.

Beckett couldn't suppress the snarl of triumph as he leaped forward, talons sweeping across to tear gouges through Carpenter's back in a gruesome X. The zombie cried out as it stumbled forward. Beckett was on the dead thing before it could turn, striking with his feet to knock it down and rip into it with all four limbs. The pistol came around and Beckett hit it away so hard it traced a glittering arc halfway to shore before plunking into the harbor. Clothing became shreds of confetti and cold, dead flesh was sliced to ribbons as Beckett's talons tore down to bone. A mortal would have been dead a dozen times over; Beckett would have thought even a zombie couldn't withstand such savagery. But Carpenter still struggled against him, the zombie's powerful arms flailing as it tried to strike Beckett a solid blow.

Then there was an oilslick glimmer and something flashed across Beckett's sight. He had an impression of bright darkness, then a hideous cold agony blossomed

along his chest and all the way down the inside of his left arm. Beckett roared in surprise and pain, rearing back to see his arm had been laid open by a blade so sharp it had cut down to the bone—had cut *into* the bone. Skin was ripped open, tendon and muscle torn away. He tried to command the wound to heal, but this was no mundane bullet hole. Something preternatural had cut him; Beckett could not order his flesh closed merely with an effort of will. The Beast surged forth, overcoming the pain with one overriding desire—destroy the thing that had caused the hurt.

Beckett came at Carpenter again, his left arm held tight against his body as his right swung down. The zombie followed up on its lucky shot, moving to Beckett's left and forcing him to turn and cover his weak side. Despite the shocking injuries it had suffered so far, the zombie moved as fast as before. Beckett saw the strange glimmer again and barely threw himself aside in time. There was a clang and sparks as the weapon chopped through the top of the metal container on which they fought. The devastating blow proved to be a feint— Carpenter's left hand thrust forward and grabbed Beckett.

With strength to match Beckett's own, Carpenter yanked him by the collar up and over the side. Beckett's feet shot out and ravaged the zombie's face, tearing skin and puncturing bone. Then he was flying through the air and plunging into the channel. The shock of the frigid water restored Beckett's reason. Still holding his wounded arm close, he struggled to the surface. He treaded water as best he could and tried to get a good look at the *North Llorca*'s receding shape. The zombie had surprised him with its sheer toughness and whatever it was that carved so painfully into him. But could the zombie have survived the savage wounds Beckett had inflicted upon it?

Spying a form struggle to its feet atop the back row of containers and thrust its index finger in his direction, Beckett had his answer.

• • •

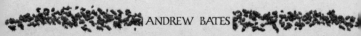

Beckett's body screamed for blood as he dragged himself through the freezing waters to the shore. He savaged an unfortunate pair of dockworkers strolling off-shift, but even the blood from two grown men wasn't enough to heal the vicious wound the zombie inflicted. Time is what he needed. Time and rest.

Bloody and savage, his arm and chest burning with the awful cold of the wound, Beckett dumped the bodies into the back of the battered Lincoln Continental they'd been walking toward and drove it away. He headed north, to upstate New York. He'd built a cabin there a century ago, not far from the Stillwater Reservoir. Covered in blood, talons of his hands and feet apparent, crimson eyes blazing, Beckett made an extra effort to avoid populated areas along the way. He drove on back roads, finally turning off onto a disused maintenance road. After dragging the dockworkers into the underbrush for scavengers to pick over, he left the Continental, taking pains not to leave any tracks through the woods. The cabin was about ten miles distant, built on an outcropping far from the nearest road and accessed only by game trails. He would be safe there, could rest and decide what to…

Beckett's thoughts trailed off. Safe from what? He realized he felt a sense of… perhaps not danger, but of deep disquiet. Nothing he could define, a mere whisper of unease, but Beckett hadn't endured for as long as he had by ignoring even these faintest of instincts.

His cabin could wait a little longer; he had a call to make first. He slipped into the town of Big Moose and contacted his agent, Manfred von Reis of the Witz-Kohn Bank of Geneva. Beckett had directed von Reis a few weeks before to look into satellite phones as a way for Beckett to more easily contact people, even when far from civilization. The agent felt the new Motorola 9505-Iridium most closely matched the specifications Beckett had given him, capable of voice, paging and even data transmission over most of the globe. Beckett ordered von Reis to send one, along with a half-dozen extra batteries and a couple battery chargers, to his

post office box in the nearby city of Carthage. The Swiss banker was used to far more unusual requests from his clients, and assured Beckett it would be taken care of.

Beckett made his way to the cabin and bandaged his wound using gauze from an old first aid kit kept for those rare instances when he suffered a wound his blood couldn't heal. The next few days and nights passed in a dragging haze of pain. The sun forced him into slumber, but the pain kept him from succumbing fully to sleep. He awoke in the evening, the edge of the wound etched in an aching chill. He became the wolf to more easily hunt—even with only three working legs he could bring down deer and other animals on which to feed. He gorged on blood, forcing it to the wound in hopes that the sheer amount could overcome the injury. No matter how much he drank, Beckett found he couldn't accelerate the healing.

By the third night, he resigned himself that it would take weeks, perhaps even months, to recover fully. The injury was down to a dull ache at least, and he felt clear-headed enough to head into Carthage and pick up his package. The city was thirty miles from the cabin; he'd rented a large post office box there some years ago for those occasions when he needed substantial items shipped to him. The main post office was locked, but the post office box wing was accessible at any time. He reached Carthage in a few hours traveling as the wolf, but returning to the cabin took a great deal longer. The package he extracted from the post office box was too bulky to subsume into himself when he changed forms, so he was forced to carry it in his human shape. Beckett wasn't an expert on the metaphysics behind these transformations; he couldn't give a clear reason why his clothing and smaller belongings stayed with him when he turned to bestial forms or even to mist, while larger items stayed as they were. It was enough to know that it wouldn't work. So he slogged through the old snow back to the cabin, reaching it shortly before sunrise.

The next night he read through the Motorola user's manual. The device proved easy enough to operate, looking and functioning like a typical cell phone. There was even a hookup he could use to connect a computer to transmit online. Beckett commended von Reis on the choice. The phone, a pair of spare batteries and a plug-in charger would fit in his leather jacket he wore, replacing the sheepskin coat he'd ruined in his fight with the zombie. Once he felt familiar enough with the satellite phone's operation, Beckett placed his first call.

The call connected easily; he was close enough to civilization that the Motorola routed through a standard cellular linkup. A woman's voice, husky and with a lilt of humor, answered on the third ring.

"Good evening, Nola. It's Beckett."

"Twice in as many months," Nola Spier replied, warmth suffusing her words. She was mortal, a wizard of long acquaintance Beckett first met in Los Angeles during the Great Depression. Nola was among his more trusted contacts spread around the world. "To what do I owe the pleasure?"

"I am calling about the bracelet you gave me."

"Hmm. Interesting tone you have there. Something wrong with it?"

"I don't think so." Beckett looked at a bracelet of braided silver strung with opalescent stones that hung around his left wrist. "Instead, I'm curious about what it might take to pierce through the aura it projects."

"Something pretty powerful, I'd say. You wanted me to create something that would keep you off the psychic radar. That bracelet should do the job—at least for another month or so. It should be effective against most any extra-sensory capabilities."

"What scale are we speaking of?"

"There really isn't a standard scale for what we're talking about," Nola admitted. "You wanted something potent, so I designed it to trump anything in my experience. But that doesn't mean there isn't something out there that could still see through it. If there is, though, it'd be something of mind-boggling power."

Beckett nodded to himself. Nola Spier had amassed significant mystic knowledge over the years and wasn't prone to exaggeration. He trusted her expertise. "Thank you, Nola."

"Sure." After a beat, Nola said, "Sounds like there's a wrinkle here. I might be able to help if, well…."

For beings such as they, knowledge was power and even the strongest ties could be sundered by unforeseen circumstances. It was understood and accepted that seldom was more than the barest necessity divulged. But Beckett had spent the past few days in an internal struggle, looking for some measure of objectivity in hopes of determining where he truly stood in recent matters. He had to admit that such a viewpoint might well be beyond him now. He might be best off taking a confidence, allowing some measure of trust in someone else. Trust tempered by instinct, anyway. Nola Spier was as close to a friend as a creature like him could have, and the deepest parts of himself felt he could confide in her—had to, if he had any hope of getting a handle on the turmoil surrounding him. He would have to take a chance. Drawing breath, Beckett explained his discovery of a powerful force under the streets of a major metropolis and the ancient artifact it hoped to use to arise from its long slumber. He stayed in the realm of the general, refraining from naming the parties involved or even confirming that he was speaking of the undead. Nola likely knew this anyway, but such details were incidental to the meat of the matter.

He listened to the crystal clear silence on the digital connection as Nola Spier mulled over the tale. At last, she said, "Comes down to this, unless I miss my guess: You're wondering if this slumbering giant might have its hooks in you despite the precautions you've taken."

"Or looking for a way to get a hold."

"That's a tough call, Beckett. We both know that slipping into someone's mind like that—subtle and pervasive—takes a lot of time and finesse. My initial response would be to say that, with the help of the bracelet, you're okay. But… well, you're usually cool-headed about things. Charging after this guy who has the artifact? This 'Heart'? Something about it…"

"Doesn't ring true."

"Yeah. A touch of the reckless."

Beckett thought about Critias and his thoughtless plunge out of the Sears Tower in pursuit of the Heart of Osiris. "So, where does this lead your thoughts?"

Nola Spier sighed heavily into the mouthpiece. "Maybe you got me all hyped with paranoia so I'm looking at this too hard, but… Okay, look. You said this artifact is heading *away* from where the creature is buried? To the place it's originally from?"

"Yes."

"Well, I'd say that's the right and proper thing, isn't it? Do you really see any reason to get mixed up in it any further?"

"But there is the possibility—"

"Yes, there's always a possibility. Long as I've known you, Beckett, you've always charted your own course, beholden to no one. I guess, if you have any doubt that you're not making the best choice for you…" Her voice trailed off into another sigh. "Comes down to it, this is all just chitchat. There's a simple way to determine if you're still your own man."

"Which is?"

Nola chuckled. "Stop trying to chase after this Heart thingy."

Beckett smiled and thanked Nola for her help. He set down the Motorola and plucked at the silvery bracelet, pondering ancient influences and free will.

He was easily intrigued by mysteries, but he never allowed himself to be seduced by them. Yet recently, he'd been drawn into machinations involving an ancient undead and its insidious effort to attain an artifact of untold power, not to mention conflict involving mortal hunters of the supernatural, a powerful zombie, and at

least one of the rare immortal mummies. He felt confident that he was still his own man, as Nola put it. Yet here he was, suffering a wound that could easily have destroyed him, all for the sake of some object that had nothing to do with his own research or even the mission he'd agreed to take on for Inyanga. The Heart of Osiris was halfway across the Atlantic, heading for a land populated by countless creatures older and more powerful than he. By the time he was healed to full strength, there was no telling in whose hands the Heart would be. It seemed likely that it would be a force with no inclination to put it within Menele's grasp, though.

Beckett shook his head in bemusement. He might never know if he was free of Menele's influence, but he knew himself well enough. Others could vie for control of the Heart of Osiris. Beckett would chart his own future.

EIGHT

"My husband," Newa Ghandour said, "your father, drew me into the Cult of the Sun-Disk when I was but a girl. I might still be there if not for you."

"*Me?* What? Why?" Thea was having trouble processing the strangeness her mother was laying out, and she suspected it was only the tip of hugely bizarre iceberg.

"I was a confused young woman when I met your father. He was a handsome man with a mysterious, worldly air. I was drawn to him, and soon into his life. At first, the Aton-u seemed nothing more than an entertaining diversion, a bit of obscure culture from our past, yes? But it grew to take ever a larger part of my life. In time, I forgot the teachings of Islam in favor of Akhenaton's heresy. There was nothing terribly sinister about that time. 'Pathetic' might be a better word. We reveled in what we thought were secrets of the ages—but that I now suspect were merely drug-induced visions spewed forth by the high priest. It went on like this for... I do not know how long. Then, I became pregnant." Newa's body drooped in an embarrassed slump as she spoke, her fingernails tapping idly at the china cup in her hands. But when she spoke of her pregnancy, some measure of strength returned. Newa directed bright eyes tinged with sadness at her daughter. "When you were born... My daughter, this new life, there in my hands! I realized they were nothing more than fools playacting at deeper mysteries. And I was no better. A charming, charismatic man had lured me from my faith in Allah, lured me from sanity to take part in his madness."

Thea felt Jake's stare; a glance showed his brow furrowed and dark eyes intense as he took it all in. At the other end of the table, Margie sat with her hands toying with the china coffee cup. If anything, she looked bored with the entire conversation.

"Something doesn't fit. My father pulled you into this? What would an American soldier be doing with some Egyptian cult?"

Newa shook her head. "I misled you there as well. Your birth father was a Cairene, like me. I left him behind when I took you from Egypt."

"What?!" Thea felt close to losing it. In the space of five minutes she was discovering her entire past was a lie. "*Took me* from Egypt? I was born *here*. That temple's right downtown. What the hell are you talking about?"

Those same sad eyes. "I did not know there was a temple to the cult in Chicago until years after we settled here. The one your father belonged to was in Egypt. And you... you were born in Egypt."

"Why... what the hell?!" Thea gobbled air for a few seconds as her brain hit the boiling point. "So you're telling me, what? Everything I know is a fucking *lie*? What—"

"Show respect!" Newa's tone of shock, outrage and embarrassment would have made a saint feel ashamed. Her fist smashed against the table so hard the cups jumped, sloshing tepid coffee into their saucers. Newa Ghandour was not prone to physical displays, making her action all the more startling. "How dare you come into my home and speak to me so!"

Then they were both yelling, twenty-some years of buried grievances spilling over in an instant. A voice cut into the cacophony, strong and full of anguish to match their own shouting. "Stop it! Just stop!"

Thea turned to see Margie leaping up so fast her chair tumbled over. She trembled like a newborn foal, tears streaming down her plump cheeks. "Enough!" Margie yelled, "Just stop it!"

She dashed from the room before anyone could respond. Jake was up a second later. "I'll make sure she's okay," he said.

Although no less concerned about Margie's welfare, Thea was thrilled at the outburst. They were the first words her best friend had spoken in a week. For the first time in too long, Margie seemed all there. Traumatized she still was, but no longer adrift mentally.

In the lull that followed, Newa Ghandour spoke in a calmer tone. "I do not claim to have made the right choices. I understand your anger, Thea, but that does *not* give you the right to use such language."

Thea nodded. She wanted to go after Margie, make sure her mind didn't slip back to wherever it had been. That would have to wait; ugly secrets remained to be probed here. Jake should be fine taking care of Margie. He had a good bedside manner… and was probably glad not to have to be a spectator to the bickering between Thea and her mother. With a closer eye on her language, Thea said, "I just don't understand. Why would you lie to me about this? What's the deal with my father being in the military?"

"I met a soldier after I fled the temple with you. We… grew close, and we came to America together, where we were married." New pain flickered across Newa's face. "But that soon changed. He became… abusive, and I would *not* tolerate myself or my daughter suffering under another's will."

"Mom, I swear… And I thought *I* had bad taste in men. You go from one guy who's a nutjob to another who smacked you around? How could you be so obtuse?"

Newa's eyes flashed, but she didn't upbraid her daughter again. "Your father was dangerously charismatic, and I was weak then. The soldier… it was different. He was not that way at first."

"I suppose that's why you never told me his name. *Their* names, I guess I should say," Thea muttered as her

memory churned. Something in her mother's hesitation when talking about the American soldier… If the part about her dad being a soldier was true enough in its own way, perhaps other details had similar ties to the truth. "It was a pregnancy, wasn't it? You got pregnant by him and that's why you got married. But something happened with the baby, and that changed things. Right?"

"You make a good journalist, Thea." Newa rubbed the back of her neck. "Yes, I had a child, another daughter, after we moved to America. It was a difficult pregnancy, and she was born too soon. She did not live long. It was too much for him… That is why I left."

"I don't remember any of this."

"You were but a year old; fourteen months. And I… I did not have the strength to tell you of it when you grew older."

An odd detail came to mind. "Wait; how come I have an American birth certificate if I was born in Egypt?"

Newa looked even more agonized than she'd been before. "You… I used…"

A horrible realization came over Thea. "You somehow used the certificate from your other birth, didn't you? I've had my dead sister's birth certificate this whole time! Did you ever tell me the truth about *anything?*"

Thea didn't wait for an answer before she fled the dining room.

• • •

She found Jake outside the bathroom upstairs.

"Margie's in there crying," Jake said. "We've talked a little bit but she won't let me in."

"How's she seem?"

"Pretty shaken up—not surprising, all things considered. But I don't think she's, y'know…"

Thea nodded. Margie wasn't the suicidal type. She rapped on the door. "Hey, Margie? It's Thea. Can I come in?"

A sniffling mumble seeped through the door.

"If you're trying to tell me to go to hell, I can't hear ya, hon," Thea said. "Open up so you can at least yell at me face to face, okay?"

After a few seconds, they heard some fumbling and the bathroom door opened a crack. "I've got this," Thea murmured to Jake before she stepped inside.

The hall bathroom contained a sink, toilet, and shower stall with frosted glass walls. Margie was sitting on the closed lid of the toilet, holding about half a roll of wadded toilet paper that she used to dab her face. Noting how Margie cringed away from the open door, Thea closed it behind her and hunkered down on the floor. She sat Indian-style, her back to the shower stall, and offered her friend an apologetic smile.

"Sorry about all the craziness you've gone through, Margie. You have no *idea* how sorry. It's all my fault."

"Yes, it is," Margie said, letting out a heroic snort as she blew her nose. "Feel like I'm in a movie. And not in a good way."

Thea nodded. She felt the same way much of the time. "How're you feeling? You had me scared for a while."

"Good! You've had *me* scared and pissed off for a while myself. I feel okay, as much as I could in this nightmare." Margie directed tear-reddened eyes at her friend. "I just don't get it, Thea. I don't get what this all about. Why me? Why you? Why all of it? And now your mom, too? Is it all something about your family?"

"I wish I could tell you, hon. I'm as much in the dark as you." Thea took Margie's hands in her own, looking up at her friend in earnest. "I don't know what it's all about. The only thing I do know is why you, and that was just to get to me."

"Lucky me."

Thea gave her hands a squeeze. "I know, and I'm sorry. I did all I could to protect you."

Margie pulled her hands away and wiped her nose. "Sound like your mom, there."

That gave Thea a better idea of how Margie felt toward her right then—and how her mother might feel. A lot to take in, maybe too much to keep their relationship intact. Thea felt awful about Margie being captured by vampires, but she couldn't think of anything else she could have done about revealing the horrible truth. No matter when she'd taken the opportunity, Thea was sure that telling Margie would have resulted in her friend thinking she'd gone off the deep end. Only seeing the truth for herself had pressed the point home. *Yeah; look how that worked out.*

"You're right, hon. I screwed up big. I don't know how to make things right between us, but I'll do whatever I can."

"Can you turn back time? No? Then maybe you could just leave me alone for a bit, all right?"

● ● ●

Thea was not in a mood to confront her mother again, so she retreated to her old bedroom. Newa Ghandour had remade it into a second guest room after Thea moved out a few years back. Aside from the room's dimensions, it lacked any intimate familiarity. Considering the rest of her stuff was so much trampled junk, Thea would have to take what she could get.

It was all full-on insanity now, with no hope of anything ever being normal again. Even that wasn't necessarily the worst of it. Thea was used to her life being out of the ordinary; present circumstances could be viewed as just the most extreme range. Lying on the bed in the dark, listening to the faint hum of traffic along Lakeshore Drive, Thea realized the most disturbing part was not knowing what came next.

She wasn't the type to have detailed plans. Still, for most of her life she'd carried a confidence within her, an intuition of knowing the next step to take. The powers born in the hunt might be a supremely heightened aspect of this self-confidence. Regardless, she could take a big picture view and plan the next few steps of her life accordingly. Until now, that is.

People close to her were dying, others being manipulated by forces beyond her control. Her past was proving to be a lie, her mother a total stranger. There was nothing to hold onto, nothing to use as an anchor, no solid vantage point from which to make sense of all the rest.

She drifted in spirals of thought for an indeterminate time. At some point she finally slipped into a fitful doze, awakened later by a quiet voice.

"Thea? You in here?"

"Hmmm? Hey, Jake. What's up?"

"Beginning to wonder what happened to you." A silhouette of movement thanks to the distant glow of streetlights resolved itself into Jake feeling his way toward a chair by the bedside table. "Must've dozed off, huh."

"Must have. What time is it?" The alarm clock sat so all she could see was a foreshortened series of red vertical slashes.

"It's a little after eleven."

That woke Thea the rest of the way. "So late? We should get going, find a place to hide out."

"Actually, that's one of the things I came to talk to you about." It seemed like Jake was being fidgety, but it was hard to tell in the dim light. "Your mom says we can stay here if we want."

"What? Hang on." Thea slid over to the bedside and fumbled for the lamp switch. Jake appeared in the warm light, looking faintly embarrassed.

"After sitting around feeling really uncomfortable for a while, we got to talking. I figured it'd be best to give her some kind of explanation of what was going on. Plus, I wanted to understand better what she was saying before. Anyway, by the end of it, she offered to let us spend the night."

Thea directed a withering look his way. "Just what exactly did the two of you talk about?"

"Hey, don't make like I'm the enemy all of a sudden. I was trying to get a clearer idea of your family, is all. Context. Look, Thea, she knows she messed up, I mean, huge."

The hurt surged up like lava through a crack in the earth. "Do you even understand what she *did*, Jake? I mean—"

"I have a pretty good idea, yeah. Your mom got sucked into some cult, but she woke up to her situation when she gave birth to her daughter. So she packed up and got out, and hooked up with the first guy she met who she felt could protect her. Emotionally, if nothing else. They come to America; it's a chance for her—and her daughter—to start a new life. Then she's pregnant again, but this one doesn't work out, and her husband turns into a major prick. But she can't rely on someone else to protect her and her daughter, so she does it herself. She leaves the guy, takes her kid with her. Starts over again, tries to put the past behind her, thinks up a story to protect her daughter from the mistakes she made." He paused, returning her glare with a shrug. "Should she have told you the truth? I dunno; probably. Sometime, anyway. Do I understand why she didn't? Sure. I'm not excusing what she did, Thea. Just trying to wrap my brain around it."

Thea scrunched her eyes closed and tried without success to figure her mother out. "It just seems so *insane*."

"Kind of like going around hunting monsters, eh? I think it's telling that she was so forthcoming, especially in front of other people. Took a lot of courage. At the risk of getting my head bit off, I'd say your mother loves you." Jake made the sign of the cross with his fingers. "Stop it with the evil eye, jeez."

"Hrmph. Don't expect me to do some After-School Special bonding. She still has a lot to answer for."

"That's for you to work out with her," Jake said with another shrug. "Listen, I know this isn't your favorite topic right now, but we should go over some things that might help you make up your mind whether to stay here or not. Personally, I think it might be good for you and for Margie, but whatever."

Thea sighed. "All right; what?"

"It sounds like all the stuff your mom went through was run of the mill bad luck and dumb mistakes. After talking to her some more, I didn't hear anything that sounded like she'd rubbed elbows with the supernatural. The cultists she hung with in Cairo were all talk, I think. I got her believing what we ran into at the temple here was more of the same. I don't know if she believes we're ignorant of what the fight was all about, but I'm pretty sure she doesn't think we're behind it. She brought up the white supremacist angle the media slapped on it before and I didn't say anything to contradict that."

"Which is your subtle way of saying Mom's not some spy for the nasties who'll turn us in at the first opportunity."

Jake muttered something in flustered confirmation.

Thea fell back across the bed, trying to organize her thoughts. "Fine. We might as well stay here. At least tonight."

"I talked to Margie, too. She's out of the bathroom now; seems good. Well, better, anyway. More like when I met her when you were in the hospital a few weeks back." His lips pressed into a thick line. "She's still shaken by everything, but I don't think she's going to wig out again. Despite all the yelling and stuff I think it's doing her good to be here."

Rolling to her side, Thea propped her head up with her hand to look at Jake. The movement stretched her abdomen, and an ache flared where she'd been wounded. It wasn't painful, though, just tight. Felt like she was healing well. "We need to talk to her some more, make sure she's okay and find out what she saw."

"I tried to find out what she might've learned when… well, when they had her."

"And?"

Jake pursed his lips and exhaled. "It's all hazy. Like she was drugged, or a dream. She understands she was in danger, and remembers us protecting her. But otherwise nothing useful."

"If she's no worse off than that, I'll take it," Thea said with a weak smile. "You think that her spotty memory's because of the vampires' influence or what?"

"Might just be a defense mechanism of her own, suppressing the trauma."

"Well, I don't want to push it trying to pull details out of her, Jake. Margie doesn't need to be dragged into this any further."

Jake looked ready to disagree, then waved a hand. "Yeah, I hear you. I'd like to find out if she could help us, but there's no telling what asking a bunch of questions will do."

"Right. So, you think that Earl guy bought that whole thing about Margie being dead?"

"I think so. You were pretty believable." When Thea kept staring at him, Jake laughed. "I guess you're wondering if I think it'll help, right?"

"You guess correctly, sir."

Jake assumed a contemplative look. "Based on what I've seen of the rots' habits over the years, I'd give a solid maybe. Their main beef is with us; she just got caught in the middle. I don't imagine they'll bother checking into your story if they have us to chase after. The one that seduced her to begin with might have, but he's been destroyed."

"Good fucking riddance, too."

"The trick, I think, is what it will do to Margie. Will she be able to get her old life back, and all that. You know?"

Thea knew all too well. She'd been able to think of little else, even in the face of her mother's incredible revelations. "And?"

"Hard to say," he shrugged. "The question, aside from how well she recuperates herself, is whether there is somebody on the lookout for her to pop back up."

"Yeah. Well, fuck. There has to be something we can figure out. She doesn't deserve to have her life destroyed by this."

"I agree. I can check on hunter-net, see if anybody can offer helpful information. Otherwise, only thing I can think of is to hunt down the woman vampire who got away—Sylvia? Her and anyone else in her group or cabal or whatever they call their gangs."

"Oh, right. What a bitch."

One corner of Jake's mouth quirked. "You know something, Thea? You swear a lot."

She laughed, surprised. "Do I? Yeah, I guess, maybe. Could probably chalk that up to the whole rebelling against Mom thing."

"It's not a big deal; just begun noticing it now that we've been hanging out so much."

"Yeah, well, it's not like I'm going to stop just because you brought it up, you prude."

• • •

Thea spent a restless night, drifting off for no more than a few minutes at a time. Confronting her mother had run in a direction she hadn't conceived. Add to that potentially ruining Margie's life and Thea had a tough time getting any sleep.

She staggered down to the kitchen a little after ten to find Jake and Margie chatting over coffee, juice and oat bran.

"Good morning," she said, directing it at no one in particular. Jake murmured a reply while Margie sipped orange juice.

"Your mom went shopping a little while ago," Jake said. "Don't think she felt too comfortable sitting around with us this morning."

"Yeah, I figured," Thea replied, fixing a bowl of cereal and some coffee. "That's why I didn't come down till now. Waited to hear the garage door go."

She carried her breakfast to the kitchen table and sat across from Margie, with Jake to her left. Thea had decided that the only way she could hope to repair her relationship with Margie was to be as honest and

plain-spoken as possible. *No time like the present.* Without preamble, she said, "Margie, I want to apologize again for everything I've put you through. You deserved the truth from the beginning, no matter how crazy it may have sounded. I know saying 'I'm sorry' doesn't begin to make up for all this. To be honest, I don't know if anything can. But from now on I'll dedicate myself to doing whatever it takes to get you your life back."

Thea trembled with the effort of looking her friend straight in the eye while pouring all this out in a calm, reasonable voice. She didn't quite have the willpower to sit still waiting for Margie's reply, so she took a hefty bite of cereal and washed it down with a gulp of coffee. When she looked back up, Margie was sitting in the same position, juice glass halfway to her mouth. Thea sensed Jake looking back and forth at the two of them.

After an eternity or two, Margie stirred, taking a sip and clearing her throat. "I've been thinking for a while, ever since... since that night. I don't remember much, but I can't deny what's happened. Jake's been helping me figure some stuff out—not that understanding makes it any more rational. I guess I know enough by now to know I don't want anything to do with it. But I'm not going to sit here and be a victim, either. Apologizing doesn't make it all go away, you're right. I'm still really pissed at you, but I can't blame you for it all."

Thea returned Margie's smile and hunched over her coffee till she had a handle on her composure. They weren't even close to back to normal, but this was a start. Knowing Margie was willing to fix things—not just the chaos of the undead but their friendship as well—Thea breathed easier than she had for weeks. Margie was closer to Thea than anyone; losing that friendship would destroy her.

"One down, one to go," Thea muttered into a spoonful of bran flakes.

"What's that?" Jake asked.

"Just thinking. If you're feeling better and don't want to tear my head off, Margie, it might be best if we all found a new hideout where we can plan our next move.

"Oh, boy," Margie replied. "I can't do… what you do. I want to get as close to normal as I can."

"I know, Margie," Thea said as Jake nodded. "Believe me, we'd like nothing better ourselves. But I don't mean you're going to have to walk across the country like in *The Fugitive*. Just saying, this place doesn't feel remotely like home to me right now thanks to the bombs Mom dropped last night. I can only imagine how uncomfortable it must be for you two."

"Wait," Jake interrupted as Margie was about to speak. "It's not really my place to say, but don't you want to try and patch things up with your mother?"

Thea sighed. "I just don't know. Well, okay, maybe— probably—but not right now. There's just too much going on. Dealing with Mom on all this would be the proverbial straw that broke the camel's back. Plus, I've screwed up Margie's life; I'd prefer not to suck my mother into this, too."

They nodded their understanding. In the lull that followed, Thea finished the last couple bites of cereal and refreshed her coffee. As she sat back down, Margie asked, "Is there any reason I can't go home? Not the apartment—at least not right away—but my folks' place. And school. I need to get back to my lab work."

Thea looked at Jake, who shrugged. "She asked me before, and I think it'd be okay. Based on what she's told me and the shape your place was in, Graham trashed the place 'cause he was pissed at you. It didn't seem like anyone gave it a hard search. Margie's wallet and whatnot were still in her room, so I don't think they know where her family lives or that she's a grad student or anything. And if they think she's dead, well…"

"Yeah, that makes sense. We could take you to your folks' instead of hauling you around after us." Thea gave

a rueful smile. "I guess I'm just nervous about letting you out of my sight. I want to make sure you're protected."

"I'm a big girl, Thea; I can take care of myself."

"I'm not saying you can't. Just that this is a different situation. There's trouble just waiting to jump on you."

Before Margie could retort, Jake said, "That raises a point, Thea, about you and your life here."

"You mean whether I can get things back to normal." Thea rubbed a fingernail against a scratch in the table. "Well, our faces haven't been plastered all over the news or anything, so on the surface of it I could try. But realistically, I'd have to say my life—in Chicago, anyway—is finished. The nasties around here want me dead. Makes sense, considering we destroyed those two vampires, Critias and Graham, and injured Sylvia— maybe even destroyed her, too, though I don't think we could be that lucky. I don't like the idea of hitting the road, but staying here will just get the people I care about in trouble."

"Yeah, that's what I was thinking."

"So, what?" Margie pursed her lips in a frown. "You two just run away?"

Jake poked with a spoon at the soft dregs of his cereal. "What we do is get the rots'—the vampires'—attention and make sure they *know* we're running away. They're not going to stop until they catch us. We need to get out of their home turf, get some friends to help put together a trap for them."

"Plus, that way they're not looking around here any more, and you're safe, Margie." Noting Margie's expression, Thea added, "Never said it was a perfect plan, hon. We have no other choice right now. Jake and I have to take the initiative, otherwise we'll be sitting ducks."

"I guess so." Margie shook her head. "This whole situation is just crazy."

"You got that right."

• • •

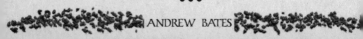

Thea wanted to leave a note and hustle them all out the door before her mother got back. She had a pretty good idea that Newa was running errands to give her that exact opportunity. But no; they'd both been avoiding truth and confrontation for too long. There was too much to resolve in an afternoon, but her mom at least deserved a good-bye in person.

They packed up what little they had and spent the next half hour scanning TV channels looking for any new reports about the Sears Tower or any one of them. The Sears Tower attack got a few seconds on CNN—no new information, authorities suspecting organized crime rather than terrorists—but nothing else of note. Looked like no one heard the shots fired in their apartment, and presumably Earl was resourceful enough to get himself loose and sneak away without freaking out the neighbors. After cycling through the channels again, Jake finally suggested it would be best if they got a move on.

"I don't mean to brush aside what you have to deal with regarding your mom, but we can't waste the day away here."

Thea nodded. "You're right. Maybe a little more cool down time would be good, you know? I'll make sure to see her before we head out of town."

Jake had just finished calling Lupe Droin for a pickup when the garage door rumbled, heralding Newa Ghandour's return. Thea's mom entered with a bag of fresh fruits and vegetables and another with sundries. She nodded hello on her way to the kitchen, where she busied herself with putting the groceries away. Jake and Margie didn't need any prompting to slip upstairs and get their meager belongings. Drawing a deep breath, Thea marched into the kitchen.

"We just called a cab, Mom. We'll be heading out in a few minutes."

Newa Ghandour stepped over to the large stainless-steel sink and began rinsing and trimming some celery. "All right," she said, her tone mild. "Where will you be going?"

"Probably best if you don't know that." She waited for her mother to turn from the sink. "Uh, Mom? Look, we have to go, but I wanted to talk to you about, well… everything."

"That sounds like a lot to cover in just a few minutes, Thea."

"What, now you're a comedian? Mom, this is important!"

Newa laid the celery on the counter and leaned on the sink's edge for a moment. Finally, she shut off the water and turned around. Newa was flushed, her eyes red and puffy. Her voice remained as calm and controlled as ever when she said, "Yes, it does appear to be important. I know very little of what you are involved in now, but I suppose I do not have the right to ask."

"Because of what you told me last night? Maybe so. Then again, I guess I can understand why you'd want to keep something like that from me." Thea chuckled without humor. "It must be clear what's happening with me now is something I'd prefer you remain in the dark about. At least until things are more stable. We're practically strangers, you and me. There are a lot of things we need to talk about to change that, and I wish we could do that now. But, well…"

"Now is not a good time."

"No, it's not. I'll be in touch soon, and we can try working through everything. Or at least agree on what we're going to lock away and act like never happened." That got the ghost of a smile out of them both. "Until then, I need you to do me a favor."

Newa Ghandour tilted her head a bit. "And what favor is that?"

"I need you to not tell anyone that Margie was here. That the last you saw her was the night you brought me back from the hospital a couple weeks ago."

"That seems a strange thing to ask, Thea." Her tone almost insisted on an explanation.

Thea frowned. "You know how you decided not to tell me all that stuff about Akhenaton and my dad before now because you thought it would protect me? This is like that, except I know without a doubt that doing this will protect Margie, and maybe you as well. But that's all you're going to get for now."

Newa looked at her daughter without expression, then nodded. She stepped over to the cutting board where she laid her purse. As she rummaged in it, she said, "If that is what I must do for us to remain family, I will. In return, I have a favor of sorts to ask in return. Here, take this."

Thea opened the envelope and laughed in shock. "Holy— Mom, how much money is this?"

"Two thousand dollars. I stopped at the bank this morning. You have never been good with your finances; you might have need of it wherever you are going."

Thea babbled for a few seconds but couldn't deny that the money would come in handy. "I don't know what to say… oh. Except: What's the favor?"

"I left my family out of shame and confusion. I thought I had drifted too far. I felt I could never return. Do not make that same mistake. Always remember that you are welcome here, Thea."

Two short honks sounded from the street.

It was hard to say which of them was more surprised when Thea suddenly embraced her mother. "I will, Mom. I love you."

Thea dashed out of the kitchen, barely holding back tears, her mother's words following her out into the freezing March afternoon: "God be with you, my daughter."

● ● ●

Thea felt guilty. Or at least selfish. Her best friend in the whole world was safely stowed with her folks and promised to keep a low profile for the next few weeks. But Jake was still with Thea, a guy barely out of his teens who she'd known for not even a year. The kid had joined the Van Helsing brigade to help them learn more about the things they hunted. Now the team was destroyed, so there was little reason for him to stick around. Beyond loyalty to Thea, which had a good chance of getting him killed. But here he sat at the desk in the Best Western motel room, discussing plans with her and checking options on hunter-net, not the slightest bit hesitant about sticking with her through the bitter end. Saying something about it wouldn't assuage her guilt and would embarrass him, so she kept her thoughts to herself and focused on their nascent plan.

They were agreed the best option was to take Amtrak out of town. They'd disembark in another city and do a poor job of losing anyone shadowing them, buying tickets for two different departures and choosing one at the last minute. Then, at the next destination, they'd again leave a trail a blind man could follow—that is, until they reached a spot worked out in advance with some local hunters. There, they'd do their best to lose any tails for real, and retreat to the local hunters' safe house. This should keep the rots interested enough that they wouldn't bother with minor loose ends like checking whether or not some bystander really was dead. So they hoped, anyway. Thea wished her sixth sense could be used to plumb for any pitfalls in the scenario, but the plan was too abstract. She should get some helpful epiphanies once they were underway, at least.

The main difficulties lay in deciding which city was best to travel to, and in finding other hunters to help out at short notice. Although they enjoyed a global communications network thanks to hunter-net, most hunters were paranoid about revealing their identities to anyone except those they felt they could trust beyond a shadow of a doubt. The nasties had been known to send in their living followers to draw out hunters. These Renfields posed as hunters themselves, and although they seldom did a very effective job of it, the threat was no less real.

It was a lucky thing Thea had Jake there. She was still fairly new to the hunt and had very little presence on hunter-net. As "Bookworm55," Jake was among the first and most respected of those on the network. The trick, then, became deciding who—or, more properly, where—they felt most comfortable working with someone. Jake finally made an executive decision and named Baltimore.

"Fine, but let's not take too long getting all this going," Thea grumped. "It's been a week since the Sears Tower and the nasties must be pretty pissed they haven't found us yet, especially after smacking around one of their goons. I bet we have maybe a day before they pull out all the stops and sweep the city from top to bottom, if they haven't started already."

"What makes you say that?" Jake wondered. "Your 'spider-sense'?"

"Nah, just what I'd do if I was sick of trying to find a couple pain-in-the-asses and had a bunch of resources to throw at the problem." He smiled, but Thea could tell his heart wasn't in it. She imagined she was as worn out as he looked. "All right. That's it for me; I'm going to crash. If the monsters come a-knockin', you're on your own."

"Okay." Jake tapped his fingernails against the side of his Compaq. "I just need to send out a nice, cryptic request to the list. Then I'll hit the sack myself."

They'd decided on a double. Thea looked on Jake as the little brother she'd never had, and while she suspected he might have a bit of a thing for her, he'd never be dense enough to act on it. Any possible sexual tension rated not at all compared to the threat the supernatural posed. Getting separate rooms was asking for some undead thing to slip in and pick them off one by one. Thea paused halfway into the bedroom, a memory she'd been doing her best to suppress bobbing unbidden to the surface. Ever since they'd started talking about other hunters, she'd had flashes of a body, limbs flung out at odd angles. Now the memory grew more vivid, and in place of the motel bathroom she saw a dark temple chamber, a man in a bloody black suit lying before her, his life blasted from him in an instant too fast to conceive. Thea wasn't sure how long she stood there before she shook

herself back to the present. Blinking away tears, she stepped back from the bathroom.

"What about Carpenter?" she asked.

Jake jerked like he'd been poked in the colon with a cattle prod. He cast a wide-eyed glare over his shoulder and snapped, "Jesus, Thea! You scared the hell out of me!"

Thea moved over to lean against the edge of the desk. "Well?"

"You mean, why haven't we gone after him this whole time?" Jake said, shaking himself to burn off the adrenaline surge.

"That, and now we're planning on leaving town without having done a thing to find him."

"I was wondering when you would bring that up."

"Yeah? How come *you* didn't?"

Jake offered her a humorless smile. "Because I don't feel like committing suicide."

A retort was already on its way, but Jake waved her down. "Listen, Thea. Going after Carpenter now wouldn't be part of the hunt; it'd be revenge. We'd be trying to get him back for killing Romeo and Lilly… and, by extension, Parker and Dean. Hell, maybe he was even behind Carl and Wayne's deaths, like Parker thought."

"What's wrong with a little revenge? Don't forget that son of a bitch also killed who knows how many members of the Sforza family. And those're only the people we *know* he clipped."

"If anybody's at the top of my 'deserves it' list, it's Maxwell Carpenter." He pushed the chair back and crossed his arms to lecture. "But you know me, Thea. I think there's something worth saving in almost every one of the things we encounter out there. Destroying them may be necessary, but when there's no other choice. But let's put that aside for the moment. For all the horrible things Carpenter's done, I don't think his motivation is evil. Probably not too different from the reason you want to chop him up in bitty pieces."

"Oh, you are *not* comparing the two of us."

"I did and I am. You already know all this, Thea. It's just easier to give in to the pain and lash out than to see the reasons these things're happening. Carpenter's a mess thanks to a tough life and a really horrible death. All those years being dead have just made him all even more twisted. Take how you're feeling and multiply it by a million and maybe that's where he's at. I can see why he should be destroyed, yeah—not because he's a monster, but so he doesn't suffer any more."

"Come on, Jake," Thea pleaded. "I can agree that not every one of those things is bad to the bone, but *some* are. Evil does exist, and its name is Maxwell Carpenter. Maybe he started out just a poor, fucked-up mobster, but he's been eating peanut butter and evil sandwiches for twice as long as we've been alive. We've seen firsthand that everything he touches is corrupted in some way. The rest of our gang is dead, my life's ruined, Margie's probably too—and he wasn't even after us! We were just a means to an end for him. Take off your fucking rose-colored glasses and take a hard look at him! There's not an inch of that bastard that's worth redemption."

Thea hadn't meant to lash into Jake. But those innocent, glass-half-full assumptions of his were going to get him killed one of these days.

"All right, Thea; all right." He scrubbed at his face, showing a little more self-control than she had. "I've been around on this issue before with people. It's nothing new and we won't solve anything by yelling at each other. This is beside the point anyway. You want to know why I didn't want to talk about going after him? Because he's hiding somewhere in Chicago. Right here—a city that's crawling with vampires who'd love to get their hands on us. We can't keep on with the hunt like nothing's changed. We're outclassed right now. The

smart thing to do is retreat and regroup. Live to fight another day, right?"

"As long as you can live with yourself in the process, Jake," she snapped, heading for the bathroom. She slammed the door, drowning out any response he may have given. Thea turned the shower on hot as it would go, then tore off her clothes in a series of jerking, angry moves. Scalding herself under the water, she tried without success to let her mind go, to capture some measure of calm.

Thea was willing to grant the wisdom of avoiding certain death at the hands of bloodsucking freaks. But whatever rationalizations Jake wanted to make about Carpenter, she knew the truth. He was a monster in the purest sense, a thing of corruption who had torn her life apart at the seams. And he was still out there, doing God only knew what.

NINE

The diesels were slowing. Not much, but the sound was unmistakable. Carpenter had been hearing the steady drone of engines for long enough to become attuned to the slightest changes of tone. He stopped his rat-hunting, debating whether to slip up on deck and get a lay of the approaching land. Might be best to stay below. If the arrival in New York was typical, it'd be hours before the ship was close enough to port for it to matter. Plus, this was the time the crew was most active, getting ready to hit land. They were jumpy enough from the trip without him popping up and giving their fears focus.

They had a right to be spooked. His scuffle heading out of New York Harbor left behind bizarre evidence—blood spatters, scraps of clothing, dead rats, a railing sliced clean through—but nothing to give a clear idea of what caused the mess. Not that the crew got a good look at it before the next morning. They contented themselves with further sweeps with the bridge spotlight, its beam registering small dark lumps on a far stack of cargo bins. It seemed no one was curious enough to go clambering over a series of containers to check it out up close. By the time they saw the gore, they were twelve hours out from New York. Given that there was no body (no human body, anyway; plenty of rat carcasses…), it appeared the crew was willing to dismiss the odd traces in favor of sticking to their schedule. People were great at rationalizing. Carpenter had seen it often enough. The ship's captain probably did a head count and, finding all his crew accounted for, declared business as usual. A vigorous hosing down followed by some quick welding of the vandalized cargo bin the next morning and nothing remained to make the crew uncomfortable but a patch of solder.

Except "out of sight, out of mind" didn't usually apply to ship crews. There was little to do on a long voyage besides gossip. Carpenter imagined the mystery he'd left on the aft deck was a favorite topic of conversation. The crew knew something wasn't quite right on *North Llorca*, but none was interested in scouring the ship from top to bottom in case there was a killer or worse on board. That was fine by Carpenter. He needed a quiet place to recuperate, and wasn't in any shape to move if some overly curious crewmember started checking out the ship.

Lacking any tangible cause of the mystery—and, to be honest, not interested in finding the solution—the crew had blamed it on the rats. Carpenter knew the rats were the damn vampire's fault—though explaining that wouldn't help the crew sleep better. The important thing was that the crew restricted its movements to the common areas in the central tower and the engine room, not wanting to take on the suddenly vicious rats that swarmed through the ship, attacking anyone they came across. That was fine with Carpenter. He didn't need anyone tripping over him, and not just because he was stowing away. He'd never win a beauty contest looking like he did now. His second pair of dungarees and a heavy wool sweater covered most of his wounds, but his face carried a series of vicious gouges, parting shots from the vampire.

The vampire—Beckett, he'd said his name was—had really done a number on him. Mean motherfucker, Carpenter would grant him that. If not for his trusty hammer, Carpenter would have been done for in the hours following the fight. He'd drawn strength from the hammer, dragging himself out of the spotlight's sight barely in time. He left no noticeable blood trail—mainly because there was nothing with which to leave a trail. The fight had relieved him of what fluids remained in the husk he possessed. And getting belowdecks to a corner of the hold where he could recover drained him of what energy he had left.

Carpenter spent the transatlantic trip doing little else but concentrating on getting all his parts in working order. Only now, after days doing nothing but healing—though he wasn't sure how many days, since he'd been hiding belowdecks the whole time—was he back to full strength. The damage was repaired, but the results weren't pretty. His torso, arms and thighs were a crosshatched mess of ugly scars. He was glad he didn't have a mirror down in the hold; the scars on his face had to look at least as unnerving as they felt. The wounds' ugliness, combined with spending uncounted hours in a dank, filthy ship, had been as hard on his mind as the injuries were to his body. Carpenter wanted nothing more than to stand under a shower for a week, then put on a crisp, starched shirt, tailored suit and silk tie, and slip his feet into some hand-made leather wingtips. He had all of that in the garment bag, but he forced himself to wait until he disembarked before changing.

He wasn't sure how much more of this he could take. He was holding on to this parody of life by pure will-power. Formidable as Carpenter's will was, focusing so intently for so long was taking its toll. And making it even more difficult was the torture of hope, the idea that he could return completely to life—not just that, but to live forever. And even if he didn't go nuts from the idea, there was no guarantee this body would last long enough. It had done very well for him ever since he'd possessed it a few years back. And even if it looked like shit, it felt restored to working order. But how many more beatings like he'd suffered lately could his body take before it no longer bounced back?

In the past month he'd been shot, what? A couple dozen times? Had a stake shoved through his chest (though he did that to himself, so he couldn't really bitch about it). Losing two fingers of his left hand, that was a serious pain in the ass. Even worse, being plugged in the gut by some magic bullet. And now mauled by a vampire.

He willed the body to heal most mundane wounds, but the last couple of injuries were a problem. The gut shot; Nicholas Sforza had done something to the bullet he'd shot Carpenter with. It actually hurt going in (and blowing out the back, just missing his spine), and refused to heal completely. Now, same with the vampire Beckett's claws. He cursed vampires for the millionth time since he'd been in the hold, fashioning a new refrain that focused on freaky bloodsuckers who could turn into bats and summon hordes of rats. And claws. He had some choice words to say about big-ass claws that carved you into hamburger.

If it weren't for the bizarre piece of… whatever… that he'd stolen from the top of a parking garage, Carpenter would still be a mangled lump of torn flesh, shredded muscles and exposed organs.

The Heart, everyone called it. Carpenter supposed it could be a heart. When he'd first grabbed it, it had looked like a dried out old moldy tomato. Now, though, in better light, it looked more as if it was rough-hewn from stone. No denying what it could do, regardless of what it was made of. Carpenter was living proof of that. Metaphorically speaking.

The wounds he'd suffered were too great for the hammer that was his anchor in the living world. Too great even for the dark power of the straight razor to fix. He'd been weak enough to succumb to the razor's siren song, choosing thrall of the razor's homicidal thirst over the endless hell of being a disembodied spirit. *Whatever it took*; that was Carpenter's mantra now. Whatever he had to do to become immortal. Nothing would stop him.

But hammer and razor had failed him. Drawing upon his treasured hammer lent his dead muscles strength enough to drag himself to a hiding place after the fight, but little more. The straight razor's power could only repair the minor injuries he'd suffered. Then, lying in the dark hold wracked in agony, inspiration struck. The thing he carried, the so-called Heart, throbbed with a life force stronger than anything he'd ever encountered. He'd sensed it first inside the Temple of Akhenaton, where it rested under the protection of Nicholas Sforza. Then, interrogating the punk, he'd learned the Heart was somehow tied to Sforza's own immortality. So Carpenter hadn't hesitated when he'd had the chance to grab the Heart and run.

The lack of planning showed. Here he was, riding a damn freighter across the Atlantic Ocean with nothing more to his name than a hundred grand, a few changes of clothes and three supernatural artifacts. Worse, he had absolutely no idea what to do once he got to Egypt. Sforza told him he'd undergone a ceremony there, something to do with the Heart, that had made him immortal. Okay, fine. Carpenter had the Heart and would be in Egypt soon enough. But then what?

No point whining about it. The other choice was to try and recapture Nicholas Sforza and squeeze more information out of him. But damned if he would hop another ship back after all the time and effort he was spending to get to Egypt. Besides, now that the punk knew Carpenter was gunning for him, he'd be prepared. Much as Carpenter hated to admit it, he wasn't sure how well he would do against Nicholas Sforza straight up. The best choice he could've made, all things considered. Zig when they expected him to zag. He was a smart guy; he'd figure out what to do sooner or later.

Though not smart enough to have imagined a vampire would try for him in New York. He hadn't expected to run into anyone who knew about the Heart, least of all when he was on his way out to the high seas. Didn't seem like Beckett was in cahoots with Sforza, but that he wasn't too friendly to Carpenter was all that mattered. He should have ditched the ship after he knocked the son of a bitch over the side, taken a different route. But at that point Carpenter was in no shape to do anything besides scoop his guts up and head for cover.

Carpenter wished many bad things upon the son of a bitch. He wasn't naive enough to think one blow of

the razor was enough to destroy Beckett. It was a nasty piece of work, that straight razor, but the vampire had proven himself no slouch. Drowning was out of the question, too. The best Carpenter could hope for was that the prick was too fucked up to stay afloat long enough to reach shore. There was a thought—a vampire having to slog his way through the crap on the bottom of New York Harbor. How long would that take? Long enough. The red-eyed freak was going to be one pissed motherfucker by the time he reached dry land, that was certain. Unless something got him while he was down there. Stories of giant alligators in the sewers and whatnot and probably lot weirder things besides. Carpenter had seen a lot of strangeness in his years as a ghost; he wouldn't be surprised if there were some things in the Hudson River that'd give a vampire a good scare.

Enough with worrying about that piece of shit. Carpenter decided to chance taking a look topside. He wasn't accomplishing anything down here besides wallowing in the past.

He slipped along the narrow gap between the top stack of cargo bins and the ship's hold, moving as fluidly as before the accident. Again, he marveled at the recovery possible thanks to the Heart. It hadn't been easy, tapping into the Heart's power. Carpenter was used to dealing with the energy of death. That's what ran his motor, that was why it was so easy to fall under the straight razor's spell. The Heart was the opposite end of the spectrum. But after focusing on it for some time, he'd at last sensed a kind of rhythmic pulsing to its aura. Working on instinct, Carpenter had found a way to "tune in" to that pulse. Then the danger was in being overwhelmed by the artifact's raw power. It surged forth with an eagerness far beyond Carpenter's own. Battered and tossed by the flooding energy, Carpenter realized he couldn't stand against the power for long. With difficulty, he'd finally staunched the Heart's flow to a trickle. Just enough to siphon off what he needed to force his ruined body to heal.

While the Heart restored his body to working order, it did nothing to repair the cosmetic damage he'd suffered. Nor did it strengthen his failing senses. It seemed his dim eyesight and poor hearing were due to spiritual possession rather than the body's weakness. It was a small price to pay, all things considered, and his ghost sight was a fine substitute. Plus, he was pleased to note the Heart seemed to pulse more strongly the closer they got to Egypt. Carpenter may not know where to go himself, but perhaps the artifact could be used as some kind of divining rod.

Also thanks to the Heart's influence, he felt more calm and clear-headed than he had in a while. The artifact's aura, he realized, was lending him the strength to resist the dark taint of the straight razor. Carpenter had fallen deep into its thrall when he almost lost his hold on the body he possessed. Ever since, the weapon had tried to seize an ever greater degree of control over him. Difficult as it was to resist, Carpenter knew he felt only a fraction of the straight razor's power. The razor was chaos given form, a manifestation of the underworld he'd fled. It still had a direct connection the spirit world, could draw that vast turbulent energy over here to the living world. He wasn't sure what it wanted with his body, but damned if he was going to kick back and let it take over. He had no interest in being possessed by some supernatural shaving implement. Embarrassing, if nothing else.

Emboldened by the energy siphoned from the Heart, Carpenter tried to rid himself of the straight razor. It had been of tremendous use, but he had enough trouble on his plate. But he soon found he couldn't bear to part with it. Standing on deck in the dark of night, he grabbed the closed handle his pocket and whipped his arm in a wild arc. Even as he flung, Carpenter realized his hand was empty. He'd never actually pulled out the razor. He discovered he could draw the weapon if he wanted to use it—but he couldn't even find the thing if he thought about throwing it away. It was tied to closely too him

now, could sense his intent and protect itself accordingly. It was a stalemate. The razor had lost the strength of its control over him, but neither could he rid himself of it. Carpenter decided to take a philosophical view: corrupting and evil the razor might be, but it was also one helluva useful weapon.

Once he felt sufficiently recovered and came to terms with his new relationship with the straight razor, Carpenter roamed the *North Llorca*'s hold. He tracked down every rat he could find; teach them to take sides with vampires. Only a handful remained by the time he heard the engines change their tune, heralding their impending arrival. The remaining rats could count their blessings.

The most convenient way out of the hold was via one of the stairwells in the central tower that housed the bridge and crew quarters. There were also access ladders fore and aft; Carpenter made his way to the rear of the ship and climbed one of the ladders. He emerged below a stack of cargo bins. This gave him an impressive view of the ship's wake, but not much of the approaching coastline. He climbed up the stack and moved to a spot where he could command a good view while staying out of sight of a casual glance from the bridge. It was mid-afternoon, the sun descending to his right as it blasted the Mediterranean Sea with tremendous heat. It was hot enough that even Carpenter's long-dead bones felt the warmth. Reveling in the sensation, he looked around. A long, low coastline stretched before him, with a dense scattering of buildings and towers immediately ahead. Port Said.

He'd chosen the *North Llorca* because it seemed to be the fastest, most direct route to Egypt at the time. From what he'd learned through quick questions along the docks in New York, any ship headed this way would stop over in Portugal, Spain or Italy before hitting Egypt. *North Llorca* was headed for Port Said by way of Italy, all told saving him almost two weeks' travel time compared to staying aboard *Meroe Atlantic*. After they arrived in the seaport of Gioia Tauro on the lower curve of Italy's western coast, he'd planned on hopping to another ship to save time, as he had in New York. Except that nothing else was headed for Egypt before *North Llorca*. He'd waited out the two day stopover variously avoiding the crew switching out cargo containers and hunting down rats. Didn't compare to taking in a show, but it passed the time.

Every minute he'd expected an attack. The vampire Beckett knew what ship he'd used to leave New York. Considering the hard-on Beckett had for him there, Carpenter could about guarantee some of the bloodsucker's pals would be waiting for the freighter to arrive. Daytime wouldn't much matter; vampires had a shitload of the living working for them, and often made up in number what they lacked in individual power. Hell, if Beckett hadn't been too fucked up in their earlier fight, he might even have flown in to get a piece of the action. But after the first day with nothing more exciting than a run-in with one of the crew—easily resolved by forcing his will upon the man to make him forget the brief encounter—Carpenter wondered if there would ever be an attack. It took eleven days for *North Llorca* to cross the Atlantic—plenty of time for Beckett to round people up for a reception at Gioia Tauro. Unless... if Beckett could do that, why hadn't he in New York? Puzzling over that, Carpenter concluded that the vampire was working on his own. There had to be other undead around here Beckett could get ahold of, but for whatever reason, he wasn't. He'd have to come out himself. So did Beckett pass on Gioia Tauro because he was working alone, maybe waiting more time to heal? Carpenter thought maybe so.

As long as *North Llorca* hit Egypt during the day, Carpenter would have a head start getting the hell out of there. Let Beckett try for him in the desert or wherever the hell Carpenter ended up. As *North Llorca* entered the mouth of the port, he realized the error. Greedy vampires didn't matter one good goddamn. The real problem was Nicholas Sforza and his pals. Sforza may not know what ship he was on, but the punk, and any other mummy, must be able to track down the Heart's emanations. They surely wanted the thing back. And Carpenter was heading right into their home turf.

Carpenter knew it was a chance in hell that there wasn't somebody on land waiting to kick his ass and take the Heart. He could have dived into the water and slogged his way ashore, but the ship was heading into the thick of the harbor. There was no telling if lookouts already had an eye out for something like that. Which would make him a sitting duck by the time he got to shore. More importantly for Carpenter, he was sick of getting filthy and had no interest in flailing around underwater. So he'd have to ride this behemoth all the way into port and try to sneak off as best he could. It wasn't bound to be that easy. Carpenter felt certain he'd end up fighting his way through. And with no good idea where the hell to go after he did.

Fuck. He just couldn't catch a break.

● ● ●

You've seen one harbor, you've seen them all. This one was sunnier and hotter than Chicago, New York or even Gioia Tauro, but otherwise Carpenter didn't see much difference. Huge ships loomed all around, the docks bustled with workers and forklifts, cranes shuffled cargo bins back and forth between ships and shore. Port Said sure did a lot of traffic. Carpenter thought his chances were good to slip through the bustle without getting tagged by a mummy with revenge and larceny on the brain.

North Llorca approached a berth, guided along by tugboats. Carpenter used the time to move around the container stacks from port to starboard and get a good look at the approaching docks. Then he slipped back below and gathered up his garment bag. It held two suits—a Navy summer-weight cotton and a cream linen, both double-breasted, and appropriate for the Egyptian climate. It also contained most of the cash he'd fled Chicago with (he carried only about ten grand on him), his last remaining automatic and one hundred rounds of .45 caliber ammunition. The bag itself was leather and folded over to zip the top and bottom together, with a convenient carry strap along the mid-length. He slung the strap across his chest and shifted the back around till it rested comfortably against his back. It'd jostle when he moved, but nothing he couldn't handle.

He took the Colt from his garment bag and slipped it into the left holster of the double rig he wore. His hammer he'd fit into the right holster, having lost that gun during the fight with Beckett. The straight razor was in the back pocket of his dungarees. He'd change out of this merchant marine outfit soon as he got ashore. The Heart was wrapped in canvas and tied around his waist using an Ace bandage he swiped from one of the ship's first aid kits. Despite what it had done for him and what it promised, the Heart still scared the hell out of Carpenter. He didn't want to touch the thing, didn't want it anywhere near him. But it was too important to stick in his bag or even a pocket, where it could fall out or be torn away. So strapped to his body it was, his dead flesh crawling in disgust at every phantom pulse the thing emanated.

Heading back up, Carpenter heard the dim clanking and felt the vibrations of *North Llorca* shouldering up against the pier. It would be a few minutes before they got the gangway hooked up, maybe a half hour or more before they finished with customs and got to work unloading the cargo bins. Carpenter wasn't sure he wanted to wait, but leaping off the ship would call undue attention. It would be best to slip off after the unloading began, when people weren't paying attention to who was coming and going. He killed time hunting rats; after an hour, he felt it was time to make his move. Moving to the stairs leading up to the gangway, he listened as best he could. From the tenor of the voices and movement above, sounded like someone was heading outside. He gave them a minute, then moved swiftly up the stairs and around toward the gangway.

His timing could have been better.

Just beyond the main hatch, *North Llorca's* captain was pocketing a wad of cash while he waved on a small group. In the lead was a huge black guy, thick from shoulders through the waist, limbs like tree trunks, head a wide slab with two glittering black eyes staring out over a pug nose and thick-lipped mouth. The man wore a loose tunic and trousers with sandals and some kind of bandoleer slung across his chest. A trio of Egyptians, two men and a woman, tagged along behind the guy, midgets next to his tremendous size. There was no way Carpenter could avoid being spotted, so he got ready to charge through the group.

Sure enough, the captain looked surprised to see him standing there... but the visitors looked like they were *expecting* him. Big ol' Simbah stepped forward with a huge grin across his ugly mug and his thick arms spread wide in greeting. Strange words tumbled out of his mouth, something foreign—sounding a lot like the bizarre yelling Nicholas Sforza did just before he croaked when Carpenter held him hostage. Carpenter took another look at the big black guy and realized the son of a bitch had the same vibrant aura Sforza did. *Fucking mummy's standing here waiting for me!*

Carpenter didn't understand why Simbah was being so friendly, but the warmth didn't last long. Even as the mummy and his helpers stepped forward, the grin was dimming on his face. More words in that same funny language, this time interrogatory, and a look of confusion tinged with concern spreading across his dark features. One of the Egyptians spoke rapid English to the captain, who looked equal parts baffled and irritated, while the other two looked between their leader and Carpenter in growing puzzlement.

Simbah was barking something now, and Carpenter figured he was about out of time to figure out a plan. He didn't like his chances getting past the mummy and the rest without getting knocked around, so he turned and sprinted for the stairs. He burst onto the bridge a minute later, surprising a couple of guys standing by the ship's controls.

"Who the hell are you?" The guy on the left said, his face souring into an aggressive pout.

"There any way off the ship besides that gangway?"

"What? Listen, buddy, I—"

Carpenter didn't have time for this. He drew his pistol. "No, you listen. Simple question: any way off the ship besides the gangway down there?"

Respect via firepower. As contrite as he'd been belligerent a second ago, the man said, "Uh, no; not unless you jump over the side."

Good idea. But not into water; no telling what kind of crap was down there. The bridge was situated a little more than halfway back along the *North Llorca*'s length, and extended entirely to the sides. Rushing over to starboard, Carpenter could see straight down to the water line. This side didn't have a pier; perhaps fifty feet separated *North Llorca* from the next ship over, this one a large tanker. Although it rode low in the water, the tanker's deck was higher than *North Llorca*'s. However, the container ship was still stacked high with palettes. A crane moved at the front of *North Llorca*, removing a series of large cargo bins, but there were plenty left Carpenter could use as a running start across the gap.

The two crewmen took advantage of Carpenter's distraction and fled down the stairs. Shouts arose seconds later—Simbah was coming up the stairs. The mummy burst onto the bridge a second later, pulling something from one of the pouches on his bandoleer. Whatever the guy had, it was bound to be bad news. Carpenter blazed away with the pistol just as the big guy swung. A liquid the color and consistency of cooking oil splashed in an arc before him. There was a sizzling flash as it caught one of the bullets, but the other two slammed past too quickly. One crashed through the other side of the bridge, the other caught Simbah in the side and spun him around.

The oil still hung between them, falling as if in slow motion. Anything that could disintegrate a bullet was something Carpenter didn't want to mess with. Before the mummy recovered, Carpenter ran for the front window, crashing through to land twenty feet down on the unforgiving metal of a cargo bin. He was up in an instant, running toward the port side. He heard a yell; instinct told him to duck so he flung himself to one side. There was a tremendous flash as a supernova went off. Carpenter smelled singed hair and his clothes were smoking, but otherwise he felt unhurt. As he scrambled to his feet, he saw the container he'd just been running on was white hot and melting in on itself.

What the fuck is this guy using? Carpenter hustled beyond throwing range before he got another chance to find out. He ran further forward, leaping between rows until he was directly above the pier on the port side. Simbah was coming for him across the bins, having jumped out after Carpenter. He wasn't running, though; more like... *bounding.* Like a frog or a kangaroo or something. *Christ; mummies are pretty fucking weird.*

Carpenter looked down over the side as he heard shouts along the pier. A small crowd was gathering, trying without success to see what was happening on *North Llorca.* Carpenter recognized two of the camel-jockeys who'd been with Simbah, both pushing through the crowd back toward the docks. Their mummy pal, meanwhile, was closing fast and digging into his bandoleer for another surprise. Carpenter took off at full speed, flashing across the width of *North Llorca.* Simbah wasn't a complete idiot. While trying to adjust his own momentum, he whipped a glass vial. He didn't lead Carpenter enough, and the beaker hit a few feet behind. Another flash and wave of intense heat that threw Carpenter off stride for a second. "Jesus fuck!" Carpenter swore. Charging at full speed, he launched himself off the starboard side. The stacked containers gave him an extra ten yards of elevation, and he let out a whoop as he saw he was arcing down perfectly to land on the tanker's deck. He hit the deck in a hard roll that carried him across to the opposite rail. The landing broke his left arm in two places and cracked a few ribs. His spine didn't quite feel right, either. Focusing his will to heal these minor wounds, Carpenter struggled to his feet. Simbah was just turning away from *North Llorca*'s edge and gesturing to someone else. The last of his little brown friends, probably.

Not his problem. Important thing was to get off this tanker and out of the neighborhood before any more damn mummies showed up. *Gangway should be nearby on this side, right?* Carpenter dashed over, knocking aside a pair of filthy deck hands who'd come over to check out the commotion. Just as he reached the gangway, his long-dead ears caught a hearty yell and a dull *thwam!* Looking up, he saw Simbah had leaped off the side of the other ship. *Son of a bitch; doesn't this guy ever quit?*

Pound for pound, he thought he had a good chance of taking Simbah. No telling how many more like him there were, though; his little Egyptian buddies might've run off to grab some more. Best to get out of there quick as he could. The big guy landed better than Carpenter had, a controlled roll that ended in a combat-ready crouch. He growled something as he dug into one of the bandoleer pouches. Carpenter whipped the Colt around and fired a rapid series of shots as Simbah's hand was trapped in the pocket. The first smashed through the mummy's hand and shattered the container it held, the rest marching down the bandoleer. Not every shot hit a pocket, but the results were still spectacular.

Molten liquid sprayed out from underneath the mummy's hand, melting cloth, flesh and bone in a heartbeat. The next pocket released a cloud of blue smoke that dissipated as fast as it spewed out. Liquids burbled from a couple other pockets, but the strange lava was the big winner, melting through Simbah like piss through snow. With a hideous, strangled cry the mummy snatched at the bandoleer with his good hand and flung the whole

thing away. The bullet wounds, the molten liquid and the other vials' contents left Simbah a mess of mangled flesh and charred meat. He crumpled to the deck, burbled once, and died.

Which was fine by Carpenter, except the bandoleer wasn't done spewing out damage. The sizzling fluid ate through the cloth as well as the objects inside. A rainbow of explosions erupted, flinging Carpenter over the side of the gangway. He tumbled through the air and smashed into the side of another tanker docked in the next berth. He hit badly, the impact snapping his spine and one of his legs. He fell away, plunging through the narrow gap between the pier and the ship. His injury, like most he suffered, was little more than a dull pain. He concentrated on mending the wounds as he sank through the warm Mediterranean water. Then a brilliant flash swept across the water above him followed by a deep coughing boom, and God reached down from the heavens and punched him in the chest.

The concussion shoved him into the thick, silty bottom of the seaport, where he could just make out a firestorm on the surface. Then came a second tremendous explosion that kicked him further along the sea bottom. The two blasts hit him with such force that it was a minute or two before he could even gather a coherent thought. When he could focus, he struggled to free himself from the muck while channeling his will to repair the damage he'd suffered.

He'd extracted an arm from the viscous sea bottom when movement above caught his attention. An inferno still raged on the water's surface, but now a huge dark shape descended in the water. *Can't catch a fucking break*, Carpenter thought as the ruptured tanker sank down over him.

PART III:
DEATH AND ETERNITY

TEN

"Thea, you might want to take a look at this." Jake sat at a rickety table in the living room of the squatter's apartment in Baltimore they'd been living in for the past week. Only the best accommodations for the monster hunting set. "A post from a guy in Cairo; some interesting stuff just happened there a few hours ago."

"Egypt, eh? This something about the Temple of Akhenaton?" Thea set down the disassembled components of the MP-5 she'd taken from Earl the vampire stooge. She was the type who preferred to wear shoes as seldom as possible, normally kicking off her footwear soon as she got home. But the place their contacts in Baltimore had found them was cold and drafty, with only a pair of space heaters for warmth, so she clumped over to Jake in her hiking boots. She and Jake were bundled up in jackets and boots practically day and night, in fact. The dingy apartment reminded Thea of the Van Helsing brigade's old convenience store hideout in Chicago, a memory she could have done without even if it hadn't been the place the last two members of their team died.

"Nope. But there is something I think you'd like to see." He swiveled the Compaq to give her a better view.

There were hunters around the world, but those in poorer nations didn't have easy access to hunter-net. Case in point: Egypt was notorious for having a horrendous phone system, where completing a local call to the number you wanted was cause for wild celebration. Finding a telephone line that would sustain an Internet connection for any length of time was a task of Herculean proportions. Cable or DSL was but a dream to all but the wealthiest and most influential. Despite this, a hunter who went by the handle of "Fatwa243" somehow logged on to hunter-net with fair regularity, passing along what discoveries he and others had made in the hunt.

"Hmmm. 'Unusual series of events…' blah blah. Writes pretty good English, I have to say. 'A fellow kiswah found'… what's 'kiswah'? Wait, don't tell me; might have enough Arabic still rolling around in my noggin to remember… ah. Roughly translates to 'hunter,' right?"

"You got it."

"I'm a regular font of knowledge. Okay, what about this fellow kiswah? Let's see…" The next paragraph offered a surprising collection of events, but nothing that tripped her spider-sense. "I don't know, Jake. Sounds like some weird shit, but why do I care? We see stuff like this all the time on hunter-net."

Jake gave her a mirthless smile. "Yes, we do. But I did a little digging before I showed you this that should put things in better context."

"I appreciate a flair for the dramatic as much as the next gal, but sometimes you can be downright irritating."

"Just hang on. Let me walk you through this." He pointed at the computer screen with the stylus from his palmtop. "We got a couple oil tankers blowing up in Port Said harbor. I checked some online news reports; final death toll was eighty-six, with almost two hundred more people suffering serious injuries and another fifty or sixty people still missing. Tragic, but nothing to do with us, right? Then, later that night near the harbor, we have a policeman murdered as he tries to stop what appears to be the kidnapping of an American tourist. Witnesses were too far to see what happened, but they found the suspected kidnap victim's mud-encrusted garment bag at the murder scene." With his other hand, Jake rolled his thumb over the mousepad square. The cursor clicked open a window to the *London Times* online paper, showing the report of the harbor explosion—CONFLAGRATION IN PORT SAID—and a smaller sized headline titled OFFICER BEHEADED DURING SUSPECTED KIDNAPPING. "Here's the interesting part—"

"A cop getting his head chopped off isn't the interesting part?"

"Not compared to this. Tag in the luggage gives the name of one David Kuhn, a professor of economics at Northwestern University, just north of Chicago."

Faint warning bells jangled in Thea's mind. "Okay, the Chicago thing is kind of interesting, but how's that a big deal?"

"Normally I would've thought the same thing. But what with recent events, all that stuff relating to Egypt and whatnot, figured I'd poke at it a little." He flashed a grin that was one part mirth and two parts unease. "You'll die when you see this."

He ran the cursor over to another window, clicking it open to reveal a face burned into Thea's memory. Spiders skittered down her spine as she stared at the laptop screen. "Carpenter."

"David Kuhn, actually," Jake corrected. He scrolled down to show the rest of the article from the *Chicago Sun-Times*: EVANSTON MAN MISSING ON HUNTING TRIP. "This is from a few years back. I'll paraphrase. The good professor was an avid deer hunter. He enjoyed bow- and rifle-hunting up in Wisconsin and, from what the article says, was pretty good at it. Until a couple years ago, when he never came back."

"That's fucking Maxwell Carpenter," Thea said, unable to take her eyes from the image. "Holy shit. But… what? He possessed Kuhn?"

"Yup. Explains why Carpenter doesn't look anything like his picture from the 1930s, right?"

"Why this guy? Who is he to Carpenter?"

"Well, here's what I think happened," Jake said. "We've seen stories on hunter-net about possession, but nothing I've read indicates a ghost could stick to a living person this long. Carpenter has one heck of a strong hold on this body, and we've seen first-hand that he's not alive. I think Kuhn was just the first convenient dead body Carpenter came across."

"So... Jesus. This Kuhn must've suffered some sort of accident on that deer-hunting trip, right? And Carpenter's ghost swooped in and took over the poor guy's body."

"Pretty much. Must have found where Kuhn lived from his driver's license or something, drove from the back woods of Wisconsin to his place. Stole what he needed—including the guy's garment bag—and began his whole revenge routine."

"Son of a... right; okay. This isn't too weird, not at all." Thea scrubbed her face with her hands. "I think we can assume it's outside the realm of coincidence that luggage belonging to a man reported missing two years ago who looks exactly like Carpenter shows up in Egypt a couple weeks after our favorite zombie disappears from an Egyptian temple with a kidnap victim, yes? So, what's he doing over there?"

"Aside from probably blowing up half of Port Said? Good question."

Thea strode over to her backpack and dug through the various pockets.

"What're you doing?" Jake asked, shifting in his chair to watch.

"Bought this pack for my trip through Europe a few years ago. Internal frame, ergonomically designed, all that fun stuff. If I recall correctly, should have... ha!" She yanked a small blue book from a side pocket and waved it in triumph. "How 'bout it, Jakester? Up for a trip?"

•••

It didn't take that much convincing to get Jake on board. They'd been running on fumes for a while now, with no real plan but to get out of Chicago and deal with whatever nasties followed after. They were both tired of reacting, of feeling like forces beyond their control were driving them along. Carpenter wasn't the only reason for this—plenty of monsters to go around—but he had played a major role recently. Payback was past due.

They didn't know why Carpenter might secret himself—and possibly his captive, Nicholas Sforza—aboard an ocean tanker bound for Egypt, but whatever the reason, it couldn't be good. The key was Nicholas Sforza, of course; he of the sudden interest in Egyptian temples and jewelry. Jake hadn't found much of substance on the topic of mummies, so their working hypothesis was that Sforza might be some fashion of walking dead not unlike Carpenter. It was possible he was a living guy, but it seemed more likely he'd become some breed of supernatural. Based on those assumptions, they figured there was something in Egypt that was of interest to the undead, maybe something that gave them greater power or a longer existence or maybe a really cool clubhouse. Who the hell knew?

At this point they had nothing to lose by looking into it. Indeed, hopping a plane across the Atlantic should be a move the vampires after them wouldn't expect, giving Thea and Jake breathing room on that front as well.

They pooled their money to buy tickets. A last-minute flight leaving in mere hours came to a jaw-dropping amount, more than three grand altogether. Thea had the American Express, but she didn't want to use that except in the absolutely most dire of emergencies. Plus, no sense taking chances the nasties were connected to the credit card companies. Instead she used the cash her mother was kind enough to give her. Jake paid cash also. He could have charged it—as far as they knew, the nasties hadn't learned his identity. He kept his old driver's license and passport in his bags, never carrying ID on

the hunt, and during their Sears Tower stay had only said his first name.

Lacking useful stuff like forged passports, they had to travel under their real names. There was still a chance that the vampires would check into various airlines' passenger manifests, but that involved more effort than keeping tabs on a single citizen's credit report. Thea was betting they'd be out of the country by then. Just in case, she and Jake got separate bookings. She didn't want to put Jake in any more danger than he already was by having him get a ticket sitting right next to her. The nasties might know he was on the plane, too, but without a name to match up he should be safe.

Jake shot a quick email to Fatwa243 and got the ball rolling for their arrival. He supplied enough details to show the urgency of their trip, but held back the majority of what was going on for when they'd meet. He sent a separate message to the Baltimore hunters saying only that they were moving on in a few days. Best to keep the need-to-know to a minimum, just in case. They made a hasty trip to Mondawmin Mall for summer clothes, then on to the Baltimore-Washington International Airport.

The first leg of the journey was on a Delta connector up to New York, where they switched over to Flight 120 which would take them straight on to Cairo. The large jet left JFK a little after sunset and made its way east into the heart of the night. Thea had an aisle seat on the right, with Jake somewhere on the other side and up. Although overcome with exhaustion from the stress of being on guard at all times for the past month, Thea had trouble relaxing. Her mind insisted it was safe; she was on a plane, after all. A big MD11 jetliner, winging its way over the Atlantic. After an hour and a couple cocktails, she finally fell into a fitful slumber.

She wasn't sure how long she was out when something snapped her awake. Thea rose from her seat, eyes roaming over her fellow passengers in the cabin. Not a one was awake, and the utter silence was unnerving. She couldn't remember where Jake was seated, so she moved up the aisle and soon found herself by the first class curtain. Her sense of unease mounting, Thea pulled back the curtain and stepped through. There were six rows of plush leather seats, then the front exit and the cockpit. No Jake, flight attendants, just a dozen sleeping passengers. Then the rustle of movement. Thea whirled around. Relieved, she saw a handful—no, maybe a dozen or more—people moving in the main cabin, stepping into the aisle and looking around. They smiled, catching sight of her, and started up the aisle. Seeing the pale skin and sunken eyes, Thea realized these weren't people. Looking down at the person next to her in a plush first class chair, Thea saw a moldering corpse, its flesh sagging off the bones of the skull like wet clumps of paper towel. Then the thing shuddered and lunged at her. Thea leaped back, slamming against the cockpit door. The corpse was held in its seat by the seatbelt, but continued reaching for her hungrily. Behind it, dozens, scores—perhaps the entire rest of the plane—was rising now. Moans and horrid shuffling, thumping footsteps were headed for her. Fear seized her mind. Thea hammered on the cockpit door, summoning the strength of panic to smash at the locking plate. She flung herself into the cockpit, where brilliant morning sunlight poured in through the windscreen, and began gasping out the horror that had overtaken the rest of the plane.

The pilot's chair swiveled around, revealing a black clad figure with a gaunt face, in which a pair of dead eyes burned with the light of hell. "Excuse me, miss," Maxwell Carpenter said, "but passengers aren't allowed in the cockpit."

The copilot's seat turned and Thea was looking at Samuel Zheng—Romeo—dressed in a blood-spattered pilot's uniform, his eyes empty holes in which maggots squirmed and fell down his face like obscene tears. "Thea!" Romeo said. "Carpenter has been showing me the ropes. What do you think?"

Thea awoke screaming, bringing a squadron of flight attendants running and almost giving heart attacks to the old couple next to her.

• • •

Thea apologized for disturbing the other passengers, but still had to suffer through a stern lecture by the head flight attendant, performed in a whisper loud enough to be heard by half the plane. It took a while, but Thea finally convinced the woman that she wasn't going to freak out again. The elderly couple wasn't thrilled with having her still sitting next to them, so Thea was led over to the other aisle and brought to an empty seat as far from an exit door as they could find. She passed Jake on the way and favored him with an embarrassed half-smile and shake of her head. A while later she followed him to stand waiting for one of the restrooms and gave him a quick whispered recap of her dream.

"Oh, man," he said, eyes wide behind his wire-rimmed glasses. "Must have been horrible! You sure you're okay?"

"As okay as I can be. I mean, I've had nightmares before, but that one… brrrr." She gave an exaggerated shudder. "Felt pretty real, my man."

Jake looked around, then whispered. "You don't think it was, like…"

"Some kind of vision? No. I focused my 'intuition' once I settled down. I haven't felt any bad vibes; except…" She leaned in close, shooting a look toward the back of the plane.

"What?"

"I wouldn't order the chicken."

• • •

The Egyptian hunter Fatwa243—who'd offered up his first name, Rafiq, but wanted to wait until after they met to disclose his full identity—had provided the address of a decent, inexpensive hotel off Maydan at-Tahrir, a public square in downtown Cairo. Thea had been through the country years back during college, the last leg of a backpacking trip through Europe and the Mediterranean. She remembered how crowded and turbulent the city was. Stumbling off a plane after too long in the air, it was a relief not to have to think about something as basic as finding a hotel. They took a taxi from the airport, the noonday sun pounding down from on high, wanting nothing more than to crash for a few hours. Once they adjusted to the local scene, they could look forward to wasting a day in many lines waiting to get a visa. By then, this Rafiq should be available to act as their guide and help search for Carpenter.

Jetlagged and culture-shocked, Thea and Jake sat in a daze as the cab descended into the vehicular chaos of downtown Cairo. After a heart-stopping ride, they stumbled out of the dented taxi into the human equivalent of the mess they'd just ridden through. Once she was in the place again, Thea remembered that Maydan at-Tahrir was literally the center of Cairo. The square was gigantic, with no fewer than six major thoroughfares meeting there. Aside from the tourist attraction of the Egyptian Museum and the bureaucratic sinkhole of the Mogamma—the place to go for visas—that loomed in immediate view, a spate of foreign embassies, a university, and a number of government buildings were a stone's throw away. Even in the hottest part of the day, thousands of people flowed through the maydan in churning waves of humanity that crashed into and flowed through one another on their way Allah only knew where. And the streets were likewise full of cars rushing about in a riot of incomprehensible traffic rules made up on the spot and forgotten a second later. The place was nuts.

After minutes of gawking and asking some passersby, they finally located the address Rafiq gave them. Ismailia House was a crumbling mess of a building; it looked like it might collapse at any moment. Thea was worn out enough from the plane flight that she didn't much care how the place looked. As long as it had a shower and a

bed, it was perfect. They had to go all the way to the eighth floor, and rather than plod up the stairs they crammed themselves into the tiny elevator. It was a cramped, iron-barred coffin with only a thin plywood floor keeping them from a nasty fall. There was barely room for the two of them and their single bags of luggage. The thing creaked into motion, laboring for every foot it ascended. After some disturbing groans, the elevator ground to a stop halfway between the fourth and fifth floors. Apparently it happened often, for the person coming by on the stairs who helped them out didn't look the least surprised. Finally reaching the eighth floor, they got a double room for only 35 Egyptian pounds—about $11 US. The room itself was small, with just enough space for two narrow beds, a single nightstand, and a space by the door the size of a postcard. A shared bath was nearby. The room and bath were as clean as the building was decrepit. Thea dropped her pack to the floor at the end of a bed and collapsed on the mattress, lacking the energy to take her shoes off. She was zonked before Jake had the door closed.

Despite the exhaustion of travel, Thea and Jake awoke after only a few hours. The sun had set, bringing a soothing cool to their little room. After showers and a change of clothes, they tracked down a qahwa a few blocks off the maydan that offered excellent coffee and plates of bread and white cheese. During their light dinner, they discussed Middle Eastern do's and don't's, gleaned from Thea's spotty memory of her previous trip and paging through a travel guide Jake picked up in the Baltimore airport. The most useful thing so far was making sure they were dressed appropriately—neither wore shorts, and Thea bucked her usual preferences to wear clothes that didn't accentuate her figure. Her memory of Arabic was rusted down to the bolts but she recalled enough of the basics to smooth over dealing with the locals, and Jake was good with figuring out the conversion of Egyptian pounds to American dollars. Otherwise, as long as they were polite and didn't go around attacking suspected monsters in public, they should be fine.

As Thea reached for a piece of cheese with her left hand, Jake said, "I've been meaning to ask, Thea. Where did you get your tattoos?"

"Huh? I had them done. Took some hunter signs and hieroglyph elements and combined them into different designs." She looked at the back of her left hand, turning it so the setting sun caught the design clearly. "The last few months they've started to… respond, I guess is the word, to the supernatural. But things have been so nuts that I haven't taken the time to look into it."

"Yeah, but what made you get them?"

"I don't know. I've always wanted tattoos but my mom wouldn't let me. And I couldn't think of anything I wanted to get. But after I joined the hunt, well; these ideas popped into my head and I thought, why not?"

"So you don't know about the Bedouin practice of henna tattoos?" Jake smiled at her puzzled look. "I was checking archived posts from Rafiq and he mentioned something about them. Sounds similar. Something about a sheikha, he called them—wise woman or something like that—who would cover herself in detailed designs that served as a focus for these amazing powers."

Thea looked at the back of her left hand, then lifted up her blouse to look at the tattoo on her stomach. "Wow; really? Sounds about right. I'd never heard that before, though."

"Not a big mystery as these things go, but something to check into after all this insanity is over, huh?"

"Yeah, whenever that is." Thea leaned forward, lowering her voice. "Speaking of which, this is about all the vacation we're going to get. Tomorrow we'll go for visas, then meet up with this Rafiq guy."

"I'm surprised we didn't need them coming in," Jake said, his own voice grown softer now that they were talking about the hunt.

"I thought that, too, my first time through. You can apply for visas in advance, but I guess they don't have a problem if you wait to get hooked up once you get in the country. That huge ugly building where we got out of the taxi before? That's the Mogamma. I think just about every part of the Egyptian government is crammed in there. That's where we'll have to go tomorrow to get them." Thea remembered from her previous trip that getting a visa was a full-day affair. She'd spent long hours in the ugly Mogamma building before emerging, wilted and dehydrated, with her tourist visa. Going through again with Jake would be like some long, painful déjà vu trip.

Jake nibbled at some bread. "Then head up to Port Said."

"I guess. Though it's a safe bet Carpenter isn't there any longer. It's been, what? A day since those tankers blew?" They shared a moment of silence as each considered that, mere hours before, they'd been thousands of miles away in a freezing apartment in Baltimore, Maryland. Thea knew they were counting down to something big and time was fast slipping through their fingers.

Jake shook his head in bemusement. "No other way I know of to get on his trail, though. I suppose, if we wait long enough, he'll end up blowing something else sky high."

Thea pursed her lips, considering. "So, you have any idea about that kidnapping angle the newspaper mentioned?"

"Nope. When I emailed Rafiq with the basics of why we were coming out here, I asked him to see what he could find out. Haven't heard anything, yet. Why, you have a thought on that?"

"Not sure. The dead cop sounds like something Carpenter might be involved in, but kidnapping? The only thing that comes to mind is if he still has Nicholas Sforza hostage, some of Sforza's friends found them, maybe?"

"Mummies?" Jake said.

"Not as funny when we're sitting within spitting distance of the pyramids, eh? Remember, we still haven't figured out the deal with Sforza and that temple of his."

"True enough. Can't wait to meet with Rafiq. I have yet to find any evidence there are mummies, other than what you'd find in stories and legends. I'm hoping he has some insight."

"For as often as he posts to hunter-net, you'd think he'd've mentioned by now if he knew anything about mummies."

"Good point." Jake sighed and slouched down in his chair. "I don't know, though. I've been thinking some more about Carpenter. You know how we hear about zombies from others on hunter-net? Everybody says they're strong and all but seldom, if ever, approach the degree of cunning, let alone intelligence, that we've seen with Maxwell Carpenter."

Thea nodded. "Yeah, he's a breed all his own."

"That's a good way to put it. What if the things like Carpenter, the walking dead we call 'hidden,' account for the stories of mummies? Powerful, clever, unstoppable…"

"Yeah, maybe," Thea shook her head. "I don't know. The more I think about it, the more I wonder that maybe mummies do exist. Things out there that really are immortal. Live forever; that's a pretty attractive idea, y'know?"

"What're you getting at?"

"Well, Carpenter's plenty powerful and all, but he's not *alive*, right? What if we were wrong about his motivation? You know how you've said zombies have an overriding goal?"

"And they're usually none to subtle about going after it."

"Right. Thing is, with Carpenter… we figured before that his whole thing was getting revenge on the Sforza family. And we've seen him pull some pretty blatant maneuvers going after this guy, Nicholas. But if all he wanted was to payback on the Sforzas, what's

he doing over here? Motivation aside, Carpenter's also been cunning and subtle. Think about how he tricked us into going to the Temple of Akhenaton. Spun some truth and some lies, read each of us well enough to know what buttons to push, and even after we thought we figured out what he was up to, we ended up doing pretty much what he hoped we would."

"And?"

"Well… what if Carpenter was after Nicholas Sforza this whole time to get some elixir or something that would make him immortal? Bring him back to life permanently as, for lack of a better word, a mummy."

"Elixir?"

"Whatever. Who's to say this doesn't go all the way back to… what's her name? Annabelle Sforza? Maybe that's really what they had a falling-out about. Well, maybe not; that gets farfetched." Gears churning away in her mind, it took Thea a little while to notice Jake looking at her with a half-smile quirking his face. "What?"

"Full steam ahead down Tangent River!"

"Yeah, yeah. Answers a lot of questions if we begin with the hypothesis that mummies are real, though."

"And us without Brendan Fraser," Jake muttered.

"Very funny."

•••

Thea and Jake wound down as the jolt from their coffee began wearing off. Jet lag was sneaking up on them fast so they headed back to Ismailia House. Once in their room, they crashed like bricks dropped from orbit.

Their body clocks still weren't up to speed the next morning, but they weren't quite as wrecked as the day before. Struggling through their lethargy, they cleaned up and prepared for a long day on their quest for visas. Emerging from the hotel, they saw the Maydan at-Tahrir was thick with vehicle and foot traffic. Thea and Jake had spent plenty of time downtown in large American cities, but this was a new experience. All they had to do was get from one side of the square to the other. The trick was figuring out the best way to get to the Mogamma without getting carried off by the crowd's momentum or accidentally run over by one of the dozens of cars that swooped through the maydan.

Focused as she was on the issue, Thea didn't register at first that a man stood watching them from just a few feet away. She didn't think she was being ogled—Egyptian men didn't stare blatantly at women and her peasant's blouse, low-slung cargo pants and hiking boots were appropriate enough attire. *The guy must be hanging around waiting to play tour guide*, she thought, turning to give him a brush-off. Thea's mouth dropped open. His hair was a lot shorter and his skin was a bit more tanned, but she recognized the man instantly.

"Sforza!" Her voice was a breathless gasp.

"Nicholas, please," he replied, crossing his arms and looking them over with an odd smile on his face. "Hi, Thea; Jake. Welcome to Egypt."

ELEVEN

After Ibrahim revealed he'd brought the ruined compass scarab to Egypt, Nicholas' mind was afire with possibility. Once they reached Cairo, he headed for the workshop Basel Nyambek-Senemut had set up in the Mausoleum of al-Qalarayn and began work on a new tracking amulet.

Nicholas felt the pressure of time like a physical weight. The longer the Heart of Osiris was loose in the world, the greater the possibility of disaster. There was no danger Carpenter would somehow harness the artifact's power to be resurrected as a mummy. The Heart had nothing to do with that closely-guarded treasure, the Spell of Life. And just as he couldn't use the Heart to become immortal, there was no way that Maxwell Carpenter would find anyone willing to perform the resurrection ceremony.

No, Nicholas' greatest fear was that the Heart might fall into the hands of a threat far greater than a single zombie. The Followers of Set and the Bane mummies alike could perform the most terrible acts should they gain possession of the ab-Asar. As a conduit to Osiris, the Heart offered inestimable power to those who could discover the means to tap into it properly. That power could be twisted to any number of depraved ends. Beyond that, some among the Amenti believed it might be possible to use the Heart—or any of Osiris' scattered body parts—to harm the god himself. Eternal Osiris could not be destroyed, but it was possible the enemy could inflict upon him incalculable agony should they capture the Heart.

The irony was not amusing: That the mightiest of all immortals could not draw together his body and return to life—something even the newest of the Undying could do. Thanks to the efforts of accursed Set, Osiris could not influence his physical form. Osiris remained a being of spirit, his only link to the living world the portions of his flesh spread about the globe. Yet the limitation that made the deity vulnerable to the dread Apepnu offered Nicholas the key to recover the Heart. The energy that flowed from the ab-Asar found its source in the Lord of Life. If Nicholas could only get a new compass scarab working, he could trace that energy back to the Heart itself.

He spent a solid week working on a new compass scarab, pausing only to eat hasty meals and nap a few hours at a stretch. Ibrahim and Faruq took turns bringing him food and drink and shoving him onto a cot when he'd been at the workbench for too long. As Nicholas was busy in Basel's workshop, the two cultists put feelers out for anything unusual that could be linked to Maxwell Carpenter or the Heart of Osiris. Each Eset-a had an area of expertise, Ibrahim his computer skills and Faruq his street connections. As a boy, Ibrahim often traveled to various job sites with his father, an electrician in the government's employ, where he had his first encounter with a computer. It was love at first sight. Before joining the cause of Ma'at, Ibrahim had a promising career as an IT specialist for the Egyptian government. While Ibrahim kept an eye out in cyberspace, Faruq put the word out with his street connections. The older Eset-a was what Cairenes called an ibn al-balad, or "son of the city." The label denoted a man who embodied qualities most respected by Cairo's residents, a blend of affability and cleverness not to be found among the fellahin of the countryside—and certainly not seen among the countless foreigners who thundered through Cairo like so many water buffalo every year. In practical terms, Faruq knew people who kept him appraised to a degree rivaling

Ibrahim's computer skills. Nicholas also kept in touch with other mummy groups through Lu Wen Khutenptah, an associate of the Cult of Isis, the group most closely involved with performing the resurrection ceremony that created new mummies. It wasn't a perfect arrangement, but until Nicholas got a new compass scarab working, it was the best they had to work with.

● ● ●

Nicholas pushed away from the workbench, cursing in frustration. He'd done some of his best work in the art of meket—amulet creation—in the past week. But despite his efforts, he met with failure. He'd already created one new compass scarab, but it had proven ineffective. This second attempt was almost complete; within a day or so he should have it. Unvoiced was his fear that there wouldn't be sufficient residue after the first two attempts for a third to have a chance. He had no choice but to make this second one work.

He glanced over at the first replacement, discarded next to the ruined original on a table of scrap metal and other oddments. His gaze roamed from there to take in the rest of the workshop. It was one of the larger chambers in the complex carved under Cairo's southern cemetery. Basel Nyambek-Senemut was skilled in many forms of Egyptian magic and spent much of his time in the room working on amulets, effigies, alchemy and the like. Likewise, visiting immortals were welcome to use the chamber as need be. A pair of worktables faced one another in the room's center, with additional tables and shelves arranged along three of the walls. The fourth wall held the door and a large wallboard where schematics, notes and the like could be tacked up. Equipment both modern and arcane was scattered across the various tables and poked from half-open drawers. The table Nicholas worked at had a lighted magnifier lens on a swivel arm attached to one corner, with a full set of jeweler's tools in an open metal case sitting within convenient reach. Bits of copper, silver wire and other precious metal odds and ends were swept to one side for later cleanup. Sitting on a rubberized mat before him was a sleek curved bracelet, a stylized gold and jade scarab attached to the top of the curve. It looked nice, but it still wasn't functional. And letting his attention wander wouldn't finish it, either. Nicholas sighed and leaned forward on his elbows, putting his eye to the magnifier lens and taking another look at the compass scarab.

Then Ibrahim dashed down the hall, calling his name. Nicholas looked up from the magnifier lens and cocked an eyebrow as the cultist ran, excited, into the workshop. "What've you got, Ibrahim? Something about the Heart?"

"No, Amenti, but perhaps almost as good." Ibrahim was as reserved as always, but excitement peeked from his eyes. "We have monitored passenger manifests for all incoming flights and registered ships entering Egyptian ports, yes? Aside from the name of this Carpenter, watching for those reporters who came to the temple. I think we might have something this time."

Nicholas had only heard the first names of the "reporters" who'd come to the Temple of Akhenaton, Jake and Thea. Slim as far as leads went, but they were desperate. Ibrahim had already come across a handful of hits on incoming flights and visa applications. With Faruq's help, they'd confirmed that none were the people they were looking for. Nicholas had recommended they stick with the searches, though they all figured it was a long shot. Carpenter was probably trying to sneak in and it wasn't like the "reporters'" names were uncommon in their respective cultures—if they were even coming here to begin with. Ibrahim wasn't prone to optimism, though, so he must be pretty sure of this lead. "Let's hear it."

"There is a Delta Airlines flight with a passenger named Thea Ghandour and two Jakes: a Jacob Pellitier and a Jake Washington."

"We only need one, you know."

Ibrahim was too focused on possibility to catch the joke. "I do not think both of these 'Jakes' are who we are looking for. But this is the first flight with that name and 'Thea' as well."

"Can't hurt to follow up," Nicholas said. "When does it get in?"

"It is expected to arrive in an hour. Faruq and I will go to the airport now to see if they match the descriptions you gave us. If so, do you want us to bring them here? Faruq has a friend with a taxi we can borrow."

"Don't want to tip our hand. Do what you can to have them take your cab, but drive them wherever they want to go." Nicholas wondered if Carpenter might be on the same flight under an alias. *No; he's not that obvious.* "There's every possibility that they're here to meet with Carpenter. Once we know where they're staying, we can watch them and maybe figure out what their plan is. Then we can grab them up or trail them to Carpenter as the situation warrants."

Ibrahim nodded his understanding and headed for the door. "I have a feeling about this, Nicholas."

"Here's hoping. We could use a breakthrough about now," Nicholas replied, curling his lip at the amulet on the workbench.

●●●

Nicholas shuffled the photos around on the worktable. He couldn't stop grinning. "Fantastic work, Ibrahim! And Faruq's trailing them now?"

The cultist nodded. "He left after I returned. You do recognize them?"

"Oh, I recognize them, all right." Nicholas flicked a finger at a shot of Thea Ghandour and Jake Washington standing on the sidewalk in Maydan at-Tahrir, backpacks in hand and jetlagged confusion on their faces. Ibrahim had been on an errand when the attack went down at the Temple of Akhenaton, so he'd had to go by Nicholas' description. He'd explained to Nicholas that he had

little doubt once he'd spotted them getting off the Delta flight, but he was determined not to take chances. He'd been able to finagle them into the borrowed taxi and dropped them off by the Ismailia Hotel. There, Ibrahim had snapped some pictures with a disposable camera and rushed it to a one hour photo lab. "Incredible break, Ibrahim. Really. Nice job with everything—monitoring flights, getting these pictures, the whole deal."

"What is next?" Ibrahim was afire from the praise, doubts of his worthiness voiced a week before but a distant memory. Like Nicholas, he was ready to exact vengeance for the loss of his comrades and the Heart.

"I wouldn't think they'd be up for anything after a long plane flight, so we have a little time. You and Faruq keep on them. See if you can find out if they're meeting with anyone, renting transportation, that kind of thing. If you think you can do it without them noticing, go through their stuff while they're out of the hotel. Meantime, I'll keep working on this damn compass scarab."

Ibrahim looked at the amulet, his excitement dimming somewhat. "It still does not work?"

"I've been at it night and day and *pffft*! Nothing," Nicholas griped. "Structurally, it's sound. I can feel the enchantment, but it just sits there. No indication that it's picking up anything."

"Just as with your first attempt," Ibrahim noted.

Nicholas shot a dirty look at the first replacement. Like the one on the table in front of him, that bracelet was a marvel of simple elegance that tracked the Heart's mystic resonance from the residue infused to its design. Or so it went in theory. Neither one showed the slightest inclination to work.

If only I hadn't misled Carpenter, Nicholas thought. If he hadn't tried so hard to resist the zombie's mental compulsion, he would have revealed that the Spell of Life had to be performed by the living upon a prepared corpse. The Heart played no role in the process. But in trying to retain the secrets of his kind, Nicholas had inadvertently implied that the Heart was the key to resurrection. So now the prick was heading for the Near East with the ab-Asar in his pocket and not a clue what to do with it. And who knew how many of the enemy's minions could sense the thing? They were sure to be drawn to it like bees to pollen. The intensity of the Heart's aura disguised its exact location, but with enough people to throw at the problem it was only a matter of time before someone stumbled across it.

Only the damned bracelet had a chance to pinpoint the Heart's location. But he had two strikes, and there just wasn't enough left of the original to allow for a third. Days wasted when they could have—

Nicholas blinked, something striking him as odd. "Ibrahim, have you done anything with the first replacement?"

"I have not, Nicholas."

"You haven't been dragging it across the table so it left little tracks, then."

The Eset-a glanced over at the side table in puzzlement. The complex underneath the Mausoleum of al-Qalarayn was as well-ventilated as Basel had been able to make it. Even so, by nature of the desert climate and stone construction, dust and sand were impossible to keep out. Nicholas kept his work space brushed clean, but didn't wipe down the whole room. The nearby scrap table had a thin film of grit... which showed a pair of needle-thin lines that ran about three inches to the edge of the first replacement compass scarab. The amulet was fashioned as a U-shaped bracelet; the open end slipped over the wrist with the sleek scarab on top rotating like a compass to track the Heart's position. The two ends of the U matched up with the pair of lines in the yellow dust on the table.

Nicholas snatched up the replacement and slipped it onto his wrist and laughed. "It's responding, Ibrahim! It's weak, but I can sense a connection." He scrutinized

the amulet further and determined that the replacement compass scarab functioned at a greatly reduced range from the original. He hadn't expected it to operate with the same strength as the original, but it seemed it was even weaker than his calculations suggested. "The first one I made could track the Heart up to half a world away. It's hard to tell distances with this one... at a guess, I'd say maybe five hundred miles?"

"Can you tell where the Heart is?"

"Damn. It's here, not far at all. Somewhere in Lower Egypt." He looked at the marks on the table. "Look, you can see from the marks in the dust, right? Must've come in... let's see, north is that way... north-northeast. And see how it dragged in a slight curve to the east? From how the amulet feels, it's somewhere to the east now. Still can't say how far away, though."

Ibrahim frowned, thinking, then his mouth dropped open. "Port Said!"

"How's that?"

"An accident in Port Said yesterday. Tankers exploded, many people dead. It was in the news."

"But Port Said is northeast of Cairo... given the drag marks on the table, the timing is right. So Carpenter came in by ship and something happened. And now he's east and, what? Going through the Suez Canal? On land, heading for the Eastern Desert?" An awful realization hit then. "Oh, shit. Remember when we got back from Edfu? Lu Wen mentioned some of her Isis people were headed to Port Said to gather up someone coming in on a hajj."

Ibrahim paled. "They left before Lu Wen could contact them, Nicholas."

Nicholas cursed. While he'd gone to speak with Mestha, Lu Wen had traveled to the few sites the Cult of Isis had in the northern part of the country. Since hidden temples and underground mausoleums didn't normally have phone service—the Eset-a safe house being an exception—Lu Wen went to the different resurrection sites in person. She'd returned to the Cities of the Dead a few days after Nicholas got back and related that the group in charge of a hidden site at Saqqara had seen portents of a new arrival. The cultists who remained at the site told Lu Wen they'd already sent a group out. They hadn't thought anything of it at the time, but the problem was painfully clear to Nicholas now. The new and old spirits who joined to become an Amenti were trapped inside the dead flesh of the newly deceased until the Spell of Life could bestow the resurrection. In other words, they animated the body to make the journey to Egypt—ghosts possessing a corpse. Something not too different from Maxwell Carpenter. "Son of a… If the Cult of Isis misread their visions, they could have mistaken Carpenter for a mummy on the hajj. They might've run right into him, Ibrahim."

"But would they not sense the Heart?"

"Mortals wouldn't, of course, but even though a mummy would feel the aura, he wouldn't necessarily know what it was. And once he passed inside the aura's perimeter, he would have no idea where the emanations were coming from. He could walk right up to it, but until he touched it he'd have no idea it was there." Noting Ibrahim's downcast look, Nicholas added, "You can see why I want to get this damn compass working, eh?"

The cultist nodded. "But… surely we would have heard something?"

"Well, you did mention something about tankers blowing up, right?" Nicholas smiled without humor. He had no doubt that mass destruction might result if Carpenter encountered mummies. "I need to talk to Lu Wen right away."

He tried her cell phone and was pleasantly surprised to get through. It didn't take long to bring her up to speed on his suspicions. "What do you think? Have you heard anything from that group?"

"Not yet. I have been researching the Sphinx." Lu Wen was one of a small group who suspected the Sphinx

might be some kind of effigy, an enchanted construct like the mastiffs she'd given Nicholas. Every so often, she would investigate an obscure new line of inquiry in hopes of discovering its intended purpose. "This is the first I have heard of any disaster in Port Said. It happened just yesterday?"

"Yep. It's possible that's just a coincidence, but I don't think so."

"Neither do I. Though we should not assume our people were caught in it. It may be that the group did, indeed, gather someone on the hajj and even now is returned to Sanakht Nebka." A plateau south of Cairo, Saqqara was the home of the famous Step Pyramid of Djoser. It also served for over three thousand years as the necropolis for the dead from Egypt's ancient capital of Memphis. Following the recollections of the Imkhu, the Cult of Isis had re-discovered another step pyramid near there, long buried in the sand, dedicated to the pharaoh Sanakht Nebka. Built in a place of great spiritual power, it served as one of the mummies' resurrection sites. A pause, then Lu Wen suggested, "It may also be that this Carpenter was destroyed in the accident. Perhaps some other force has the Heart now."

Nicholas looked at the compass scarab. "I won't believe Carpenter is dead for good until I see his body turned to ash. And if he's still around, it's a sure bet he still has the Heart with him."

"I shall go to Saqqara immediately and see if they have returned. If not, perhaps those who remain have heard fresh news."

"You need any company?"

"No. You must pursue the Heart, now that you can sense its location again."

She was right, of course. It would be tragic if they lost people to the conflagration in Port Said, but that was the way of things. Warriors fell in battle. He had to focus on recovering the Heart of Osiris. "All right. I need to tie up a few loose ends before I head out, so you can still find me here until, say, tomorrow morning."

"Very well. I wish you luck."

Nicholas ended the call and turned to Ibrahim, standing pensive nearby. "You got the gist of that?"

Ibrahim nodded. "We do not go after the Heart now?"

"Much as I want to, I think it's best if we find out what part our 'reporters' play in all this first. I don't want them sneaking up on our ass when we're about to nail Carpenter."

•••

"I am sorry I could not hear more," Faruq apologized that evening. "When they started speaking so softly, I would have had to join them at their table to hear them!"

Nicholas smiled. Faruq exaggerated, of course. He'd followed Thea Ghandour and Jake Washington to a coffee house and eavesdropped on them from the next table over. He hadn't heard everything the two had said, but what he had picked up was enough that Nicholas was certain they weren't working with Carpenter. In fact, it sounded like quite the opposite. The Heart remained the big mystery. Knowing they shared an enemy in Maxwell Carpenter was good, but if those two wanted to swipe the ab-Asar from him? A complication Nicholas didn't have time for. "So they're after Carpenter. Question is, are they gunning for him to get the Heart or is it something else?"

"I do not know, Nicholas. I did not hear them speak of the Heart, but that does not mean they did not talk about it."

"And you're sure they said something about visas?" Thanks to Ibrahim's ties to the bureaucracy, Nicholas didn't have to waste his time on such things, but he'd heard horror stories from others. "Good. Okay, same plan as before. Let's get everything ready now. Tomorrow morning we'll pick them up for a chat. Once we know what they're up to, we go after the Heart."

"You do not want to get them tonight, while they sleep?"

"Too risky. They're, what? On the eighth floor? Too many opportunities for things to go wrong, getting them down to a car. Better to surprise them on the street in the crowd. I don't think they'll try anything with bystanders around." He shrugged. "Besides, I'm burned out from spending a week in that damn workshop. Be nice to get a good night's sleep for a change."

A bribe to the desk clerks at the Ismailia Hotel—night and morning shifts—and they could expect a phone call if the "reporters" so much as poked their nose out their hotel room door. Now that things seemed to be going his way again, Nicholas had his first restful night in some time. He awoke, refreshed, at dawn and took a quick workout in the mausoleum courtyard. When he came back downstairs for a shower and breakfast, Faruq reported that the hotel had called. The desk clerk saw the young guy, Jake, headed for the communal bathroom. They were up and getting ready; it was time for Nicholas and his people to get moving also.

Fifteen minutes later they were in the borrowed taxi, a battered Audi, and heading for downtown Cairo. Traffic was insane, as always, but Faruq handled it like an old pro. They made it to Maydan at-Tahrir with only a couple fresh dings. Nicholas and Ibrahim got out at the corner and split up to cover each side of the hotel. Faruq stayed where he was parked, the car halfway up on the sidewalk. Other cars honked and scraped their way around him while pedestrians cursed him cheerfully as they slipped between the Audi and the crumbling building.

Nicholas waited with more than a little impatience. When he'd donned the compass scarab that morning, he'd seen the scarab reorient to point almost due south. It had faced east the previous evening, and it concerned him that Carpenter was covering ground so fast. He was tempted to forget about these "reporters" and get after the Heart before it got out of range. Now was not the time to go off half-cocked. *Decisive and bold is good,* he cautioned himself. *Rash and impulsive, not so much.* Dealing with Thea

Ghandour and Jake Washington should take no more than an hour or so. Easy enough to get on the Heart's trail after that was resolved. It didn't make the waiting any easier to take, though. Thankfully, they were there just a few minutes before a man and a woman came out of the building, their attention focused across the square on the huge Mogamma government building.

Nicholas recognized them instantly. Jake Washington was a thin black kid barely in his twenties, wearing an anime T-shirt with jeans and Nikes. Thea Ghandour was a few years older, mid-twenties, wearing a peasant blouse with cargo pants and hiking boots. Nicholas recalled from their first meeting at the Temple of Akhenaton that she was attractive, but the sudden attack had shoved any appreciation from his mind. He took a moment now to note a curvy, athletic figure not quite hidden under the loose clothes. Her skin was a deep copper and her hair a mass of thick, loose curls still damp from a shower. She turned slightly, giving him a good view of striking Arabic features with a hint of African ancestry mixed in. Brilliant green eyes ringed by thick lashes and full lips… Nicholas realized he was staring.

A little embarrassed with himself, Nicholas gestured for Ibrahim to be ready on the other side and stepped forward. The woman saw him and turned, amazement spreading across her face. "Sforza!"

"Nicholas, please," he said. He thought telling them his full name now would make for a needless distraction. Best to keep it on a first-name basis. "Hi, Thea; Jake. Welcome to Egypt."

He felt the surprise rolling off them like heat from a stove. He and Ibrahim took advantage of their startled state to herd them over to the Audi. "It's best we don't make a scene here, don't you think?" he continued as they started sputtering protests. "Let's all hop in and go someplace where we can have a nice talk."

They got themselves under control fast, although Nicholas could still sense a riot of emotion—wonder,

fear, concern, anger—continuing to simmer behind their calm exteriors. The kid, Jake, shot a questioning look at Thea. She said nothing at first, just fixed Nicholas with an odd, penetrating stare. "We should be all right," she said, more like she was talking to herself than anything. "Yeah; it's okay, Jake. Let's go."

Nicholas recalled from that that Jake was definitely the follower. He directed the kid to the front seat, then put Thea in the back with himself and Ibrahim on either side. Faruq jerked the taxi into traffic, laying on his horn and trusting someone would clear a space for them. Navigating the streets was too hair-raising a proposition to allow for any conversation, so they rode in silence until they were well into the southern cemetery.

Nicholas was quite aware of Thea's muscular thigh pressed against his own in the cramped back seat. As one of the Amenti, his immortal senses reveled in all manner of sensation. Seemed his body was reminding him it was some time since he'd indulged in any form of physical encounter. It wouldn't do to hit on someone during such a time of crisis, especially a potential enemy. *Get control of your hormones, idiot.*

"You mind if I ask where we're headed?" Thea asked.

Nicholas was glad of the distraction conversation provided. "Right now we're in what us Westerners call the Cities of the Dead. It's safer for us here than in Cairo itself. Anyway, it encompasses two big cemeteries east and south of the city. It's not just a graveyard, though; people live here."

Their passengers looked around with interest, but the sightseeing was over soon enough. "It is time, Nicholas," Faruq said as he turned the taxi in to a narrow alley between crooked rows of tombs.

"Right." Nicholas gestured at the cloth sacks Ibrahim pulled out. "Put these over your heads. I know it sounds sinister, but we need to keep a few secrets. Long as you continue playing nice, you'll walk out of here safe and sound."

Thea Ghandour directed that same unnerving look at him, but took the sack. "Go with it for now, Jake."

"If you say so," the black kid replied, muttering something else as he pulled the bag over his head.

Faruq drove them through the winding alley and circled around to the tunnel entrance hidden in the cluster of date palms. Ibrahim led the way down with Jake and then Thea coming after, feeling their way down the ladder with the slow determination of the blind. Nicholas came last after sending Faruq to the Ismailia Hotel. Depending on how things went in the next hour, Thea and Jake would be joining the hunt for Carpenter or would end up permanent residents of the cemetery. Either way, they wouldn't have an opportunity to collect their things from the hotel.

After shuffling through the tunnel and into the underground chambers, Ibrahim led them up through the tomb and into the open air courtyard. The walls were high enough that their guests couldn't determine where they were by surrounding landmarks. And in case something went wrong, they wouldn't have free reign of the subterranean complex. Ibrahim removed the sacks, then, and indicated they should sit in the chairs provided. The seats were arranged in the mausoleum's shadow, providing some relief from the ascending sun. Thea and Jake sat facing out from the mausoleum, Nicholas in a chair opposite. Nicholas had no weapons visible—with the number of amulets and charms he now wore, he had no need for any. Ibrahim, mild-mannered in appearance as always, now sported a Kalashnikov assault rifle on a shoulder strap. The Mamluk fountain that Lu Wen designed rose behind Nicholas, the muscular, fierce stone figures lending additional gravity to the scene.

Jake looked around with frank interest, while Thea gave only a cursory glance at her surroundings before directing her attention at Nicholas. Brushing a strand of hair from her face, she said, "Just what are you, exactly?"

Still trying to decide on the best way to begin his interrogation, Nicholas was thrown off balance by the question. "You're blunt, eh? We're not here to talk about me—"

"Sorry, but that's exactly why we're here. To start with, how did you get free from Carpenter? Why is he over here? What the—"

Nicholas quieted her with a flash of an upraised hand. "No. You're on my turf now. I'm calling the shots."

"Nope," she replied, full lips curled in a smile that didn't touch her eyes. "This won't be a one-way deal. I can tell you're not going to just waste us, but I'm sick of being a mushroom."

"'Mushroom'?" The black kid wondered, giving her a puzzled look.

"Kept in the dark and fed a lot of crap," Thea muttered back. To Nicholas, she continued, "So how about it? You play straight with us and we'll do the same in return."

Nicholas could sense her honesty and commitment, as well as Jake's fierce loyalty. *What an odd pair*. He wondered if they were together, as in *together*. It didn't scan, but he'd seen stranger pairings. Probably wasn't the smartest question to toss out there right now, though. "I don't have time to waste negotiating, so let's say 'okay.' But only about what I think we're all here for. I'm not divulging the full details of what I'm involved in; likewise, I wouldn't be surprised if you had a few secrets you'd like to keep yourselves."

"All right, we'll start with that. What do you think we're all here for?"

Carpenter was a sure bet, but Nicholas wasn't concerned about him. The next words he spoke would decide it. "The Heart of Osiris."

Nicholas sensed brief confusion, genuine and undiluted by deceit, flare from both his guests for a fraction of a second. Then Jake's puzzlement gave way to relief and Thea's to irritation. *They don't know what it really is*. Barely restraining a relieved sigh, he shook his head minutely at Ibrahim.

"Osiris, eh?" Jake had a smile of discovery on his face. "I was wondering just whose heart it was."

"Sorry," Thea said, "but the last I saw that thing was when I threw it out a window."

Nicholas laughed in disbelief. "That was *you*? Son of a... You know what kind of hell you've put me through because of that?"

"We were about to get our asses handed to us by some very bad people. Pardon me if I don't get choked up because it put you in a bad spot." Thea's anger was a palpable thing. She leaned forward, thrusting an accusing finger at Nicholas. "I know this Heart was yours to begin with—and better believe I'm sorry that I ever took it—but let's not forget that a bunch of your goons killed two of our friends trying to get it back!"

"You had no right to take it," Nicholas replied. His ancient self stirred with anger of its own. "What happened as a result rests on your shoulders."

"Bullshit. If your guys had bothered talking to us like you're doing now instead of charging in, you'd have your precious fucking jar and our friends would still be alive. But no; had to be all guns and testosterone and screw up all our lives!"

"You aren't the only one who lost people important to you," Nicholas replied, forcing himself to assume a reasoned tone. "If you're not interested in the Heart, why did you take it to begin with?"

Thea swore, not through with being upset. The woman had a mouth like a sailor, but somehow she made it work. A cautionary look and some whispered words from Jake helped calm her down somewhat. At last she threw up her hands in a shrug. "I don't know. I just..." she paused, looking nonplussed. "Wow. I really *don't* know. It was so overpowering, feeling this energy, like a physical thing pressing around me. And then after Romeo... after it all, I just felt *drawn* to it. But once we left... remember later, Jake? It all kind of faded—at least, until the Sears Tower."

Nicholas understood Thea somehow tapped into the Heart's wavelength, and to a greater degree than what the supernaturally sensitive might pick up. He was curious to know just what this might mean—was there something in her heritage? Some of the cultists, he knew, were descendents of priests from ancient Egypt, and showed particular aptitude in performing the Spell of Life and other duties. So there was a precedent. Of course, it could just as likely be something else altogether. Whatever the case, he didn't have the luxury of investigating now. *A mystery for another time*, he thought.

"I think it's clear our involvement with the Heart of Osiris was a mistake," Jake offered. "Of, like, cosmic proportions. We can't help you with it any more than we have. Like Thea said, last time we saw it was in Chicago weeks ago."

"I know," Nicholas replied. "That was the last time I saw it, also. Right before Carpenter stole it."

"He was there, too? Oh, man. Listen, I know the whole thing at your temple looked really bad, but we didn't know Carpenter was going to attack the place and come after you."

"Speaking of which," Thea said, having shaken off her fugue from contemplating the Heart, "he kidnapped you, right? What was that all about? How'd you get loose?"

"That falls under the category of irrelevant to the current situation," Nicholas said.

"Oh, come on—"

"Thea, do you want to shoot the shit about some old grudge or do you want to find out where Carpenter is right now?"

"If you actually know where that prick is, to hell with the rest of this Twenty Questions. Just tell me and we'll be out of your hair. Or what's left of it, at least."

Nicholas rubbed the dark bristle of his scalp and smiled. "So you did come all this way just for some good, old-fashioned payback. Sorry, but I can't tell you where he is."

"Listen, you jerk, you just said—"

"—That I don't know where he is. However, thanks to this—" he tapped the slim compass bracelet on his wrist "—I can lead us right to him."

"What about our visas?" Jake asked. "And we're supposed to meet someone, a local contact. He could be a big help in this."

"That's up to you," Nicholas said with a shrug. "Our timetable is set for right now. You want to get all legal with your visas and hook up with friends, fine. We'll drop you back in Maydan at-Tahrir. But after that, we're gone. You're on your own, and you won't have a chance of finding Carpenter before we get to him. But if you're in, you say so right now, and no turning back."

Thea's eyes flashed. "Oh, we're in, all right."

TWELVE

Carpenter found extracting himself from the bottom of Port Said Harbor to be one hell of a chore, stuck as he was beneath a large fragment of the oil tanker. Despite his tremendous undead strength, Carpenter couldn't make the steel hull budge. The sea floor was more forgiving. With an effort, he dragged one hand over to his pocket and fumbled to extract the straight razor. No good; the pressure of the tanker was too great. He couldn't cut his way out. So that left giving up or trying to crawl out from underneath a thousand-ton hull. Undead muscles straining with effort, Carpenter started pulling himself along the rough surface of the tanker.

It took hours to get free. The effort, already difficult by the ceaseless pressure of the hull upon him, was made even more uncomfortable by the garment bag that dragged against the muck. He'd have torn it off, but he didn't have the room to maneuver. Then there was the hard knot of the Heart that jabbed into his midsection. Considering a number of his bones and internal organs were damaged when the ship landed on him, Carpenter was surprised at first that the Heart was still in one piece. Having plenty of time to reflect on the matter as he slogged his way along, he decided it wasn't remarkable after all. The Heart carried a major mojo; things like that were hard to wreck. Still, it got him to thinking. Powerful and durable this Heart was, but how far did that go? Was it indestructible? Doubtful. Carpenter had seen enough in his time to know that everything had a weakness. He pondered what the Heart's might be, but

he didn't have enough to go on to draw any conclusions. Then his reaching hand was no longer pressed between the wet clay of the harbor bottom and the unyielding metal of the ship's hull. Energized by the thought of freedom, Carpenter pawed at the curve of the tanker hull. He was finally free.

Although out from under the ship, Carpenter had no idea where he was—aside from a hundred feet underwater along the coast of Egypt. He couldn't see through the dark, silt-impregnated water and his spiritual awareness didn't register much at all, so he spent a good long while wandering around under Port Said harbor, half-swimming, half-stumbling until he reached a pylon he could climb.

He emerged along the docks a half-mile from where the tankers exploded. It was dark out and he could see fire crews on the docks and in boats spraying water on scattered clumps of flame. The place was black with burned wood and scorched metal. A thick residue covered the water and chunks of debris covered everything. Carpenter had no idea how long he'd been trapped under the tanker. From the blanket of stars and chill in the air, he suspected it was the middle of the night. Maybe six hours or so to crawl free. *Unbelievable*, he thought. He looked on the bright side. If he hadn't been knocked off the deck from one of the bandoleer's first explosions, he would be part of the ash fouling up the harbor.

Carpenter's skin crawled under his befouled clothing. He couldn't even change into fresh clothing since everything in the garment bag was as waterlogged as the rest of him. The discomfort of being filthy was fast becoming the entirety of his existence, and only a supreme effort of will kept him from rampaging through the streets in search of a decent clothier's. He found a spigot and washed off as best he could, which took the edge off. He also removed the Heart and stuffed it in a pocket, unable to take its unnatural warmth and psychic pulses any longer.

Carpenter had never been in a foreign country before (he didn't count liquor runs to Canada during Prohibition; the Canadians were all wannabe Americans anyway). He wandered along the docks for a while, out of place, a fish out of water. Given his condition, he didn't expect anyone would want to stop and chat—not that they could understand him, since he spoke only English. While he didn't know where he was headed yet, it wasn't a good idea to hang around there. No telling if the mummy who'd come after him before had friends combing the area. In fact—

He lunged behind some crates as a pair of towelheads approached. They walked with the cautious pace and alert movements of people searching for something. They'd seen him, but it looked like they hadn't identified who he was. The two crept toward his hiding place, whispering to one another and calling out in soft tones. Carpenter was startled to realize he recognized one of the words: "Amenti." Where had he heard that? *Sforza. Just before he died, he said that's what he was.* Carpenter was right; mummy fuckers *did* have people searching the area. Just his luck to stumble right on them.

He readied himself to attack, but paused when inspiration sprang forth in his mind. His deathsight showed these two were just a couple mortals. No danger of overpowering him. Even better, they worked for the mummies. They should know something about this whole ceremony business. Crossing their path was lucky indeed—a couple hostages should take him where he had to go.

He'd lost his trusty Colt in the explosion, so he'd have to do this up close. He dumped the garment bag, useless at this point, and dashed from his hiding place. Carpenter was upon them before they could process that he wasn't the Amenti they were looking for. He grabbed the one on the right by the throat and lifted him a couple inches from the ground. He pointed his ruined left hand at the other one—a

stocky woman, he saw now that he was close enough—and said, "Make a sound and I'll pop his head like a fucking grape."

Carpenter was on a roll. Looked like the woman spoke English. She nodded, eyes wide to watch her buddy struggle against Carpenter's iron grip. Something about her... he leaned in closer, trying to get a decent look at her in the illumination shed from lights along the docks. "You came to the ship with that big bastard, didn't you? How the hell did you survive?"

She shook her head, out of fear rather than denial. "I... not there," she said, and pointed to the other one. "Sent to get driver. For help."

"Driver, eh? So you got transportation somewhere?" Getting better all the time.

"You... no escaping! We have help, coming here. They catch you!" The stocky broad was trying for righteous anger, but it was coming across as panic.

"So you're saying they're not here yet? Good to know." He shook the guy, well on his way to unconsciousness. "You speak English, too? Fantastic. You do what I say and you'll live to tell your hundred little brown grandkids about it. First thing, you're going to take me someplace I can get some decent clothes. Then we're going to wherever you do your hocus-pocus. You know: 'Amenti,' right?"

Even in the dim light and with his atrophied eyesight, Carpenter saw the woman grow pale. "No," she said, her voice but a squeak.

"Oh, yes," Carpenter replied. The straight razor appeared in his left hand as if by magic. Even missing his first two fingers, the weapon rested comfortably in his grip. The blade flicked out, an unnatural shimmer coursing along the metal as Carpenter pointed it at her. "You see this? Yeah, you can feel it; I can tell. You know what it's like getting cut by this little beauty? You don't play nice, you'll find out."

A shout came from nearby. A guy in a white uniform was pointing a gun. So much for the run of good luck. Carpenter dropped the man he'd been holding. The cultist collapsed, retching as he tried to suck down air. The woman cried out something in Arabic as she crouched to help her friend. The cop yelled in return and fired when Carpenter turned to face him. The bullet caught Carpenter in the thigh, knocking him off balance. He staggered forward as the cop fired again, the second shot going wild. Carpenter covered the distance before the policeman could squeeze off a third shot and plucked the automatic from his grip. Carpenter didn't realize his left arm had swung until a spray of red warmth showered him. The cop's face, frozen in agony from the brief moment of soul-searing torture inflicted by the razor wound, rolled back… and kept rolling. The razor blade had cleaved deep through the man's neck. The spine kept the head attached, but only just. Red staining the front of his uniform, the cop dropped to the ground with a wet thud.

Carpenter felt the razor's eagerness like a vibration up his arm. "You little fucker," he said, watching as the blood along the blade appeared to seep right into the metal, "just waiting to pull something like that, eh? Gonna have to keep my eye on you."

He had to move fast; even his weak ears picked up the sound of approaching shouts, calling out in response to the gunshots. It took an effort, but he was able to fold the blade closed and stick it back in his pocket. After stuffing the cop's pistol in his waistband and grabbing the handcuffs and keys, he returned to the cultists. The woman was helping her pal shuffle for cover; Carpenter reached them before they got more than a couple feet. "Don't even bother. You saw what happened when you fuck with me. Now take me to your car and let's get the fuck out of here."

• • •

Forcing his hostages to take him to a clothing store was a risk, but Carpenter would have gone nuts if he'd stayed in his mud- and blood-encrusted clothes any longer. Turned out these two didn't know the city that well, so they drove around for a good hour before they found a store that looked like it sold suits. After hours, of course, but that just made things easier. Carpenter broke in and cuffed his hostages around a pipe, using ties to gag them. Looked like there was an apartment above the shop; Carpenter slipped up there and, sure enough, found the shop's owner and his family. Just in case, Carpenter tied up the lot of them, then took advantage of the opportunity and had a long-overdue shower. The straight razor whispered that the family was a liability, but Carpenter saw no reason to kill them. He repeated that to himself until he was back in the shop. With distance, the razor seemed to forget about the family upstairs; its siren song sank to a murmur. Carpenter looked through the selections and was surprised with the variety available. The building might be sagging and the apartment upstairs little more than a hovel, but the shop had decent selections to choose from. He picked out a nice summer-weight suit in a modern cut. The only real problem was the shoes. After washing the muck off, he kept the boots he'd worn with his dungarees. Didn't match the suit, but there it was. Probably be better slogging through desert, at least.

They were gone as the sun was turning the eastern sky pink. A pall of oily smoke hung over the harbor, hidden in the night but all too apparent in the new day. Carpenter recalled the woman's claim that she had friends coming to the harbor. He hoped that, if they knew about him, they would think he was still somewhere among the wreckage. He had a plan now and didn't want it all to go to shit before he got properly started.

Carpenter reclined in the back seat of the cultists' Ford Expedition and watched the desert roll by in the early morning light. He was surprised they had such nice vehicles over here. He would've thought these people would all be driving some unpronounceable brand of East European crap, some tiny go-cart that'd fit in the back of this monster of a four wheel drive. Or camels; on the way out of Port Said, he'd seen people actually riding fucking *camels*.

His directions to the cultists were simple enough: take him to their temple or ceremonial chamber or whatever they called it, and they had his word they'd live. Carpenter knew they had no reason to believe him, but he'd seen plenty of people who were quick to fool themselves. There was a chance he was telling the truth, or that they might have a chance to escape, or who really knew? The future was unwritten. Carpenter had a fair idea what the future held in store for these two, but let them have their fantasies. Anything to make them easier to manage.

Even so, he figured his captives might try to get clever sooner or later. Carpenter considered forcing his will on the driver—he'd already done so to confirm that they did, indeed, know of a ceremony that could bestow immortality. Carpenter was tempted to make him take them to wherever it was they needed to go to perform it. But the power didn't allow for full-on mind control. It only worked well with simple, straightforward—and here was the important part—*short-term* commands. Carpenter had learned that trying even specific long-term commands—"don't say anything for another hour" or "forget you ever saw me"—did something to the subject. Carpenter wasn't worried about inflicting brain damage on people. His concern was that they were harder to control afterward. Unpredictable, like wires got crossed in their heads. He'd seen it happen with one of those hunters, that other chick in Chicago… Lupe Something-or-other. He'd planned on using her for his ruse to go after Sforza, but he'd pushed too hard. She was fine most of the time, but anything to do with "Maxwell Carpenter" sent her into a spiral

of frustrated anger. Too much trouble to manipulate like that, so he'd started over with the Thea woman and her friends. Guile instead of supernatural powers. *Live and learn*, he thought. *Well… learn, anyway.*

So instead of forcing his will, Carpenter remained in the back seat, the cop's pistol—a Sig-Sauer, whatever that was—pointed through the seat at the driver's spine. He kept them cuffed together also, which afforded him some amusement when the guy had to yank the woman over to his side to steer with both hands. The cultist took the Ford down a major highway, a straight shot south paralleling the Suez Canal. Carpenter knew this due to the sporadic signs that had Arabic squiggles and English subtitles. Well-traveled roads suited Carpenter just fine. He had no idea where he was; his knowledge of Egyptian geography amounted to picturing a huge desert with a couple pyramids stuck in the middle. As long as they were on a major thoroughfare, Carpenter felt comfortable that the guy wasn't trying to pull a fast one.

They stopped off in the city of Ismailia, about an hour south of Port Said, and fueled up the Expedition. Carpenters kept a close eye on his two captives—Ahmir and Sherin, he discovered were their names—but they were quite well behaved. After leaving the gas station, they wound through a series of meandering surface streets until Carpenter realized Ahmir was just trying to waste time. Carpenter was irritated with himself for not figuring it out sooner. He'd been too quick to assume that the mess of winding streets, lacking even a nod to any kind of traffic plan, was typical of the city. A quick nudge of his will and Carpenter discovered that the driver was, indeed, trying to give him the runaround.

"Where is this hideout of yours?" Carpenter demanded, eye flaring with an unclean green light.

"Desert… It is hidden—ruins," the cultist replied, sweat pouring off him so thick he might have been standing under a faucet.

"Does this look like the fucking desert?" Carpenter asked, more conversationally this time. The neighborhood they were in did, in fact, have a parched and windswept look, but even with a poor command of English, it was clear Ahmir got the point. "How far is it, smart guy?"

Ahmir stammered and shook his head, casting a panicked look at the woman. They both looked scared enough to play it straight. Carpenter shouldn't have to waste energy trying to control them. He pointed the pistol at Sherin, who was marginally more calm than her friend. "You. How many miles is it to get there?"

"Many miles," she nodded.

"Fucking Christ. How *many*? Huh? How *far*?"

"Miles? Do not know miles. Is many kilometers. Uh… hundreds! Yes?"

Ridiculous. Like pulling teeth, this was. "All right, fine. Get us back on the goddamn road before you really piss me off. And don't try to pull this shit again."

The driver, nervous sweat dripping off him for the next half hour, took them to a smaller highway continuing south that brought them to the city of Suez a couple hours later. Curious, Carpenter had them drive to overlook the Gulf of Suez and the marvel of engineering that was the canal. He was feeling good about his progress; he could afford to take some time out for sightseeing. Who would have ever thought that a punk kid from Chicago's South Side would someday be looking at the Suez Canal? It would have been something to tell the gang back home… if any of them had still been alive. That was all right. After he became immortal, Carpenter would have plenty of time to find a whole new gang of friends. He chuckled, spirits high, and hopped back in the Ford.

"So how did you find me so fast, anyway?" he asked after a while, more to break the monotony of travel than any real curiosity. "Come on; what's it going to hurt to make a little conversation?"

At last, the woman said, "We did not look for you."

"'Did not look'… what, you were expecting someone else?" That was puzzling. He spent a long time on that freighter and didn't come across anyone besides typical crew members and rats with attitude. "What, that vampire, Beckett?"

She turned, surprised, then revulsion twisted her features. "A ghul? You are offense enough."

"Hey, be nice. So, wait. If you weren't expecting me… were you even looking for the Heart?" The two cultists looked at one another in mild confusion, but Carpenter didn't catch any dawning enlightenment. *Strange. Seemed like a big damn deal to Sforza and his buddies.* Taking out his handkerchief—a fresh one he'd grabbed with his new outfit—Carpenter extracted the Heart from his pocket. Holding it, he was certain it was significantly heavier than it had been. That was odd; it didn't seem to pull on the line of his jacket any more than before. He took a closer look. Its texture, previously porous and rough like stone, now appeared smooth, marble-like. In fact, the Heart didn't even seem to have the same shape it had before. It was hard to say for certain; thinking back, he tried to recall if it had a different form on the ship than when he'd first seen it in Chicago. Subtle changes, maybe, alterations he overlooked thanks to his weak eyesight. But yes, he felt pretty sure there were differences.

Physical appearance aside, the Heart's psychic pulses continued much as they had before. Reduced to a faint tingle when in his pocket, the beats attained a steady, thudding rhythm when the Heart was in his hand. Carpenter felt that the pulses didn't occur in response to his holding it. They were probably going all the time; he just didn't feel them unless he held the Heart close. The sensation was at once soothing and unnerving. As if he was touching a cable that hummed with tremendous power, but it might deliver a devastating shock at any moment.

Forcing himself not to squirm, Carpenter leaned forward so his traveling companions could get a look at the Heart. "You telling me you never heard of this? How about Nicholas Sforza? Him and a bunch of camel jockeys like yourself were pretty excited about this thing."

Their confusion seemed to increase when they glanced at the Heart, but Sforza's name caused a reaction. The guy barked, "Amenti? Nicholas Sforza-Ankhotep?"

"Right, yeah. Amenti. Like that big pal of yours, Simbah. You've heard of him, then."

The woman jabbered something fast in Arabic at her friend, and they were soon spitting words at each other and getting more excited by the second. Seemed they had fair idea what Carpenter was talking about now. He didn't like being left out of the dialogue, though. He shoved the Heart back in his pocket and called out to get their attention. It took a couple tries, and he finally had to wave the pistol between them, but the two chatterboxes finally shut up.

"What was that all about, huh? Looks like I struck a nerve. Huh? Oh, and now you're not talking?" He looked from one to the other. They stared out the front, watching the road with grim resolution. They might put on a brave face, but Carpenter could feel the outrage and fear radiating from them. Drinking in the emotions with relish, Carpenter decided to let it go for the time being. Remembering his interrogation of Sforza, he had a fair idea why they were so worked up. *Just wait till I'm one of these "Amenti," too. That will give them something to talk about.*

● ● ●

Every so often the road curved to the coast and gave them a glimpse of the Gulf of Suez, but otherwise desert stretched to infinity around them. Carpenter supposed you could hide a lot in such a huge expanse of nothing. He decided it'd be a good idea to have them point out the hideout's location on a map, just in case they tried something sneaky again or he had to dump them. Of course, there was no map in the four wheel drive. It was mid-afternoon by the time they reached the next town. *These people can't even spell right*, Carpenter thought as they passed a sign that declared the city was called "ᶜAin Sukhna."

It was some tourist kind of place near the beach. The gas station they pulled into wouldn't have been out of place in America. Although Carpenter couldn't read anything except "GAS," he saw it had a small convenience shop that should have maps and the like. A street vendor was hawking food across the street, which prompted the woman to make some noise about getting something to eat. Carpenter debated, finally deciding against it. He didn't want to take the chance they'd say some kind of warning in Arabic while they faked haggling over falafel or whatever the hell they ate in this Godforsaken country. These two could survive for a couple days without food, and being a little weak should make them more manageable. Carpenter did get them some water as he paid for the gas and the map.

He used money he'd taken from his captives and the shopkeeper in Port Said. In his frustration, he'd left almost all the money he'd brought with him in the damn garment bag. American dollars, but he was sure these camel jockeys would snap up good old greenbacks. Instead he was reduced to robbing his kidnap victims. *A fucking joke, is what this is*.

The map had all of Egypt on one side and the Nile valley on the other. Carpenter laid it on the Expedition's hood, opened to the Egypt side. It was easy enough to find where they were, just at the start of where the Gulf of Suez curved in a final arc before the canal. There was a whole lot of country left, all of it colored a bland light gray except for the thin green ribbon down the center that was the Nile River. Plenty of places to hide a temple in all that desert, that was certain. Feeling a sudden delicious rush of fear, Carpenter cast a glance into the Expedition, where Ahmir and Sherin were cuffed through the steering wheel. They were looking at him—no, at the map, and the man was speaking rapidly. Much as Carpenter enjoyed drinking in their renewed panic, he didn't like what he saw. They had the look of people caught in the act.

Carpenter crumpled the map in one hand and stalked over to yank open the driver's side door. He shoved the printed paper in Ahmir's face and growled, "Show me where your fucking temple is, shitbird."

The guy was worked up, looking everywhere but at Carpenter and jabbering away. Carpenter had enough. He grabbed the cultist by the jaw and wrenched his head around. Looking him full in the face, Carpenter slammed him with his will and ordered him to calm down. Ahmir slumped in the seat like he'd been injected with a hefty dose of morphine.

"That's better," Carpenter said, maintaining eye contact. "Now, *show me* where your temple is on this map."

Ahmir groaned but his free hand flattened the map against the steering wheel and dragged in fits and jerks across it. Carpenter's anger before was nothing to the cold fury that possessed him when he saw where the finger stopped. The cultist was pointing to a place on the map about a hundred miles, as the crow flew, from their current location… a distinctive spot to the northeast, away from where they were headed currently.

"What; Cairo?" Cairo was a big city. But this guy had replied to the compulsion before that their temple was hidden in the desert. So somewhere around Cairo, then. "Where exactly? What is the name of the place?"

The cultist shook his head, but couldn't resist the command. "Saqqara. Pyramid… Sanakht Nebka."

Carpenter saw, then. A red star on the map, indicating ruins. Saqqara, all right. No names of any pyramids, but how hard could it be to find a pyramid? So then… "Where were you taking me instead? Huh? Tell me!"

Straining muscles relaxed; Ahmir had no problem revealing this. "To the Imkhu. Horus, the elders... they shatter your bones to powder. Scatter remains to the four corners of the earth!"

"Already been through that, buddy. Didn't take." Carpenter didn't need the editorializing; he got the point. He fought to stay calm. He needed these people still, needed whatever they knew about the Spell of Life. But he was done being nice. "All right. You had your chance, and you blew it. *You will take me to the pyramid of Sanakht Nebka now.*"

Carpenter pushed the command with every ounce of his will. It hit the cultist like a physical blow, rocking him back so hard his skull slammed against the headrest. All expression vanished from his face, his mouth hanging slack and eyes filming over. His cuffed right hand scrabbled for the Ford's ignition, the left moving to the ten o'clock position on the steering wheel. Carpenter saw the woman's face transform from concern to dread. She called Ahmir's name, then tried shaking him by the shoulder.

"Leave him be," Carpenter snapped. He took the map, having to tear it away since Ahmir's hand had closed around it when he grabbed the wheel. After climbing in the back, he handed the car keys forward. The cultist, moving in a determined yet clumsy motion, like a drunk automaton, started up the big four wheel drive and pulled out onto the road. As they swung around to head north, Carpenter noticed a handful of other patrons at the gas station watching their departure with puzzlement. He grinned and waved.

There was a turnoff about five miles north of ʿAin Sukhna; soon they were driving along a narrow two-lane road, heading toward the setting sun. Carpenter cooled from his fury and pondered whether giving the command had been a smart move. It was precise enough in its way, but it would take hours to complete. Sneaky old Ahmir would be under the compulsion until he drove them up to the front door of this hidden desert temple of his. There was a good chance his brain would fry as a result. Carpenter didn't care much about that in and of itself. But what if he needed the guy to do this immortality ritual? Too late to do anything about it now. He'd have to hope the woman could handle whatever needed doing.

And if not? He'd made it this far. He'd figure something out. He always did.

Darkness came fast upon them as they drove, the sun dropping below the horizon despite their best efforts to catch it. Some gusts of wind poked at the Ford a couple times, then the sandstorm was upon them. A mountain of blackness that Carpenter had assumed was nothing more dangerous than nightfall swept in like the end of the world had come. Visibility was gone in a heartbeat. The SUV rocked on its heavy-duty suspension as blasts of wind savaged it left and right. Tons of sand dropped on them out of nowhere only to be swept away in the next instant. The sand scoured hungrily at the Ford's finish and struck the windows like millions of tiny fists pounding to get inside.

As the sandstorm moaned and howled around them, Carpenter felt a thrill of unease. He recalled from his living days the tornado season in the Midwest, the savagery that could descend out of nowhere and go just as fast, leaving utter destruction in its wake. And during the interminable decades in the underworld, spirit-storms that arose out of nothing. Winds of chaos and oblivion that could shred a ghost to pieces in an instant. Undead he may be, but if they got in a wreck and he ended up with these two dead, he'd have a tough time getting resurrected as an immortal.

"It is early for khamsin," the woman said suddenly.

"What?"

"Khamsin—uh, sandstorm, yes?" Fear of the storm made her unusually forthcoming. "Winds... they come up in desert and go for many hours. Sometimes days. But not always so big so soon. So early in year."

Hours, maybe days, like this? Fuck. Only the insane or suicidal would keep going under such conditions. He tried to get Ahmir to stop, but the cultist was lost in the grip of compulsion. Carpenter could try another command, but that would probably burn out whatever was left of the fucker's mind.

Ahmir and the storm took the decision out of his hands. The road took a curve, but with about six inches of visibility they didn't even know it until the Ford was already thundering down a slope. The cultist remained aware enough beyond the scope of his orders that he'd shifted the vehicle into four-wheel drive when the sandstorm first hit. The Ford handled as well as it could over the shifting surface and went quite a ways before it hit a dune too steep to climb. As none of them wore seatbelts, the impact threw them forward. Carpenter bounced off the driver's seat and fell sideways onto the floor. Ahmir slammed into the steering wheel then ricocheted back into the seat while the woman, Sherin, cracked her forehead against the dashboard.

Carpenter was embarrassed but otherwise uninjured. His captives were dazed, though while the woman shook it off after a minute, the driver slumped into unconsciousness. Carpenter figured that was all for the best. He reached forward, shifted the car to PARK, shut off the engine and flicked off the lights to save the battery. Darkness engulfed them, gray swirls of sand moving around them in the night, the only sounds the moaning wind. After she got her bearings, the woman checked on her friend and then shot a look back at Carpenter. He couldn't see her face clearly enough to read her expression, and simply said, "We wait."

• • •

Carpenter wondered if that sandstorm was a sign. Halfway to this Saqqara place and they get a whole desert dumped on their heads? Thinking about it, he'd suffered one setback after another ever since he got to this country. Not all on the same scale, of course—the tanker rated a little more problematic than this cultist taking him on a tour of Ismailia. But if Carpenter was the superstitious sort, he might have thought there was something more at work here than mere coincidence.

Whatever the case, sandstorm did nothing more than cause a delay. The storm continued blowing for a number of hours. After cuffing his captives through the steering wheel, Carpenter took advantage of the time by dropping into a slumber. He'd been going for a while without a break; even the wicked had to rest sometime. His hammer clutched in the crook of his arm like a parody of a child's stuffed animal, Carpenter slipped into the dreamless catatonia that passed for sleep among the undead. When he roused himself six hours later, the night was clear and still. Ahmir and Sherin were asleep—though the man looked like he hadn't come to since ramming the dune.

Carpenter saw the Ford was about half-buried in sand. He got out on the passenger side and scrambled up to the top of the dune they'd run into. It rose over ten feet above the vehicle, and from atop it he had a decent view of the area. Stars shone down with brilliant clarity over the desert. There wasn't even a hint of wind; aside from the dark shape of the Expedition poking out of the sand dune, Carpenter wouldn't have believed there was ever a sandstorm. He couldn't see the road, but it couldn't be far. After sliding back down, he looked the Ford over carefully. It was pretty well stuck, but he was unwilling to just leave it there. The alternative was hitchhiking, and he didn't think that would work too well. *Walking down the highway with a couple handcuffed camel jockeys. Right.*

He took one more look at the SUV. Sand had swept up on the driver's side and the front was buried about a third of the way up the hood in the sand dune. He could

get it out, but he'd have to do some digging first. A look inside showed his captives were still out—not that they'd be much good, he suspected, being weak from hunger and all. That was all right. Carpenter was used to doing things for himself.

He stripped down to his undershirt and slacks and spent a few hours shoveling sand. It went much faster after he ripped the lid from the cubbyhole between the front seats to use as a scoop. It was still dark, dawn maybe an hour or so away, when he felt ready to get going. He tossed the cubbyhole lid away and caught movement out of the corner of his eyes. Reaction took over, days' worth of anticipation and frustration released in an instant. Carpenter had the pistol out and was firing before he fully registered what the target was.

The rounds from the Sig-Sauer tore apart the small shape, spraying flesh and gray matter with lethal effectiveness. Carpenter trudged over, his deathsight having as much trouble making out what it was as his normal vision did. Once he saw the victim, he couldn't help but laugh. He'd blown away a baby zombie.

It was, indeed, the corpse of a child, maybe ten years old. The gunshot wounds were only the latest injuries the decaying body had suffered. The flesh was torn and gray and withered almost down to the bone. Mummified by the heat, though not in the same fashion Carpenter was interested in. He understood the zombie couldn't have been very powerful. He barely sensed it to begin with, and four rounds from the automatic were sufficient to destroy it. Still, it got him to thinking.

This little zombie must have been drawn to Carpenter, just like the walking dead he'd run into back in Chicago. Made sense. He'd been on the move ever since he got to Egypt, which made it tough for an animated corpse to catch up. He was stuck here plenty long enough for one of them to get his scent. Carpenter thought about the corpses he'd collected to aid him in the States, first to take out the weak links in the hunter group and later to help him steal the Heart. He'd taken advantage of coincidence then, the happy accident that these creatures gathered near him when he had need of some extra muscle.

But what if it wasn't coincidence? Perhaps his subconscious was tapping into some new way of using his mental compulsion, but focused on his fellow walking dead. Carpenter shrugged. He could debate the theory of it with himself later. For now, it was enough to know that he had access to resources other than just himself. In fact…

As he walked back to the Ford, Carpenter focused his thoughts, calling out with his mind as hard as he could. He'd been able to boss around the animated dead with nothing more than strong mental commands. Perhaps he could also draw them to him in force doing the same thing. He didn't expect them to pop up from the ground, but hopefully some would show up in time to do him some good.

Carpenter was in better spirits as he stepped up to the four wheel drive. Popping open the driver's side door, he unlocked the handcuffs and manhandled Ahmir none too gently into the bed of the SUV. He gestured that Sherin should get in the back seat and cuffed her to Ahmir's ankle. Didn't look very comfortable, but Carpenter had other concerns. He'd hoped to have kept his shirt and jacket free of sand by removing them, but looked like sand got everywhere in this country. He suspected his dead flesh was chafing from deposits in creative locations, but his sense of touch was almost nonexistent by this point so it remained no more than an intellectual concern.

It took some grinding of gears and a lot of swearing, but Carpenter finally got the Ford moving. He had cleaned off the hood and most of the sand from the side, but there was still some solid resistance as he backed the thing up. He stayed in reverse all the way back up the slope, then turned on a fairly level patch and headed

northeast. Carpenter wasn't sure which way the road had curved during the storm, but if they didn't hit it going cross-country they should still run into the Nile sooner or later. His luck was up and running again, for they crossed the sand-covered asphalt only a few minutes later.

The desert turned to green within another hour. Coming over a rise, Carpenter saw the Nile stretched before him. He'd seen the mighty Mississippi, but he had to admit the Nile did it one better. It was a wide, calm brown ribbon running as far as the eye could see from the north and away south, as impressive in its quiet grandeur as Niagara Falls was in its raucous turbulence. The Nile lost some of its magnificence as they drew closer and found the view obscured by terrain and a roadway that paralleled the river. Carpenter referred to the torn map as he drove and saw that Saqqara should be just to the other side of the river and north a few miles. *Almost there*, he thought.

●●●

Saqqara was on a plateau that rose above the surrounding desert. Carpenter pulled the Expedition off the main road toward a ticket booth situated at the bottom of the plateau. He thought it was silly to pay for a tour when you could just walk in off the desert, but hey. He continued up and shortly reached the ruins. He was surprised at how expansive they were. A large blocky step pyramid was the focal point, with an enormous walled enclosure running around it, complete with a number of unearthed buildings. There were squat blocky shapes to either side of the central complex, more substantial than the buildings but not approaching the step pyramid in scale. Numerous low structures excavated to varying degrees wandered to the north. The Step-Pyramid of Djoser easily dominated the site. Huge and weathered, its once-crisp six steps had been eroded by time, giving it the appearance of a melted layer cake. Even so, the sight was impressive, especially when Carpenter spied the Great Pyramids of Giza off to the north.

He wasn't sure he could trust his weak eyes, but Sherin gave grudging confirmation that the ancient wonder was, indeed, but ten miles away. *Might just have to take in some sightseeing when this is all over.*

Carpenter put the Ford in gear and steered around the first tour bus of the morning, currently disgorging a small group of old men and women. Some pointed questions to Sherin, his remaining conscious hostage, had informed Carpenter that the temple, the so-called Pyramid of Sanakht Nebka, was actually west of the Djoser complex. It was part of a new excavation site. Driving around with a plume of dust in their wake, Carpenter saw an adjoining plateau with some marker boundaries denoting an archaeological dig. He didn't see any pyramid, just a lot of sand and a couple half-buried buildings. Drawing closer, Carpenter realized his deathsight was picking up a ghostly shimmer through the area, a spiritual vibration that was starting to interfere with his vision.

An armed guard stood near the trail and waved them down. Carpenter rolled down the window and smiled as the man approached. He was too close to success to bother with this idiot. As the guard opened his mouth, Carpenter said, "Forget we were ever here," and pushed hard. The man blinked hard a few times, mouth opening and closing like a fish gasping for breath. As Carpenter drove on, he noted in the rearview mirror that the guard was still standing there, looking around in mild confusion. *Another lobotomy to add to the list,* Carpenter thought. Feeling a brief wave of dizziness, Carpenter realized abusing his ability in this fashion was taking its toll. He drew upon the power in his hammer to shake off the lethargy seeping into his bones.

The track dipped through a depression that separated the Djoser complex from the new excavation site and came around to an ad hoc parking area. The spot was nearest a few low buildings, apparently unearthed only recently. The plateau continued to slope upward

from that point. Two other vehicles were already there; Carpenter pulled up next to a twenty year old BMW and cut the engine. He glanced in back; the woman had the broken look of someone who's committed the ultimate betrayal and now waits for judgment to be passed upon her. Carpenter couldn't see the man, but assumed he was still comatose. He had some more questions for Sherin about this place, but wanted to wait until he gave it a once-over himself.

That opportunity didn't come. He was still looking around from the comfort of the Expedition's driver's seat when he spotted movement in the rearview mirror. A slight Asian woman had emerged from one of the partially excavated buildings and was headed his way. He wasn't concerned; this was the cultists' car to begin with, so they belonged, as far as anyone knew. Looking back through the rear window, Carpenter's deathsight showed the vibrant spirit of a mummy. "Son of a bitch."

The cultist in the back seat turned as well and started shouting as soon as she saw the Asian lady. Carpenter tried to shut her up but she wasn't facing him, so his force of will was useless. The mummy heard the yelling and slowed to a stop, reaching into a satchel she carried slung over her shoulder. If she had anything like the crap Simbah was throwing, Carpenter was in for a bad time of it. He had to stop this before it got out of hand.

Carpenter popped the door open and sprinted toward the mummy. Her head snapped around at the sound and her eyes grew wide. She cried out something in Chinese that sounded suspiciously like it ended in his name. "Stop!" he yelled, slamming his will toward her and hoping she understood him. The command held only for a second, but that was all Carpenter needed. He caught her with a right hook that cracked her jaw and sent her sprawling in a heap. He shot a quick look around. The tourists were almost a half a mile away, but if they were paying attention they might've seen something. He just had to hope they were too busy oohing and aahing over the ruins. Carpenter checked to make sure she was out before taking off her satchel and throwing it as hard as he could. Then he uncuffed Sherin from Ahmir and dragged her over. "Help her up," he directed, hustling them both to the building the Asian lady had just come through.

Straight razor in one hand and Sig-Sauer in the other, the Heart of Osiris pulsing quietly in his pocket, Maxwell Carpenter entered the lost pyramid of Sanakht Nebka.

THIRTEEN

Nicholas made a patting gesture with his hands. "You'll get your chance at Carpenter soon enough, Thea. But first, we're going to wait for Faruq to return with your things—"

"Hey!" Thea and Jake cried out as one.

Nicholas went with a diplomatic explanation. "I suspected you'd be eager to head out once you learned what I was offering, so I sent Faruq to get your belongings to save time."

Jake seemed to buy it, but Thea wasn't in the mood to cut much slack. "Right; whatever. So what's 'second'?"

"Second we can actually do first, since we're waiting. I want to make sure you understand the gravity of what's involved, here. I might do things that don't make immediate sense, or that may appear to be downright threatening. Especially when considered in your current frame of mind, which I expect is pretty paranoid. That's understandable. You're totally out of your element here, and dealing with forces whose agendas are mysteries to you. I'd like to make sure you're totally comfortable with the situation before we hit the road. But we just don't have time for that. So I'm going to ask you to take it on faith that we're not going to double-cross you when things get hairy— and in the same vein, we'll extend our trust to you."

Thea cocked her head to one side. "You realize you've just made me more suspicious."

"Whups!" Nicholas chuckled. "Look, I'm saying this now simply because I don't want to stop in the middle of

something so I can reassure you that I'm not about to screw you over."

"Incidentally," Jake said suddenly, "is there a native Egyptian bird with a long, skinny tail, kinda like a lizard's?"

"What?" Nicholas gave Jake a puzzled look. "Of course not."

"Huh. Maybe it's migrating, then." He pointed into the brilliant blue sky, shielding his eyes with his other hand. "That, or there's something kind of unusual flying above us."

They looked up. Nicholas gave an excited yell and held his arm up, elbow crooked and fist high. Thea and Jake watched in astonishment as a whip-thin black lizard with a glossy feathered wings swooped down to alight on his arm.

"What the hell is that?"

"This is Xian," Nicholas said, smiling at the small dragon held tight to his wrist, curling its long tail up his forearm. "Belongs to a friend of mine. Haven't seen you in a while, big guy. What are you doing here? Where's Lu Wen?"

Xian minced along Nicholas' arm, its needle-sharp talons dug into his skin. Nicholas ignored the discomfort as best he could. The dragon was agitated, which meant something was wrong with his creator. Smart as the enchanted creature was, it couldn't speak, so Nicholas interrogated it with simple "yes/no" questions.

"Is Lu Wen all right?" This got the creature even more worked up; Nicholas took that to mean she was in trouble, but Xian didn't know how much. "Is she at the lost pyramid?" This got a decisive nod. Nicholas didn't need to frame another question. Realization hit him head-on. He checked the compass scarab. He couldn't tell how far the Heart was, but there was no mistaking the compass pointed almost due south. The direction of Saqqara, and of the pyramid of Sanakht Nebka.

In the modern day, Saqqara was just one of many locations where excavated ruins gave evidence of the majesty of ancient Egypt. Like Edfu, it was also a place of great spiritual power, one of select sites in the Near and Middle East that housed a wellspring of supernatural force. Perhaps a dozen other locations in the vastness of Egypt held similar power. These sites had gained newfound importance after mighty Osiris' awakening. When he bestowed the new Spell of Life to his faithful, he revealed it was necessary to perform the ritual upon one of these places of power. The vibrant energy was a key component to the ceremony; without it, the expectant spirit would never be bound to the prepared corpse.

Nicholas had led Carpenter to believe the Heart was the key of the resurrection, not these special sites. So how did Maxwell Carpenter learn of it? The cultists, of course. The zombie must have used that mind control ability to interrogate them in Port Said. Then blew up the tankers to cover his trail? No way of knowing. Important thing was that Carpenter was there now, and was past due for an ass-kicking.

●●●

Carpenter found the spiritual dissonance increased as they made their way down a tunnel carved under the desert. The barrier separating the realms of the living and the dead was very thin, here. Carpenter thought he could almost reach out and tear aside the fabric of reality, step through to the shadowlands. He felt the straight razor tremble as if in eagerness at the thought. But he was here to do the opposite. He searched for immortality, so that he would never again face the chilling realm of the underworld.

The cultist shuffled along in front of him, half-carrying, half-dragging the mummy chick. The tunnel headed down at a steady angle for a couple hundred feet or so. Lights spaced evenly down the length provided adequate illumination. At last they turned a corner; the tunnel opened onto what looked like a long antechamber. Two guys, a towel-head and a white fella, were brushing the dirt from some mural along one wall. Identical expressions of shock and dismay appeared on their faces as they took in Carpenter and his captives. "Hey there, you sorry sons of bitches," he said with a grin. "Feel up to a little hocus-pocus?"

Some shouting and feeble efforts at resistance followed. Two more cultists rushed through the doorway in the wall opposite the mural, but numbers made no real difference. Carpenter had the physical advantage of power and the psychological edge of having just kicked the ass of their mummy friend. With the Asian honey as an object lesson, he herded the five cultists back through the doorway into what turned out to be some kind of burial chamber.

He understood that he was inside the so-called pyramid of Sanakht Nebka, buried underneath a whole lot of sand. It looked like this chamber was the main room in the place. It was sizable, almost thirty feet long and fifteen feet wide, with a ceiling twelve feet high. It had a series of small alcoves running down each of the long sides, with statues in six of the alcoves. An alabaster sarcophagus dominated the chamber's center. The room had two entrances—the doorway they'd just come through and a central shaft that went all the way to the top. From the look of the shaft, the pyramid wasn't completely buried. He could see a brilliant blue rectangle of sky three hundred feet up.

Seeing some toolboxes to one side, Carpenter laughed. He snatched up a roll of duct tape and directed a couple of cultists to wrap up the mummy. (From their blubbering, Carpenter figured her name was Lu Wen Koo-something). Even if she was as strong as Carpenter, she'd have a tough time getting free of the tape that wrapped her arms tight against her torso and bound up her legs. And with a strip of tape for a gag, she wouldn't be raising a ruckus with sudden commands.

ANDREW BATES

The mummy might help with the ceremony, but Carpenter was playing it safe. These immortal types had power; he'd have an easier time keeping the mortals in line if she was rendered harmless. He considered just killing Lu Wen, but then she might come back to life at some critical point and screw everything up. Besides, he might need to extract some detail the cultists didn't know, which would be tough to do if she was dead.

She was just coming to when he dragged her to a corner just inside the burial chamber entrance. He smiled and patted her on the head, then moved over to stand behind the sarcophagus by the exit. The cultists were clustered at the opposite end of the burial chamber. Sherin had chattered away in Arabic while the mummy got taped up. Seemed she filled them in on just how bad-ass Carpenter was, for they looked utterly cowed. Aside from staring at Carpenter or Lu Wen, all they did was stand there and tremble.

"How many of you speak English?" Carpenter asked. Sherin, of course; only the white guy raised his hand. From the blank stares the others gave him, Carpenter felt confident the others weren't faking. To the woman and the white guy, he said, "Cooperate and I'll let you walk out of here. Got that?"

He was telling the truth; he didn't care about these people as long as they could give him what he wanted. It appeared Carpenter could make whatever claims he felt like. From the looks on their faces, the cultists didn't believe a word he'd said. No problem; if he couldn't coerce the information, he'd just force it out of them. Try the easy way first, at least. He reached into his pocket and slapped a bound object on the center of the sarcophagus.

"You know what this is?" he asked, flipping away the cloth from around the bundle. Exposed to the halogen lights hung in the burial chamber, the Heart of Osiris was a roughly pear-shaped object with a red cast to it so dark it was almost black. Again, it had a different appearance from

before. Carpenter suppressed a shudder and tapped the sarcophagus lid next to the Heart. "See this? Huh? Take a good look."

There was a collective intake of breath. Yes, it looked like Sherin had told them everything. Carpenter looked over at the mummy. Her eyes flickered between Carpenter and the artifact, a mix of emotions scampering across her face.

The white guy stepped forward, swearing at Carpenter as he grabbed for the artifact. Carpenter backhanded the guy, slamming him into one of the alcove walls and fracturing his jaw. "Cut that shit out," Carpenter said. "Time to get down to business. So, you going to tell me how this thing can make me immortal?"

Sherin seemed to have forgotten she knew English. Sure; now that she was with friends she'd found her backbone again. She picked up where the white guy left off, firing Arabic swear words and getting her pals all riled up to boot.

Carpenter slammed a hand on the sarcophagus lid with a hard crack that silenced everyone. Pointing a finger at the woman, Carpenter focused his will and demanded, "Can you tell me how to do a ceremony that can make people immortal?"

She gurgled and spat, then said, "Yes."

Green light flared in Carpenter's eye. "All right, then. What's the first step?"

• • •

Thea wasn't happy with the way things were going. This guy Sforza teased them with the possibility that they could track down Carpenter but he refused to give them any significant details of who he was or what was really going down. And now, they were about to go after the zombie son of a bitch but Nicholas wouldn't cough up any weapons for them. She wasn't big on guns, but she felt naked going on a hunt without at least a pistol. She and Jake hadn't brought their weapons from the States.

She'd figured they might get something from Rafiq, but it didn't look like they'd meet up with him until after all this was over. *Assuming we make it through this alive.*

"I thought we were on the same side," she said, trying one last time. "You don't even have some old .38 Special lying around? What, are we supposed to rely on our wits and a swift kick to the head?"

"I agree we have a common interest, but I don't know yet if we're on the same side." He moved the weird flying lizard to his shoulder and muttered something to Ibrahim, who dashed into the mausoleum.

"Thea, I don't mind not having a gun," Jake said.

She shot him a look. *You are not helping.* "Fine. Even granting that, what was it you were just saying about trust? This would go a long way to easing our own minds about you guys, if nothing else." Her sixth sense told her that she could, in fact, trust what Nicholas Sforza had been telling them. The threads of possibility seemed favorable concerning him. Even so, that didn't mean she was just going to roll over and do whatever he said.

Nicholas seemed to ponder that and nodded. "That's a good point. I can see how it might look if I were in your shoes. All right; come on."

He led them into the tomb and past an ornate sarcophagus. A narrow panel in the back wall opened onto a staircase, the one they'd come up blindfolded a short while before. Thea had suspected they'd gone through some underground rooms on their way here, but she was surprised at what she saw. The chamber they stepped into was large; electric lights set in torch brackets provided plenty of illumination to reveal vibrant murals on the walls done in the style of ancient Egypt. Doorways opened off in a number of directions. Clearly, this was part of an extensive complex.

Nicholas led them down a tunnel to a smaller room that looked like it was set aside for storage. He left them standing in the hall, so Thea only got a

glimpse of unlabeled boxes and half-open wardrobes with clothing. Nicholas stepped back out, holding a shotgun and an automatic pistol. "This is about all we have, besides the rifle Ibrahim's carrying, of course."

"Fantastic; thanks." Thea took the pistol, a Glock 9mm. "Any extra clips?"

"Just one." He pulled a clip from his pocket, then held the shotgun toward Jake.

"This is a little heavy-duty," Jake said, eyeing the Spas-12 with distrust.

Thea chucked him on the shoulder. "Chicks dig guys with big guns. Really, Jake, do you want to take the chance of not having it?"

Jake took the shotgun with a heavy sigh, though he held it carefully with his fingers away from the trigger.

"Amenti?" Ibrahim's voice echoed down the corridor. "Faruq has returned!"

"Right. If we're done with all this, what say we get on the road?"

"Lead on," Thea replied, checking the safety before dropping the Glock in the side pocket of her cargo pants.

"Let me ask you something," Nicholas said as they hustled down the passageway. "How did you get dragged into all this to begin with?"

"You mean Carpenter and monsters and mysterious artifacts?"

"Yeah."

"Chalk it up to a terminal case of curiosity." She flashed him a mischievous smile. "You never answered my question, you know."

"What question was that?"

"Just what are you? Your… employees or whatever you want to call them called you 'Amenti.' We, well, we kinda think that means 'mummy.'"

Nicholas laughed. "Yeah? That's funny. And what do you think a mummy is?"

"There's the question, isn't it?"

"I'm nothing like Carpenter, if that's what you're wondering. I'm a living, breathing person."

Thea had noticed Nicholas Sforza breathed, moved and acted in all ways like a normal human being. In contrast, although Carpenter gave the appearance of life, a sharp eye could discern that he was somehow *wrong*, that he didn't fit in. So Nicholas' claim wasn't exactly news.

She caught a playful glint in his eye. Apparently if she was going to be coy, he'd be coy right back. *Fine by me, tough guy. I'll figure you out soon enough.*

•••

Carpenter felt the presence of the first zombie just as he began extracting the resurrection ceremony from the woman cultist. Turning to face the doorway, Carpenter saw an animated horror, its bony fingers scraping at the stone wall as it shuffled in. Once it saw him, the corpse grew more animated, faint grunts gusting from its half-rotted throat.

Carpenter felt nausea in his atrophied stomach even as a smile drew across his face. The creature stopped a few feet away and did a sloppy job of clicking its heels together, one arm shooting out stiffly before it. Looking closer, Carpenter saw the zombie wore the remains of a German military uniform. *A fucking Nazi zombie? What the hell would a German be doing dead in Egypt?* Carpenter was dead when World War II started, and he ran across a few restless spirits in the underworld who'd died during the fighting. It took a minute, but at last he recalled that there was a whole theatre of battle in northern Africa. Carpenter wasn't sure he wanted some Nazi helping him out, dead or otherwise. Still, he didn't exactly have much else to work with.

The zombie was in surprisingly good condition, especially considering how long he'd been dead. Though not as whole as Carpenter, the soldier was merely gamey instead full-on decayed. Carpenter had run into few

zombies that were close to being as self-aware and physically restored as he was. The majority was husks in an advanced state of decay, all dried sinew and rotting flesh. The soldier landed somewhere in the middle: clearly a mess, but not reduced to an automaton. Carpenter recalled the zombies who'd been drawn to him in the past had all been in pretty sorry condition.

Was it something to do with his superior state? Did they sense his power and, what? Think he could show them the trick? "Is that it, Fritz?" he asked. "You hoping I can show you how I got this way? Not much better than where you're at, believe me. Why d'you think I'm in this Godforsaken country, anyway?"

The dead soldier worked its ruined jaw and groaned something in puzzlement.

"Good point." Carpenter replied. *No philosophical talk with the corpses,* he chastised himself. *Too much for the mush in their heads to take.* "Okay, Fritz. Why don't you wait out by the tunnel entrance and keep watch? Make sure nobody tries to jump us. Oh, and knock out all the lights in the tunnel when you go, too."

The soldier shuffled off after another salute. Carpenter was just continuing the arduous process of extracting information from Sherin without frying her brain when two more animated corpses showed up. Apparently Fritz understood that others like him had permission to pass. Each of these was so far gone it was almost impossible to determine what they'd been in life. Didn't matter; they were more muscle and would help keep the cultists under wraps as Carpenter got deeper into things. As he had them move into position—one to stand by Lu Wen and the other over with the cultists—Carpenter realized he didn't have to speak his orders; a focused thought did the trick. He needed to think hard to get the corpse's attention, but it wasn't very difficult. From personal experience, Carpenter knew ghosts didn't have any problems understanding one another. The language of death was universal. He must be tapping into this somehow to communicate with fellow walking dead.

Carpenter still had no idea why the walking dead were drawn to him. Similarly, he'd had no way of knowing if focusing on bringing them to him would even work. He was quite pleased with the results. There was no telling how many animated corpses would come to him if he were to stay put. For now, three should be enough.

• • •

Nicholas clutched the door handle as Ibrahim drove the Audi with a recklessness remarkable even for Cairene drivers. Faruq stayed behind to contact any other groups he could reach. In case Nicholas failed to recover the Heart, forces would be converging on Saqqara by nightfall. The Amenti would recover the Heart one way or another.

Thea and Jake shared the backseat with a cooler stocked with bottled water that smacked into them as it slid with each one of the car's sudden twists and turns. As far as Nicholas could tell from reading the replacement compass scarab, the Heart hadn't moved in some time. Whatever Carpenter was doing, he should still be in Saqqara by the time they arrived. The ruins were only fifteen miles south of the city, and the way Ibrahim was driving they should reach it in as many minutes… if the Audi didn't get wrecked on the way.

Despite the air conditioner's best efforts, the Audi was a sauna. Nicholas was glad he'd used henna that morning to paint symbols on his left biceps that protected him from the oppressive heat. The charm was temporary, lasting no more than a week, but it should be enough to keep him from collapsing due to dehydration and sunstroke. Nicholas shot a glance at Ibrahim, who drove with fevered intensity. The amulets he wore—gifts from Nicholas, the last remaining in his leather case—caught the sun in brief flashes as the Audi caromed down the road. The charms would offer Ibrahim some protection against harm and

bestow enhanced reflexes. Nicholas had also cautioned Ibrahim repeatedly not to be a hero; he suspected such words fell on deaf ears. He had to hope that the amulets were enough to keep his mortal friend alive in any conflict to come.

Thea and Jake didn't have any supernatural protection. Nicholas had considered lending them something, but he only had so many amulets and he and Ibrahim took a higher priority. They seemed to have a good idea of the stakes involved, and he couldn't waste his time holding their hands in this. The only important thing was recovering the Heart; everything else was just distraction.

The drive settled down somewhat when they broke free of the tangle of city traffic. The Audi roared onto a southbound road that took them past the Great Pyramids at Giza. Saqqara was only minutes away.

"What's so special about this place?" Jake asked when it looked like they weren't about to tumble into a fiery crash.

"Saqqara? It's where the pyramid was born. You've heard of the Step Pyramid of Djoser? It's the work of a guy named Imhotep. He gave those who followed the inspiration for those things right over there." Nicholas pointed at the mammoth pyramids looming off to their right. "The foundations at Saqqara were laid almost five thousand years ago. Civilization was a little less advanced back then, y'know? And this one man, Imhotep, had the vision and brilliance to create things others of his time hadn't even dreamed."

"And what's this 'lost pyramid'?" Thea inquired. She rested an arm across the back of the driver's seat and directed a frankly curious look at Nicholas.

Momentarily dazzled by the brilliant green eyes so close, Nicholas turned to look at the pyramids. "Okay, we've danced around the issue of the supernatural, but it's clear we're talking about some ancient powers, here.

There are places of spiritual strength throughout this whole region and extending into the Middle East. Saqqara is one of them. I suppose it's possible that this force, this power, is what led the pharaohs of the first dynasties to build their tombs there. Among them was a pharaoh of the Third Dynasty, Sanakht Nebka. He ruled following the brief six-year reign of Sekhemkhet, the successor to Djoser. Djoser was, among other things, patron to Imhotep. The original Renaissance man, was Imhotep—he was a scribe, architect, physician, priest and seer. Intellect without equal. Anyway, in addition to designing the Step Pyramid of Djoser, Imhotep also designed Sekhemkhet's tomb—but it was never completed due to the pharaoh's early death. Though quite old himself by then, Imhotep dedicated himself to preparing the funerary complex for Nebka, modifying the designs meant for Sekhemkhet. He died before it was finished, so they only ever completed the step pyramid and core temple—normally a whole enclosure wall and supporting structures were built as well. The finished tomb for Nebka was a grander version of Djoser's step pyramid, a wonder of its age."

Thea pulled her lips down in a frown. "So how come we've never heard of it. I mean, Djoser and the Giza pyramids, sure. But this Nebka guy?"

"Yeah, well, unfortunately for his role in history, Nebka didn't choose his burial site as well as Djoser did. He had the pyramid built on a plateau maybe a half-mile from his predecessors. This gave him a commanding view of the west—kind of a big deal among ancient Egyptians. The setting sun, following Ra's chariot into the afterlife, that kind of thing. Problem was, thanks to a quirk in geography, the pyramid caught the brunt of weather patterns sweeping down. Sand slowly covered the step pyramid over the course of centuries. By the later dynasties, people remembered something about a pyramid to Nebka but nobody knew where it was."

"Okay, smart guy. How did you find it, then?"

"I didn't. But if you mean the archaeologists, I expect they stumbled across it. Saqqara's riddled with about three thousand years' worth of lesser burial tombs aside from the ones we already know about. It was a matter of time, y'know?" That wasn't quite accurate. In truth, some of the Imkhu recalled the long lost pyramid of Sanakht Nebka and directed a Cult of Isis sect posing as ubiquitous archaeologists to find it. Nicholas hadn't been there himself, but Lu Wen had told him they had already opened an access tunnel from a nearby mastaba and had unearthed the lost pyramid's capstone. They were in the process of refurbishing the interior—at least, they were before Carpenter showed up. Nicholas had a suspicion that the pyramid would be in need of extensive repairs when the day was done.

•••

Carpenter knew things would go wrong sooner or later. The guy with the fractured jaw groaned something in Arabic to his buddies while Carpenter was busy pulling information from Sherin. A second later they'd all pulled knives and attacked. Carpenter realized almost immediately that the aggression was a feint. As three of the cultists came at Carpenter and his zombies, the fourth drew his blade across the woman cultist's, then tore the blade across his own neck. The zombie standing behind them didn't react fast enough, and could only watch as the cultists bled to death.

Carpenter knocked the knife away from his opponent, breaking his forearm in the process. The straight razor was in his hand a heartbeat later, but Carpenter resisted using it. He needed these people alive. Instead, he grabbed the cultist's other arm and squeezed hard enough to snap the bone, then tossed the punk aside.

Carpenter yelled for his zombies to restrain themselves, but it was too late. The other English-speaking cultist tried to get past the other zombie and free the mummy, who was struggling against her bonds in the corner. The zombie was having none of it. The thing lashed out, its right hand snatching the cultist's wrist and twisting while its left swung up to the neck and wrenched the man's head around. The cultist dropped to the floor like a broken kite.

The last cultist had grabbed up the Heart and made a dash for the exit. Carpenter and his zombies were slowed just enough by their own attackers that the little bastard actually made it out of the burial chamber. Carpenter ran after him, sending his thoughts ahead to the thing guarding the other end of the tunnel. Courageous the guy might be, but he never had a chance. Fritz was on him before he got halfway up the corridor. One solid backhand caught the cultist on the temple and bounced him off the wall. He fell in a heap, the Heart falling from his fingers into the dirt.

Carpenter snatched up the Heart and dragged the dazed cultist back to the burial chamber. The cultists' attack was surprising, and embarrassing. He'd been so overconfident he hadn't bothered frisking them. But it was the committed look in the cultists' eyes that got to him. To kill your friend and then yourself like that? It took balls. Huge ones, dragging in the dirt. "Zealous bunch of idiots," he said, his voice a mix of disgust and respect. Futile gesture, perhaps, but it'd been damn effective. Two cultists who remained alive... and neither one spoke English. Carpenter wouldn't get anything out of them. He couldn't make them do anything if they didn't know what he was saying. He'd noticed how they were worried when he was grilling their friend. The fuckers didn't actually know what Carpenter was doing until the white guy regained his senses and told them.

After dumping the guy to the sandy floor, Carpenter noticed the straight razor had leapt into his hand again. In the past, he'd been disturbed when the thing moved with a mind of its own, but now a smile blossomed on his face. Hefting the Heart, Carpenter turned

to Lu Wen, still bound and gagged in the corner. "I know you understand me," he said, readying his will. "Looks like I'm not going to get the blow-by-blow on this Spell of Life thing. Can just two of these guys do it?"

Forced by the compulsion, Lu Wen gave a grudging nod.

"All right then, since I can't order these guys to do it, let's try some old-fashioned persuasion instead."

Carpenter placed the Heart on the sarcophagus. After flicking the razor open, he dragged the glittering blade across the artifact. Smoke curled up as the unnatural metal scored the Heart's surface, and a few thick drops of some golden fluid welled up in the cut. At the same time, a tremor shook the room, a faint shower of grit falling from the ceiling. The cultists cried out in dismay and clutched one another while the mummy Lu Wen screamed through her gag and strained against the duct tape that bound her. Carpenter looked over at her. "That was just a scratch. Unless you want to see what happens if I really slice into it, I suggest you order these guys to deal straight with me."

Palpable hatred burned in Lu Wen's eyes, then her gaze dropped to the wounded Heart. She nodded, her head moving the barest fraction.

● ● ●

Thea had focused her sixth sense when she saw Nicholas Sforza outside the hotel that morning. She'd kept it going ever since, and was feeling the mental exhaustion from trying to hold her heightened perception together. When the Audi turned west to head up to the plateau, Thea got her first good look at the ruins of Saqqara. The shock of it knocked her right out of her hyper-aware state.

"Oh, wow," she gasped.

Jake looked around. "What?"

"There's a… holy… it looked like the end of a rainbow." She laughed in delight at the marvel, even as a wedge of pain dug into her temple.

"What do you mean?" Ibrahim asked.

"I saw this shimmering light coming down in an arc," Thea explained. She'd seen it only for an instant, but it was burned on her memory. Even with her mild color-blindness, the tones had been breathtaking. Less a rainbow than a grand curve of aurora borealis, rising high into the midday sky. "It was glowing and fluxing—is that a word?—and went waaay up… It was *beautiful*."

Thea saw Nicholas Sforza and his Egyptian friend giving her a strange look. *They don't know about our sixth sense.* "Uh, I can see things, sometimes," she said with a lame smile. Nicholas had said something about this area being a place of great spiritual power; had she seen that on some level beyond normal sight? Thea wanted to look again, but she decided to wait until her headache eased off a little.

"Right," Nicholas replied. He seemed about to say something, then shook his head. "Much as I'd like to talk hallucinations, we have to figure out an approach. You see around there, past the Djoser ruins? Couple of cars and some fresh excavations. That's the tunnel entrance to Nebka's tomb. I can confirm the Heart's about two or three hundred feet to the north, which should put it right inside the lost pyramid."

"Is there any other way in?" Jake asked.

"A ventilation shaft that goes straight down to the burial chamber."

"How far is that?"

"About three hundred feet."

"Okay, so only one way in or out, practically speaking."

"Unless we need to get in there fast," Nicholas confirmed. He didn't look like he was joking about jumping down the ventilation shaft, though. "I can go down the shaft, but I'll knock down a bunch of dirt and sand as I go. Big giveaway."

"So—" Thea broke off what she was about to say as they pulled up next to a guard watching the approach

to the excavation site. There was something strange about him… "Look at this guy. Like he's having some kind of fit."

Nicholas and Jake leaned over to the driver's side to get a decent look. The guard was looking right at them—more correctly, about a foot over the top of the Audi—but it was obvious he didn't actually see anything. His eyes were wide open with a washed-out, filmy look. Salty tracks of dried tears coursed down each cheek, and his mouth fluttered like he couldn't think of what to say.

"Jesus," Jake said, "looks like he hasn't blinked in hours. See his eyes?"

Thea nodded, her mouth dry. Just the kind of twisted thing Carpenter might pull. Grimacing through the pain in her skull, Thea called forth her sixth sense. Wasted tendrils of possibility withered around the guard like leaves scorched by the sun. Whatever else he may have done in life, the chance had been stripped from him; he was nothing but a shell now. *Soon, Carpenter,* she promised. *You'll get yours very soon, you son of a bitch.*

• • •

Carpenter looked down at Lu Wen. "You care to repeat that?"

The mummy sat straight as she could, bound as she was. Carpenter had removed the tape from her mouth so she could talk to the two remaining cultists. Instead, she'd started in on some crazed attempt to talk Carpenter into surrendering. He was too amused to do anything at the moment but stare at her.

"Stop this now." Lu Wen said. "You cannot hope to succeed. Even if you somehow learn the Spell of Life, your soul will not survive judgment. Your spirit will be destroyed by the Judges of Ma'at, your existence ended. We care only about the Heart. Leave it whole and depart immediately. You may yet survive for some time, even if only in the awful parody of life you now suffer."

"You know what I've been through to get here, honey? I can't begin to tell you all the shit I've had to deal with. But I'm supposed to drop everything and walk away on your say so? You got some nerve, I'll grant you that. But if you don't cut the shit and get these guys to work, I'll have Fritz here start slicing your precious Heart into lunch meat." Carpenter had brought the Nazi corpse down since it was the most self-aware of his charges. Guard duty was brainless enough, so one of the decrepit zombies had that post now. Carpenter felt confident Fritz could carry out his orders without screwing up at some crucial moment. The only thing that bothered him was putting the straight razor in the soldier's hand. Leery as Carpenter was of the thing, he felt naked without it. Indeed, he'd expect it wouldn't allow itself to leave his possession. To his surprise, it had slapped easily into Fritz's palm. The zombie now stood by the sarcophagus, straight razor held over the Heart. Carpenter had instilled a command that Fritz should cut the artifact at the first sign of danger to Carpenter. He'd spoken the words aloud although it was literally the thought that counted. From Lu Wen's expression, it was clear she had no doubt the corpse would carry out the order. Despite this, she continued to defy Carpenter.

"You would do nothing more than assure your own destruction," she countered.

Carpenter felt the heat of anger steal over him. "Yeah? Maybe I should have Fritz practice on you a bit first, then. Think that might change your tune?"

"Perhaps you don't truly grasp what it means to be immortal. Threats such as yours mean nothing to someone for whom death has no meaning."

"I got a million ideas on how to kill someone. Love to try 'em out on you." Carpenter's lip curled at barely contained anger. "You don't think death has meaning? Spend some time with me."

"What can you do? You are nothing more than a corpse that is too stubborn to lie still." Lu Wen gave

Carpenter a cold look. "You have no chance of succeeding in this. Even now our forces are converging. My brethren will take the Heart of Osiris from you and then send you and your fellow abominations back to the realm where you belong. Every second you stand here, you come that much closer to destruction."

"You better be sure you do the job right, lady. 'Cause if you don't, you can damn well bet I will never rest until I track your ass down."

"I have given you fair warning," she said. Then, after taking a deep breath, Lu Wen barked something in an ancient tongue. Another tremor went through the chamber, this one not as strong as when Carpenter wounded the Heart. Carpenter's weak eyes almost didn't catch the sudden motion in time to dodge as one of the statues leapt from an alcove and swung its staff at him. He saw all six of the statues were moving, in fact—though his deathsight didn't register anything at all. *What the hell are these things?* No time to worry about it. He commanded Fritz and the other zombie to attack while he went for the mummy.

But she was already getting free, another of the statues cutting away the tape that bound her. Carpenter reached for the pistol to drop her fast when something whipped past him. It was his other zombie's head. Two of the statues had chopped it to pieces in a few seconds. Carpenter glanced around and saw that Fritz was accounting for himself well enough, thanks to assistance from the devilishly sharp razor. Then Carpenter saw the last statue was moving for the Heart as its compatriot beat Fritz back toward one of the alcoves.

Everything's going to shit again! His clever plans dashed, just when he'd been so close. Lightning-quick, Carpenter grabbed the Heart and ran for the doorway.

• • •

Nicholas looked at the tunnel entrance with a frown of frustration. They'd parked the Audi as close to the tunnel as they felt comfortable. They sat inside with the windows rolled down, but with no breeze it was breathtakingly hot. "Okay, Thea. I don't disagree that it'd be a bad idea to just go charging in, but do you have any reason why? If it's just Carpenter, I'd assume he's with the Heart. By my reckoning, it's still in the burial chamber."

"Remember when we met the devil Carpenter in Chicago," Ibrahim asked. "By that building?"

"The Sears Tower? Shit, that's right." He looked back at Thea and Jake. "That's where Carpenter jumped us and stole the Heart. He had, like, four or five animated corpses in a truck with him."

"So, he might have some here, too," Jake said.

"For all I know, the prick has a dozen walking corpses hidden around here just waiting for us to show up."

Thea shook her head. "I don't sense danger from the surrounding area. It's all coming from inside this pyramid of yours."

Nicholas quirked an eyebrow. *"Don't sense danger"?* "Okay, but I still don't see an alternative to—"

Just then something black streaked through the passenger side window. Xian ran around across Nicholas and Ibrahim's laps, making odd croaking noises and fluttering its wings.

"Where's that thing been?" Thea wondered.

"I think it's been keeping an eye on Lu Wen from the ventilation shaft." From Xian's immediate loud squawk, it appeared Nicholas was correct. "Considering how he's acting, I'm guessing something bad is going down. That means end of planning; let's go."

Thea's hand clamped down on his shoulder in a surprisingly strong grip. "Wait! You're right; there is something... and it looks like the variables have changed."

"We do not have time for this cryptic bullshit, woman!"

"No, listen! I think... Yes, if you can, get the hell down that shaft right now. We'll go in the front."

There was something to her tone that made Nicholas want to jump up and go. Since he didn't have time to argue, he decided to go with it. They piled out of the Audi and headed for the tunnel, Xian shooting into the air in a fast arc as they went. Nicholas dug something from his pocket as he ran and tossed it ahead of them. Channeling the vibrant energy of his spirit, he muttered a command. The carving swelled and gained substance, and Sherlock crouched before them. The enchanted dog, as black as coffee left too long on the warmer, looked around with expectant eyes. Nicholas sprinted for the capstone, calling over his shoulder, "Take Sherlock with you. Just make sure you stay out of his way!"

• • •

Carpenter felt the Heart throbbing in his grasp and oozing that same odd, bright substance. Lu Wen stood in the doorway, murmuring something as she grabbed a charm from her necklace.

Fury arose within Carpenter. Infinity were its measurements, forever was its depth. *This bitch thinks she can stop me? Fuck her.* Carpenter pulled his hammer and summoned forth all the power at his disposal. Dark forces coursed through his soul, bloating him like a tick. His spirit shrieked for retribution—on the creature before him, on anyone who would stand in his way. He would not be denied success when he was so close! Immortality had been within his grasp—could still be so. He cast the energy outward, searching for anyone, anything that would help him achieve his victory.

The charm in Lu Wen's hand had grown into a glittering katana. "Your time here is done," she said, swinging the blade in a few deadly practice cuts. He sensed four of the statues moving in position to attack him as well.

"Not quite yet," Carpenter said just before the alcove walls exploded inward and a sea of undead surged forth.

• • •

Thea and Jake shared a shocked glance when the big black dog appeared as if out of nowhere. But it was a momentary distraction compared to the tunnel. The only viable options she saw required her to go into that passage, but that was also where she felt a screaming, off-the-scale sense of danger. No choice but to take a deep breath and dive in.

She charged forward at full speed, the mastiff loping beside her and Jake and Ibrahim hustling to bring up the rear. Sure enough, a zombie popped out of the darkness, lunging for the attack. Thea planted herself to launch a high spinning kick, but suddenly there was no target. The huge dog had leaped forward and clamped its jaws around the zombie's upper thigh. Still running forward, Sherlock shook his head from side to side and smashed the animated corpse repeatedly into the tunnel wall. The zombie came apart after a few good hits and lay twitching for a moment after the dog dropped it.

"Wow," Thea said as Jake and Ibrahim ran up next to her. *Maybe this wouldn't be so tough after all.*

Then the ground shook and dozens of skeletal figures started erupting from the desert sand.

• • •

Nicholas reached the capstone, pulled free and set to one side to reveal the rectangular gap of the ventilation shaft. An inhuman chorus of shrieks boiled up from below. He could see intermittent flashes as shapes moved in front of the lights far below. It was like a direct line to hell.

Xian flew down the shaft and came back out a few seconds later, cawing wildly. Nicholas took that to mean things weren't good down there. Drawing upon the amulet of Selket, Nicholas had the agility of a scorpion. He took a deep breath and leaped into the shaft, bracing his arms and legs on the sides and skittering down at breakneck pace.

• • •

Carpenter wasn't entirely sure what he'd done, but was nonetheless pleased with the results. The things that boiled from the earth were animated corpses, and he knew he'd somehow called them forth, but beyond that it was a mystery. They weren't even worth calling zombies. He could see the weak life force flickering within them, barely enough to animate their long-dead bodies. There was something familiar about that energy, though...

Then he realized it was *him*. He was pouring his own power into these things. Carpenter could feel the energy coursing through him, a web that was spreading farther every second, firing a spark of vitality in every corpse it encountered. But despite the hideous power this required, Carpenter felt absolutely brimming with energy, with life. That's when the greater realization struck. He might be channeling this energy, but he was getting it from the Heart.

Carpenter looked down at the thing pulsing in his hand, a film of golden fluid covering his fingers. He could feel the vast depths of power at his command, an ocean of it he could use for any purpose he could imagine. He sensed the secret of its control was just on the tip of his tongue. He could taste it, so close...

The blow shattered his left arm and broke most of his ribs. His hammer flipped into a mass of churning undead as he slammed into a wall. Even as he drew on the Heart to heal his injuries, further blows, powerful enough to pulverize stone, rained on him. Carpenter found he couldn't react, his senses were too diffuse, his attention being sucked back to the Heart. Crying out in frustration and agony, he flung away the artifact. In an instant, his perceptions snapped back into himself. Nicholas Sforza stood above him, just turning to see the Heart of Osiris vanish amid the horde of animated corpses. Carpenter took advantage of the moment's distraction and flung himself toward the doorway.

27

Although he broke the connection with the Heart's power, Carpenter still sensed the energy flowing into the creatures he'd summoned. The things piled on Sforza, the other mummy and her statues, and fought with furious intensity. The power was waning fast, but if he hurried he might still take advantage of the distraction to reach freedom. He sprinted up the tunnel, shoving his way through dozens more animated corpses. Along the way, Carpenter realized the straight razor had somehow returned to his newly-healed left hand. Weak as he felt now, he didn't think he could resist the weapon's allure any longer. But the alternative was destruction. *Get out of here first; deal with the consequences later.*

Carpenter burst out into the desert, the razor pumping him with the energy to run all the way to the Atlantic Ocean if he had to. Hundreds more undead rioted on the plateau around him, though already he could feel those farthest away faltering and falling inert. He had to go, had to run now. But then someone was before him, a woman dressed in khakis and with blood trickling down her face. The intense light that blazed from parts of her body blinded his deathsight.

"You son of a bitch," Thea Ghandour said. "Just what the hell have you done now?"

● ● ●

Nicholas lost it when he saw Maxwell Carpenter standing with the Heart of Osiris in his hand while dozens upon dozens of corpses tore at Lu Wen, a pair of hapless cultists and some guardian statues. Seized by the red haze of vengeance, his ka spirit wrapped around him like a protective cloak, Nicholas dropped from the ventilation shaft and charged Carpenter. Calling upon the full strength of his amulets, Nicholas smashed the zombie to the ground. Animated corpses grabbed at him, but he tossed them aside. Dead hands clutched at his arms and legs, ripping and pulling at him. His ka twisted the threads of fate just enough so that he slipped through their fevered grasp and fell upon Carpenter.

A twinge upon his arm shook Nicholas. A dim part of his consciousness realized the compass scarab registered sudden movement by the Heart. *Carpenter no longer had it—where…*

Following the amulet's tremors, Nicholas plowed into a mass of corpses that were savaging some cultists. One of the creatures, more substantial than the rest and wearing some kind of soldier's uniform, snatched up the Heart. Nicholas was upon it before it could move a step. He battered the thing into the wall, fists striking so hard they punched through flesh and bone and cracked against the tomb. A dozen more corpses jumped him then, their determination and numbers overwhelming his spirit's subtle protective aura. Nicholas clutched the Heart close to his chest as he struggled against the undead. Adrenaline slammed through him as he labored to tear the creatures off. As he cast aside the last of the corpses, Nicholas was surprised to see a semblance of peace had returned to the rest of the chamber. Lu Wen was covered in blood on the other side of the tomb, looking around in dazed wonder at the piles of bodies.

Nicholas stripped off his torn, bloody shirt and found a relatively clean spot with which to wrap the Heart of Osiris. He stepped under the ventilation shaft, the noonday sun spearing down and illuminating the Heart. Nicholas looked upon the ab-Asar, a smile growing on his face. *At last*, he thought. *Home and safe at last*.

●●●

Thea felt calm, strangely detached from her surroundings. Carpenter stood before her, outlined in sharp relief. She could see every wound he'd suffered like it was some kind of diagram; she understood the severity of each, and how much she might injure him by striking each one a certain way. Yet even as she looked, the options decreased steadily—the prick was healing himself. She had to move before he could become whole again.

"Looks like someone put out a fire with your face," she said, circling left, away from the razor he held.

"Hey, why do you have to be that way?" he replied, offering a smile that was surprisingly warm and disarming despite his ruined face.

"Don't make this hard, Carpenter. You've caused too much pain, ruined too many lives, for this to end any other way than it's going to."

"Funny. I was about to say you shouldn't throw your life away on futile gestures."

Thea could hear the roar of Jake's shotgun and the staccato clatter of Ibrahim's assault rifle, as well as the occasional growl and snarl of the strange, enchanted mastiff. The animated corpses were swarming all over, but for some reason they left Thea and Carpenter alone. That was good. She'd already used up the Glock's ammunition on the things, and Carpenter required her complete attention. Thea watched him like a hawk, all the variables laid out before her.

Her left hand, a blazing comet of light, smashing into the side of Carpenter's head. She saw his feint and counterstrike, knew she could spin around and catch him from the side. But as she turned, Thea saw the oilslick flash and knew she hadn't moved fast enough. Cold fire burned down the side of her face, a pain more horrible than anything she could encompass. The razor blade tore down her left eye, through her cheek and out the side of her jaw. Incredible as the pain was, more terrible was the damage to the core of her soul. Words failed, comparisons could not do justice to the degree of agony that coursed through her.

As if down a tunnel, she saw Carpenter's cold grin, misshapen where her strike had smashed in the side of his head. Falling, blood coursing warm down her front, Thea saw the shimmering black rainbow of the blade he flicked up for another stroke.

Anger as blazing hot as the cold pain within her surged to life. Defying the inevitable, denying the agony she felt, Thea lunged as the razor swept down. Her right hand, plain and unadorned with any mystic charms, grabbed Carpenter's wrist and twisted around. Crying out in equal parts torment and triumph, Thea jerked the hand across. The blade cut deep and clean, slashing Maxwell Carpenter's head from his body.

"Race you to hell," Thea whispered as she collapsed beside him.

EPILOGUE

Beckett scrambled up the ice cliff, the fever of discovery upon him. Centuries before, an elder vampire was said to have hidden some tomes in a cave among the fjords of Norway. There was conjecture as to what the books held—were they journals of his contemporaries from the time of the fall of Carthage, a translation of the precursor to the Book of Nod, or merely Lapplander mating customs? Beckett suspected they were musings on the power of the blood, a treatise that might bestow insight as to where vampires' abilities came from and what else Cainites might be capable of.

He'd spent the past month crawling around the most remote and inhospitable parts of the country, spending his days beneath the ice-covered rock and his nights exploring every crevasse he came across. Based on nothing more concrete than instinct, he felt confident the small opening he was headed for was the lair he sought.

It had been centuries since Beckett felt the need to prove anything to anyone, even himself. Decades since he had doubted himself—his intellect, his prowess, or his power. But since Chicago, an insidious worry blossomed within him, a seed that threatened to grow into full-blown fear.

Although he felt he was his own man, that no one held influence over him, he hadn't felt *certain*. He had thought he escaped the snare of Menele's power, that the choices he made were his own. But he couldn't say what might have happened if he had gone after the Heart of Osiris. While he liked to think he would have hidden

it away forever, a part of him feared he might have brought it to his new lord and master.

Even though weeks had passed after Nola Spier's bracelet had become inert and he'd felt no drive to pursue the Heart, Beckett felt concern that he continued to think about it. At last he shook off his lethargy and threw himself into his current search. Struggling up the cliff face, battered by midnight winds and stinging sprays of ice, Beckett felt an exhilaration he'd long forgotten. Rather than be fearful of the kernel of doubt within him, Beckett embraced it. He reveled in the sensation of vulnerability. It sharpened his senses and quickened his spirit. He felt reborn.

Teeth bared against a savage gust of wind, Beckett continued climbing.

●●●

Nicholas Sforza-Ankhotep stood on the rise at the edge of the cluster of mastabas and watched the workers puzzling over the Pyramid of Sanakht Nebka. The lost pyramid was lost no longer, as far as the world was concerned. The hundreds of ancient Egyptian corpses scattered around the area were already almost forgotten, unable to compare in surprise and wonder to such a find. The explanation most in vogue claimed that a localized earthquake had shaken the bodies free of substandard mastabas and revealed the entrance to Nebka's tomb.

The Amenti would maintain control of the site for the time being, but it was too high profile to serve as a resurrection site any longer. Unfortunate, but by no means catastrophic. There were other sites, and there would be more mummies. The enemy was still out there, and the Amenti would not rest until balance was restored.

Hearing the crunch of tires in the sand, Nicholas turned to see the battered, dust-covered Audi pull up. "What's the word, Ibrahim?"

"Nothing yet, Nicholas," the cultist replied as he walked up. He carried himself with a confidence gained from victory against overwhelming odds. Ibrahim had given a good accounting of himself in the battle, but almost didn't survive the overpowering number of undead that swarmed over him. If the things hadn't fallen, the energy that infused them finally wasted…

Nicholas shook off the thought. Enough pessimism. He should be filled with pride and optimism. Victory against the Corrupter was one step closer to realization. The Heart of Osiris was safely ensconced in Horus' complex at Edfu. The Eset-a had been proven worthy of respect from the other Amenti, even if they still didn't approve of the cult's tactics. Vengeance was realized against Maxwell Carpenter for the atrocities he inflicted against Nicholas' family and far too many others. The cursed razor blade he used was stored away in the Eset-a safe house, where Nicholas and Lu Wen would study it to find the best means to destroy it without any unfortunate side effects. All true enough, but he would rest easier when he had one more piece of the puzzle. "They're sure?"

"They have gone through the burial chamber twice, and are now looking in the maze off the antechamber. If the hammer is there, we will find it."

"You think I'm being paranoid, Ibrahim?"

Ibrahim shrugged. "I saw him fall. Even if he is undead, I do not understand how he could return from a beheading. But if you think it best to recover his anchor, who am I to doubt you?"

"Did you just poke a little fun at me? The wise, all-knowing mummy?"

Face studiously blank, Ibrahim looked at Nicholas. "I have no idea what you mean."

"This is what it's all about, you know," Nicholas said as they watched the work continue around the pyramid.

"Amenti?"

"Being able to stand here with a friend, wasting an afternoon watching the find of the decade—well, the year, anyway. To be able to enjoy life without being

crushed by fear. To live life, instead of merely existing." Nicholas burst out laughing at Ibrahim's expression. "Are you blushing?"

The Egyptian had, indeed, gone red in the face. After some more prodding, he finally admitted, "I was surprised, that is all."

"Surprised about what?"

"Well... you said to stand here with a friend..."

Nicholas laughed again, but sobered somewhat when he saw Ibrahim's wounded expression. "Sorry; I'm not laughing at you. Look, Ibrahim. It's not easy, this situation. Being chosen for this struggle that will go on for... who knows how long? And most of the people around me... everyone dies, right? So it's easiest, safest, for my kind to keep our relationships at arm's length. Just as you're getting to know a mortal, well. And then I feel like an asshole for pointing out that you're going to die someday.

"But listen. For all that you're overly formal with me and still doubt whether you can cut it even after kicking ass out there... I'm proud to call you my friend, Ibrahim."

They lapsed into silence, somewhat uncomfortable as two men unused to sharing intimacies is bound to be.

"You are, you know," Ibrahim observed after a while.

"I am what?"

"An asshole for saying I will die someday."

"Oh, boo hoo. I've been there. It's not that big a deal."

"Amenti?"

"Yes, Ibrahim?"

"How do you say 'fuck you' in the language of the ancients?"

● ● ●

Thea Ghandour walked up the steps to the towering apartment building and pressed the button for apartment 909. A harsh tone buzzed from the door accompanied by a click. Thea pushed through and made her way across the sparkling black and white tile to the stairs. An elevator stood to one side of the lobby, but ever since her stay at the Ismailia Hotel, Thea preferred the stairs.

The past year and a half kept her in good shape, so the trek of nine flights left her just a bit winded. She counted off the apartment numbers until she reached 909, then knocked on the thick wood panel in which the brass numbers were nailed. A faint voice called for her to enter, so she turned the knob and stepped in.

The apartment was spacious. A simple decor helped with the impression of expansive space although the floor plan for the entire place probably didn't cover more than twelve hundred square feet. A couch and matching chairs faced a blond wood entertainment center in which rested the usual 21st century electronics entertainment gear. End tables to either side of the couch held lamps that contributed warm light to the room. The wall to Thea's right opened on a balcony that gave a view of the Chicago skyline right up close, thousands of lights twinkling in the night. The opposite wall was actually a counter that divided the living room from the kitchen. Margie Woleski stood scrubbing at the sink.

"Hi, Thea!" she said brightly, her attention focused on the sink. "I'm so glad you could visit. Sorry I didn't get back to you sooner. I just got this job at a think tank and been putting in long hours. Only got home a few minutes ago myself!"

"That's okay," Thea said, checking out the rest of the living room. A few potted plants in the corner, some nice prints on the wall hung in expensive double mats. "This is a nice place; a step up from the old place, huh?"

"Yeah, isn't it? Who'd have thought all that would be good for me? With my life all up in the air, I met with some people and lucked into a sweet job, found this place and, well… here I am!" She waved her hands to prove she was, indeed, there. Pointing at the sleeve of her

blouse, soaked through, she explained, "I gulped down some yogurt right before you got here and spilled some. Of course; brand new blouse."

Margie came around into the living room, dabbing at her sleeve with a dry cloth. "Anyway, come on in. Have a— Thea! What happened to your face?!"

Thea fingered the velvet eyepatch self-consciously. "Would you believe I cut myself shaving?"

"That scar… all the way down your face! Does it hurt? I mean…"

"No, it's okay." In fact, it still ached with a fierce coldness. She took it in stride. After all, without Nicholas Sforza and the strange healing bandages he'd wrapped around her face, Thea would be dead. Then there were the nightmares, images of cold steel and even colder eyes, intimacies of dead flesh that startled her awake screaming every night. But it was a small price to pay if it meant Maxwell Carpenter was gone for good. Her mind started to wander, thinking about Nicholas and the incredible things she'd learned about him and others like him. She shook herself mentally to get back on track. "Anyway, it's part of what I wanted to tell you. But I should really start from the beginning."

Margie nodded, apparently having trouble taking her eyes from Thea's face. Still waving her arm to dry her sleeve, she sat on the couch and gestured for Thea to sit in one of the chairs.

"Well, don't rush on my account. Oh, hey, how's that boy; Jake? You two ever get together?"

"No, thank you very much," Thea said, blushing. "Anyway, he's doing okay. Last I heard he was headed down south to look up some people he met online. I expect we'll keep in touch."

Margie nodded. "Well, that's good. He seemed very nice."

Thea fidgeted and cleared her throat. "Look, Margie, before I get into things… uh, I wanted to apologize again for everything that you went through."

28

"Oh, don't worry about it! I'm fine, really! Matter of fact, probably the best thing that could've happened to me."

Thea was thrown off-stride by her friend's cavalier response. "Margie, I thought... well, because of me you were put through some pretty awful stuff."

"Yeah, I suppose so. It was all so crazy, though. You know? Hard to believe it really happened." She looked down at her sleeve, rubbing at the stain. After a few seconds, she looked up. "But, you know, I would like to hear how it all worked out. Really; it would mean a lot to me."

Thea frowned, worried at Margie's manic behavior. Perhaps she hadn't recovered from everything as well as they'd hoped. "Okay."

A door opened behind Thea then, and someone approached from one of the bedrooms. Thea turned to see a willowy young woman with straight caramel-colored hair that hung down to her shoulders. The woman reached up with her left hand to brush a hair aside as she walked in. The skin on her hand was the raw angry red of burned flesh.

Margie's face lit up. "Hey, this is great! Sylvia, Thea's about to tell us all about her adventures. Thea, you remember Sylvia, don't you?"

• • •

Chaos reigned in this place. Storms of nothingness pounded at remnants of dream, raging across a landscape of insanity and torment. Amidst these winds of madness a spirit was buffeted. The soul was but a speck of distracted thought to the scouring nothing of oblivion, yet it clung to identity with a tenacity that the ghost storm's strongest gale could not shake.

In the midst of the ravages of hell, in the depths of the fractured underworld, a lonely soul railed against the limitless expanse of the beyond. Carpenter tore at the barrier dividing soul from flesh, nightmare from reality.

His fingers, curled like claws, found little purchase, what few gouges he made in the wall of the real healing even as they were cut. But Carpenter did not stop, did not slow for an instant. His spirit felt no fatigue, for he was fueled with a passion that burned with blinding fury, with the driving need to escape damnation. He would not rest until life, until the physical realm, was his once again.

He would never stop, even if it took an eternity.

Δ NOTE ON ΔCCURΔCY

While writing the **Year of the Scarab** trilogy, the author abided by real-world history and geography when possible. However, he took the liberty to alter certain historical details as well as topography, street layouts, weather patterns and other trivia to better suit the plot. (It is the World of Darkness, after all, and not our own reality....) As with any errors of fact you discover while reading this tale, any mistakes rest on the author's shoulders, no matter how much he may protest.

AUTHOR NOTE

Andrew Bates spends his time wandering the contiguous United States. He visits towns, befriends the locals and rights wrongs before moving on down the road.

Land of the Dead is his third novel for White Wolf. His previous credits include the first and second installments of the **Year of the Scarab** trilogy, **Heralds of the Storm** and **Lay Down With Lions**, as well as a short story featuring Maxwell Carpenter for the **Inherit the Earth** anthology.

Visit http://www.devilbear.net and http://www.white-wolf.com for more information.